Hayner Public Library District

☑ O9-BSA-063

RECEIVED
AUG 2 9 2019
By_____

No Longer the Property of
Hayner Public Library District

HAYNER PLD/ALTON SQUARE
OVERDUES .10 PER DAY. MAXIMUM
FINE COST OF ITEM. LOST OR
DAMAGED ITEM ADDITIONAL $5.00
SERVICE CHARGE

WILLA & HESPER

WILLA
&
HESPER

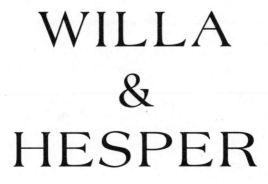

Amy Feltman

GRAND CENTRAL
PUBLISHING

New York Boston

This book is a work of fiction. Names, characters, places, and incidents are the product of the author's imagination or are used fictitiously. Any resemblance to actual events, locales, or persons, living or dead, is coincidental.

Copyright © 2019 by Amy Feltman

Cover illustration by Hsiao-Ron Cheng
Cover copyright © 2019 by Hachette Book Group, Inc.

Hachette Book Group supports the right to free expression and the value of copyright. The purpose of copyright is to encourage writers and artists to produce the creative works that enrich our culture.

The scanning, uploading, and distribution of this book without permission is a theft of the author's intellectual property. If you would like permission to use material from the book (other than for review purposes), please contact permissions@hbgusa.com. Thank you for your support of the author's rights.

Grand Central Publishing
Hachette Book Group
1290 Avenue of the Americas, New York, NY 10104
grandcentralpublishing.com
twitter.com/grandcentralpub

First Edition: February 2019

Grand Central Publishing is a division of Hachette Book Group, Inc. The Grand Central Publishing name and logo is a trademark of Hachette Book Group, Inc.

The publisher is not responsible for websites (or their content) that are not owned by the publisher.

Print book interior design by Marie Mundaca
Interior illustration by Peter Bernard

Library of Congress Cataloging-in-Publication Data

Names: Feltman, Amy, author.
Title: Willa & Hesper / Amy Feltman.
Other titles: Willa and Hesper
Description: First edition. | New York : Grand Central Publishing, 2019.
Identifiers: LCCN 2018023076| ISBN 9781538712542 (hardcover) | ISBN 9781478999812 (audio download) | ISBN 9781538712566 (ebook)
Classification: LCC PS3606.E45 W55 2019 | DDC 813/.6--dc23
LC record available at https://lccn.loc.gov/2018023076

ISBNs: 978-1-5387-1254-2 (hardcover), 978-1-5387-1256-6 (ebook)

Printed in the United States of America

LSC-C

10   9   8   7   6   5   4   3   2   1

3668491

FEL

For my grandparents: Stan, Vivian, Al, Judy, and Bud,
with all of my love.

WILLA & HESPER

1.

It happened quickly. It happened, to me, quickly. Then it stopped. Tree-scales scraped barkily against the cotton of my T-shirt. The boy was walking away. My earbuds had fallen out of my ears, dangling over my collarbones. The boy's figure disappeared, duskily camouflaging into the New Jersey night. Past the green-glowing empanada store; in front of the synagogue where I'd been bat mitzvahed. *He's gone,* I told myself, but even my own diction seemed hazy, baffling. I didn't know who *he* was. I didn't know if *gone* was a permanent state of being. I didn't remember how to propel myself forward. I watched my legs move as though they were someone else's legs and I was a camera, capturing it all. Spidery voices slid into the world from the earbuds. My body felt thick, full of cement.

What had happened? Ten minutes earlier, I was getting off the bus. I was visiting home for the weekend from graduate school. Bergen County skies, glazed pink with pollution, leered over my head. I had a backpack filled with toiletries, books. My sweater was missing a button. I'd walked up this hill innumerable times before. I was only one and a half blocks from home, I thought, though it was less my home now.

There had been nights when I'd been afraid, but tonight wasn't one of those.

Now I was late for dinner. My mother would already be annoyed, and then: how would I say it?

Why couldn't it have happened somewhere else? I thought, glancing back at the temple. My temple. The place where I felt most myself, sequestered by neatly clipped yarmulkes and swathes of lace on pious heads. The place where I'd won the Purim carnival in my shiny blue dress with the lace collar. Singing, unfettered, the mellifluous bounce of Hebrew prayers. My parents sat obediently twice a year, measuring the number of pages of the service between two fingers in the prayer book. But I loved it; the standing and sitting, bent knees during the *aleinu*. It was the only place that I ever sang. That was what I wanted to think of, here. Not the boy. His hands on me.

I tried to talk to God. I whispered, "I'm sorry."

In the space where I usually felt an undulating presence, there was nothing. "I'm sorry," I said again.

The street was hushed. Shelled insects scurried into the porous earth. The sky, crepuscular and unending. I heard squirrels rattling in the branches overhead, the far-off sweeping whirr of an airplane. I could see no one—no silhouette of a boy sneaking into the living room to play video games, no khaki-adorned dad rushing to the market to retrieve a forgotten head of lettuce. Suburban streets, devoid of eyes, slouching back to status quo. Nothing ever happens here, I'd complained as a teenager, and I had believed it.

AT MY PARENTS' HOUSE, I was greeted by the stale smell of lasagna, old furniture polish from a can. Mom ate blueberries from a plastic container at their kitchen table, carefully laid upon a square of a paper towel so that no drops of condensation would stain the wood. "You're late," she said. She popped another blueberry onto her tongue. "You were supposed to help me cook."

"I can help now."

"I thought you'd be here every weekend," she said. "I thought that was one of the benefits of going to Columbia. Within commuting distance."

"I'm sorry," I said.

"Every day I do this by myself," she said. "Every single day." She didn't notice my hands, which were trembling conspicuously. I knitted them behind my back. I imagined what her shocked expression would look like if I said it. I imagined her, staring into that container of blueberries and not believing me. *Things like that don't happen here,* she might say. *That's why we raised you in the suburbs, close enough to the city to get there in twenty minutes without traffic but without the risk of someone grabbing you in the—*

And then, what would we do with Dad? We couldn't bring him to the police station. The chairs would hurt his back.

Why would the police care? They wouldn't. They'd say, *Why did you wear that sweater? Don't you know what a missing button looks like? Why were you walking alone at night, with your earphones in? Don't you know that makes you a target?* They'd think, *You're the one with a body that someone can't help but*

Twice I refused my mother's offer of blueberries. I opened a plastic bag full of frozen, fetus-y shrimp and filled a pot with water. I squinted into the liquid, waiting for the beads to flicker to the surface. My heart felt pinpricked.

I kept my arms away from my sides, maintaining space.

I remembered that Jews weren't supposed to eat shellfish because they're the smallest animals that feel pain. My mother didn't follow those rules, and discouraged me from doing so, too. "We're not *those kind* of Jews," she said. "You don't need to be a fanatic about it." The water boiled, beads of heat and movement. The clumps of crystallized shrimp bodies transformed from gray to pink, unfurling.

"I'm positively engorged," my mother declared, popping another blueberry in her mouth.

"After dinner, I'm going to head back to the city," I said.

"I already washed the towels," she said.

"I'm sorry."

"My time is valuable, too, you know. *I* can't just decide to jettison back to fun whenever I feel sick of being here, Willa."

If my mother asked why I was leaving instead of staying for the whole weekend, as originally planned, I didn't know if I would lie. I have a lot of homework, I could say. Or.

But she did not ask. A sliver of fruitskin swam between her front teeth as she complained about the obligations of caring for Willa's dad, for the house, the new roof, the gutters leaking, the clanging radiator in Willa's bedroom. She narrated it to me as if Willa were not me, but a stranger who had been dropped in the middle of her life. *So let me use an old towel,* I thought, but I couldn't say it.

"Don't forget to say hello to your father," Mom said, standing to take over dinner preparations. But I knew, first, I would have to retreat to my childhood bedroom to "gather my feelings," as I'd been trained to do. In the dark, cluttered room, a litany of glow-in-the-dark stars watched me from their position on the ceiling. I told myself: *Try to conjure all the joy you've ever felt.* I remembered being hoisted onto my father's shoulders, the warm sunshine on my four-year-old face. A gorgeous, light blue sweater I'd been given as a birthday gift that was the softest material I'd ever felt. The satisfying crunch of salted sidewalks against the soles of my shoes. Then nothing remained, all the joy slid away; only the sensation of a mortar and pestle, mashing my feelings into a paste. I could do this; I could hide it.

In the living room, the coffee table had carefully laid out piles of medical bills and appeals, like place settings for imaginary visitors. Dad had his face nestled in a warm, well-knit afghan. He was lying across the length of the sofa, wiry ankles propped up against the adjacent wall. My father was perpetually in a state of deterioration from a serious back injury. He'd been in an accident, and instead of

recovering, he didn't. I hadn't known that this happened to real people, only characters in medical dramas, but here we were. It had been
years. His disks were unsteady, a doctor explained, wiggling his fingers to illustrate the undulating spinal fluid. It seemed like my father's
vertebrae were performing a well-coordinated baroque dance. The
only upside was that medical emergencies had left him sweet, gra-
cious. Once he'd been the sort of man to hurl an empty soda can out
of a moving car rather than deposit it in a recycling bin. No longer.

"Your shrimp smell delicious, Turnip," he said to me, and I kissed
his air-conditioned cheek.

I could never tell him about the boy. I knew, if I did, my father
would not understand. His eyes were gooey with morphine. He
wouldn't be able to call me Turnip anymore. This, more than anything besides the lasting and impervious smell of my childhood home,
felt like the truth.

At the dinner table, I used a fork to dig into the shrimp's body.
My mother talked about going on a juice cleanse. "I suppose it's not
exactly juice," she admitted. "Rice bran, rice syrup, and encapsulated
bark enzymes.

"I'm going to be as thin as I was when I was your age," she vowed.
"Not a pound heavier." I watched her, evaluating my body, calculat-
ing how many more pounds I weighed than she ever had. I thought
of the willowy, obedient daughter that she'd envisioned for herself. A
person who washed towels and counted calories by her side. A person who craved, above all else, a husband to cherish and please. But I
wanted cake, and literary acclaim, and women. Well, just one woman,
really.

"That sounds extreme," I said.

At first, he'd covered my mouth. His skin was salted, firm. The
hands of a child straining to catch a tadpole. He pushed me against the
birch tree, his arm a bar over my neck. Then he'd moved his hand.
I hadn't made any noise. *How had he known that I would stay quiet?* I

wondered as Mom listed all of the parts of her body she wished she could replace. The loose skin where her neck met her chest.

Why hadn't he been afraid?

᠅

LATER, ON THE WAY back to New York, I felt the knot inside my chest loosening. I imagined the tiny, L-shaped tool I'd used to put a bookcase together, bringing me back to equilibrium. One turn counterclockwise at the pho place in Ridgefield Park where I'd once gotten a parking ticket; another as the bus made the wide turn at the Dairy King. A gummy, kalamata-olive taste lingered in my mouth. By the time I arrived at the congested, twinkling Port Authority, I no longer had to concentrate on the rhythm of my breathing.

I thought about texting Chloe. Now that we were roommates, I told her basically everything out of a combination of intimacy and convenience. But she was visiting Graham this weekend at Yale, and I imagined texting her in the middle of their blissful, long-distance-relationship reunion that I'd been . . . what? Fondled. Traumatized. She would call me right away, want to talk to me about it until I cried and she cried from me crying, and then I'd abruptly hang up and she would worriedly text me to see whether I wanted her to come home and I didn't. The imagined conversation exhausted me. I wanted to concentrate on a destination. One foot, then the other.

"Last stop," the bus driver announced. I descended: steps from the bus, steps down to the subway entrance. I gave the pruneish, slippered homeless woman in the concrete tunnel between Times Square and Eighth Avenue an extra fifty cents, pressing each coin into her hand fervently. *We made it,* I told the woman with my facial expression. We're alive. Everything remains possible. On the subway, I watched a young girl in a soccer uniform dangle her infant brother's head back and forth against the sticky floor—a game. He's a broom! He is invincible! Overhead, an ad for an introductory philosophy course taunted: WHO DO YOU WISH TO BE?

❦

I TOOK THE N train to Union Square. I took the L train to Williamsburg. I got off and onto the L train three times. Where was I going? It didn't matter. Williamsburg was where your night ended; that much I'd learned from graduate school so far. I felt the bruises forming on my breasts, my rib cage, the pillowy insides of my thighs. Or could I be imagining the bruises forming? It happened. Something happened to me.

❦

ON THE TRAIN, THREE girls my age were going to a party together, each holding a tin-foiled platter of brownies on their American-Appareled laps. Ankle boots and ill-fitting patterned pants. Chin-length haircuts and mascara-coated eyelashes. Entranced, I followed them off the train. I followed them into a diner and waited by the gumball machine in the carpeted space between front and middle doors. The gumballs were stationary, covered in dust. For a moment I regretted giving my extra quarters to the homeless woman. I wanted to hold a dusty gumball. Suddenly I had never wanted anything so much in my life, to feel the grime against my skin.

"Excuse me?" a stranger prompted me. *Let's move this along,* the stranger's face expressed. She did not have time for yearning. This was a business; it was inappropriate. I mumbled an apology, allowed myself to be swept into the restaurant. Tall columns of yellow-lit cheesecake slices stood on a mirror-covered table. A cash register trilled excitedly; a waitress astutely gathered that I was not with the impatient stranger. "One?" she said, nodding, a thick plastic menu in hand, escorting me to the nearest, saddest table, only a few feet from the bar.

I thought of my mother's guilt-ridden expression. *Engorged,* she'd said, leering at the blueberry pile as though it were impious. Maybe what she meant was, *If you were smaller, no one would notice you.* If you had worked harder to be contained—birdish and compact, like the girls on the train. I knew that I took up too much space in the world. Not only with my body—I saw bodies all the time that were more expansive. But my feelings spilled outward, puddling like oil underneath a car. "It's like you're emotionally immune deficient," I'd been told by an ex-best friend in high school. "When I'm around you, everything hurts a little bit extra."

When the waitress returned, cloaked in tobacco-scent, I ordered French fries and a slice of peach pie. I felt, instantly, that I'd missed something. An important element of the order. Regret rose steamily inside of me. I stared at the advertisements on the paper place mat cloaked over the table: confident dermatologists, beekeepers harvesting their own honey. The waitress rushed past me with a plate of accordioned French fries; they were not for me.

Across the room, I caught the eye of someone I recognized. Hesper, with her luminous strawberry blond hair pulled back from her small, rounded face. Beautiful Hesper, from workshop; we had participated in sanguine exchanges about the mild weather and Karen Russell. I could recite each of those exchanges.

She was wearing a puzzling dress. The top, knitted ivory fabric looped in a kind of cape, swirled over her shoulders and breasts, but with a strip of translucent fabric below her ribs before expanding outward into a swingy A-line. *Is that all one dress, or has she layered different thrift-store purchases on top of each other?* I wondered. *What does her body even look like?*

Hesper met my eyes and smiled primly. Waved.

I'm sorry, I told Hesper's face. I was bleary-eyed and staring at a place mat. I hadn't even given myself the luxury of pretending to read an engrossing book, or scrolling through a Facebook feed of Friday night updates. I wished I were holding the dusty gumball. I wished I could put my hands somewhere that the boy had not touched.

Hesper approached me at the saddest table. Her hands were splattered with freckles, and she smiled crookedly, baring an overbite. I waited for Hesper to ask what I was doing here, in the strange not-quite-Greenpoint pocket of Williamsburg, by myself on Friday night. Instead, Hesper sat and rested her elbows on the table and said, "My sister's cat just had kittens," and I swelled with gratitude for this easy, though foundationless, familiarity.

"Are they okay?" I asked. I thought of the kittens being pummeled by a stream of relentless water in a large, metallic sink. Were they drowning or just taking a very forceful bath?

"What do you mean?" Hesper asked. "They're adorable."

"Right," I rushed. "Of course."

Hesper's head drooped into her open hand. "We found someone to take each one. Poor Tibby. She'll be so sad to lose her kittens. But you can't have that many cats in one apartment."

"Tibby? Like tibia?"

"Tbilisi. Georgia. It's where our grandfather is from." Hesper smiled. "Do you usually name your pets after bones?"

"I've never had a pet."

The waitress returned with the fries and pie, each thickly jarred peach slice spectacularly glittering. I thought I should say something about Eastern Europe that didn't involve Stalin. Probably anything Soviet was a touchy subject. Hesper ordered chicken noodle soup and a Bloody Mary.

"The president of Estonia went to my high school," I said.

"Estonians are dour," Hesper said. "And taciturn. Wooden, really."

"I've never met one," I replied. "Is that true?"

"I think that was Calvin Coolidge, actually. Oh, no. Willa?" Hesper said, leaning forward across the table. "Can I tell you something?"

She doesn't believe me about the Estonian president, I thought. It was true. I wouldn't have said it otherwise. My eyes felt liquidly, about to spill into something incriminating and vulnerable. "What?"

"I'm substantially high right now. Everything feels so . . . easy."

A bashful blush crept over Hesper's cheeks. I instantly felt as light and feathery as if I were the Molly-afflicted; I could say anything I liked to Hesper, the guarantee that it would be misty and surreal tomorrow. The bright white lights of the diner suddenly seemed illuminating, cradling boldness. Hesper's gold necklaces jangled as she reached for the fork, capturing a peach slice with a jubilant stab.

"Did you know Hemingway's estate is crawling with polydactyl kittens?" I offered. A French fry burned against the roof of my mouth. Hesper organized her hair into a donut-like bun.

"I hate that story we read for workshop," Hesper said. "Masculinity 101."

"They have thumbs," I said. "You can hold their little paws."

Hesper slurped her soup ravenously.

"I heard Liam tearing Isabel's story to shreds in the lab," I said.

"It deserved to be shredded," Hesper said, between noodles. "She used the word *electric* eight times. I counted. Not everything is electric, Bells. Some things are just lackluster."

As Hesper continued, I felt electrically toward her—the brushing of our bare knees underneath the small table, the warm orb of wanting Hesper's puffed, silken lips on mine. Hesper moved the peach pie plate closer to her soup and fragrantly tomato-ish drink. "Sorry to colonize your dessert," she offered.

I made a robotic gesture that I hoped conveyed generosity. We insulted the work of our classmates: Liam's blatant misogyny; Elisabeth's overuse of quilting imagery. Hesper's laugh was low and melodious.

Our knees knocked fortuitously. I couldn't seem to find a way to broach my gayness in the conversation. If gay was even what I was. Queer felt too political; omission and long hair rendered me a straight person. I wanted to avoid the confessional, desperate-for-support tone that so many of these conversations led toward. If only I had a prop. The gumball—I could roll the gumball at Hesper across the table, skirting around our plates of food and perspiring glasses, and if Hesper rolled it back, I would know.

Did you bring her here? I thought. I waited for God, for a squeeze in my chest to let me know someone was there. If not answering, then not answering for a reason. But I felt no squeeze. Hesper was looking at me.

"Where is the rest of your family from?" I asked, leaning forward to retrieve the pie. Hesper hollowed out most of the peach slices, leaving a buttery crust-foundation slumping in the center of a white porcelain plate.

"Pale-skinned places. Ireland, England. Wales." When Hesper said Wales, she made an ocean-wave motion with her non-soup hand and then laughed, embarrassed. *Oh, no,* I thought, falling a little bit in love. "What about you?"

I mused. I hadn't properly thought about a response to this question. "I come exclusively from people that don't exist anymore. I mean—places," I clarified quickly, as Hesper emitted her alto-toned, harmonious laugh. "Prussia, the Austro-Hungarian Empire, the Soviet Union."

"People that don't exist anymore," Hesper repeated. "I only sleep with ghosts!"

I looked into her lap. I thought of the boy's thumb, digging.

"Ghostgasm," Hesper continued, buoyant. "Do you want to leave?"

I nodded encouragingly.

"Let's go right now," Hesper said brightly, uncrinkling two twenty-dollar bills from underneath the cape's folds. "Don't forget the crust," Hesper advised, so I broke the remains of the pie into transportable pieces.

ON THE TRAIN, I refrained from asking about logistical considerations.
I wanted to appear nonchalant, unconcerned about getting eight
hours of sleep and whether it made more sense to transfer to an express train. Hesper leaned close to me on the tiny cold seats, her
slender body a force field of expectation and knobby joints. I tried
not to think of that word *electricity*—the sharp hook of the *c*, submerged between two prominent *i*'s. Hesper entwined her fingers with
the strands of my hair, seemingly reveling in the intricacies of texture.
I ballooned with self-consciousness, thinking of adjectives I could use
for my curls: fluffy, diffuse. Triangular. My hair had become awfully
triangular.

"Your hair is so frothy," Hesper said finally. "Like a latte's milk hat."

I thought: she has to be gay. She has to at least be in the vicinity of
gayness.

"Do you want the crust scraps?" I asked. Hesper wrangled her fingers away from my scalp and scooped the bits of pie from my careful
grasp. When our skin touched, my entire body liquefied, a sloshing
outline of a girl, waiting to condense back into herself. Then I did.
Then I did, and was looking at Hesper, who was feeling the tulle of
her skirt with incredible focus and precision. Like someone on drugs,
I remembered. I kept forgetting. I, too, was partially submerged in a
place that was not-here.

"You're sunburned," Hesper observed, pushing her thumb into
my arm.

"It's my natural color," I said apologetically. "Not the sun's fault."

I watched the mark of Hesper's touch disappear and felt the salty
taste in my mouth return. A tiny cactus was growing at the base of my
throat, itching up to my esophagus. I thought of bruises. I thought
of Hesper marveling at the pattern of my bruises in the serene yellow
light of a reading lamp.

"Do you want to feel my dress?"

I let Hesper guide my hand, warmly, across the fabric pooling over her knees, her hidden thighs and hip flexors and motion-related muscles. The ivory skirt was scratchy, protrusive tulle. The sensation of ballet practice, secondhand prom attire. I wondered if I should move my hand away from Hesper's knees but lingered there. These were her knees. My fingertip slipped comfortably, serendipitously, into a small cave between Hesper's kneecap and bone.

Everything feels so easy.

"We fit," Hesper said, mesmerized, and I tried to keep my balance with my other hand, knuckles whitening as I pulled hard on the bottom of the subway seat. It was a miniature miracle. A polyp, if polyps could be engorged with romantic potential. I wouldn't ruin our puzzle-piece quality because of the train's jostling as we pulled into and from each station. I would conquer the subway's unsteadiness; I would preserve this, like a fly cushioned beneath layers of amber.

WE TRANSFERRED TO A different, ricketier train that seemed swollen with light. Hesper's skirt shimmered, fish scales of ivory and metallic sheen. Each station we passed looked deserted. Hesper and I sat on a glossy bench, several seats distance from a mangy, pallid man with a large plastic bag balanced between his oversized feet. In slow motion, he folded in half, retrieving a stuffed banana wearing a pair of sunglasses made of black felt. The banana had a large, menacing grin, each tooth elongated into the shape of a carrot.

The man began to laugh.

I covered my mouth. I didn't want him to see my lips.

Hesper's expression shifted from perplexed to amused. The other passengers, too, seemed to regard the laughing man with a distanced sense of entertainment. I arched my neck back to examine what else may have been in the plastic bag. An ear of corn? A handgun, glinting with possibility? If it were a gun, I knew, it would have to go off. But I couldn't distinguish any of the objects; just dark, untenable shapes. The man wrapped his stolid arm around the banana, as though it were a child needing support for its journey.

At the next stop, a group of teenaged boys sporting NYU lanyards trailing from their pockets boarded. Draped in nearly identical outfits: hipster plaid shirts and Warby Parkers. Immediately they pointed at the man and his banana companion, dipping their heads low. Bellowing with judgmental laughter. I did not want to look at them. I felt his fingers, everywhere. Marking me.

I reached for Hesper's hand but ended up instead resting my own nervous fingers in the crook of her elbow, a warm spot that exuded safety. Hesper seemed entirely at ease, her limbs loose and ethereal. She could have been doing anything: examining plums for dents in their violet skins, outlining a hopscotch board on planks of sidewalk with thick pastel chalk. How was it possible she seemed so unthreatened as the voices increased in volume, insistent in their aggression of Banana Man?

"Shit," the boldest boy said, pointing at the banana and its keeper. His laugh felt like fingernails. His friends chorused around him, mutinous. Warmed by the attention, Banana Man swept his arm back and punched the banana's eye. I could hear the distinct sound of his fist meeting stuffed fabric. He began to hit the banana faster, faster, until the boys' cheering became a continuous wave of sound.

Hesper tucked a loose curl of my hair behind her ear. "Don't worry," she whispered.

"Bet you I can pull out his eye," Banana Man boasted toward the boys.

"I bet you're too *weak* to pull out his eye," the boldest of the boys yelled.

"Oh, shit," one of the friends said. The others clapped, delighted. They circled each other.

"Oh yeah?" Banana Man said. In a sudden motion, he toppled the banana to the floor, pummeling its face with his raised fist. His cheeks exploded with color from the exertion. Each new passenger avoided the violent exhibition, skittering toward the opposite end of the train. The boys hollered, watching rapt as Banana Man draped himself across the stuffed animal. In victory he raised a fist, having retrieved the plastic eye.

"What should we name him?" Banana Man asked.

"Andy?" one of the quieter onlookers suggested. His suggestion was rejected.

"Bubbacunt," Banana Man said. "Bubba-*cunt*," he repeated, striking him again.

I watched the banana's still body on the floor of the train. *That could be me,* I thought. That could have been me, my arms scraping against the sandpapery texture of the tree in the dark. With each meeting of the fist against the banana's face, I felt it against my own. I imagined all the tiny, unnamed bones that formed the infrastructure of my cheekbones caving in under the pressure of Banana Man's unstoppable fist. His knuckles, tinged with white.

When the boys shuttled off the train, they shook hands with Banana Man. "Peace," they said to each other. "Peace."

"At least they left his hair attached," I said. My voice trembled feebly.

"What?" Hesper asked.

"Weren't you..." I began. "Didn't you find that disturbing?"

"It's the New York experience," Hesper said. "I felt like I was watching it on YouTube."

I tried to concentrate. I imagined my discomfort as a dining room table that I could transport once the leaves were safely removed. "Yeah," I managed. My voice was tart. "Me too."

"You are not a good liar," Hesper said, and ran a pinky along the slope of my nose. Her tone was dulcet, not admonitory. "I'm an incredible protector, luckily."

"Are you?" I searched Hesper's eyes. Within them the pattern of bloodshot lines were mesmerizing, tributaries of pink. They were the color of the center of a rare cut of meat. "How do I know if I can trust you?"

I intended for this to be an extension of flirting. Instead it seemed elegiac, searching.

"I'll make you a solemn promise. That means five Mississippis of eye contact."

"Okay."

"Willa Greenberg," Hesper said. I felt a flutter that filled my whole body. I hadn't realized that Hesper knew my last name, or that Hesper would want me to know that she knew my last name, and it felt incredibly significant. I knew how I would read this, if it were a short story. This was the moment when things would become permanent; when their tectonic plates would twinge into a new position.

"You can trust me," Hesper said. Her teeth were such small, lovely squares in her mouth.

"I can trust you," I repeated.

"I won't let anything hurt you."

"You won't let anything hurt me," I said.

"Do you feel satisfied by the terms of this agreement?"

I nodded. Drugs, I reminded myself. Hesper was on them.

"One Mississippi," Hesper counted, but I had to avoid her gaze. It was too much.

AT THE 7TH AVENUE stop, I followed Hesper down a long, hilly corridor. Unblemished advertisements stared at me and Hesper from their positions on the station wall. *80 Years of Secrets!* exclaimed a poster for Russian vodka. Hesper's skirt swept baggily across the backs of her knees, occasionally brushing my leggings. The desire to ask where we were going eddied inside my chest. I had never been to this bloodclot of Brooklyn, though I knew by reputation that it was diffuse, decorated with flea markets and artisanal popsicle stands on Sundays.

Exiting the subway station, I stayed quiet, growing increasingly wary of the less-trafficked paths. After we passed a bodega on the corner, with its brightly advertised breakfast specials, the likelihood for commerce disappeared. An occasional sign demarcating an optometrist or acupuncturist's office aside, there were only houses. Four-story brownstones crowded around wide streets like soldiers. We were traversing a seemingly unending number of blocks. Not electric, I thought, startling as I mistakenly identified a crumpled black plastic bag as a threat. Interminable.

There was no one else outside.

Trees stretched upward into the darkness.

He hadn't been afraid.

"Do you ever feel like nature's really dangerous?" I asked Hesper.

"I once slept through a huge earthquake," Hesper said. "Four point six."

"I meant more like everyday nature," I said.

"Are you one of those people that's really into the moon?"

"No."

"I'm an Aquarius, but people always say I'm more of a Pisces."

"It's like being stuck in an elevator shaft," I explained. "Feeling all these—trees around. Closing in around you."

I gestured outward with my hands, like someone demonstrating the girth of a deeply pregnant woman. Hesper was looking at me very intently, even though we were walking next to each other speedily, and I felt flattered by her efforts. It was worse than being stuck in an elevator shaft, because then there was a large, clearly designated HELP button. Besides Hesper, there were no living human beings around. A green water hose coiled like a snake against the side of an adjacent building. Grandly designed churches, stocky mailboxes with their legs low to the ground.

"I can't understand you," Hesper lamented. "Oh, no. Is it the drugs?"

I felt immensely grateful for the existence of drugs. "Probably."

"But you're sad," Hesper said, dream-voiced.

"Scared," I corrected.

"What would make you less scared?" Hesper asked.

"I want to go to Times Square," I said. "I want to be squelched by all those tourists and caricature-makers and places to buy individual slices of red velvet cake."

Hesper laughed. "Times Square is the worst place in the world. The world!"

I thought of being sandwiched among businessmen, the miserable souls hidden by Dora the Explorer and Elmo costumes in the blocked-off street by the TKTS line. Clusters of teenage girls swingsetting between American Eagle and Forever 21. Everyone struggling across midtown, politely ignoring the makeshift entrepreneurs with their burned mix CDs and relentless promotion. I thought of all the eyes that would be able to see me.

I watched Hesper slide her finger across the smudged universe of her iPhone screen and type furtively. Of course, I thought— I had damaged the affection polyp with my innate, incomprehensible weirdness. It was only a matter of time. But then Hesper passed the phone to me with a dimpled smile. On her screen, the first image of Times Square was garishly pumpkin-colored, golden arches of McDonald's glowing benevolently. Bank of America, Kodak, Toshiba, Toy Story. Smudges of bowling-pin-shaped people dashing into a taxi. Pearly skies hidden behind towering, safeguarding skyscrapers.

"You can carry it with you," Hesper offered.

I accepted, eyes blurring against the colors. I wished I knew Hesper well enough to ask: *What are you thinking, underneath all of that ivory fabric and secretive layered hair?* I cradled the phone in my clammy palm. Lending someone your phone was an act of trust. It said: *If my best friend texts me a picture of a watermelon wearing sunglasses, you will see this and it is okay because I would never need to hide my love of accessorized fruits from you.* It said: *When I am with you, I don't need to be with anyone else.*

HESPER STOPPED ABRUPTLY IN front of a tall brownstone. The steps outside were the color of dried figs. I blinked expectantly; this was it, the moment of reveal. I knew it wasn't Hesper's apartment; she walked to class, cheeks flushed from running across campus. Every four seconds I touched the iPhone screen with my fingertips and there it was, comfort in visually arresting shades of neon, tall metal flagpoles in the center of the frame. Hesper and I trudged hurriedly up the five flights of stairs in the building. As Hesper dug for her key ring in a buttery leather purse, her elbow touched my arm. We were careening toward an increase in contact. An attraction, pooling like a blister in a hidden place.

"Are you excited to meet her?" Hesper asked, winded on the landing between the third and fourth flight of stairs. My knees were mildly, hopefully imperceptibly, shaking as we moved toward the top. It was the type of building where residents kept their well-polished oxfords outside their front doors, perched on sprightly welcome mats.

I imagined a guest of honor in a garish, metallic throne. "Of course."

On the fifth floor, Hesper tried each key on the ring before the door opened. I followed her hesitantly down a narrow, pale hallway into a large, wide room. A girl with dark blue, pixie-cut hair and a small gold nose ring glittering between her nostrils crouched in front of a cream-colored mannequin, pinning a hem. She was swarmed by swaths of fabric—an ocean of patterns, obsequiously floral fabric, peach and lilac-colored flowers clustered around leafy spurts of green, splotches of jewel tones, stiff lavender felt.

It's her beautiful, talented girlfriend, I thought. Making another mystical, strange outfit for Hesper to experience the world in. Her own Technicolor dreamcoat.

The nose-ringed fabric-hemmer said, "Are you really wearing that? It's hideous."

"You're the one who made it."

"As an experiment, Lemon. Not as evening wear."

"Lemon?" I asked. What a perfect nickname for Hesper.

"I'm Ada," said Ada, leaning over her many cloths to shake my hand. "Sister of this caped creature."

I smiled with my lips tightly pinched together. The girlfriend assumption felt inordinately creepy. Ada continued to criticize her own garment on Hesper's small body, and Hesper argued in an escalating, delighted defense, especially of the cape's wayward strings. I averted my eyes from their affection. Even though the relationship had been clarified, I still housed a prickle of competitiveness with Ada, the kind that only children feel when they witness interactions of love between siblings.

Two other mannequins loomed in the corner of the living room against a large, obtrusive sofa. I stared at their plastic torsos, swanlike necks. The places where their hands and feet would be. Lumpless hourglasses, as smooth as china. I looked at the things that they were missing.

"The kitchen's on the other side of the apartment," Hesper informed me.

"What?"

Hesper reached for me, gripping each of my shoulders with a smooth hand, leading us out of the living room and into the narrow hallway. It was like a kindergarten chain of students, marching out to the playground for recess. At first, the contact between Hesper's fingertips and my cotton-covered shoulders was a beguiling jolt. But her touch was so gentle, and in the dimness of the corridor, with Hesper's breath collecting in the hollows of my ear, the jolt soured into a rolling, unshakeable sensation. The presence of another body, so close to hers—but imperceptible, distanced. Without the ability to see Hesper, the voluminous ivory skirt, the floppy, Thousand Island–colored hair, she could be anyone. She tightened her grasp on my bones.

"Before you came to the diner," I began, my voice tremulous.

I felt the rays of Hesper smiling, and then the wobble that remained post-smile.

Hesper stopped walking toward the kitchen. We stood, motionless, with Hesper's fingers kneaded into my shoulders. I knew that I should continue, but saying it out loud would have been like parting my lips and conjuring up the dusty gumball instead of the consonants and vowels that make up language. I listened to the hum of Ada's sewing machine.

"It wasn't like a real assault," I said finally. "It was . . . small. Assault Junior."

"Assault Junior," Hesper said, quiet. "A.J."

"Right."

"What happened?"

"He followed me. And then."

"And then," Hesper repeated.

"You don't have to let go of my shoulders."

"Okay," Hesper said, returning to her original position.

"He had me pinned to this tree. I could feel it rubbing against me."

Hesper was waiting for me to continue, but I wasn't sure that I could.

"He just touched me, he didn't... It wasn't very... thorough. He didn't get..." But I didn't want to say the words *inside me.* "Invasive," I finished, finally. *But he could have,* I thought.

"God, Willa. Are you okay?"

Her touch felt delicate now.

"I thought I would feel better if I said it, but it didn't work," I said, throaty.

"Do you want to tell anyone? The police?"

"I just want to tell you," I said. "They don't do anything anyway."

A silence unfurled between us.

"I shouldn't have nicknamed it," Hesper said.

"No, I liked it. Thank you."

"Do you want to talk more?" Hesper asked, in a tone of gentleness that dismantled something I was trying very hard to contain.

"No. I want to meet the thing that's in the kitchen."

Hesper led me into the kitchen. I bent to peer inside a cardboard box, at the tailed clumps of animal, curled with their pink triangular ears plastered tight against their heads. They looked frighteningly new and fragile, as though missing a layer—raw, skinned. I swallowed. Mother Cat stood, slinking, her torso swollen against the box. Hesper was speaking, identifying the names of each claimed-for kitten. I watched Mother Cat's eyes glistening greenly, her graceful, acerbic movements as she suddenly jumped from the box and bounded across the tiled floor, the sound of her claws clattering dramatically.

"What's going on with you?" Hesper clucked, intrigued.

We followed Mother Cat, who was taking steady, deliberate steps across the room. I crouched on the floor, knees heavy and spread, approaching Mother Cat, who swept furiously with her sharp nails at something underneath the refrigerator.

"There must be something under there," Hesper said, straining to see what Mother Cat was hunting. But I saw only dark, empty space in the tiny curtain of black between the bottom of the refrigerator and the clean, Swiffered floor tiles.

My leg muscles started to ache, the pain of stillness and balance, but I didn't change positions. My thighs trembled with effort. Hot sweat formed in the space beneath my breasts. Mother Cat swiped her paw relentlessly underneath the machine, concentrated. I forgot that I was in Hesper's sister's apartment; I forgot Hesper's iPhone in her back pocket, the chrysalis of comfort that I'd found in images of Times Square; I forgot Hesper. I forgot the boy. I forgot the texture of the tree that he pressed me into. The notes that were playing into my ears, the bruises that had formed underneath my clothes. Transfixed, I watched Mother Cat tuck her head underneath the refrigerator, lunging at the unseen. She bared her teeth.

2.

I hadn't remembered falling asleep on the sofa, and I hadn't remembered Willa falling asleep on the floor of Ada's living room, either. In the morning, my eyes blurry with sudden awakeness, I took it in fragments: the sprawl of her dark curls against one of the ivory, fuzzy pillows that belonged on the futon; an exposed ankle, pale, bent like a wishbone. Tibby was circling Willa's head, her little paws menacingly stalking the space surrounding the wooden coffee table with its fashionably gold-painted legs.

I cranked myself from supine to upright, and without meaning to, I moaned. I moaned because the comedown from the Molly was so terrible already and I'd been awake for three Mississippis, tops. My eyes felt leaky. Ada's living room, dappled with midmorning light through her bird-covered curtains, was an obstacle course of mannequins with hastily pinned fabrics, and I knew if I tried to stand and grabbed at any of those creations, I would rip them apart.

Then: Willa. She slept in the shape of a comma. Even in the haze of my depression, with its weight in the space underneath my sternum and the feeling that all of my life had been hopeless, forever, and I had just realized it right now, that all of life was a hospital waiting room where someone else was in the only bathroom and it smelled of bleach and individual apple juices in plastic cups, even through that, I noticed Willa, how her hair looked like that of a mermaid, how her body looked so soft, so curveful, underneath her shirt. I saw the space between the bottom of her T-shirt and the top of her leggings and I wanted to lay my head there and use it as a pillow.

I lifted Tibby into my arms and she first lovingly and then combatively nibbled my pinky. She stared at me with judgy, glowing green eyes, squirming, until I dropped her. Not on Willa, but near enough that she woke up to the clatter of Tibby bolting back underneath the sofa. Any sense of tranquility, scalded. The sound of Tibby, scurrying out of sight and then down the hallway, had the cringeworthy effect of radio static, stretching into my headache and elongating it like taffy.

"Sorry," I said. "I didn't mean to drop her so close to your face."

Willa sat up. Creases from the pillow's texture, and from the blanket she'd been using as a bed, covered her in a verdant linear pattern. She smiled warily, in a way that made me think she ached from the uncomfortable sleeping place, and I wished I could remember the conversation that led to us sleeping here in the first place. She made a visor with her hand. "When I was in sixth grade, I woke up to my friend's cat licking my nose, and it scared me so much that I screamed."

"Tibby's not licking anyone's nose. She's a killer."

Willa blinked. "She hasn't ... brought you any conquests?"

"Ada probably wouldn't tell me about that. She's squeamish." And probably awake, eavesdropping on this conversation and ready to heavily reprimand me for crashing here without asking. Never mind Willa. My shoulders bunched together, caving up to my ears. I thought about lying down next to her, there on the floor. There was no reason to think things would improve from here. I didn't even know what day it was.

"I feel awful," I announced. "I'm sorry. I'm not going to be ... good company."

A smile crested over Willa's face. She had a dimple. It was the kind of dimple that looked etched in with a knife, not one of those flimsy dimples that came and went. "My mom uses that phrase when she thinks I've brought up an unpleasant topic. She says, 'Willa, you're not being very *good company*.'"

"What kind of unpleasant topic?"

"Oh, you know. Like whether your cat's brought any dead mice to you as treasure."

In spite of myself, I smiled. "Have you ever done Molly?" I asked. She hadn't. "It's the most miserable hangover you can have. Seriously, there have been studies. It can plunge you into a clinical depression. But the good part," I said, trying to remember: the exuberance, the light, the love I felt for everything in that diner, especially the aluminum siding and the salty broth of chicken soup. "The good part is unbeatable. What's the happiest you've ever been?"

Willa looked at the ceiling as she thought. As soon as I noticed, I knew I would never not notice that again, and the knowledge that I knew her thinking face felt strangely satisfying.

"When I was four, on my first day of preschool, my dad came to pick me up as a surprise. He worked all the time when I was that young, so it was really rare for me to see him before I went to bed, much less for him to pick me up at school. Anyway, he hoisted me up on his shoulders and we walked all the way home like that, but midway through the walk, he gave me a peppermint pattie. I couldn't believe it. I never got to eat candy during the day."

I waited for the story to continue, but it didn't. "That's the happiest ever?" I asked. "He gave you a peppermint pattie?"

"I saved the wrapper, even."

I laughed, harder than I meant to. "You have the lowest expectations I've ever heard."

"*Thanks*," Willa said, a blush creeping down to her neck. "I'll take that as a compliment."

I looked at the bunched-up blanket, the scanty space that Willa had curled herself into, and a cascade of guilt whirled through me.

"I'm sorry that you had to sleep on the floor like a vagabond. I wasn't thinking...super clearly, when I brought us back here. My sister's probably going to hang me out to dry for this whole...adventure."

"She went to the co-op," Willa said. "She left a note, and like, forty vitamins."

"You were up, earlier?"

Willa shrugged. "I didn't sleep well."

My gaze settled on a bruise, purpling onto Willa's skin. It was shaped like a thumb. The vestige of her Assault Junior. Willa saw me see it and her entire body changed, her posture pulled into a straight line. The spine alignment of a ballerina, ready for a performance. Without thinking, I reached for it, and she flinched.

The moment when I should have asked if she was okay, or if she wanted to talk, passed in glacial slow motion. But what if she said yes? What then? I was ill-equipped for other people's traumas. My go-to move was the forearm pat, and without that, I didn't know what I would do. In some ways, around Willa, I felt as if we'd been orbiting each other for years—when, from across our classroom table, I watched her start to smile at something she shouldn't be smiling at, and watched that smile poorly compress back into the architecture of her face. But then, moments like this emerged, and I realized I didn't know her very well at all. Not concretely.

"You should take the vitamins," Willa said. "Before you feel worse."

"Thanks," I said. I found my way to the kitchen. "Do you want any orange juice?"

"Only if it's incredibly pulpy, or not pulpy at all."

I checked the pulp factor. "You're in luck. You're going to be choking on these vesicles. There's no turning back." The violence of my quippiness hung between us like a blackout curtain. "Sorry. I—"

"Perfect," Willa rebounded, bouncing into the kitchen. I couldn't tell if I was moving at 100 percent sluggishness or Willa was an En-

ergizer Bunny in the morning, but she broke out two coffee mugs
and poured the juice and drank it down before I weebled my way to
Ada's kitchen table, where there was just enough room for two cups
and nothing else, between the microwave, a vase of browning dahlias,
and a lazy Susan crowded with packets of gourmet mayonnaise. Willa
shook out a vitamin from each bottle that Ada prescribed. "Open,"
and I unlocked my jaw.

"I meant your hand," she said, laughing a little.

"Right, right."

"So after you replenish your serotonin levels," she read from Ada's
note, "and have some vitamins A, C, and E, we should go for a walk
and look at trees? What's forest bathing?" She'd Googled it before
I had a chance to formulate an answer. The pills chalked down my
throat. "So it's not just looking, but...smelling trees lowers your stress
hormones? That's bananas."

"That's why everybody's happier in Northern California. It smells
like eucalyptus." The last pill, the important one, tasted like fake
"mixed berry" and I felt my nose wrinkle up my forehead.

Willa glanced up from her phone. "Were you happier in Northern
California?" she asked.

I thought of my new apartment, on Claremont and La Salle, with
my roommate Kate, who'd said less than five words to me since we'd
moved in three weeks ago and how she'd taken over the living room
with her kinesiology flash cards mounted to a bulletin board as tall as
I was. I couldn't open my closet door and the bedroom door at the
same time, and how we were both too afraid to kill the cockroaches
so we just trapped them underneath salad bowls but now we'd run
out of salad bowls and it was impossible to walk from the kitchen to
the bathroom in a straight line. I thought of how I'd wanted to live
with Ada, but Mom had insisted that student housing would be better, would help me make friends.

"Nope," I said, which was true.

WE ASCENDED THE HILLY block between Ada's street and Prospect Park, covering basic details: Willa's hometown in New Jersey, my parents' status as divorced with a side of maybe-they'll-get-back-together-someday, the beautiful architecture of Park Slope's brownstones and occasional flickering gas lamp. At the entrance near Grand Army Plaza, flowery urns adorned with slithering snakes guarded the stone perimeter. The sun shone cavalierly on my bare shoulders while dutiful runners with French bulldogs weaved past us on the main path.

"I've never been here," Willa admitted. "Prospect Park always seems really far away."

"I've only spent time in Brooklyn," I said. "When I visited, I stayed with Ada. Manhattan is like this weird collage of places I've seen in movies. This, here, is what I think of when I think of New York."

"Did you always want to move here?" Willa asked. "Or did it just happen for the MFA?"

I didn't want to tell her the truth, which was that I'd followed Ada here because I had no real plans of my own; that I'd taken exactly one creative writing class and the professor was so sleep-deprived with her new baby that everyone had gotten an A that semester; that I'd only applied to Columbia because Ada told me it was a big program that didn't need the GRE, so I had a pretty good shot with the two sto-ries I'd written in my life, both of which I'd worked on for over a year. After Northwestern, I hated the idea of moving back into my mom's house in Marin, becoming the focus of her twitchy, postwork attention day after day. I was an adult. I was skittering toward becom-ing an adult. And I'd been good at school. I came close to deadlines but didn't miss them; I knew when to emphatically nod and keep eye contact with professors so they knew I was listening. It was more about playing a part than having talent. But I liked the idea of Willa thinking that this was some kind of writerly destiny and not a series of surreptitious mistakes.

"Yeah," I said blandly. "And, you know, I missed my sister."

"Who wouldn't? The vitamin provider," Willa said.

"What about you?" I asked, trying to talk over the sound of Ada's future lecture in my head. "Did you always want to end up in the city?"

"When I was younger, I hated it here. I was convinced somebody was going to jab me with a hypodermic needle in that giant Macy's." Willa laughed, although that particular visual made me a little queasy. "Once I got older, and all the concerts were here, I got obsessed with it. I used to take the bus in on weekends and walk to the Village, and think about Kerouac and Gertrude Stein, and all the other writers who were inspired by the city... you know. It sounds cliché."

"A little. Maybe more romantic. Capital R romantic."

"I love it," she said. "I love it even when I have to haul my laundry two avenues and it's so heavy that I have to rest a few times. Plus, living with my parents was..." She paused.

"No more peppermint patties?" I asked.

That dimple. She lowered her chin, bashful. "Yeah. Less peppermint patties. A few years ago, my dad was in a car accident that really fucked up his back. It caused all this damage to his disks, and once the damage started, it's just gotten worse. He had to go on disability and now he's really... out of it, from all the painkillers."

"That sucks."

"Yeah. My mom is super resentful about caretaking. She's more of an executive type. So... I'm loving having my own place," Willa rushed on. The Great Lawn stretched before us, an expanse of manicured green. In the distance, a children's birthday party with paper plates and red and yellow balloons bobbled in the wind, like living creatures straining against their leashes. "I live with Chloe—do you know Chloe? Straight hair, gold glasses?"

"Everybody knows Chloe."

"We went to Vassar together. She was my sophomore year neighbor; we've been really good friends since then. We live right around the corner from Lion's Head," she said, "and we have this little basement, so whenever a group of fictioneers go out and somebody gets too wasted, they usually end up staying over on our couch, and I make them tea in the morning. It's a good routine."

"So you're good at taking care of people," I said. She looked at me with her dark eyes.

"Yeah," she said. "I am." Her purse swung listlessly at her side. We folded into single file as a woman with an enormous, bearlike dog passed us, and I felt the current between us then, the presence of her body right behind me. She could have kissed my neck, I thought, and imagined her lips finding my pulse.

"Do you think the trees are healing me?" I asked.

"Definitely," Willa said. When she reemerged at my side, her thighs brushed mine.

We kept walking, deeper into the park than I'd been in a long time: past the bandshell, a bird-watching tour with their binoculars clutched in hearty anticipation, the Boathouse with its grand, pastel tiles. The lake glowed its algae-laden green. We talked about our favorite writers, about the best kind of jam, about where we'd traveled and where we wanted to go. Willa, mysteriously, had never been on an airplane. I felt the leaden drumbeat of my hangover start to dissipate. Feathery leaves skirted white clouds, arranged in bunches as if they'd come from a spout. Willa's face was smudged with light.

"What would be your ideal day?" I asked her. "If there were a Willa Greenberg day."

"First, I'd get the pancake special at Community. Do you know the pancake special?" she said. "It's ten dollars for the best pancakes in New York, plus coffee and orange juice, but it's only until eight a.m."

"That's obscenely early."

"They're the world's best pancakes. I work at the business library—in real life, not in my ideal day—at eight-fifteen, so sometimes I treat myself and get there at seven, right at opening." She absentmindedly twirled a curl around her finger and it bounced back, in perfect formation. "Then I'd go to Neue Galerie and see the Klimt paintings they have. He's my favorite. And at the museum, they have this Austrian cafe with perfect cake and Viennese coffee with whipped cream. It's my *favorite* place."

"So your ideal day is just dessert and art?" I said.

"Basically. I'd probably see a concert at night. A female singer-songwriter with a guitar."

"That's my zone, too," I told her. "Cat Power. A side of Laura Marling."

"Yeah?" Willa said brightly.

"Yeah."

"Then I'd go to bed early," she said. "That would be the end to my perfect day. Sleep." She smiled at me. "What about you?"

I shrugged. I was never the planner; that was Ada's job. I thought of the night before, with Adam and Haniya, who I'd known since high school, and their new friends from Stanford who'd thought it would be funny to tinfoil the walls of their living room, and their drug dealer, Q. It was easy to be with people who plotted their destinations in terms of procuring drugs, then reclining at someone's apartment, then finding garlic knots or fries blanketed by saucy cheese. Dancing at a place with no cover. Getting thrown out of that place with no cover because Adam, even on Molly, couldn't help fighting if there was a line for the bathroom. I didn't really think about what I wanted to do, most days. I went along with a plan, or I read glum stories about blue-collar Americans from the '80s and ordered pad see ew. I liked to feel the noodles slide down my throat. I barely even chewed.

"With the exception of my hangover," I said. "I guess . . . this is."

"Yeah?" Willa said. Her smile had taken over the bottom of her face and it lightened me.

"Yeah."

We'd been next to each other, but now her body faced mine.

"Come here," she said. And then, I didn't realize we were kissing until we were. It was a kiss that spread wide inside of me, an eagle's wingspan. Her hand reached for the top of my spine and stayed there, the lightest possible contact, and I felt it traipse all the way down the length of my back. Her lips were even softer than I'd imagined. I found the rhythm of her kissing: furtive, but constant, a surge of wanting. She tasted like the orange juice. Our mouths matched, I thought.

I had kissed girls before, but at parties, and not soberly. Not without plausible deniability.

And: I had wanted to kiss girls before, but I had not.

In a faraway place in my head, the place that wasn't thinking of Willa's body against mine, or the ebb and flow of my breath hot on her neck, or the quiet crunch of foot traffic avoiding us, here, in the leaf-laden park on a beautiful day, I thought of yesterday. I thought of the bruise that squinted out from underneath her pale skin, and whether there were others. Whether it was right to make out with someone who'd just been sexually assaulted, even if she tried to downplay it by saying it was a little assault, and what did that really mean? Was I supposed to stop her? She'd kissed me. She was definitely kissing me now. She'd slept on the floor of my sister's apartment to conjure this moment, I thought.

"Are you okay?" I asked, mid-kiss. My voice rumbled. I touched her bruise, the evidence, to show her what I meant. She lowered her gaze from mine. Beneath us, the ground was spongy, pockmarked with mud in places where yesterday's rain hadn't yet been absorbed.

"I don't want to think about that," Willa said. Her fingers pressed against my neck. "I just want to think about you, Hesper. Okay?" She adjusted her posture so her lips were flush against my earlobe. "I've been thinking about this since the first time we saw each other. I've been thinking about this every time we're in workshop, across that giant table."

"Really?"

"You're even better than the peppermint pattie," she said, and pressed her lips to mine.

It seemed impossible, as we headed back to the subway, that the previous night had been less than twenty-four hours ago. It felt like time had unshuffled from its usual pattern to deliver us into a new, shinier reality, in which a person that couldn't wait to kiss me, and a person that I couldn't wait to kiss back, was at my side. Dopey, doe-eyed, we sat so close to each other on the train that I could feel Willa's exhales balloon, then shrink. All of the other passengers nearby seemed out of focus, painted in sepia tones somehow, with their earbuds and phone swiping. Couldn't they feel it, the frenzied, hamster-wheel energy circulating from my legs to hers? Didn't they see we were radiating?

All other infatuation I'd experienced was like having too much coffee: heartbeat rapid, a little nauseating. Willa made me feel as if my life was about to get so much better, that the current motion of the F train was interminable. I was walking in circles in the rising action and then, I'd be where I was meant to be, hiking up the narrative of my own life. The F train skittered through Brooklyn, sweeping out from Gowanus to look out over the water, sunshine glinting metallically, before we plundered back into the darkness underground. Jay Street: Metrotech. We transferred to the A, where a panhandler played a large steel drum with his hands and, for the first time, I gave him a quarter.

"You're so generous," Willa said, brushing her shoulder against mine. I was not terribly self-aware but knew that I was distinctly ungenerous. But it occurred to me that I could fall in love—not just with Willa, but with Willa's idea of me.

We chatted around lukewarm topics—not going to talk about the press of her finger on my wrist, or the way that she licked her bottom lip, not going to talk about the long, rapt eye contact that defined our conversation on the subway even as we were discussing our professor's socks and clogs combination, and would it be more comfortable to wear clogs barefoot, but then if you were barefoot, would your feet get cold in the overly breezy classroom? Clogs, Willa said, and she continued to talk but all I heard was *clogs clogs clogs*, and all the while her eyes lobbed with possibilities that involved: me, my body, her, and hers. I saw it all. I was latticed with wanting and distracted by the squeaky brakes and the guy across from us eating a strawberry yogurt with his face in the absence of a spoon. Anticipation spread, a rush of toppling dominoes. Then we were on the 1 train, and 79th, 86th, 96th, and soon if no one did anything it would be Willa's stop, which was not also my stop.

I could have said: *Come over.* I could have said: *I want to see your apartment.* I knew she would have agreed happily. But I remained soundless, skittish. Anxiety fluttered up my throat like a moth searching for a source of light. The truth was, for all of my yearning, for all of the time I'd been gathering queer signifiers and incorporating them into myself—collecting fedoras, watching *Buffy the Vampire Slayer* on Netflix, the Virginia Woolf quote underneath my senior portrait—I'd never considered that I might not be good at sex with women until this moment. Or that there was such a gulf between knowing something and acting upon it, when acting upon it was a possibility that grazed your arm.

When we got to 110th Street, Willa squeezed my hand. "See you tomorrow," she said. For class. For a class that would be my turn to hand in a story, and that story didn't exist yet. But for now, that didn't matter. For now I was going to get a paper cup filled with sour frozen yogurt and eat it until my teeth went numb with cold, and I wouldn't even notice.

In line at the frozen yogurt store, I stared at a man in a 49ers jersey with a rainbow ribbon pinned to his backpack. I thought about saying something to him, but I didn't. I'd grown up just outside of San Francisco, perhaps the gayest place in the world. Gay pride flags swung vibrantly in front of brunch spots with huckleberry smoothies and waffles dotted with raspberries. Cable cars chugged uphill. Whole neighborhoods of bandana-wearing folk music fans with rescue dogs handed out fliers for social justice. But: still. I'd never tried to talk about it, and the longer I tried not to talk about it, the stupider it felt, since the only person making it an issue was me. I could so easily imagine Mom's tone of voice on the phone as she called Dad to tell him—a little too loud, with her syllables crisp and practiced, adding some comment about how she'd never thought I cared much about any of my (many) boyfriends, anyway, it all made sense now. I could so easily imagine a bouquet of rainbow-hued flowers in my room with a little card about how my happiness mattered more than anything, and I didn't want it. I didn't want an announcement or a premade, sculpted tale of acceptance that may as well have come in a kit called "Supportive Liberal Parents of LGBTQIA+ Children!!"

Besides. I'd never had any reason to tell.

I texted my sister: *I think I'm in love.*

She texted back: *You better be, Lemon. The roommates are chewing me out so hard. Don't ever have a sleepover in my living room without asking again. (But: !!!!!!)*

THEN IT WAS THE afternoon and I realized I had a document with no words, not even a handful, to describe a plot that everyone had read already. I had a stomach full of overpriced Pinkberry and a computer that I'd very recently spilled coffee on, so each word came with a trail of R's afterward as a frustrating bonus to my writer's block. I'd been a procrastinator for my entire life and the deadline hummed merrily in my ears as I snacked on almonds covered in cinnamon sugar and looked at pictures of baby hedgehogs and returned to Willa, to our kiss, to the tunnel of trees that sheltered us in the park and the way her breath had percussively slowed, then quickened.

I couldn't think of anything else. *Every time we're in workshop, across that giant table.*

For hours I tried to construct a world as far away as I could imagine. A middle-aged accountant describing the death of their daughter's pet turtle. An entire page devoted to the methodical ritual of rolling one's own cigarettes. I teetered through the story, constantly glancing at my phone (had she...? No. Not yet. But maybe she would. Or maybe I should...?) The child mourned her dead turtle. She blew through a kazoo. She had asthma now. Was she dead? Not dead. Just sad about her turtle. I drained cup after cup of coffee that my roommate had definitely brewed for herself. We'd run out of regular sugar so I substituted confectioner's, and it clumped eagerly along the surface like a powdery rash. It wasn't such a bad story. The asthmatic kazooer learned how to masturbate, alone in her polka-dotted bed, remembering the shell of her turtle's body. Was that...okay to write? It was edgy, I decided, my head pumping with wanting, so much wanting that I couldn't block it out long enough to write this paragraph.

I closed my computer. It was definitely done, I thought, my fingers already starting to move.

IN THE HAZE OF Tuesday morning, after a desultory conversation about the humidity with my roommate and another cup of coffee, the first thing I thought of was Willa. Willa Greenberg. It took longer for me to remember that, for my first story in my graduate-level creative writing workshop, I'd decided to write a story about a child masturbating to the memory of her dead pet. Scrolling through my ten mealy-mouthed pages with one finger while I funneled cereal into my mouth, I confirmed that it was, in fact, just as bad as I remembered.

I knew how gossip went. I'd overheard enough catty conversations from the plush, brown sofa that served as the epicenter of the computer lab about people's repetitive sentence construction or use of old-man idioms to know that this was the thing that people would remember about me next week, and the next month, until we graduated. A faint but insistent purr of dread amplified in my ears. Gracefully, the dredge of the coffee swished against the bottom of the pot, and I couldn't even bring myself to drink it, I just put it back down; rubbed the makeup from my eyes and rushed to the computer lab to try to salvage whatever reputation I would have after today's class.

At school, I darted into the lab and stood uncomfortably behind someone I didn't recognize until they relented their seat. *Come on, come on,* I thought, logging in to a blank screen decorated with anonymously pleasing fireworks. I had to make the child older; that seemed the most obvious way to subvert at least some of the controversy. A teenager. Sixteen, I thought; nobody was uncomfortable with a sexually curious teenage girl. Frantically I scanned through every tag of dialogue, every mention of age, and I hunched toward the computer as if it were an enemy in a duel.

I didn't even notice Willa there, in my extreme focus, until I heard her. "Hey, Hesper."

"My story is garbage. I need to change . . . all of it. Everything."

Willa bent behind me to glance at the screen. "I'm sure that's not true," she said, her voice balmy. I could feel the sway of her hair against the back of my shoulder blade and it was enough to make me start to cry a little.

"I'm at a tipping point," I said. "I'm sorry."

"I used to be a proofreader as part of my job," Willa said. "Tell me what you want to change and I'll do it fast."

"Really?"

"Yeah," she said, dragging an orphan chair closer to my screen. I mumbled the changes about the girl's age, and how I wanted to make the kazoo a clarinet, and for her mother to be older so they didn't seem too close in age, all the while keeping an eye on those digital numbers in the upper right hand corner, ticking down closer to my workshop humiliation. On the other side of the wall, the copiers pleasantly spit out stapled, collated packets of other people's thoughtful, researched stories. I could hear the crunch of the staples and, even as Willa wound through my story correcting, restitching the connective tissue that held my words together, I braided and unbraided my hair so that my fingers had something to do.

"Five minutes," I said.

"Almost . . . there. Print it. Print!" Willa exclaimed. She looked at me with that smile. "We did it."

"You did it. I just turned myself into Heidi," I said. The printer rushed, warmly, in a paginated flurry of something resembling my work. "Thank you. Seriously, I don't know what I would have done."

"It's not a big deal," Willa said, pausing before she added my name at the end. "Hesper."

"I'll make it up to you," I said. "I'll build you a castle of peppermint patties."

Willa scanned the room to see if anyone was looking near us. She touched my hand. "Okay," she said. "I accept."

THE NEXT WEEK, WHEN it was my turn to be critiqued, our professor—a lanky woman with sleeves of floral tattoos and an eyebrow ring that was maybe ironic—stretched her arms out on the table. She drummed all of her fingers in unison. "This next one is a real doozy," she said. "Hesper, you want to read a page to get us kicked off? Then you're in the *cone of silence*."

Willa kept her eyes on me as I read; my voice cracked on the word *pulsing*. Laughter rolled toward us from behind the closed glass door. I took a long sip from a bathroom-sized Dixie cup of tepid water. I wanted to be less nervous. I wanted to care as little as I'd cared all through undergrad, when a professor noticed me texting underneath my individual desk in a lecture hall. But this was different. What you chose to write was a statement on what you thought was important, or at the very least, it was an avenue into what you thought about. Everyone already knew that Marisa was obsessed with her cousin, and Ingrid described alcoholics with too much detail to be a casual observer. Willa's story, which had been about the granddaughter of a Holocaust survivor who discovered her girlfriend was cheating on her with a White supremacist, also contained the residue of truth.

Willa raised her hand. "I love the way Hesper takes objects and makes interesting verbs out of them, like 'marionette-d' on page ten. I think it's a really smart choice to contrast with the conservatism of the mother's career and personality."

She'd read the comment, word for word, off of the top of her page. I could tell, and it endeared me to her like nothing else had. I pinched a smile gratefully in her direction.

"Can I say something?" Megan said. "I don't know what this story *is*. Why do we need another story about a teenage girl experiencing her first orgasm? Can't teenage girls do something outside of sexual

awakenings? Why couldn't she become a coder, or get involved in ro-
botics? And who could possibly love a turtle this much?"

"I don't think that having a female-centered coming-of-age story
without a male love interest is trite," Willa said. She'd never spoken
this much in class before and her whole face bunched with pink
splotches. "And why should we center the experience of someone in-
clined toward mathematics as a more valuable perspective?"

"I had a turtle," Ingrid said. "I loved it. I mean, not like this, but—"

"And the mother," Megan said, with a sigh. "What's her motivation?"

"She's inert," Willa said. "It's a commentary on the motivation that
she's lost throughout her life." Willa stared in Megan's direction. "At
the end, there's a note of hope when she takes the clarinet back to her
room, implying that maybe she'll learn to play it herself."

"The *clarinet* is a symbol for hope?" Megan asked. "Come on."

"Whether or not you feel the clarinet is a worthwhile instrument
is not the discussion," Willa said, dipping into a tone of hostility that
I hadn't heard from her before, and I could feel the gratitude all over,
like pain. "We're supposed to evaluate each story on the terms the
writer sets in the opening pages. The clarinet is important. It's on
page one."

"Good gravy," the professor said. "Let's hear from someone on a
non-clarinet issue."

"I feel like— Am I the only one who thought the daughter might
be dead?" Ingrid asked. "Like, is *she* the turtle?"

"Great," the professor said. "Let's go with that."

AFTER CLASS, MY CLASSMATES (not including Megan) spilled into the
hallway and stood in a glob, weakly exchanging compliments and re-
assurances in my direction. Ingrid told me more about her pet turtle,

who was named Curtis. Willa stood protectively next to me, a thick pile of workshop submissions camouflaging her chest. I could feel her, evaluating my reactions, the slippery smile on my face that felt it might slide right off if I didn't concentrate on seeming fine. I was. I was fine. It was a stupid class in which overly invested intellectuals tossed around theories about fictional people who didn't mean anything to me. That's all it was. Somebody laughed and I laughed, too, my gaze focused on a blackboard with a Toni Morrison quote: *If there's a book you want to read, but it hasn't been written yet, then you must write it.*

"Sorry, I have to— See you guys," I said, my voice frosted with faux-casualness. I waved.

"Like a literal bloodbath," I heard Ingrid say as I headed down the main staircase. "Well, not a *literal* bloodbath."

I stood in the foyer of the Creative Writing building, with its TV screen by the vending machine boasting of previous graduates' success, and the guy who worked at the snack counter with its individually wrapped Macintosh apples, and even though I wanted to leave desperately, I couldn't get my feet to work. I coated and recoated my lips in citrus-scented gloss. Through the glass doors, I could see the familiar oak trees, the tall, marble columns where, though the smokers themselves were hidden, I could watch plumes of cigarette smoke phantom into the sky.

"Quite the getaway," Willa teased behind me. "Hey. Are you okay?"

"Sure," I said.

"Your hair is stuck in your lip gloss," she said, tenderly unsticking my hair from my face.

"Thanks."

"Let's get you immersed in some trees," she said, nodding in the direction of Riverside Park.

"Don't be *too* nice to me," I warned. "You can be nice, just not extra. Like, five out of ten."

She nodded. We scattered from the building, careful to look so engrossed in conversation that our classmates turned into unrecognizable shadows, coagulated on seating next to our building. Down the colossal, iconic Columbia steps, we navigated around undergrads carrying salads in clear plastic domes, across Broadway toward the park. Grand brick buildings with seafoam green roofs looked golden in the sun. At the water's edge, trees heavy with ivory and peachy blossoms sunk, crooked over a row of benches. We sat there, looking at the texture of the Hudson chopping along with its serene, chemical-tainted water. I slipped off my shoes, crisscrossed myself on the bench until my thigh muscles ached from the stretch.

"Not to be a bad feminist, but Megan really is a bitch," Willa said finally. I laughed.

"She really doesn't like clarinets. Or turtles."

"You know what's weird?" Willa said. "I don't find any comfort in looking at water. Even though it's been, like, scientifically proven to reduce stress and create that feeling of awe of nature, I just... don't see it."

"Really? What do you see?"

Willa shrugged. "Live action wallpaper."

I laughed. "What?" I said, lingering on the surface of the river. Although I knew it wasn't, the water looked completely still. The sky above the current was dusted with mist. I missed San Francisco, the way that the fog veiled the Golden Gate Bridge's red paint in swatches of translucent gray. The Hudson didn't compare to the ocean, the scent of the salt in my nostrils. But it helped. It made me feel small, and manageable. It made the wary anxiety that snagged throughout workshop fade.

"You're incredulous."

"I won't deny that. And, also... I meant to say before," I offered. "Thank you for defending me." Willa laid her hand out on the bench between us like a starfish. She bristled, then smiled past it, as I inspected her hand like it was a road map. She had a beauty mark, or some kind of freckle, on the right side of her palm. "I wanted to say something else."

Her eyes felt welded to mine. Dark with vigilance.

"I've never had a girlfriend," I said. "I mean . . . you would be my first. I've wanted one, I'm not, like . . . wavering in what I want. It's just never worked out, exactly."

Willa opened her mouth to say something but then didn't. The extent of my vulnerability revealed itself in a somersault below my ribs. It wasn't doubt that she felt the same; it was doubt that, by voicing it, something would go wrong. Possibilities of catastrophe inflated as soon as you spoke it, that much I knew. I plucked a dandelion that had clustered in the grass near our feet, a little yellow lollipop, and handed it to her. Willa's hand quavered. But her face was gridded with tentative joy.

"So now you know," I said.

She gazed at me, adoringly but unblinking, as if seeing a premonition. "Now I know," she said.

3.

With every new love interest, there was research to be done. It was tradition. Chloe bought Red Vines and bit both ends so they'd work as straws for boxed cabernet sauvignon, and I clustered onto her bed with our laptops next to each other. Though our apartment was on the first floor and every conversation on the stoop was audible from Chloe's exuberantly plush-pillowed bed, I felt sequestered. We snooped. A kaleidoscope of Hesper's past: her emerald green prom dress, her summer working as a camp counselor, a throwback photo of her as a baby, swaddled by a diaphanous orange pumpkin outfit. There was a ten-year limit on Facebook stalking, Chloe decreed, but Hesper was younger than we were. Ten years earlier, she'd been twelve.

"She's a baby," Chloe said. "Twenty-two."

"That's only four years younger than us."

"Yeah, but four years can be a lot. Four years ago I didn't own a pair of flats. Plus, you know. Emotional maturity."

"She's emotionally mature," I argued. "And so beautiful. Don't you think she's so beautiful?"

"She's so squinty in this picture," Chloe said, turning the laptop toward me for confirmation. "Like the flash is a solar eclipse or something. But yes, on a whole. Super beautiful. And that letter was dreamy, Will. She just snuck that in your mailbox?"

I flushed. "It was a thank you for helping her with her story." *But she hadn't just said thank you,* I thought, the love-potential flurrying across my thoughts so that I was somewhere else, a quiet room with Hesper's voice low in my ear, so that all other sensory input had been muted and it was just me, and Hesper's voice, thanking me. Closing the letter with the admission: *I keep thinking of you and I can't stop. —H*

Last month, I'd lived in my childhood bedroom, its walls painted a juvenile shade of bubblegum. Pictures of friends that I'd stopped speaking to years earlier were clipped into photo holders adorned with tropical fish from bar and bat mitzvah favors. Last month I'd been in charge of pleasant dinnertime conversation topics because Mom was usually mad and Dad was starting to drift off, drift away, three white pills and his pain abated but not enough to concentrate, to follow a thread. Last month I'd packed a suitcase full of loose cotton T-shirts and leggings, leather boots that came up to the knee, and moved seven miles away to live with Chloe, who already had furniture and dish towels and bowls from Anthropologie in dainty Victorian florals. Now we were drunk on wine and straws fashioned from candy, and I had a letter that was . . . not exactly a love letter, but not *not* a love letter either, from a perfect person who squinted excessively in photos. I had everything. A best friend, a story that had been relatively well received in workshop, a work study job at the library that paid enough to cover groceries and utilities and student loan checks to cover the rest, mostly. I knew it wasn't really my money but it felt real, seeing a five-digit number in my checking account for the very first time. And what use did it do to worry about after graduation, anyway? The MFA program directors told us, that first day at orientation: these two years were to focus on becoming a real writer. To become a real version of yourself.

Chloe touched my arm and I felt the touch travel from my arm to my shoulder to my chest. Underneath my bra's wires, I felt the bruise's tenderness, reminding me of what had happened. But I didn't have to remember, I thought. I could pretend; people did all the time. People came home to their spouses and pretended the thing that bound them together was love, not obligation. People took sugar pills that cured their depression and anxiety. I just had to harness my brain.

"Jumpy much?" Chloe asked.

"You know I'm a skittish drunk," I said, trying to laugh.

"Are you?" Chloe asked. "Usually you're full of hugs."

It was too late to tell Chloe. It was too late because she'd ask why I had waited so long, and I didn't have an answer, and every day the problem compounded itself. Except there was no problem. There was nothing but Hesper, frame after frame of Hesper with different hairstyles, different college sweatshirts, smiling in poorly lit hallways or in front of rolling, lush Californian hills.

I clicked next. "Oh, she had late-2000s bangs!" I continued. "Perfect. I'm starting to think that she's the perfect human. Can't you just imagine it? Us in a little cabin in the Pacific Northwest, reading novels next to each other in matching red flannels. Or...us at one of those bed-and-breakfasts on an alpaca farm, petting their fluffy heads."

"You can stay at a bed-and-breakfast on an alpaca farm?" Chloe asked. "Why haven't I made Graham take me to one of those for our anniversary? I want an alpaca friend."

I laughed. "The alpaca friend is a *bonus*."

Chloe adjusted her glasses and smiled. She twisted to face me. "You're about to become so annoying, you know that? One of those people that's like, 'oh my gosh, did you say you liked cantaloupe? My *girlfriend* loves cantaloupe.' Everything will be an invitation to boast about your great romance."

"Chlo," I said, giggling before I could deliver the joke. "Actually, my *girlfriend* is allergic to cantaloupe. It makes her throat tingle."

"It begins," Chloe whispered. "It...has...begun. Let's invite her over." Chloe straightened, rustling a litany of notebooks that occupied the bed space. "Let's have a party tonight! Marisa and Ingrid and Liam went to get hot pot in Alphabet City but we're supposed to meet up later, around ten."

"I'm opening the library at eight-fifteen tomorrow. Besides"—I felt the smile controlling my face—"Hesper said she's going to meet me after my shift for some kind of surprise day."

"Stop," Chloe said, but she was smiling at my happiness. She was a good friend. "That's too much. Fine. I'll have the party without you and recap it all to you in enormous detail. I guarantee Liam will end up with something in that beard. It's like a pantry in there."

"That's disgusting," I said, but my tone was ebullient. Chloe kissed my cheek.

Throughout my shift at the library, I itched. I catalogued every instance of contact that I'd had so far with Hesper's body. I stamped little white cards reminding students to return their reserved materials to the main desk in two hours or less and sneakily slurped iced coffee from the shelf that dug into my knees as I sat in an angled-too-high computer chair and asked patron after unruly patron if I could help them, that the library closed at five today, that the bathrooms were to the left. Folding, unfolding my hands, as if in prayer. Then I actually said a prayer. *Thank you for leading me to this,* I thought. But again, a weird hollowness came where I'd once felt grasped by the warm company of believing. Maybe it was nothing. It was busy in the library, and I was distracted. That's all it was: to feel distracted by the early embers of love. It was Willa Greenberg day.

The cadence of Hesper's voice.

Those little white teeth.

I keep thinking of you and I can't stop. —H

HESPER WAS WEARING A jean jacket, a velvet leotard, and patterned navy-and-scarlet pants that somehow all unified to seem fashionable, perfectly meshed together into an outfit, although I didn't understand how they worked, exactly. She had another dandelion, a twin to the one that she'd pulled from the grass for me earlier that week. I wore what a mother of three young children might throw on to go get cereal, I thought, tugging the V-neck down over my hips. Hesper seemed aglow, effortlessly rosy, with a leather tote bag over her shoulder and a striped thermos in hand. "Willa Greenberg," she greeted.

"It's you," I said.

"It's me! So, are you ready for your dream day?" Hesper asked. "I brought coffee!"

I accepted. It was strangely sugared and clumped down my throat, but was also perfect, because everything that Hesper coordinated had a ring of surrealism around it, as if my real life had been paused and this better, impossibly auspicious replacement was running for a limited time before the regular version would pick up where it left off, with me back in my childhood bedroom in New Jersey pretending not to eavesdrop on Mom complaining to Aunt Sylvia that part of her wished he would have just died in that accident, right off the bat, instead of this new, feeble replacement husband that would never work again.

Before the accident, and the decline that followed, he'd been a fastidious lawyer, juggling a multitude of mergers and acquisitions. An office that overlooked a courtyard. A complimentary gym membership he never had time to use. He'd been a workaholic, sneaking glimpses of his cell phone at all occasions. Mom had loved that version of him, the one that was never satisfied by any level of achievement and had three different leather belts. She was an office manager who'd worked at a nonprofit, but it wasn't enough to support a family of three, and she'd moved to work at a start-up where she was the oldest person by thirty years and the most miserable on staff, and perpetually searching for a new, stealthier income with better benefits for Dad, who could no longer even follow the plot of *Law & Order*. But that had been a different Willa's life.

"Is this regular sugar?" I asked, over the sound of myself, churning.

"I had to improvise on the sugar. Is it palatable?" Hesper touched my hand, retrieving the thermos. "Oh, no. This won't do for Willa Greenberg day." She uncapped the thermos and the coffee splashed onto the cement, a rush. Hesper looked at it, pleased somehow. There was something a little theatrical about her, I thought; a way that her actions felt special, defined. Outside of the subway entrance, my hair stirring in the Tuesday breeze, Hesper leaned forward and kissed me, one hand on the small of my back, and it made me feel like I was dissolving.

"I never plan anything. You should know that. But today... today, I have a plan," Hesper whispered, and I saw that when our faces were this close, I could see the slight movement of Hesper's irises, flickering according to the supply of light. I kept my nose against Hesper's nose. I was curious about the plan, but I wanted to preserve this, the moment, I wanted it to last just the tiniest bit longer before we separated. I stood there against the cold metal rail at the entrance of the subway. We were inseparable, I thought, and everyone who stepped around us realized it; it was that obvious; it was palpable and luminescent. It was Willa Greenberg day.

FIRST: WE HAD PANCAKES. We shared a plate, thick with berries and lightly browned. We patted them with little rectangles of butter, spread them with a glowing layer of jam and syrup. Then we took the 1 train to a crosstown bus, and for a minute I forgot that I'd ever mentioned loving the Neue Galerie to Hesper directly; I thought it must have been a result of our connectedness. Sitting in the carpeted seats of the bus, Hesper cupped my knee. "I love how you have a uniform," Hesper said, fumbling with a button over a non-functional pocket of her jacket.

"I just like a V-neck," I said. "And...stretch. The occasional cardigan." I resisted the word *comfortable*.

"It's perfect on you," Hesper said. The bus squeezed slowly through traffic. Rows of red brake lights throbbed as the cars stopped, started, swooped between lanes. As we whirred through Central Park, Hesper's hair looked particularly tinged with red, and I found myself smiling for no reason, for every reason.

We went inside. The museum was resplendent, both exterior and interior. We clipped little tags onto the collars of our shirts. I pointed out all of my favorite things: the clock in the first room on the second floor with all of its gold discs, the contrast of gold wallpaper near the crown molding and the diffuse, airy gray color of the walls.

"This one," I said, stopping in front of *Adele Bloch Bauer*. A thicket of tourists lingered around the painting, too, with their cell phones zoomed in on Adele's impassive, doughy face. "I know it's a pretty common favorite painting," I said. It was, at least, better than *The Kiss*, which every freshman had push-pinned over their bed at college. Hesper leaned close to the portrait of Adele with a curious expression, the same tentative look that she had when she approached a sleeping Tibby. "But I love what she's doing with her hands, like she's trying to fold inside of herself."

"She's so uncomfortable," Hesper said.

"Yeah, but all the gold leaf is so elegant and lavish, at first that's all you see. It's like...she's at the fanciest occasion of her life, wearing her finest jewelry and clothes, but she's still in this cloud of anxiety." I took a few steps to the left, angled to properly examine the metallic sheen in the light. I crouched, scrutinized. "I love how the gold shines in person, how you can see the light move right over it."

"She looks a little like you," Hesper said.

"We both look really Ashkenazi Jewish," I replied, with a little laugh. "Is that what you mean?"

Hesper said, "Um ... I don't know. I didn't mean it like—"

"Oh, no, no," I said. "I know. I just mean ... people can tell. Looking at me." Everyone could; I was the picture of Ashkenazi Jewishness. My dad's mother, Grandma Joan, who'd died in 2003, had said, *You can't wash your star off, Willa,* when I'd tried to straighten my hair every day before school. The smell of my hair, burnt, burning, with those unreachable waves in the back that gave me away. I stopped eventually.

Hesper buttoned and unbuttoned her jacket. "It seems so weird to me that people could glance over at another person and think to himself, 'Oh, that person is Jewish.' I just ... I didn't realize it could be overt, like that."

"Because you don't know a lot of Jews or anti-Semites?" I suggested. I tried to keep my voice light. Full of air.

Hesper kept her eyes on the painting. "Maybe," she said. "This sold for a hundred thirty-five million dollars?"

I shrugged. I thought of the Nazis, slipping this into their collection of ransacked art, hanging Adele's nervous, dead face in a museum somewhere. She'd been lucky, I remembered from my last visit and ensuing Wikipedia deep-dive, to have died from meningitis in 1925. "It's the perfect painting," I said. "Don't you think? It has beauty but also it makes you feel ... like you're witnessing this private, painful moment of her life. Do you see it?" I asked, getting close enough to Hesper so that the presence of her body rippled like a wave against mine.

Hesper, ever so slightly, relaxed against my arm. "I see it," she said, quiet.

IN THE CAFE DOWNSTAIRS, we ordered coffees with blankets of whipped cream on top and three slices of cake to share. Hesper kept her fork extended in midair, unsure whether to try the raspberry or the chocolate hazelnut or the kirschtorte first. She slurped the whipped cream from her coffee until it coated her whole mouth and I thought about later, how inevitably the end of Willa Greenberg day would be sex, wouldn't it? But I tried to keep my face still, inscrutable besides a love of cake. Cake love was acceptable to express.

"Oh my God," Hesper said, covering her mouth. "That hazelnut thing is unbelievable."

"I know," I said, smiling. "It's the best. That's why it's a main ingredient in my perfect day."

"You have excellent taste," Hesper said. "This is almost as good as dessert in Paris."

"I've never been."

"That's right! You're an airplane travel virgin. Paris is, you know, it sounds cliché at this point, but it's magical. I remember, the first time we were there, Ada was obsessed with this one bus route. The Seventy-Two. It went right past the Louvre, to the Eiffel Tower, and once they let us ride for free and we were so excited. And pistachio ice cream! Pistachio ice cream everywhere." Hesper unleashed a packet of sugar into her murky coffee. "I just can't believe you've never been. There are all these pictures of me at my most awkward, middle-school phase, giving Ada bunny ears at the Pompidou while my dad harangued us about ruining our future memories.

"We'll have to go," she said. She said it the same way as she might say, "I need contact solution."

I tried to busy myself with my fork, creeping closer to the torte's marzipan layer. "You know," Hesper said, lifting the fork from my hand, "you're really cute when you're trying to play it cool, Willa. You could be a living example of the phrase *I wear my heart on my sleeve*."

"I know," I sighed.

HESPER TRIUMPHANTLY RETRIEVED THE last bite of the hazelnut torte. "Hey. What animal would you be?"

I tried to think. What animal would I be, not what animal would I *want* to be, I puzzled. I knew exactly what I'd want to be: a gazelle, so fast that by the time you realized you'd seen it, it was already gone. Fast enough to run from anything.

"Probably a bird?" I said tentatively. "My mom says I used to chirp myself to sleep, as a baby. What about you?"

Hesper scraped her fork against the plate. "Aw," she said, and cupped her free hand over my shoulder. "A little parakeet. I could definitely see that. You hold on so tight." She twisted her fingers into talons. "I'd be a koala bear."

"Why a koala bear?"

"Because they love eucalyptus leaves," she said. "The best, most Californian smell there is. And all they do is sit in trees and sleep, which is ideal."

I hadn't known that about koalas. What I remembered, exclusively, was that even though they looked adorable, they could turn violent without any notice. Sharp teeth, sharp claws.

"What about— What do you want to be when you grow up?"

I laughed. "That's cute."

It had been such a long time since anyone had asked me that. I'd been the first person to declare an English major in my year at college. After graduation, I'd taken the first job I could find, annihilating unnecessary commas in educational media catalogues in a silent office in a converted church on the Upper West Side. So quiet you could hear someone crank open a seltzer bottle, the hiss of it, as loud as a car engine turning over.

"In my dreamworld, I'd want to write the kind of book that people quoted and had lines tattooed over their hearts. I'd be a literary celebrity, I guess. As famous as Zadie Smith—recognizable, coveted to teach at fancy conferences in the summer, my choice of university for tenure. I'd be the answer to a question at a trivia night." I felt Hesper's foot tap against the tiled floor. "What about you?"

"I don't know," Hesper said.

"Come on. I just admitted my trivia night dream."

"No, I mean, I really have no idea. The future just seems . . . far away." Hesper picked a jammy corner of her mouth away with her finger-nail. "In class, with so many people that are like, full-fledged adults, it's just . . . it's noticeable. People with little children and jobs that pay for their cars to the airport. To me, the idea of having a kid is like talking about colonizing Mars. To *produce* a *child*," she said, in bewilderment.

"Without the additional complications of spacesuits."

"Exactly."

"Everybody feels that way when they're twenty-two," I said, trying very hard not to ask the question *But do you want to have kids of your own, someday, when it isn't as opaque and ungraspable as a Mars colony?* "It's mandatory. It's the emotional equivalent of getting your wisdom teeth removed."

Her sad mood was fleeting. I felt it disappear. She twisted her hair into a donut.

Hesper touched her jaw. "I still have mine!" she exclaimed. "How do I know when it's time?"

"You'll feel them starting to break through and it'll hurt . . . badly."

"Maybe they never will. Maybe I'll be the first person whose wisdom teeth never crown, and my life will arrange in perfect little boxes without any exhaustive introspection." Hesper motioned for me to finish the last of the cake pieces. Trails of jam and crumbs looped across the surface of the plate. "Maybe this is the first day of my new life. What do you think?"

"It's possible," I said. "It's definitely possible."

"I have more plans for your day. Are you ready?"

WE WALKED THROUGH CENTRAL Park, looping around the reservoir with the tourists and their selfie sticks capturing the slate-gray water, peppered with little mallard ducks and miscellaneous plants. A woman in pink suede heels scolded her unruly terrier: "Not *now*, Buttercup!" with such seriousness and volume that we started laughing and couldn't stop. Each time our laughter came to a plateau, one of us repeated the line and it was still so absurd, so funny. I slipped my arm through Hesper's, my eyes wet from laughing with my whole body. Accidentally I started to sing aloud, instead of in my head: *"Why do you build me up, buttercup, baby?"*

It had been a long time since I heard myself sing.

Hesper joined in right away, not leaving me a pause to be self-conscious. *"I need you! I need you!"* she sang, off-pitch but jubilant. It didn't even seem possible to be self-conscious, though we were singing loudly in front of a steady stream of strangers. It seemed easy. *"So build me up, buttercup, don't break my heart,"* we finished, fingers interlaced.

Visions of the rest of my life floated gently up to me. Buying Hesper a package of blackberries that I'd found at a supermarket. Ticking the box that said *married* on my W-9. Fireplaces, thunderstorms, Tibby sleeping over my toes like a blanket. We twisted through the rest of the park—the spot where the waffle truck parked, the bridge leading back up toward Morningside. We swung up my block, that indomitable incline with its newly repainted blue buildings.

I watched her, Hesper, that casual charm of her expression and her hands as she talked, the way she hooked her thumbs underneath the straps of her backpack as if we were embarking on a great journey, and I wondered if she was leading me back to my apartment. I thought of it: the rush of kissing, knowing that kissing would lead forward, forward, breathing sex into my body, and: that I wanted, wanted, but was also afraid. I thought of her fingers trailing the path between my knees and my collarbones. Her breath hot in my ear. Then I thought of the boy. His thumbprint on my arm, underneath my right breast, my rib cage where he'd pressed, the scaly tree. I was going to kiss it right out of my system; a reboot.

"You're probably wondering where we're going."

"I'm maybe wondering."

"There's this restaurant near where I live that's super romantic and cozy. Picture this," Hesper said, and I closed my eyes. "Candlelight, checked tablecloths. We're surrounded by bookcases and spaghetti. Okay, the bookcases are actually wallpaper, now that I think of it. But the vibe is like being in a cute Italian grandmother's kitchen."

The dinner was as quaint and lovely as she'd described. We shared two bowls of pasta, rich with butter, freshly grated Parmesan like a snowfall over the long twirls of each spinach-y green noodle. Hesper swept her bread in the puddled remains of sauce and I wondered how I'd never thought to do that before, how my uneaten sauce sat, untouched, at the bottom of every bowl I'd ever had.

As I pulled one sleeve onto my shoulder, I thought: *I'm in love, I'm totally in love,* and wondered how I would wait the interminable wait between when you know you love someone and when you say it to the object of your love, how would I wait, how would I even be able to finish slipping my other arm into the cardigan's sleeve space? And in the middle of my wondering, gallantly, Hesper leaned across the table to hold my cardigan open so I could snake my arm in and smiled.

Then, Hesper's apartment. She closed the door behind us. Put her lips on mine.

It was a dance: her arm moved and my arm rose to meet her arm. I took a step backward against the wall and she took a step closer to me so I was there, tucked in the corner between the bookcase and the floor lamp and I felt safe there; surrounded completely by

Hesper's body and the furniture, I felt as if nothing could find me that I couldn't see already. Hesper tucked her hand behind my head so it wouldn't hurt against the wall and the love I felt was even more acute, it had ballooned. I opened my mouth wider. I was kissing her tirelessly; maybe I would never feel tired again. I had never thought the word *kiss* so often in my own consciousness; it was like an echo of my thoughts building toward a crescendo, a crescendo of kissing. Hesper's fingers trailed down the front of my body, irrepressible as she whispered: *"Is this okay?"* and I said: *"Let me go first,"* tilting my mouth to meet her neck, her clavicle, the slant of her bones. I couldn't tell her that I loved her with my words so I told her with my hands on her chest, her stomach, the handle of her hips. I told her and told her, I slithered my fingers down the front of her silk pants. I was delicate and slow until I wasn't slow anymore at all, and Hesper exhaled, breathy, the beginnings of what her sounds were, the sounds that I would memorize and think of as I walked alone to the gym or the florist or the pancake special, that sputter of Hesper as she got close, closer.

"BE CAREFUL," SHE SAID. Leading me toward her bedroom, she asked, "Do you want me to turn off the light?"

"No," I said. "I want to see you."

I did—of course I did, but I also wanted to see everything around me; every trinket and notebook and light fixture and coffee-ringed cup; I wanted to see if there were an intruder that emerged behind Hesper's beautiful head so that I would at least know what was about to happen, so that I wouldn't be surprised, this time. *Don't do this,* I thought. *Don't think of it; don't think of him. Don't think at all.* And I reached for Hesper, I wanted to feel her uncalloused hands traipsing over my body; I wanted to watch the expression in her face change from self-conscious to sultry. *"Careful,"* Hesper said again, cradling the back of my head as it came down against her bedspread, and then I felt invigorated with energy I didn't realize I had. *I'm not fragile,* I thought, and my un-fragileness slashed through our kissing, in my motions, a kind of vehemence, or maybe it was violence. I couldn't kiss her fast enough or emphatically enough. I wanted those kisses to say: *I'm un-breakable. I'm unbroken.* But when I got closer, I had to shut my eyes anyway, and then I was alone in that writhing dark lull before it happened, and when I came it was spasmodic, like I was a puppet whose master had dropped the strings.

I pulled my knees to my chin and let Hesper stroke my scalp. I held my breath. What was the thing that I felt? It was the return of the old flutter, the return of knowing I wasn't alone. It breathed in me, a wobble of certainty. *You were right here,* I thought, and I didn't know whether I was talking to God, or Hesper, or both.

"You know what you wrote in your letter?" I said. "That you couldn't stop thinking of me?"

Hesper blinked dreamily. "Yeah?"

"I can't stop thinking of you either," I said.

"I told my mom about you," Hesper said quietly.

"Really?"

"Yeah. Although my sister definitely told her first, because she had a pretty mellow response." Hesper laughed a little. "It was like, 'Oh, I heard your good news, Lemon. Send me a picture of you girls having fun!'"

"But she didn't know you were"—I paused, trying not to identify Hesper's sexual orientation for her—"interested in women, right? She just rolled with it?"

"I guess I outsourced my coming out story to Ada."

"And she was okay with it?"

"We're from San Francisco," Hesper said. But I was from the New York metropolitan area, I thought. I'd been able to taste the dust from 9/11 in my lungs, and it hadn't meant anything when it came to my mom's response about dating women. *You, at least, could make things easy for me, Willa,* she'd said. And what else was there to say? After five years, when it came up in conversation, she politely asked questions the way you might to an annoying loquacious neighbor. It was the best I could hope for.

She tucked her fingers in the space between my breasts. "Did you like Willa Greenberg day?"

"It was perfect. I wish it could be every day."

With her other hand, she ran her pinky down the slope of my nose. "Why can't it be?" she asked, and I felt myself billow with hope.

4.

Besides naming Tibby, I hadn't given much thought to my Georgian-ness. But Willa was fascinated. *Tbilisi* meant *warm*, Willa explained one night—her Wikipedia-recall was incredible. She wanted my family story; hot springs, forest-drenched hills. And at the beginning, it was a relief to be the focus of her unwavering, rose-tinted affection lens. Everything about me was perfect, she said, including my confused, quarter-Georgian blood.

We met at the F stop to board a train toward Gravesend, a place I had never heard of. Neither had Willa, until she made it her personal mission for us to sample an authentic Georgian meal. On the train in Manhattan, we stood so close together that I could feel her breath on my lips. A Hasidic man and a black-skirted woman with cocktail earrings looked at Willa and I felt her posture slump forward, withering. She shifted her hand from my shoulder back to her side. She leaned forward to whisper in my ear.

"They're talking about me," she said. "About how I'm not Jewish enough."

"Maybe they're jealous we're going to Gravesend," I joked. "I hear Georgian food at three-thirty in the afternoon is the latest."

Willa smiled. "Trendsetters."

"All of you is Jewish enough," I said, even though this was a distinction I didn't understand at all. Couldn't she just put on a longer skirt and fit in exactly the way she wanted to? And if Willa felt Jewish enough for the God that she seemed to actually believe in, wasn't that more important than some badly coiffed stranger on the F train? What kind of religious person thought of religion as a competitive sport?

But I knew she wanted me to make another joke, not argue about theology. "Even your uncooperative bangs," I said, pushing the strands that were crimped in the center off to the side.

"Especially my uncooperative bangs," she agreed. But she was still glancing in their direction.

"Will," I said. "They're not paying attention to us. I don't think they're even speaking English."

"But what if they're right?" she said.

"What do you mean?"

"Like . . . I just get this feeling around Hasidic people," she said, her voice dipping low, hiding underneath the noise of the subway tracks squeaking. "They see me as a disappointment, you know. As a person who has the potential to live the right way and who chose, instead, to go to concerts instead of temple on Friday nights. I've done so many things that aren't . . . right with God, I guess." She dropped her voice even lower. "Sometimes I fall asleep before I pray. Sometimes I just decide not to pray because I'm tired. And those are just the little things." She gripped the subway pole until her knuckles turned white. "They look over at me and they can *tell* I'm a bad Jew."

When two seats opened up, we took them. I could feel Willa's body brush mine on the seat.

"Once," she said, "I went for a walk in Williamsburg and I ended up in that enclave—do you know the one? On Wythe? It's like you stepped through a portal into a totally different Orthodox world. Every single person on the street is Hasidic; there's a Hebrew school bus on every block. It's wild. But I stood there for a long time, because it felt like . . . I was watching this alternate reality of my life."

"One where you're not gay?" I asked, which sounded blunter than I meant it to.

She shook her head. "That's not what I mean. I meant, one where I'm more observant. More immersed in my culture. Keeping Sabbath, that kind of thing. I don't know...maybe it's naïve, or because I was raised by people who are culturally Jewish atheists, but I don't think sexual orientation really matters that much. Not to people who really *feel* it. It probably matters to people who feel it less, because you can't question old rules with confidence if you don't know what the priorities are. Or what it feels like to be right."

"But you do? Know what it feels like to be right?"

Willa dodged my eye contact. "I think so. But then, every once in a while, I see..." She looked back over at the Orthodox couple. "So I start to think, when they're looking at me like I've made this big mistake...whether I actually have. What if God meant for me to meet these people on the train and like, see the error of my ways? What if this whole day is meant to bring me to one conclusion and I accidentally miss it?"

"If you're supposed to find it," I said, "wouldn't you?"

"What if I'm too busy looking at you?" she asked. "What if I'm just...too enamored of you to be thinking about anything else? Including being a good person?"

"You're a good person," I offered. And then, not for the first time, I wondered if she loved me a dangerous amount. But every relationship had the loved one, and the lover, didn't it? It was only natural for there to be some kind of cosmic imbalance. "I can sit over there, if you want to have space to observe your epiphany."

"No," she said. "No, don't. I don't mean that I want space. It's just a weird thing, to be...tugged in this other direction. I feel..." Willa glanced around to make sure no one was listening. "It's like I have these two separate identities. Being gay is like having feet. I know I have them; they're always there. It's not especially interesting. But being Jewish is totally different. Explaining it is like . . . trying to make a balloon animal out of Chex Mix or something. Like words don't fit that purpose, even for a writer. You know . . . that . . . invisible string that connects you to your people." She shrugged. "I carry it with me all the time. Does that sound weird?"

It did sound weird. When Willa wasn't talking about religion, I often forgot she had such strong faith. Each time it came up, it surprised me. It was like listening to detailed directions within a city that you'd never visited. I only ever thought of people praying after natural disasters or mass shootings.

"I just want to be good," Willa repeated. She sounded forlorn.

"You can't be good with me?" I asked. I meant it as a joke, but I could tell she didn't take it that way.

"Of course I can," she whispered.

Then she reached for me, curling her fingers around mine so tight that I could feel the concave section on her ring finger that had been permanently dented from gripping her pencil as if it were a knife.

In Gravesend, Willa tried to navigate and we looped around a series of Dunkin' Donuts and gas stations, the sun hot on our scalps. I loved how Willa was always a little bit sunburned, flushed as if she'd just come out of the shower.

"Are we going to a culinary tour of my whole genetic history?" I asked.

"Yes!" Willa said. "But—there's only one Welsh restaurant. It's in Gowanus." She said Gowanus as though she meant Siberia, drooping her shoulders in defeat. I looked at the spot where her bangs curled inward and it endeared me to her all over again in a nonsensical rush.

"How'd you remember that?" I asked.

"You made a pun about whales," Willa said, moving her hand aquatically.

"When we were talking about ghosts?"

"My little ghost," Willa said, pulling me toward her. She was trying to make up for the seriousness of the conversation on the train, I could tell. She wanted to be fun, lighthearted; she apologized often for dipping into depressing topics. I knew that I should tell her that was something I appreciated about her, how earnestly she could broach terrible things as if they were as easy as describing inclement weather.

We stopped in front of a truck transporting the world's largest porcelain tiles. I could feel her waiting to see if I would kiss her. Our eyes met eagerly, wondering. I knew Willa would do whatever I said next, but also that she was scared, skittish about sex when she didn't know every variable. That the sunlight beating down on our heads could turn menacing as quickly as a thread could snag into something unfixable.

I whispered, "Later," and Willa pressed into me so that she could feel the spot where my hip bone protruded.

"There's khinkali to be had," she agreed.

Inside, the restaurant shook with the movement of the train passing overhead. Dark, decorative bricks climbed up the walls. A waitress gave us half-Russian, half-English plastic menus and then skulked back to a wooden chair to watch a soccer game being broadcast on a giant flat screen. We were the only people in the dining area, though a long narrow corridor extended out of my view.

The waitress came and begrudgingly accepted my order of tarragon lemonade and Willa's list of approved dishes.

"We should go someday," she said, scanning the menu. I wanted something creamy, avocado-esque. I longed for California in my food cravings—lightly fried fish in fresh tortillas, pork buns with mysterious tangy sauce. Willa glanced in my direction quickly, then returned her focus to the menu. "To Tbilisi."

"Sure," I said. "I'll wear my cape. Let's go right now."

"Maybe we should bring some toothpaste. Contact lens solution. Money."

"Absolutely not. Where's your sense of adventure?"

"It needs glasses. And financial support."

"What about school?" I said, playing along. My tarragon lemonade came in a slender green bottle, a Perrier twin.

"We have the summer," Willa said, in a plan-making tone. "It seems like it would be perfect in June. We could go . . . next June. That would be long enough to save up for the trip."

It was May. *June* trembled between us like the beginning of an earthquake. *June, June, June.* We had been together for seven months, long enough that I knew the names of Willa's aunts without having to come up with a cute factoid as a mnemonic, but not so long that I'd met any of them in person. Willa occasionally waded into our future like a shallow pool, and I tossed her a flotation device immediately to get her the fuck out of there.

It wasn't that I didn't want it, exactly. But having to say what I did want seemed impossible. Travel plans—international flights, hostels (or, worse, relatives I'd never met who definitely wouldn't be able to pronounce my name), being exposed to someone else during the microwaveish sensation of jet lag—none of it seemed appealing. How could I know what I'd want in thirteen months? How could I be with someone who knew what they'd want in thirteen months?

"June," I repeated.

"My financial aid comes in October, so . . . if I took more hours at the library, and you got some kind of work-study thing, I think it would be doable. The cost is really only getting over there, because the exchange rate is about 2.35 lari to one U.S. dollar," Willa said. Then she looked at the table. She had done enough research to recite the exchange rate. She knew what the name of Georgian currency was.

The waitress returned with a plate of slouchy dumplings and a slab of eggplant covered in herbed white sauce. The insides of the dumplings were not as hot as I'd expected, comprised of spices I didn't recognize. Willa bit into cheesy bread that looked like opaque rubber cement.

"Willa, I've got to tell you something," I said, and her eyes became full with pre-tears. "I am not allowed to leave the country during the summer. I can't explain any further, but it falls under the category of *top secret.*"

"Pop secret? Like the snack?"

I knew she was pretending to mishear me so we wouldn't have to talk about what was wrong, and I was glad.

"I didn't reveal anything about my pop secret," I said, winking. She smiled.

WE SETTLED BACK IN our chairs, satisfied that the worst of the tension had dissipated. At a table on the other side of the restaurant, four cottonball-haired elderly patrons were chattering gregariously in a language that I should've been able to understand. They'd ordered a plate of meat that steamed voluminously, billowing with smoke. Willa and I peered at their table, covered with small plates and a basket of bread. They'd brought a bottle of wine and their teeth were dyed with grape skins. My lemonade was fizzing relentlessly. Our cheesy bread was reclining in its own oil puddle.

"What is that?" I asked Willa.

"Georgian sausage."

I hated her for knowing right away. "Why didn't we get that?"

"Because I can't eat pork." She hesitated. "You know that."

"Are you mad that I don't have your dietary restrictions memorized?" I snapped.

"I'm never mad at you, Hesper," Willa said, sounding disappointed.

"Why not?" I asked.

"What do you mean?" Willa shot back.

"Explain it to me. Like a character study."

Willa blushed. She looked at the traces of spinach on her plate. "You're perfect."

I leaned close to her. "I knew it. I was just waiting for your confirmation."

"Mission accomplished," Willa muttered. She twisted her hair up into a bun and let it fall over her shoulders, dark and lovely. Under the table, she reached for my knee and clutched her fingers over my joints with the same tight tenderness that she'd shown during the subway ride. "Okay, it's not that I never feel angry toward you, because you're a person. But then it disappears so quickly because there are a million things about you I love, and they're so much brighter than the angry thing."

"So you forgive me instantly? Because of vibrancy?"

"Within two Mississippis, I forgive you."

"The angry thing is like, grayish?"

"Taupe, even. And the rest of you is . . . this like, dazzling periwinkle."

"Dazzling periwinkle," I repeated.

"Is that embarrassingly sentimental?"

"Maybe a smidgen."

"Do you feel that way about me too?" Willa asked, averting her gaze.

I had never felt that way about any person. The closer I got to someone, the more their flaws glowed fluorescently to me. Ada was my best friend and I could write a dissertation about her flaws—the

hideous face she made before she bit into an ear of corn in the summer, the mispronunciation of *cache* when her browser needed to be
reloaded. Her perpetual wallowing over her ex Charlie, who certainly
hadn't ever been worth all these many months of incessant nostalgia. Insta-forgiveness seemed webbed with complications. I wished
I'd never heard of it.

"Impossible to determine," I answered. "You never do anything to
be angry about."

"I ordered us the wrong food," Willa said. "This gloppy cheese."

"I've never had gloppier cheese," I said, beaming as though for
a school portrait. "Thank you for leading us to this, the gloppiest
meal."

"Your grandfather never cooked any of this for you?" Willa asked.

"Grapefruit and chocolate ice cream," I said. "That's all he likes."

"Does he have scurvy?"

"In Soviet times, scurvy had you," I joked, gulping the lemonade,
expecting the ten to fifteen seconds of respite to have improved the
taste. "I don't actually know anything about it. I don't even know how
old he was when he got over here. Never talks about it. My grandma
was this lovable chatterbox, and he lost his shit when she died, and
now we make paper boats together at his nursing home."

"That's so sad," Willa said.

"They're pretty magnificent paper boats."

"Don't you wonder, though?" Willa asked. "Don't you feel like . . .
history just crawls around after you, like I was saying on the train?
Like history is . . . a terrible, creepy cat?"

"I hope you're not referring to our darling Tibby. She can't help
her scoliosis."

Willa bit her lip. "I mean it."

"No," I said. "Honestly. I don't really think about it. Maybe when
I'm older."

Willa looked wounded, as though I meant that her interest in history was a product of our four-year, two-month age difference. "I'm not saying that's how a person should be," I said. "Sometimes I wish there were a creepy historical cat trailing me. It would make things more exciting. My own personal Murakami story."

"It's just...I wish I could get on a plane, and walk up to somebody's house and know that this is where I came from. You know?" Willa said. "Here's Great-Aunt Salomeya and her five squirrely kids, and this is the casserole dish that made the—whatever this cheese is called—Baba ate when he was young."

"If it happens, I'll let you know. But I believe strongly there is no magic."

"No magic?"

"They call her Magicless Sal."

"You're so hard on Salomeya," Willa said, "and so disinterested in the rest."

"You don't have any idea where you came from?" I asked.

Willa shrugged. "The Austro-Hungarian empire. That's all I've ever found out."

"Maybe you're royalty."

"When they got here, my relatives owned a tannery in Paterson. They made fur coats. What's so funny?" she asked, raising an eyebrow wryly.

"A few generations ago, your family made its livelihood skinning animals, and now you're afraid of a man hitting a stuffed banana."

She tried to laugh, but I could tell I'd hurt her feelings, and worse, there was a little part of me that liked that. Maybe now she would see I wasn't perfect.

The waitress brought us the check, and Willa scrambled to hand her the credit card. Behind her, a tiny girl clumsily balanced one little foot on top of the other. The waitress said brusquely, "The bathroom is over there," and moved her hand vaguely as though she were shooing a mosquito as she returned to the kitchen. The girl pushed her feet together into a sandwich of soles and rubber, continued glancing around the restaurant for the mysterious bathroom location.

Willa put her bunched-up napkin atop the cheesy dish and approached the little girl. I was surprised, not only because this was weirdly forward and could be so easily misconstrued, but also because Willa never sprang into action. She was exclusively devoted to research and plans, the kind of pedestrian who simply turned back to the curb if the walk figure started to blink.

"It's right over there," she said to the girl, who looked to be rapidly approaching breakdown. Willa's smile, like honey, spread over her face and stayed there.

"My nana said I could find it," the girl whispered, dismayed.

"You can. You just needed a helper along the way." Willa peered at the table of elderly, unconcerned meat eaters and found no answers. Then she pressed her pink lips together and slowly walked toward the bathroom enclave. The girl scampered ahead, triumphant once she located the wooden door, and said, "Thank you!"

Willa beamed in a way I'd never seen her look before. She glanced at the girl's heavy, dark hair and her musty floral dress. Willa's glossy, nurturing expression grew brighter. Then her gaze met mine, maternal and future-filled. I watched her eyes glistening and saw, in the subtlest of movements, that look bounding toward me like bees swooping to receive their pollen.

I realized that she was considering *our* shyly yearning, oddly dressed girl, our hypothetical child's hypothetical bladder, and I couldn't. I wouldn't. I was twenty-three, and I had only recently become aware of the fact that I didn't know anything. I wanted to apply for a credit card and move to Portland, Paris, Pompeii; I wanted to go and keep going. The bathroom door clicked firmly shut, and Willa returned to her wooden chair. The restaurant shook, trembling from the motion of the subway. Willa rubbed the mole along her jawline, at the slant of her chin, which she did when we finished having sex, or when she was at the point in exhaustion and her vocabulary was reverting toward childhood and tired became sleepy, rabbits became bunnies.

I didn't see Willa in dazzling periwinkle. I never would. I didn't know if it was because of Willa, herself—self-conscious, insecure Willa, itching for a person to need her, printing out her Google map and possible destinations even though her phone held all the information she could ever need—or because I was missing the gene that let me need, and love, in the way that she wanted.

She leaned forward and took a sip of my lemonade. "Interesting!" she said. "I've never tasted anything like that before."

I knew then that I would end things—abruptly, entirely. She couldn't tell. If I was dazzling at anything, it was hiding my feelings. For the next few weeks I'd swaddle her in my kindest, most loving self; bring her a bundle of spray rosebuds and lemon-raspberry iced teas, watch episodes of her preferred *Friday Night Lights* instead of *Veronica Mars*, until I couldn't look at her anymore. I would run uselessly away from the inevitable. And the longer it would take me, the longer it would hurt her, wouldn't it? *So enamored of you that I can't think about being a good person.*

June, June, June.

When I left, she'd follow me out of her apartment. Stand in the hallway, trying to call my name, but couldn't get her voice to work.

A deluge of emails would follow. She'd get in contact about anything she could: did I remember which story was the one we'd read in lecture where the woman became a deer? Where had we found that magic Moroccan lipstick in Williamsburg, the one that looked different on everyone's lips? Then the questions would metamorphose into apologies for her most minor indiscretions—the time she'd given her last scoop of sour cream gelato to her sulking roommate instead of me; the copy of Grace Paley's short stories that she'd borrowed and never returned. I'd close the windows.

THE DAY AFTER THE breakup, Ada called to tell me about Tbilisi. She said she'd spoken to Dad about all the questions I'd asked lately—about Baba, emigration, which of our relatives were still living there. Magicless Sal. He was surprised by my interest, and thought it would be good for us to travel together, as a family, while Baba was still alive. That maybe it would help him to see "the site of his child-hood," Ada quoted, as though we were anthropologists and not his closest relatives. I was too fucked up to get anything out besides a slow, viscous sputter that could, maybe, pass for a laugh over a bad phone connection.

Ada was the ambassador to my paternal side. When Dad and I spent time together, we could get along, but neither one of us was willing to actively foster a relationship, and then as time lapsed, we didn't know which questions to ask to begin "catching up." Ada was a born reacher. No Facebook message unread. She was too curious to shut down a whole half of our family, even if it meant talking to Dad on his own terms. He cycled through hobbies frantically: craft beer brewing, Ken Burns documentaries. He did not like: our career paths, improper grammar, night-lights.

"So we'll leave for Tbilisi on Friday," Ada was saying.

"Friday?" I creaked out. She affirmed this, and waited for me to go on.

"Is that silence indicative of delight?" Ada asked, after a few beats.

"I'm very drunk," I managed. I wanted to say: *I've hurt someone irreparably; I don't want to be in a relationship; I only know how to be alone; the restaurant was a coffin; I didn't know what to order; I don't know where I come from.* And why couldn't she just be angry, vilify me? I hated her for investigating every moment we'd been together. I wanted her to get a drastic haircut, fuck strangers, stop romanticizing me. I wanted to say: *I've made myself a mozzarella and potato chip sandwich and it still wasn't enough salt, enough texture, enough anything.*

"Drunk," I repeated.

Ada asked, "What kind?"

"I hear words coming out of my mouth, and I can touch the tip of my nose with my finger without some weird delay, but it's like I'm...a vessel. A loudspeaker full of somebody else's thoughts."

It's like my heart is being pulverized by a frenzied woodchipper, she wrote.

"Are you emotionally unraveling, Lemon?" Ada asked.

"I think so," I answered, a beat too late to realize she'd been joking. I started to cry. "I had to break up with Willa."

"Oh," Ada said softly.

"She's going to die."

"Eventually," Ada confirmed. "But not from you."

"You didn't hear her," I said. "You didn't see it."

"I'll come over," Ada offered. My crying had plateaued into gulps. "I'll take a cab."

I angled my knees so that they crushed the tender skin overlaying my ribs. That night, curled around my sister, I whispered apologetically to the phantom-Willa, my lips full of the bunched-up fabric of Ada's at-home hoodie.

I woke up a few hours later with an unbearable itch—the kind that spreads from the site of origin, expanding outward with ill intent. Do not scratch, do not, but I paddled my nails into my skin and could feel the carving of their half-moons as I scratched, finally locating the puffing bead of mosquito bite on my forearm. Flushing, heat, my skin prickling across my limbs, I scratched and scratched, I felt the white bubble swelling against the pink raw skin and I knew I should stop and I couldn't. I dragged my forearm across the thermal tank top I wore to sleep and hoped that the texture would soothe the bite, but it didn't, and I had left her.

I tried to write back to the emails. *I'm so sorry,* I drafted. *I've never felt so guilty.* But what I ended up writing was: *Please don't contact me for a while. It'll be harder for both of you. Us,* I corrected, and hit send. But maybe *you* was closer to what I meant: the you she'd been before me, and the you that she'd be after.

5.

Fuck it, I thought. *It's what Hesper would do if she were here.* Just pot; it was practically medicinal. As Chloe's cousin Emma's neighbor instructed: breathe deep. Don't worry about coughing; that just means it's working. Breathe. My lungs sharpened with their own limits; there were at least a dozen people clustered with their bare summer thighs around the sofa, Andy Warhol dictators winking in frames over an IKEA bookcase, all observing, my hair pulled back, my lips over a plastic funnel that smelled like water from a gas station bathroom. *Pull! Pull!* they chanted until I laughed, sputtering from attention, from the golden haze of observance and the acrid flutter and the fragments of pot scattered across the floor like windblown ashes.

We were on a mission, to capture each lost molecule and return them to our purpose. I was laughing and everyone to my left was laughing but those on the right who hadn't yet received were not laughing; the people on the right were grave and determined. Chloe took me by the wrist and led me into the kitchen because she needed to talk to me about something serious. It could have been another activity; this was our summer of avocations: pottery painting, making kombucha, gentle jogs in Central Park. It could have been about her boyfriend Graham, who had jettisoned to Germany for three months. But it was almost definitely not about Hesper, even though she talked to Hesper on GChat. I'd caught the name lurking at the top of a malicious blue box, my person, my not-anymore; the hurt braided itself through my stomach lining but: gone. I'd snatched the text hungrily from her laptop screen *you are right!* and thought what is she right about? Is she right about me? Were they talking about me, now that Chloe was initiated into my most terrible qualities, the way only roommates and otherhalves can be acquainted with yogurt thieving, toothpaste uncapping, mascara-splattered washcloths? These were not my vices; these were the vices I knew to avoid. I didn't even know what they could be. And Hesper would never say because she never said anything. She just left.

"Willa," Chloe said, collecting her blond hair into a ponytail. "All of the food here is room temperature."

On the fire escape, I glimpsed a flaccid arm and wondered what happened to the rest.

Suddenly the skin at the base of my neck was as rubbery as a turtle's.

"What if we could fit in the microwave?" I asked tenderly.

"I want something cold," Chloe insisted. Her lip gloss was smudged into a nebulous region of face that I couldn't identify. Post-cheek?

"I can't talk about gelato," I reminded her. Then I slid out of time, and I was standing next to Hesper on the corner of East Houston on a windy Saturday afternoon when we had gotten to a movie theater after the show had sold out and shared a cup of sour cream and rosemary gelato, syncopating our chewing and the sun illuminated her hair, spilling over the top of a thick green scarf, and we snuck clandestine fingers underneath each other's peacoats because we were in love, and if I had saved her the last bite maybe we still would be.

"Fro-yo," Chloe said, exceptionally slowly.

"I ruined everything," I said.

"Just give my cousin's neighbor twenty bucks," she advised. "You sneezed their whole night into oblivion."

"Did I sneeze? I thought I laughed."

"I need a vitamin," Chloe declared. But we couldn't reach most of the shelves, so we ransacked the cabinets close to the ground; they were filled with stained pots and a plastic colander. I found a bottle of honey shaped like a friendly bear; Chloe swiped a ladle embossed with small flowers. I thought of going outside and realized I didn't know what time it was and swapped the honey for the knife. Chloe kissed her cousin's cheek stickily and a boy with gray eyes looked at me and I curled my fist in the soup-serving spot of the ladle, silent.

He couldn't touch me, here. There were so many witnesses, so many pot-crumbs on the carpet. He was just another boy with eyes. But.

"We have to leave," I said to Chloe. "We have to leave, now."

Outside, ambulances skittered toward the Children's Hospital and the twenty-four-hour Wendy's and Chloe and I walked as purposefully and synchronized as a team competing in a three-legged race. Bright blue construction tarps shielded us from the sky. When I looked down the stairs I saw Hesper's silhouette approaching, her shyly distracted expression, her ugly handstitched cardigans with floppy hems circling her hip bones and riding up in back, her surprisingly light eyelashes, how mesmerizing those eyelashes seemed in bed in the mornings scanning dictionary.com for word of the day, even though she could just subscribe to the email list but she never did. Chloe swiped her MetroCard gracefully, whereas I slogged through the motions of feeling each frequent buyer card in my wallet because I couldn't remember that I'd stashed the MetroCard in my pocket for just this moment. My body remembered to breathe but when Chloe pushed the slick silver button of the elevator, I couldn't figure out how to get inside, or whether we would ever come out.

Slats of lightbulbs flickered. "Look up," Chloe instructed. On the smoggy exterior of the light fixture, someone had drawn a gargoyled happy face. Did Chloe think it was charming? I was cold. I couldn't shed the paranoia. Everyone must have been able to smell the weed on us. I began to apologize to the people around us, until Chloe whispered that I should give her the ladle back. We were the last to get off the elevator, Chloe's sandals snapping like chewing gum beneath her feet while traingoers splashed us with impatient glares. We survived the elevator; we were en route. This was the prelude to the beautiful journey that we'd be on for our entire lives.

We arrived. Frozen yogurt suited Chloe. She rushed to a nose-ringed woman who offered her a plastic cup or a sandpapery cone and I lurked near the door, trying to fold my tongue into quarters. Children lingered near the frozen yogurt machines, which were shaped like metal udders with those horrible pump mechanisms.

"You aren't holding anything," Chloe said, and handed me a cup for fro-yo.

"How do you make decisions?" I asked. Her yogurt was a tangled Jackson Pollock of Oreos and slithering gummy worms and different shades of white chemical cream, a terrarium of dessert possibilities.

"Quickly," Chloe answered, swooping another cup from the nose-ringed woman. She flounced the frozen yogurt into layers of flavors I didn't like—butter pecan, coconut, birthday cake. Chunks of s'mores, sprinkles shaped like asterisks. Peanut brittle! We submerged our spoons and licked them clean. Then we left the frozen yogurt establishment; then we were standing in front of Hesper's favorite brunch spot, and I could feel Chloe deciding whether to venture a breakup-related check-in or to power through, this could be the day, the first of many days, in which I talked about something, anything, more than I talked about missing Hesper, and she said, "I think Emma had a good time at the party," and I said, "I hate that place with their wily lemon hollandaise," and started to cry and generously Chloe didn't press me about how a hollandaise could be deceitful and then my face was wet and Chloe was trying to blot my tears with her oil-absorbing sheets and it was not working, my frozen yogurt was melting, dollops of marshmallow buoy-bobbed up to the surface, Chloe asked if I was having an emotional emergency, should we take a cab, should we sit on the ground and stretch our legs, should she recite "Jabberwocky"? *The jaws that did bite! The claws that catch.*

When Chloe was too maternal, I hated her because all friendships were impermanent, brittle, and one day she would leave and I wouldn't know where my sunglasses were. When Chloe was too maternal, I wondered how deeply she squelched her resentment. I was her roommate, an adhesive she couldn't scratch off. But I could never say this because worse than needing is needing and then needing to be comforted for needing. I said, "Knees" because it was almost what I was thinking and we stretched our limbs on the gravelly uneven sidewalk, a microcosm of not-quite pebbles scrubbed against the backs of my legs.

Chloe rested her frozen yogurt in the gulf of fabric between her thighs, she was finished with the word *mimsy*, she was finished with the poem and pontificating about the pros and cons of kickboxing but I was watching Hesper's face, Hesper with her sweet small incisors and the blush of her silk slick lips I was watching her sitting at the kitchen table tucking a pencil underneath her index finger in a bath towel patterned with curled flowers creeping ivily I was watching her expression change as she pondered an acrostic I was not hearing Chloe I was not dreaming but not not dreaming I was spooning a puddle of fluent not-ice cream into my mouth and it was euphoric.

"Cold," I said approvingly.

"I can't get that song out of my head," Chloe complained, squeezing the bear-shaped honey in a gush over my frozen yogurt, an amber swarm of viscosity. I thought of the clear gel doctors spread across a pregnant woman's belly, hounding for heartbeats. How I used to imagine a fusion of Hesper and me in a biologically impossible but tiny, oddly costumed girl—a notebook scribbler, wandering through a restaurant unsure of which door leads to the bathroom with eyes

like saucers, peering gingerly, and she would have Hesper's hair and
taste for citrus and we could call her a diminutive form of Lemon, it
could be a family nickname, Lemonita, Lemonlet. Our family. Now
Chloe was singing: *"I found it hard, tried to reserve, I'll get it right when
I am heard."* The honey was stuck to my plastic spoon. Our legs were
too heavy to move. "Keep singing," I told Chloe, and her soft voice
began to dip into a different register, thickening into something dark
and deep.

❧

IT TOOK ME A minute to realize I'd been asleep. It had been three
weeks since the breakup and I hadn't slept through the night since, all
of those middle-of-the-night worries and memories clanging like an
impertinent radiator. Breathing exercises, sheep counter. Were there
things more tedious than sheep? And if, by a conjuring of miracles, I
fell asleep, I woke up talking to Hesper. I woke up saying: *Wait. Can
I be first?*

What was I asking her? First to what?

From the other side of our walls, Chloe Skyped with Graham
for their long-distance together-time in her missing-you intonation;
the susurrus of their love, traveling. I listened to the arc of their
conversation—tender, lascivious, nostalgic. When Chloe left, her keys
jangled and I exhaled, alone, knowing that I could stay still for the
next five minutes or five hours and it would make no fucking difference.

The absence of sound. Of.

Please, I implored my inbox. But she wasn't there. All that revealed
itself was a world of coupons, and an email from my mother with the
subject line "?" and a blank message inside. My limbs were still heavy,
resistant to the gray summer light. I peeled myself from sweaty sheets
to press frozen spoons over my eyes: Google recommended this for

alleviating puffiness. I perched on the kitchen island with my thighs spreading outward like pudding. For breakfast I bit into a cucumber like an apple and spit the small white seeds into a takeout container that had strayed from the rest of the garbage. Chloe left my sunglasses on top of the wine rack with a Post-it: *have a great day! your room-mate xxx.* I slid them over my unnaturally cool eyes, replaced Hesper's abandoned sleep shorts with cut-offs and Toms. Double-checked the shorts to make sure they still didn't have a wisp of her scent; they did not. They smelled like me.

At the park a block from our apartment, schoolchildren in summer camp wore coordinating T-shirts and shot flaccid streams of water from fluorescent plastic guns. I watched them circle around the main statue of the park with gusto. Tanned tourists snapped photos, wiped grubby fingers on paper maps. Who was giving out paper maps any-more? I would not think of her. I would think of the maps. I would be more curious—curiouser and curiouser. Maybe that was the key to mental health, taking each grain of observance and examining it into oblivion. I had a book called *How Should a Person Be?* and I rested it on my lap and pretended to read it from underneath my safe plastic glasses. I would have an answer for Chloe when we returned to the apartment and she said *What did you do today?* and I would not say *I left while you were gone because I can't stand to be alone.* I would not say *I stared at a group of small children and picked a favorite, a little boy in a yellow T-shirt with a yarmulke pinned into his downy curls.*

The girls aimed right between his eyes.

From behind where I was sitting, on a concrete slab that substituted for a bench, a peacock slinked into the grass and raised his head to-ward the sky. The call that he emitted was a swollen noise somewhere between a seagull and a hungry stray cat, and I yelped and glanced nervously at the space in front of me but no one had heard; I was still safe, swaddled in the soundtrack of peacocks and day camps. I Instagrammed a picture of the peacock's lustrous feathers as though we were friends, and I was the kind of person who appreciated nature instead of a girl who had to cover her fear-whimpers by burying her mouth in the crook of her elbow.

Time passed, light latticed over my lap, until the yellow-shirted boy was retrieved by a tall man in a black suit and I was following them before I realized exactly what was happening, four paces behind so as not to seem creepy. The boy slid his miniature hand into his pocket to snag a cluster of gummy worms.

I would not think about her. Would not think. One foot, the other. Basic mechanics. Taxis darted between lanes; the homeless man with a burlap sack and the printed sign on cardboard: HELP ME IT'S MY BIRTHDAY TODAY. But he had that sign out every day. Had he made it for his actual birthday and then given up, or was it always crafted upon a foundation of lies? The boy walked lack-adaisically, the tall man strode with steps like gulps of water, a runner dodged in between us and I hated her, I wished I were a differ-ent person so I could yell *Watch where the fuck you're going*, I wished I were a different person so I wouldn't feel my breath skip at the idea of losing the boy and his tall companion, I was not going to lose them, they were right here, and when they turned down to-ward Columbus weaving around plump saturated trash bags, I weaved and dodged with them, and when the tall man said, "Fold in!" benevolently and the yellow-shirted boy adjusted his yarmulke pins I crumpled downward to pretend to tie my shoes, both hands laid flat against the sidewalk. I hoped they were going to see a grand-mother, a newspaper-clippings-assembler, someone mothball-scented with runny cheese on a wooden plate.

They were not going to see a grandmother; they were unlocking the door to a synagogue—a brassy star of David hinged on the door with Hebrew letters, and for a moment I couldn't remember how to read them. Then my Hebrew school training resurfaced on cue: *aleph bet vet, gimmel dallet hay*. I thought of my mother, how she always said

Judaism was the thing that killed us. She said it, faith, was: irrational. Wasn't that what faith was? But no matter. There was a membrane that separated them from faith and mine was thin, permeable, where theirs had an obstruction. Sunday mornings, around the corner at the synagogue. They wanted me to have a bat mitzvah to fulfill the contractual obligation; wrap myself in a tallit and slice through a sheet cake. Then nothing. Once you were an adult there was nothing left to do.

But I remembered feeling the buzz of connectivity in my chest with every prayer said. I cried on the high holy days in my tennis shoes and unwashed hair. No jewelry, no makeup to camouflage, just the timpani drum of a fist against a heart, an alphabetical list of every wrongdoing and the refrain: *forgive me, pardon me, grant me atonement.* And beyond that the question that echoed in the distance: *Do you believe me? Do you believe that I'm sorry?* I hadn't been to temple since it happened. I was afraid that it wouldn't feel the way that it had, once. It had been some time since I felt that buzz in my chest, and what if it didn't come back?

&

I LISTENED TO THE key that the tall man inserted into the slot turning in the lock and the yellow-shirted boy. I wanted to say, *Wait, wait.* I wanted to be inside with the velvet tufted seat cushions and tall wooden pews, the dim reddish light hinged over the b'ma, the Torah nestled in a locked ark in its fanciest clothes.

The boy and the tall suited man shut the door and I stared after them as though there would be evidence left behind. But there was nothing to see. The door was shut. I had been taken to it and then it closed. The boy in yellow was out of view and I couldn't catch up because I wasn't allowed inside. Cars swiveled around me and the closed door. Where God might be. And it was relentlessly sunny outside,

Momofuku-pastry-clutching teenagers emerged from the corner who had never seen the yellow-shirted boy, who never would see him and this felt like a tragedy, that I wanted to say look, here he is, this thing you didn't realize you had never seen.

I kept walking. In front of every storefront I was thinking, *Is it here?* wondering what exactly it could be—was I craving that croissant sandwich with the chived cream cheese, or was it something less material? The satisfaction of combing through every knot in my hair after a shower? No, it had to be tangible because I needed it, now. It was in the window display of Club Monaco where nothing was on sale, gold adorned and nautical, thickly striped to the extent that the dark lines seemed inflamed. I paused on the corner and pepperminted my lips with balm and thought, *Yes, it's here, what it is. God brought me right here to see it, to take it, to make it mine.*

Inside it lived on a decapitated mannequin, was a long golden chain with a thin whistle, dangling deep past her sternum, or where her sternum would be if she were a real person and not a plastic corpse, and I lifted the necklace up over where her head would be and thought of Ada on that first night with her fabric swatches, patchworking hideous clothes and they were, weren't they?, hideous, now I could say it, now I had no reason to shy away from my real feelings about whether I would ever wear anything Ada designed because I wouldn't! I never would! I never would because her clothes were hideous! I never would because no real girl needed a cape, I would never have the chance again. All I could think was: Hesperless, my cementfilled chest; she was the absence of my life and the fear of forgetting. I thought I could see the love on her face but the love was holefilled; that love was actually her balking and I took her fear and swallowed it so I could see what I wanted to see. What I wanted to see was me.

I was carrying the golden whistle on a golden string. At the register a woman in a black romper slid the necklace into a small box, and I slid my credit card through a machine that promised to pay for this someday, and outside on 87th Street I discarded the box and the rib-bon and the receipt and looped my head through the necklace-noose and felt the whistle lowly dangling over my actual body's sternum, the whistle with its slim gold possibilities, to hear me, to hear. I clutched the narrowness of it and stood still amidst skateboarders and speed-walking nannies and absorbed the possibility of noise, of attention. *Do you hear me?* I asked God. I could feel its weight around my neck and the cold metal against my fingers, yes, it was here, what it was, my Godmeter felt awake again. It was just for a moment but it was there, a tremor against my rib cage. Here, here; if I could just stay like this, rooted. Found.

IN THE APARTMENT I scraped crumbs from between the kitchen tiles and dispersed lemon-scented fritz over our kitchen island, the neb-ulous region between the burner and the stove, gathered dust with Brawny's strength. The whistle necklace thumped alongside my heart-beat. When Chloe returned after her shift at the bakery, I was barefoot and carting a bag full of balled-up paper towels declaring our previ-ous state of squalor. Chloe dropped a loaf of rejected bread onto the kitchen table. "I'm surveying our empire," she said. "Don't let me curtail your cleaning."

"It looks good, doesn't it?" I would scrub the spot where her shoes were. Soon.

"It really does. Thank you."

I knew I should ask her how the bakery was but I couldn't stop looking at the floor.

"Nobody was feeling olive loaf today," Chloe said. "Only rosemary."

"Maybe I should go after the molding, those curves. Where the dust is."

"You're twitching," Chloe said.

"I bought this necklace." I jerked the whistle upward. "It's helping."

Chloe ripped a fistful of olive loaf and deposited it caringly in my hand.

"I'm not a pigeon," I said begrudgingly.

"You're my favorite pigeon. Listen, I'm not sure about this," she said, through a mouthful of bread, "as a coping strategy. The OCDing can't be good."

I crisscrossed myself on the less comfortable of our kitchen stools. "Oh."

The olive loaf bits dissolved obediently under my tongue. "What about something that doesn't promote finickiness? Have you thought about sculpture? Brushing up on the catalogue of Notorious B.I.G.? That man was a poet. Or," Chloe suggested, gaining momentum, "hiking? You can take Metro-North up to those quaint little beacons and sling yourself up a mountain."

"Nature makes me nervous," I said, pawing into the breadball.

"What if you became an activist? Earlier Graham was telling me about the green energy model in Germany, that it's the best in the world. By 2050 their whole country will be running on renewables. Doesn't renewables have kind of a cute sound to it, like you could pack it for lunch? Anyway. You could campaign for like, windmills. Graham's doing a lot of important research about photovoltaic...things. He could help you." Chloe tore a large hunk of bread and nibbled at its crust.

"Does Graham like Germany?"

"Does he like Germany," Chloe repeated. "Graham is one of those people where it's like he has to shred something to pieces, even if it's a golden gift. He's always befriending old people and then complaining about how they're really racist. But then there's the bread and beer and zoos, he likes that. He has a favorite polar bear. You know, that's nice of you to ask."

"Maybe I should go there," I said, contorting my hair into a pillow as I laid my head down on the tablecloth.

Chloe chewed pensively. "I'm not sure if you want to be traveling alone in a foreign country right now," she said. "Besides, Graham's apartment is barely big enough to fit his suitcase. He has to haul out his sheets into the kitchen to fold them. Sardine syndrome."

"But there's bread and beer. The polar bear."

"Well, right, but you have to get there. It's super expensive."

"I was saving up," I began, and let my consonants flutter. "For Georgia."

"For Georgia," Chloe said. "Right. Okay, but . . . I just don't think this is a time—"

"I can't stay here anymore. Everything's . . . It's like every single thing is a flashback. I want to be somewhere that she's never been."

"What if we found some kind of group for you to go with?" Chloe suggested. I started to shake my head and she patted the top of my scalp, a slow, steady drum. "Willa, I don't mean this in a harsh, evaluative sense, okay? But I worry about you walking twenty blocks right now. Those sunglasses don't camouflage shit. You are not stable enough for transatlantic journeying."

"Can't you come with me?" I said.

"I can't."

"Don't you want to—"

"Jesus Christ, of course I want to. Are you seriously asking me that? But I don't have any money left, okay? If I had money, I would be able to go see Graham in Berlin. I have a pathetic, frighteningly low balance. My loan check might not come in until October. I need to tutor a gaggle of douchey kids from Westchester and drag myself out of bed at four a.m. to bake orange brioche knots."

"I'm sorry."

"It's okay," she said, though I could tell it wasn't. "Besides, don't you want to use the money you have for something you could enjoy? You don't seem...able to enjoy it. Right now."

"Are you saying," I proposed hesitantly, "that maybe I should save the money because Hesper could come back from Tbilisi—"

"How do you know that?" Chloe asked. "I told you not to look at her Facebook. It'll just hurt you even—"

"I couldn't help it. So, in the future...she could change her mind, and then I wouldn't be able to go with her. Next year." Chloe blinked. "If I go to Germany."

"That's not what I'm saying," Chloe said. I lifted my heavy head from the table.

"I thought you might be trying to imply..." I folded my hair firmly behind my ears. "You know, absent hearts. Becoming fonder."

"If you want to go, we'll find you a group," she repeated. "A travel group. Like camp for youngish adults with expendable income. We'll get on Google and figure this out, if you're sure it's what you need to do." Chloe waited for an answer and I couldn't conjure one.

"We'll see what we find," she said, rushing down the hallway. I could tell she thought I wasn't going anywhere.

WE GOOGLED ON CHLOE'S bed, splayed on our stomachs with patterned-socked feet in the air. With her chin creviced into her comforter, Chloe read aloud descriptions of tours to Germany: *small pockets of Alpine terrain. Complex, compelling history. Responsible travel.*

"Doesn't that have a geriatric vibe to it, like, assisted living?" Chloe asked. "What about a different, perhaps, English-speaking country?"

"No," I said, fabric filling my mouth.

"I think our search is too broad," Chloe said, deleting the phrase "trips to Germany" from the search box until only the cursor remained, an abyss of possibility. "What else are you besides a person?"

"That feels like a trap."

"You're a writer. Maybe one of those retreats? Hole up in a cabin, stern men tell you that you have no talent and then you write an amazing novel, right?"

"I think you need to submit a portfolio for those things months ahead of time."

"Okay, what about..."

And in the hush, I knew she was thinking single and I knew that if I heard her say the word *single*, the nasally lilt of the *-ng*, I would die. What did I like besides words, besides weeding through the clichés to reassemble something surprising and crisp? All I could think of was Hesper, the different places I loved on her face, her hips. But before that, there was a before that, what did I do? Before that, the boy. The tree. The bark against my back and his—

"Hey," Chloe exclaimed, in a paroxysm of inspiration. "You're Jewish!"

I thought of the couple on the train to Gravesend, evaluating my face, my gayness, my leggings.

"You're a gold mine, my Semitic sweetheart. Do you like the outdoors? Community service? It's too bad you're not an undergrad. You could be in Bulgaria right now. Oh my God," Chloe said, scrolling triumphantly. "Willa!"

"What?"

"Do you have a great-grandparent that died in the Holocaust?"

"What?"

"Do you have a great-grandparent that died in the Holocaust?" she repeated, her tone buoyant and pleased. She repeated the question a third time in an identically rhapsodic delivery.

"My mom's grandmother. Cecilia."

"Congratulations," Chloe said, inching her laptop over so I could see the screen.

INSPIRING JEWISH SURVIVOR TRIP! the Internet yelled. The

website was a rainy light gray and a tired, already-clicked-upon-link blue, framed with posed curly-haired Jews in sweaters at restaurant tables. *If one or more of your great-grandparents died in the Holocaust, this is the trip for you! Pay only for airfare; connect with members of your community. GROW. BE INSPIRED!* the text commanded, and I cracked my knees. *Spaces still available for our summer trip to Germany,* the website conceded. Chloe scooted the laptop back toward her. "Speak now or forever hold your peace," she warned. I didn't. She emailed the rabbi in charge of coordinating the trip's details. *I am interesting in the Jewish Young People's Association for Remembrance and Change's trip to Germany 2015!* the subject line autofilled, and with this typo I knew that I would go; that things would happen. *My name is Willa,* Chloe typed.

"ONE SECOND, WAIT FOR Dad to pick up," my mother instructed.

"I haven't said anything."

"Sometimes he has trouble with the new cordless phone."

"That's okay."

"Turnip?" my father broke in. "Is that you?"

"It's me," I confirmed.

"Where are you?" my mother said. "Are you elevating your head?"

"I'm in the study. Reading."

"Are the lights on? You shouldn't be squinting in the dark."

"I'm not squinting," my father said, wounded.

"What did you want to tell us?" she prodded. "It's *Sunday,* Willa. HBO night."

"I'm going on a trip," I said. The pause that followed was gristly, expansive.

"What did you say?" my father asked. "There's static."

"There is not static," my mother countered. "How long will you be gone? Send me your itinerary. Do you have my email?"

"You email me often."

"So you do receive them," she gloated.

"It's a six-day trip. We're going to Germany."

"Who's we? You and that—"

"Chloe," I finished quickly.

"Is that it?" she mulled. I longed for an old-fashioned telephone cord to drag around my fingertips until they pulsed with white. "I thought her name was more frivolous than Chloe."

"I'm not going with Chloe. It's a Jewish organization. They arrange a trip for great-grandchildren of Holocaust victims. You only have to pay for airfare," I recited. "There's a grant."

"How do they prove that?" my mother demanded. "Do they need our records? Because they weren't exactly circulating six million death certificates."

The line filled with the blossoming, hoarse harmonics of my father's snores.

"There isn't a rigorous background check. I just had to give her name."

I imagined the tight-lipped twitch on my mother's face each time we were at a supermarket or a Starbucks and the jangling clap and smooth bongo beat began as Paul Simon lullabied her grandmother's name: *Cecilia, you're breaking my heart. Oh, Cecilia, I'm down on my knees. I'm begging you please to come home.* The percussive pop of the woodblock like a gunshot.

"Well. How do we know this is even a reputable organization? Maybe they're just peddling eager Jewish young adults into a van somewhere. How do I know you'll be safe with these people?"

The snores rolled forward like a luxurious Persian carpet.

"Ariana Cohen went," I said, naming a straight-skirted, History Club sycophant from my middle school graduating class that I hadn't thought about in years. "She said it was a transformative experience."

"Since when are you in touch with Ariana Cohen?"

"She posted it on Facebook," I said.

"I'll send you my money belt," my mother said. "Strap it over the thickest part of your body and buy a man's workshirt to wear. No one will be able to tell."

"That sounds covert," I responded, conciliatory.

"Hello?" my father broke in, gasping with sleep apnea. "Are you there?"

"It's me, Dad."

"Willa's going on a trip," my mother said. "To Germany."

"Oh, how nice. Why?" he asked.

A silence coagulated between us. I wondered if she knew, if I'd underestimated her this time. Maybe I'd underestimated her every time, and she'd pretended to forget Hesper's name to sideswipe the breakup's undertow; if she could feel the end of our relationship through some kind of Mom-osmosis. But then I heard the metal spoon abrading the remains of her low-fat yogurt from its plastic container, the sound of her evening meal, and I knew she was waiting for me to lie so we could get off the phone.

"Hello?" he said again. "Are you there?"

I SPENT THE NEXT two and a half weeks doing tasks that vaguely constituted "getting ready for the trip." I bought a passport holder decorated with a cosmos of sanguine roses; learned how to ask for help in German, then how to politely communicate that I could not speak German. Chloe was impressed by my vocabulary development. We liquified our evenings with mason jars of plush Trader Joe's wine. We tried watercolors but they seeped all over our fingers, morphing into something like a Technicolor Rorschach test, and I couldn't see anything.

The night before I left for Germany, Chloe knocked on my door with an expression on her face that I'd come to associate with gentle confrontation. "I'm supposed to go to Lion's Head with Marisa and Ingrid," she said apologetically. "And I know you're leaving really early tomorrow, so."

"Are you...deciding whether you want to hug?" I asked, watching her nervously finger every necklace hung on my treelike jewelry stand.

"No," she laughed, pulling me into her. I pressed my fingers into her back like putty. Our bodies tight, taut, like at a school dance, she continued with her chin on my neck, "I'm just worried that this is too sad of a trip. I know you need to book it out of here and I get it, really, but...I mean, Willa, it is *the* most depressing mission you could've picked. I know I encouraged it before, but just...I never thought you'd go through with it. I thought it was a weird fantasy fixation. Going to tour concentration camps with a group of strangers? Really?"

"But it'll help. It'll be like...I'm surrounded by all these memories of devastation and genocide and my own stuff will be minimized in comparison. Don't you want me to gain perspective?" I asked, emboldened by red wine and the lack of eye contact.

"Have you ever heard of that as a tactic for treating psychological disorders?" Chloe asked. "Are those tour buses at Auschwitz filled with dysthymics?"

"I'm not disordered," I said, breaking the hug.

"I don't mean it in a bad way. You're just so raw right now, Willa, I think—"

"The group was your idea. *You* said I needed a group."

"I didn't think you would go," Chloe admitted.

Well, you were wrong! I imagined boasting, but didn't want to sound twelve. Besides, Chloe was my only best friend. There was only so much I could push her.

"The itinerary you printed out?" she continued. "I just looked at it. Jesus Christ, I wouldn't be able to handle that and I haven't been—"

"What have I been, exactly?"

"Fragile. I think you've been fragile."

"Everyone's fragile. I'm going to Düsseldorf!" I said hollowly.

Chloe released me from the hug and rested on the corner of my bed, and for a horrible second I thought she knew that I hadn't changed my sheets since the breakup, that I didn't want a washing machine to sterilize all of the tiny Hesperpieces that remained. But she stroked my bedspread as if it were a docile pet, and kept her eyes askance. "I'm not trying to control you. I just don't want you to go through with a really masochistic plan. I didn't expect you to really leave," she repeated.

"I bought all of those travel-sized cosmetics," I said. "And the plug thing."

"Willa," Chloe said. Then she offered me her last piece of cinnamon gum, and I told her that she should have it, and we sat quietly, not looking at each other.

"I can always call Graham," I reminded her. "We'll be on the same continent."

"I'll email you his number," she said. "And his address. Just in case."

"Okay."

"Promise you'll come back," Chloe said. I had forgotten how much she hated to be alone, too—that there had been something warm and purposeful in wine and watercolor night for Chloe. None of Chloe's other friends needed her the way that I did. My overgrown, spooling sadness wasn't just mine, but was the centerpiece on our kitchen table.

"I'll come back," I said, not promising anything.

❧

THEN I WAS ON the subway with my luggage on my way to the airport but also: standing with Hesper at the Angel Olsen concert, surrounded by bearded men and beautiful women with clear plastic glasses, waiting for sad acoustic songs in a dulcet husky voice, and as Angel Olsen trembled through "Tiniest Seed," the shifty, quintessentially bored boyfriend in the very front was fumbling through his pocket for a candy bar, and Hesper covered her mouth to muffle the sound of her laughing at the plastic wrap crackling, so conspicuous and dissonant, and we both peered around the various giants congregated between us and the stage and the candy-craver to see what he was eating and it was an Oh Henry! bar, school-bus yellow even in the dim Brooklyn concert lighting, and we both started to laugh because it was so absurd and specific, an Oh Henry! bar, Hesper's velveteen cheekbone against mine, her arm cradling my waist, our stifled laughing transforming into something rampantly raw, her whisper in my ear, "Oh, Henry," and me whispering back, and that night with our feet tingling from standing so many hours and the long trip from Brooklyn in our snowflake-speckled winter coats, calling each other Henry into the cruxes of our necks as though every mention was a succulent secret, and I loved her, and she was perfect, and then gone and I was left with my head down, eyes shut, arriving at the airport, melting into memory feeling like if I could just remember the thing that I'd done to fuck everything up forever, then we could fix it. That no one would ever love me again. She had been my only real girlfriend in four years. Maybe loving me had an expiration date, that on seven months and one day a rancid taste filled the person who loved me and they couldn't toothpaste it away, that the sourness laced through her until she just couldn't anymore, and I had to be let go.

6.

We boarded the flight to Tbilisi with Baba. Since the dementia hit, he spoke in a clumpy stew of Georgian, Russian, German, English; listening to him piece a sentence together was like a glottal review of twentieth-century history. On the airplane, we plucked the words we understood out like fireflies, made Mad Libs on napkins embossed with airline logos. Ada and I sat on one side of the aisle; Mom and Baba and Dad on the other. We came up with: Lemon, trip, noise, pretty, bathroom. Lemon was me; pretty could've been either one of us. But was probably also me. Baba had trouble remembering Ada; we all knew it. No matter how hard she tried, he couldn't recognize her with the blue-dyed hair.

Mom tried dutifully to advertise the benefits of sleeping pills during extended travel; Dad tried dutifully to ignore everyone, shifting in his seat to admire the airplane's wing. Baba was crying a little.

"I take Ambien all the time," Mom pressed. "It's a very cushiony, dreamy sleep."

"I'll take one," I said.

"I am not trying to convince you, Lemon," she said, but acquiesced.

Baba said, "Seline," and she took his warm, veiny hand and pressed it to her chin.

Baba was my dad's father, but he'd always liked Mom better—

especially since the dementia, a hailstorm of disorientation. Even after the divorce, he asked for Seline: where is she, when is she coming back? Was there soup? Often there was soup. My parents were one of those self-congratulatory divorced couples who bragged about their cozy relationship. We went out for dumplings to celebrate holidays. But the truth is their squabbling went from friendly to vicious without warning, and we were eight and ten years old again, rubbing our chopsticks together to rid ourselves of possible splinters.

"Baba," I said, leaning into the aisle, "Mom is giving you a special present."

He narrowed his heavy-lidded eyes in my direction. "What does it do?"

"You have to eat it to see what happens," I said in half-Russian, which seemed to do the trick. He held out his tremoring hand with his fingertips pointed upward, kind of mystically, and Mom dropped the single pill in his palm like a precious jewel. He swigged the pill with her SmartWater bottle and then closed his eyes.

Before we all had to shut our phones off for takeoff, Mom texted me, "It unnerves me that you're so good with him." This was the kind of compliment I'd come to expect.

We Mad-Libbed. Ada conjured her sentence before mine. She presented it to me in looped, designer script: *A pretty bathroom noise, said Lemon, tripping.* It was a dig; it had to be, about the number of times that I'd recently crawled into her apartment late at night, tripping on Molly, sleeping on the floor with her cat. I'd started keeping food in her refrigerator, including a papaya that was currently ripening into something rotten as we swirled our way skyward toward Tbilisi.

"You don't get to make *trip* a gerund," I objected. "It's a totally different thing."

"You just don't want to admit I'm a talented wordsmith," Ada said.

"What's a pretty bathroom noise, anyway?"

"I like a good water drip."

"That's where cockroaches live," I said, which shut her up immediately. But then I caught her looking at me with that older sister worry-sympathy blend and part of me wished she had stayed in Brooklyn, that it would just be Mom and Dad bouncing between jabs and jokes and me and Baba, painting ordinary actions into fairy-tale magic.

"So kill them," she said, in her older-sister voice. "You have to be able to do it yourself."

I knew Ada was thinking about Charlie, who'd taken care of bug killing. I never trusted him; he had a smile that curled up on the edges like it was molting, and a weird splotch on his back that was perpetually sweaty. Then he left her for a Rubenesque mutual friend that designed and presented PowerPoints for a consulting firm, where she was used to sixteen pairs of eyes following her directions at all times. Ada couldn't understand it then and, two years later, had come to no conclusions besides it being the worst thing that had ever happened.

Ada didn't recover. She hunted for Other-Charlies ("The OC," she'd call them, once a dating pattern had been established) and she found them everywhere: Tinder, OkCupid, the coffee shop where she got her donuts on weekend mornings. There were obvious difficulties with the doppelganger plan, and she was just becoming more and more obsessed with preserving his memory. Now, I knew that when she comforted me about Willa, she was really thinking about herself.

"Feel it, while you have the support of your friends," Ada had advised, three weeks ago, when I finally got it together to say it out loud. "Before you hit your statute of limitations. People can only deal with your heartbreak for so long."

"Do I get to be heartbroken?" I asked. "As the initiator?"

"Lemon, that girl did such a number on you."

"I did a number on her," I reminded Ada.

"Right," she said, dunking a piece of sushi into a clotted mixture of soy sauce and wasabi.

"Don't hide behind your avocado roll with your coy accusations."

"Who's being coy?" Ada said. "You're a mess."

When we were halfway to Vienna, Mom leaned over the aisle to announce in Ada's direction, "I'm so pleased that you followed my advice about the nose ring."

Ada pretended not to hear the first time. Then she shook the earphones out from the hollows of her ears and said, "Choose your battles, right?"

"I guess there's nothing we could do about the hair," Mom said mournfully.

Nothing looked quite like strawberry-blond roots against a midnight blue pixie cut.

"Aren't you supposed to be the one with the edgy hair?" Mom asked me.

Ada beamed, an opportunity for protectiveness. "Mom, you're being offensive. You're making an assumption that she should have edgy hair because she wants to sleep with women."

"Please," I interjected. "Never say that again. Not in front of Baba."

"Well, you got all pissy at me for calling you a lesbian. I don't know what you want me to call you."

"You can go back to insulting Mom. That's all I've ever wanted."

Mom waved us off, as though we'd suddenly asked whether she preferred the air conditioner be turned up. "I'm fine," she answered gallantly. "Are you offended, Hesper? Should we open a dialogue?"

"Pass."

Mom wiped at the splotch of drool collecting on Baba's collar.

"*Your* hair looks beautiful," she said.

"Thanks, Mom."

In his sleep, Baba gurgled, "Eliyana. Eliyana."

"Who?" I asked Mom, who shrugged and passed the mystery ba-
ton to Dad.

"Don't think I haven't asked," Dad said. "Believe me."

"Thanks for engaging with your daughters," Mom said. "I appreciate it."

Dad lifted the cover of his historical biography in response, then
put it back in his lap.

"Don't forget to call Christina when we land," Mom reminded
him.

Ada and I looked at each other. *What?* she mouthed, and I
mouthed it back to her. It was rare to hear Mom bring up our father's
girlfriend.

"I will not forget," Dad said, and his eyes darted toward Baba.

"Eliyana," I said. But Baba was still asleep, his neck a rippling collection of skin waves.

"It sounds Jewish, doesn't it?" Mom asked. "You can ask your
friend."

The incorrect, lightly veiled reference to Willa curdled in my
stomach.

Stop looking at me, I begged Ada, twisting my hem around my
clenched fist.

"It does sound Jewish," I confirmed.

"Anything else you want to contribute?" Ada pushed.

"Maybe we'll meet her when we get to Georgia," I said.

"She's probably dead," Dad warned, turning back toward the
window.

"WHO DESIGNED THIS FUCKING airport?" Mom hissed, yanking her bag
behind her with a swift jolt. "Is it a social experiment?"

"It's a rabbit warren," Dad agreed. We were all power-walking like retirees in a shopping mall, luggage clattering at our heels. "Is that a sign?"

"What's a rabbit warren?" I asked.

"It's an underground tunnel system, occupied by rabbits."

"A rabbit-rynth," I said, knowing it would make them both smile.

Ada wheeled Baba briskly, her cheeks flushing as we all rushed through Terminal 3. "It's clean," Ada offered, huffing a bit as we rounded a wide corner.

"It's an anxiety-laden cesspool," Mom said. "Don't *jostle* your grandfather, Ada. Smooth and steady. Should have connected in Heathrow," she said to my father. She was twisting her ex-wedding ring around with her thumb, the way she had through our childhoods. She'd never taken it off because she said it "warded off unwanted attention," but I always wondered if it was something more. "Elevator. Ha!"

Baba mumbled something in a language none of us understood.

"Where's the adventure in Heathrow?" Dad asked as the elevator rattled us toward the correct location.

"I prefer my travel plans to be adventure-free," Mom said.

"I hate it here," Baba said suddenly, in a bark. "I hate it here."

We stood silently behind him, a heap of luggage and crumpled gum wrappers and guilt.

"Good thing we're going to a secret place," I told him. His eyes were tearing.

"It's a goddamn mystery where we're going," Mom said, mostly under her breath.

"Connecting flight!" Dad said. "Connecting those dots. Aren't we, Baba?"

We shuttled to our terminal amidst bedraggled, lost travelers and overpriced restaurants selling broiled meats and warm bread. Mom shooed Ada and Baba ahead, then said quietly, furiously, "What kind of crockpot doctor told you that this was a good idea? He's obviously overwhelmed and in no condition for international travel."

"Crackpot," Dad corrected.

"Martin."

"Seline." His voice catching in a childish one-uppance. "Alright. Define good."

"You want to discuss semantics?"

"He's my father," Dad said. "You think I'd throw him to the wolves?" She bit down on her lower lip. "Do you see any wolves?"

"This conversation," my mother said, clutching the five boarding passes required for our transfer, "is not finished." She fanned herself with her passport, the navy blue stark against her hands. "Austria's nauseating me," she complained loudly, while Ada and I configured ourselves a bit farther away from her, as though her grumpiness were a wave threatening to splash our ankles.

IT WAS THREE IN the morning when we arrived in Georgia. Baba stayed asleep; Dad was the only one who hadn't dozed on the plane. At customs, the officer beamed at our passports and handed Dad a bottle of red wine. Mom stared at it suspiciously. Dad put it in Baba's lap to hold, like a well-behaved miniature dog.

"Ada," I said. "I think we found Darcy." Darcy was our hypothetical poodle.

"Darcy isn't made of alcohol, dummy," Ada said, but seemed grateful to be talking about something besides travel arrangements. Mom huffed away to exchange money into laris, Dad leaned dangerously against the wheelchair as support for his sleepy, lanky limbs.

"You girls always wanted a dog," Dad mumbled.

Ada raised an eyebrow at me to say, *Your conception of* always *is skewed.* We had done the traditional Mom-weekday, Dad-weekend dance for twelve years and the worst part was this: the sudden bursts of nostalgia, weird generalizations that held up through 1998 and then eroded in accuracy. Ada's eczema had been cured by prescription-strength miracle cream; I outgrew soccer, sailing, ballet. But we had wanted a dog, until we decided cats were more sophisticated. Their orneriness suited our lifestyle.

"Christina's iguana was doing this strange thing with its tongue the other day," Dad began, and stopped when he saw Ada's face.

"Tell me more about those reptilian features. I'd love to really delve," I said.

"Mom won't care if we're talking about Christina," Ada said, watching Dad's expression tighten as Mom approached with her pocketbook full of liras. "You don't have to do that thing with your cheeks."

"You are decidedly talented in making people self-conscious, you know that?"

I braced myself for the dreaded phrase "just like your mother," but he stopped.

"Why did she ask you to call Christina, earlier?" I asked him.

"Oh, shit. She did remind me to do that."

"What did you do?" Ada asked. "Did you kill the iguana?"

"I have never harmed the iguana. I can't call my partner without the interrogation, Ad?"

"The weird thing was that Mom was your reminder service. Calling her isn't strange in itself," Ada said.

"Ada, my love," Dad said, which he only ever said when he was trying to fight off annoyance. "Drop it. Drop it before your mom comes back. Okay?"

"I would literally commit a homicide to have access to a shower," Mom said, taking over wheelchair duty from Ada. "Alright. The good news is we have the correct currency; the bad news is we're going to hit the four a.m. traffic jam going into Tbilisi proper. All the international flights arrive in the middle of the night," she added, before we could ask. "The hotel is in a convenient location, at least. Who has something they want to say about that? Lemon? Ada?"

"I'd rather be stuck in a car than an airplane," I offered.

"What a pioneer," Ada said.

"Did you say hotel?" Dad asked as we slowly made our way toward baggage claim. The airport was hazily lit, blueish, passengers maneuvering with oversized luggage and plastic bags filled with liquor bottles and cigarettes. "We're not staying with Salomeya?"

"If you wanted to stay with your great-aunt, perhaps you could've handled those travel arrangements, Martin."

"She's going to be insulted. She's very hospitable."

"She's ancient, and I'm not sleeping on a futon with my ex-husband."

He bristled at *ex*. We all knew that he hadn't wanted to get divorced, and he was only trying to convince himself to love Christina as much as he loved Mom.

"I knew you were resentful about coming on this trip," Dad said.

"Oh, not at all. This is my dream vacation. Bring on the caretaking, I say."

"I thought we agreed that it made more sense to have us both—"

"It does make more sense, because this is a terrible idea, and I don't believe that any licensed medical professional endorsed *gallivanting across*—"

"Hey, Mom," Ada interrupted. "Why does Dad need to call Christina?"

Mom exhaled a sigh. "You still haven't called her? Why do I need to nag you about every tiny task, Martin? You can't call your own pregnant girlfriend without a declaration of intent."

There was a long pause. Only the sound of luggage squeaking nearby surrounded us. Dad's face sprung splotches of pink that looked almost magenta in the strange airport light.

I heard it, but I also didn't hear it. I also heard myself thinking, *I have to tell Willa.*

"What was that?" Ada asked finally.

"I thought you said you told them," Mom said. She rubbed her eyes wearily. "I am absolutely certain that we already had this conversation, and you said—"

"I didn't confirm I told them. We did outline a plan for—"

"What," Mom said, crisp, so that the *T* hung for a minute, "could you possibly be—"

"It's very early," Dad said, finally looking at Ada and then me. "Very early days."

"Not so early that Mom hadn't devised a plan about breaking the news," Ada said drily.

"Are you happy?" I asked. "I mean, how are we supposed to feel about this?"

Mom held up her hand before Dad could answer. "You feel however you want. Obviously this isn't the ideal location for this kind of conversation, but we should all talk about...the issue at hand. Once we get back to the hotel, that could be—"

"You're not running a focus group, Mom," Ada said.

"We're happy. Of course," Dad said, but his voice was flat. "Christina's been having a hard time, so far. Morning sickness, and... whatnot."

"Good thing you're on a trip with us," Ada said. "That's super supportive."

"Can we please leave the airport now?" I asked. "I really...I can't be here anymore."

"Of course we can, Lemon. Let me just have a quick word with your father."

Ada and I clustered around Baba's wheelchair. I ran my palms over the ridged, rubbery handle until it was hot. Around us, travelers hoisted their luggage off the baggage claim conveyor belt, an assembly line of back lunges. It felt like we had been awake for three days.

Ada said, "That was surprising."

"Do you think it was an accident?"

"Do I think Dad intentionally brought another little miracle into the world? No. Definitely not. But maybe it wasn't an accident for Christina. She seems like the baby type. I bet she's already Pinteresting up a storm."

I thought of the girl in the restaurant. The melting expression on Willa's face.

"Third time's the charm, right?" I said. "They'll probably have a perfect baby."

"Nice. Thank you."

"What do you think they're saying?" I asked. Mom had a finger waggling spasmodically near Dad's chin.

"I wonder if they'll get married," Ada said.

"They tried that already."

"Christina," Ada corrected me. "The pregnant one."

"Oh. Right."

"I bet she'd let me design her wedding dress," Ada said. "Something really creamy."

"I don't really want a new family," I said.

I couldn't stop thinking of Willa. That one night, listening to her air conditioner wheezing its lukewarm air, when she was daydreaming out loud about weddings. I couldn't believe how much thought she'd given everything: white roses, twinkling tea lights. Pistachio-lemon cake, she said, and I'd told her, "Lemon is what my family calls me," and she'd replied, already mostly descended into slumber, that she knew that. Originally she'd wanted chocolate, but this was perfect, a cake for me, and I felt all of her hopes like I'd accidentally swallowed a sparrow and there it was, avidly attempting to fly out of my rib cage. I hadn't said anything. Just waited for her to fall asleep, for her dreams to remain out of reach.

"Doesn't matter what you want," Ada said. "Things change without your consent all the fucking time, Hesper." As Mom and Dad approached her, Ada hushed them with a wave. "You're going to wake Baba."

Mom held up her hands, prisoner-style. "Sorry, Baba. Let me, Lemon," she said, swooping in. But without the wheelchair, I felt a low-level anxiety thrumming all over me, like the bass on a speaker turned up too high.

"I'll push him," I said, prying Mom's fingers from the wheelchair's handles. "Just show me where to go."

In the airport, all of the signs in Georgian looked like the outlines of clouds in cartoons. To the soundtrack of luggage wheels humming against the smooth floor, I dipped my head close to his ear and whispered, "Eliyana. Eliyana," like a prayer.

✥

MOM HAD BOOKED THE most Western-world hotel she could find; we were handed flyers advertising Zumba classes and a special brunch menu for Sunday mornings. The lobby was bright, speckle-tiled like a cheerful office waiting room. Pillows decorated with embroidered elephants were meticulously placed in the corners of sofas. Ada and Mom and I had a room upstairs; Dad and Baba were on the ground floor. I relinquished control of the wheelchair handles reluctantly, although my wrists were sore. I didn't want to be task-less. I could feel the Willa-guilt resurfacing, drawing attention to itself like the smell of something burning.

"There's a pool," Mom offered, lugging her carry-on awkwardly up the stairs. I hated her for mentioning the pool. Who was she kidding? We weren't a bunch of sweet-eyed, optimistic children that could be enticed into thinking this was going to be an awesome vacation because of a hole filled with chlorine.

"Do you think Baba will recognize it here?" Ada said. "Not the hotel, I mean. Georgia."

Mom stopped in front of a sleek wooden door and struggled to balance her carry-on and insert the key, but neither of us made a move to help her. She mumbled something about the inconvenience of having real keys instead of a computerized swipe card.

"To be honest, I'm not sure what he remembers," Mom said. "But both of you need to think of this as a possibility for you to consider your heritage, okay? Don't drag your kitten heels through the mud, sulking."

"I would never wear kitten heels," Ada said.

Mom opened the door. "I don't want to hear another punchy comment about footwear. I'm going to take a long, cleansing shower and then we're going to have a restful, perfect night's sleep. Got it?" She eyed us both in preparation for our faux-salutes, which we delivered. The room was impeccably decorated, white porcelain ashtrays on the nightstand. Bibles, old school floral stationery, a letter-opener made of lush, cherry-stained wood.

"Can you drink the water here?" Ada asked.

"Is that a balcony?" I said, peering to the other end of the room. Long, gauzy ivory curtains hung gracefully over a picture window.

"Yes," Mom answered curtly, violently dragging her zipper around the perimeter of her carry-on. She'd packed her summer robe, though it was cool and breezy here—an uncharacteristic misstep for someone who prided themselves on arranging every detail perfectly. The bathroom door clicked definitively shut.

Ada and I traipsed onto the balcony, which was cast-iron and narrow, and we sat with our legs touching, outstretched in front of us. Tbilisi glowed sunset-like in the night; rows of sparse, non-American trees speckled our view of the city. I had never seen such an orange-tinted skyline. My jet-lagged stomach cramped in confusion about mealtimes, sleep, circadian rhythms.

"World's happiest ex-couple," Ada said finally. "Alert the media."

"They've been worse," I replied, remembering a particularly

turbulent moment when we, as a family, had gone with Ada to get her nose pierced. "I guess it's just the first day, though. Downhill from here."

"Uphill. Downhill is when it gets easier. You gain momentum."

"I don't care about the hypothetical road. I care about having to listen to them bicker and then us having to play mediator, and then five minutes later being subjected to that bullshit about how well they get along."

I watched Ada pick at a scab on her forearm. "What do you think it would be like if they hadn't gotten divorced?" I asked.

"We would've visited far fewer aquariums. That's for sure."

"Besides our aquatic education."

"I don't know. They don't seem to hate each other any more than anybody else's parents. Would we be different, is that what you mean? Maybe less afraid of commitment. We're ahead of the curve, Hes. Our hearts are in their midthirties."

"Just what I always wanted," I said. "A prematurely aged heart."

Ada pulled a strand of hair from my sweater. "Is that thing happening to you where silence makes you cry a little?" she asked.

"No," I said, turning my watery eyes down toward my knees.

"It happens to everyone," she offered.

In every pause I imagined Willa's creased face, tears dripping pathetically down the round slope of her cheeks. The tremoring pitch of her disbelief. *This isn't what was supposed to happen,* she insisted. *How do you know what's supposed to be?* I asked. How could she be so confident about what kind of person she belonged with? How did she know it was me? I don't know anything about always. I don't want to have an always.

"With Charlie—"

"This is different," I interrupted.

"It will be," Ada said gently. "But it isn't yet. Every heartbroken person is exactly the same, young one."

The cold wind swooped against my dry elbows. "Who do you think Eliyana is?" I changed the subject. Ada blinked. "You know, the name Baba keeps saying."

"It's not a name. It's syllable soup."

"It sounds like a person."

"Is this your new obsession? Like when I got really into crocheting mittens?"

"Stop trying to get me to talk about it," I said, poking her so I could pass off my tone as playful.

She relented. "Maybe it's Georgian for Rosebud. Tbilisi meets Citizen Kane."

"He might not remember anyway," I said, and Ada pushed herself closer to me. Our ankles smacked gracelessly together, the hard wire of the balcony's supports digging into our backs. Ada scratched the side of her face, and we simultaneously dug our fingers into mouths, scraping the inside of our cheeks and unfurling the remains on our palms to examine our cheek-innards scientifically. We'd done this since we were children; the kind of tradition I would never be able to explain to anyone. She was my sister, and I loved her for investigating the white, pipe-cleanerish membranes to see which was more caterpillar-like. I loved her for letting me win.

DAD POURED US ALL glasses of wine with breakfast. "Saperavi," he explained as Mom covered the top of her glass with her veiny hand. "Over four hundred kinds of grapes grow in Georgia," he continued, extending the bottle again in Mom's direction. She shook her head.

"Did you stay up all night reading a travel guide?" I asked, rescuing two rolls from the basket. Our napkins were folded across a stack of increasingly larger plates. Deviled eggs with mysterious, hummus-like filling dotted with pomegranate seeds were placed on the table by a smiling waitress.

Mom cough-laughed, an abrupt save. "It's all very interesting," she confirmed.

Baba, dressed like a slick accountant in his wheelchair, mumbled incoherently. Ada and I both leaned forward to try and pick out the words we understood. Hungry, we caught in Russian; tired, ache. Ada pushed out her lower lip in sympathy. He did not want the deviled eggs.

"You didn't have to ask for the Georgian menu," Mom said. "Nobody here thinks we're native speakers. You have two blond daughters. You have two once-blond daughters," she corrected, eyeing Ada.

"Grapefruit," Baba said, tapping his wineglass with a mouse-clicking motion.

"Fruit of the day!" Dad said. "I'll get the waitress, Dad. What a great idea." He smiled wildly.

"Remember how Mom used to like her grapefruit?" Dad prompted. "With bacon."

"Martin," Mom began, but Dad was inching his way upward, trying to get the attention of any white-clothed staff person. He ordered grapefruit and pain aux raisins, even though we hadn't finished our bread baskets and Mom was adamantly anti-dried fruit. The view of Tbilisi glittered against the wraparound windows; a lone lily leaned against its vase.

"Lemon, you were on radio," Baba said to me.

"You're a regular songbird, Hes," Ada said, taking a long sip of her wine.

"Was I singing?" I asked. Dad was grimly re-buttering his bread.

"You will not be singing," Mom said, preemptively raising an eyebrow.

"Very good," Baba said, nodding. "Very good volume."

"And she used to let the fat from the bacon drip onto the slices," Dad said.

Mom touched his hand. We watched their hands converge like cells colliding underneath a microscope. We bring out the worst in each other, Mom had explained—the cornerstone of their divorce talk. Easier to respect someone, love them, when you don't have to fight about vacation destinations, financial priorities, brands of salad dressing. But in moments like this, the tiny gestures of tenderness fell into the shaky, irrational chasm in my heart where I thought: *what if, what if,* and it seemed right.

"Christina has a nice voice," Ada said icily. "That karaoke machine never knows what hit it."

Mom's jaw set in a firm lock. Dad uneasily slid his hand from underneath hers.

"Do you think the baby will be a good singer?" Ada asked, a little smile blooming.

"I have no idea," Dad said, folding his napkin into neat thirds before he stood up. "When I come back from the bathroom," he said, "perhaps you can be a little less terrible, Ada."

"Was that necessary?" Mom asked.

"You're the one always talking about being clear with your boundaries," I said.

Ada looked at me gratefully. But she was being awful, and if I could've paid her off to be more pleasant, just a little, I might've. My Willa-induced mosquito bite was bulbous, needling. Ada ripped one of the leaves from the sad lily and rolled it into a joint between her palms.

"Alright," Mom said. "Point taken. But you need to apologize to your father."

"Christina has a mediocre voice, at best," I said. Mom smiled, wrinkles at the corners of her eyes like tiny branches.

"What's her karaoke standard?" Mom asked.

"'Girls Just Want to Have Fun.'"

Mom laughed, a low rumble of comfort, and Ada smoothed Baba's arm so that all the thick, blond hairs were moving in the same direction.

"Here's your grapefruit," the waitress chirped, approaching our table with one of those trays meant to accommodate an entire company's celebratory lunch. And then, unprompted, Baba said something to the waitress that made her laugh. Ada and I looked at each other as they spoke, sentences that befuddled us in their rhythm. Mom closed her eyes as she sliced the grapefruit with a butter knife.

"Your father is very funny," the waitress said to Mom, who did not correct her.

"Typical Baba," I said. "Chatting up strangers, binging on citric fruits."

Ada laughed, and then her face grew pensive. "Did he say anything about us?"

"He used to be very shy," Mom said. I had no idea if that was true.

The waitress smiled wryly. Was she so used to having this effect on the elderly?

"What brings you to Tbilisi?" the waitress asked, in perfectly rehearsed English, and I cringed at the difference between her pronunciation of the city's name and my own.

Ada said, "Pleasure," and Mom narrowed her gray eyes in amused condemnation.

"Visiting family," Mom countered. The waitress nodded encouragingly.

"Is it safe to walk around Dry Bridge Bazaar?" Mom asked her. "Pickpocketing?"

"My mother sells antique toothbrushes there," she answered. "Very nice visit."

We considered this. She continued. "Very safe. Nothing bad happens in Tbilisi." Her English was starting to show its holes, now that we were getting off-script. "Only good times now, since the Soviets left. Nothing...undesired," the waitress said. "Good people living the good life."

She was wearing a brass cross necklace. The kind of person that would hate me, if she knew the truth. But for now, she was more suspicious of Ada, the blue-haired, pixie-cut Helena in *A Midsummer Night's Dream*. The waitress skirted back toward the kitchen and I stuffed my mouth with bread.

When Dad returned, Ada said, "You missed Baba small-talking our server."

"What were they talking about?" Dad asked, still angry but trying not to be.

"It was in Georgian," I volunteered. "She said he was hilarious."

"She was just trying to be nice," Dad said.

Ada covered her smallest plate with deviled eggs. "Perfect brain food," she said, and Dad knew this was her apology and accepted it with a warm nod.

We made a plan: Ada, Mom, and I would take a walk through Old Town, which was too narrow and cobbled for Baba to traverse in his wheelchair, so we'd meet them back at the hotel. Dad thought Baba might like sitting at the pool with a puzzle. Later that night, we would have dinner with Salomeya & Company. Baba sucked on the rind of the grapefruit in quiet reverie while we planted chaste kisses on his crepe-like cheek.

&

"THAT IS...A LOT of Stalin portraits," Ada said, grimacing a little as we passed a seemingly infinite number of red-cloaked tables boasting pieces of Soviet coins, knives, rusted medical equipment. Women with scarves pulled austerely over their foreheads and shoulders moved slowly, lackadaisically, in the direction of the water. A line of clothes-pinned, screen-printed portraits of Soviet leaders smirked at us. Lush green trees stood overhead. Mom scooped some antique tea tins into her arms; Ada fingered a fur hat dusted with mothy remains.

"That's filthy," Mom pointed out.

"Authentic," Ada corrected, wiping her free hand against her dress.

"What kind of tea is that?" I asked Mom. "Sham-omille?"

She laughed, then shifted into a stiffly worded exchange with the merchant, a bearded man with a wooden crucifix swinging against his belly. He swept our treasure-garbage into a plastic shopping bag and smiled, snaggletoothed, in my direction.

"Your daughters are very beautiful," he said.

"My daughters are also very smart," she said. "And thank you."

His eyes were pale and determined, hungry.

She put a hand on my back and steered us toward the other side of the bazaar, where the items were laid out on picnic blankets.

"What's the matter, Mom? Why are we booking it from Ada's future husband?" I asked.

"Something about the market," Mom said, flourishing her hand. "It's too much."

I knew what she meant. It was a sensory overload—the stale scent of vodka, leather, darkroom chemicals. Old photographs swaddled in thick plastic sleeves, surrounded by twentieth-century camera lenses, suitcases, gold-plated medals. I couldn't tell whether there were more pictures of Jesus or Stalin and the juxtaposition made me twitchy. *This is your history,* I thought, but it didn't feel like mine. I grew up eating organic macaroni and cheese from a purple box. I'd only crossed myself during fifth-grade sleepovers to copy my friend Lisa, who was afraid of the *Poltergeist* movies. The sky was a sumptuous shade of blue, twigs silhouetting over our heads. I could feel my mind dipping into Willa—her profile in the sunlight at Central Park, the way she capped and uncapped her pen when she was planning what to say during workshop—and I rushed ahead, caught the eye of the nearest vendor and yelled, "How much is that?" with no real idea of what I was asking about.

The vendor was strong-boned, her cheeks like crabapples, and wearing a long dress that scraped against the ground. She was beautiful. I was surprised, which made me feel like an asshole, and smiled extra to show that I wasn't the close-minded, ethnocentric American that I was.

I could feel Mom at my heels, keeping an eye on Ada as she rubbed her hands over every available swatch and blanket. I would be wearing these weird tapestries as cape-dresses and coats with arm-slits for the rest of my life.

"This?" the vendor asked, holding up the most exceptionally ugly golden swan candle holder I could imagine. Its long neck was spotted with age, its one eye a splotch of ink across the left side of its under-sized head. The wings sprawled outward, the underside coated with wooly felt held on by glue globs.

"Oh, Hesper," Mom sighed. "Please."

"I love it," I told the girl. She smiled, teeth layering over each other. Her eyebrows were thick and impervious, curved in the style of a Depression-era movie star.

"Very unusual piece," she responded. I noticed a habit of trilling her fingers in that space between chin and neck when she spoke. "Has been in my family a long time," she said with a little laugh. "My sister added the wing fur."

"Sisterly wing fur," I repeated in Mom's direction.

"Fine," she said, handing the lari to the beautiful girl, who thanked her effusively.

"What's your name?" I asked. Something in Mom's face hardened, stone.

"Lali," she said.

Lali's wide, pouting lips were stained red, a smear of lipstick blurring over to her regular, non-lip skin. When she leaned forward, the fabric of her shirt shifted, and I caught sight of a healed burn that ran from across her collarbone, an archipelago of mottled olive skin. Parts were light, the splotched texture of wood that's been exposed to water; others were deep, etched like tree bark. The scar dipped below her neckline into bra territory and I kept looking, wondering if it trailed off into regular, non-dimpled skin.

"Thank you for the unusual piece," Mom said, clipped. I could feel her glaring at me and I ignored it. Lali smiled uncertainly and Mom thanked her again, pulling me by the wrist with her clammy fingers clamped against my bones.

"What is wrong with you?" I asked, shaking her off. "I'll pay you for the swan."

"It has nothing to do with that hideous bird," she snapped. We were standing amidst a sea of blankets covered with commemorative medals, dangling earrings made from Russian kopecks. The consonants of Georgian cycled around us like a wind tunnel.

"You have to be more careful," Mom said. "This isn't Brooklyn."

"What are you talking about?" I asked, though I knew exactly what she meant.

She lowered her voice. "You can't just go around *leering at women* in a country like this."

"I wasn't *leering.*"

Mom curled her lips inward, then exhaled slowly. "I need you and your sister to try and blend. Do as the Romans do. Is that so supremely difficult? You can go back to being one hundred and ten percent yourself in a week, okay? You and your Jewish girlfriend can paint the town red for all I care. Ada can pierce every inch of her pretty little nose. But while we're here, can you please just behave?"

"You are so racist," I said. "Do you think there are men with guns hiding in the trees, ready to pounce at every blue-haired fashionista?" But I was already starting to cry. I wiped my eyes with my wrist, determined not to ask Mom for one of her travel-pack tissues.

Hardening myself. I would observe every detail of the trip with the commitment of someone planning an exhaustive travel recap for a devoted listener. *The raisins here are plumper than American raisins, you can actually tell they used to be grapes. The Bridge of Peace looks like a knitted strand of DNA.*

"You are so naïve, Hesper," Mom said, reaching to tuck my hair behind my ear. "It's because we've raised you in these bastions of ultra-liberalism. But there are places where it isn't safe to be..." She looked at my face. "It's my job to protect you."

"Nothing's happening to me. You're just paranoid because we're not staying in a five-star hotel in Paris, Mom. The wrong side of the curtain."

"Listen to me," Mom said, so close to my face that I could see the spots where her mascara was unevenly applied. "Do you know what happened to the people who marched at the gay pride parade here last year? They were torn to pieces, Hesper. The things that they shouted...I couldn't repeat it to you. Okay? I love you and if you think I'm a bigot, I can live with that. I'm not bringing you home in a body bag because you want to make eyes at someone peddling garbage."

"What do you mean, torn to pieces?"

"Promise me you won't Google it when we get back to the hotel."

"Okay," I said, although my voice had the quality of an animal trying to speak English.

"Let's find your sister," Mom said. We walked in silence, stopping every few steps to peruse the basement-concocted grape vodka, dolls propped in slouching positions against wooden slats.

Torn to pieces.

"She's...not my girlfriend," I said finally, and covered my mouth so I could retch behind my cupped hand.

"Your Antonia?" Mom asked, waving the clean white tissue for an invisible bull.

"Not anymore," I said, accepting. "I don't know, I . . ."

"Did she say why?"

"No, that's not— It was my decision."

"Lemon," Mom said. "You can't withhold all of your information and then get angry when people misunderstand you."

"I don't do that," I said, curling my fingers into a knot.

"Was it the wrong decision?"

"No," I said.

"I need at least one more piece of information."

"She loved me too much. I tried to ignore it, but it kept . . . popping up. Between us."

Mom nodded sagely.

"She knew what kind of wedding cake she wanted us to have."

"How many months were you together? Six?"

"Seven."

"You know, I felt that way about your father," Mom said. "He was so invested, so certain of everything we did. Very grandiose, in those days—*always, forever.* I had twelve jobs, before you girls were born. I wanted to swim in the coral reefs, do investigative journalism abroad. It's not that your father didn't support me through all of those things but . . . I wanted to do them alone. I wanted to do them on my terms and I didn't want somebody waiting up for me at night with a grilled cheese sandwich and fifteen questions about my day. I know that's cold of me, but it's how I felt. It's how I still feel."

"I want to make my own grilled cheese, too," I said, tears still peeking through my voice.

Mom put her arm around me and I rested my forehead against her shoulder.

"It's a good thing we bought that disgusting bird to keep you company," she said.

"He's a swan."

Ada approached us with her arms full of fabric rolled into logs.

7.

At the airport, I loitered near a water fountain where a group of twentysomethings had congregated, loudly bemoaning the early hour of the flight. There were eight or so of them, all dressed in chinos and button-downs, combed cotton, covered knees. They looked like adults. People rushing from cubicles toward happy hours. I stared ruefully at my exposed, pink toes. None of them were wearing sandals, I realized—loafers, oxfords, ballet flats. My own feet slid sweatily across the bottoms of my four-dollar flip-flops. When I looked up, a girl in a sundress and hair the same shade of mustard had established an unwavering line of eye contact, evaluating me for a few beats before a tentative smile germinated on her mouth.

"Hey," she said. Her name was Samantha. "Are you attending the Jewish Young People's Association for Remembrance and Change's trip to Germany?" She recited the name of the organization without any self-consciousness.

I nodded, and briefly contemplated making a joke, or even expressing my consideration of making a joke—*wouldn't it have been funny if I had said no?*—but got swallowed into a group-wide declaration of gratitude relating to missing work. A girl with a slick, wilted ponytail praised the genius of the program coordinator—she'd only need to use two vacation days, which was brilliant because she'd already missed six days for an impromptu foray to the UK. Vacation

"How do you think this would look as a poncho?" she asked, her c
lected treasure toppling down from her arms. We all bent to res
the cloth; Mom grimaced as she paid for each parcel. Ada kissed
on the cheek, then took the fabric that looked most like a rug fr
IKEA and unrolled it.

"Maybe you should wait until we get back to the hotel," M
said.

"I just want to make sure I have enough," Ada said. "Hold yc
arms out." I extended as far as I could in either direction while A
measured the cloth against me. I felt the eyes of the vendors, t
other tourists, Tbilisi-ans, staring in my direction. "Maybe more
a muumuu," Ada said, "just those little slits where your arms wou
go." My muscles began to tingle, and I kept reaching, reaching.

days! It was a conversational gold mine. The others burbled about their sordid or serene travels, working in collusion with the calendar's national holidays to swindle as much time away as possible. I had three and a half months of summer vacation, and during the school year, worked eight hours a week at a library desk where my most challenging task involved straightening the spines of textbooks about econometrics. I was untethered—not Hesper's girlfriend, not Chloe's roommate. I didn't know what to say. I had nothing in common with these well-dressed, sensible people who had smartly decided to hide their toes.

"What seat are you?" Samantha asked, come-hithering my ticket. "Thirty-eight C," she said. "Guys, I found thirty-eight C. Mystery solved."

38C sounded too much like my bra size, and I concentrated on not blushing. Samantha handed the ticket back, and I was careful not to touch the place where she'd gripped it. A faux British–accented girl smiled wanly, finishing a bagel. She barely even needed her napkin. I remembered the ease of those girls at day camp, pulling their shirts over their heads while the rest of us wiggled with chicken-dance arms underneath, bulky elbows jaunting against a tent of polyester. "I'm thirty-eight A," Samantha explained. "Kyle is between us," she continued, in a voice that indicated she was very enthused by her proximity to Kyle, or by her distance from me.

"Hi, Kyle," I said, my gaze bouncing among the three eligible men, semicircled.

"Nice to meet you," the tallest one said. He was wearing pink shorts.

"Oh my gosh, Kyle," whined the girl standing next to him. "My *plants.*"

"What about them, babe?"

If Kyle and the plant owner came here together, I realized, everyone might have done the same. This could be a universe of pairs—people who are well acquainted with each other's coworkers and know their vacation day tallies offhand. It could just be me and Samantha, skulking around the circle, trying to poise ourselves next to the right person for a transatlantic flight. I shrewdly tried to observe the body language among everyone in the circle. Please let us all be strangers. A metallic monotone told us that the flight was about to begin boarding, and we each bent to pick up our carry-ons. Samantha eyed me like a derelict, then pronounced to the bagel-eater, "It's unbearably early. I'm the walking dead."

We shuffled in line; I hung back, knowing that avoiding Samantha was futile because of our seating. I was broad-thighed in a cluster of slender, stiff non-creatives with Kate Spaded ears and 401(k)s. Polite discussion of traffic on the way to the airport, a Starbucks barista who made a macchiato instead of an Americano—already-forgotten phone chargers. The rabbi was meeting us upon arrival, said a girl with an L-initial necklace dangling around a potentially cancerous beauty mark. Nobody said the word *fun*. I breathed in, in, in. *Your passport is a fraud,* the austerely bunned security woman would say. *You are a fraud, Willa!* Willoughby, wallaby, a mouthy third grader used to call me when I had to tutor for National Honor Society, and his bouncy voice wrapped around me like a shield of fog: *Will I be, will I be, will I?* She would put down my navy blue identity and sigh. *What the fuck are you doing?*

I'm waiting for you, I told her, because she was Hesper.

The narrowest of the three men offered me a Kit Kat. "It's six a.m.," I said.

His hair was a coppery, shining mop. "You're . . . not Samantha," he said.

"You're not Kyle," I confirmed. He smiled with a shy, cartoonish upturn.

"Bren," he said.

"Bren?"

"My parents couldn't decide between Bryan and Ben."

"The great compromise."

"Is that the one where a slave is three-fifths of a human?" he asked, after a pause.

"I think it was before that. I don't know, it just kind of—leapt out." I wrapped a plume of hair around my fingers and pulled. "Maybe I should keep the U.S. history references to a minimum since there's so many terrible things to dig up."

"You could make it your thing. See how many you can do per hour."

Samantha shifted to glance back at me, then Bren, then back at me with a bemused half-smirk, her hammock of a mouth tilted as she slyly meangirl-nudged the bagel-eater. I felt their muddy eyes on mine and remembered how this worked from middle school; how they'd both like me more and consider me a threat now that I'd made a boy laugh. How, during the bat mitzvah years, I had only three boys at my party, compatriots from Hebrew School, and it was considered an automatic failure; floppy-haired dancers with their awkward Nordstrom's suit jackets during Coke and Pepsi, a game that I didn't remember clearly but involved two teams, Coke and Pepsi, girls sprinting from one side of the room to the other and sitting on someone's lap. With our soles squeaking, girls plotted their kidnapping and I, the bat mitzvah girl, knew that the key to a successful occasion was someone being kissed, and I hid in the bathroom after my great-aunt stomped on my toenail and it was bleeding through my stockings. I was an adult who had thrown a terrible party. My cake tasted like Bath & Body Works.

I had conveniently forgotten until now that I had never once in my life had a Jewish friend.

In 38C, I pulled the tongue of the seat belt over the bulk of my body and ignored Kyle, ignored Samantha, ignored the cheerful instructional video in case of emergency. I prayed. I prayed in the candied Hebrew paragraphs, the same blocks of text that my parents and grandparents had never understood. Squeezing my knuckles, I added my own, lachrymose lassitude: *I know I've asked you for so much. But, please don't let me die like this, in an airplane over the sea.*

SAMANTHA ORDERED A WHISKEY sour; Kyle was asleep. "A white Georgian," I said.

"Excuse?" said the stewardess in her brusque, unidentifiably European voice.

"White Russian," I corrected. Samantha raised a threaded eyebrow. "Don't you mind your alcohol mixing with cream?"

"It's like dessert," I said protectively.

She squeezed a lemon slice into her drink and Hesper thunked into my ribs.

"So what do you do?" she asked. Miraculously, none of the seeds had scattered.

"I'm getting my MFA in Fiction Writing?" I suggested. The sky was studded with cottonball clouds, venturing across the window next to Samantha's head.

Samantha laughed. "You would have to kill me to go back to school."

I tried to think of a swift parlay into casual banter and failed. "What about you?"

"I'm a consultant at a market research firm," she explained. "It's stimulating. Have you been to Germany before?" she asked, swiveling a slender crimson straw throughout her alcoholic concoction.

"No," I said, gulping my Kahlúa with gusto. It was sweet, throat-coating. "I've heard there are wonderful bears at the zoo in Berlin."

She paused before a polite, baffled chortle. "I suppose that's true."

"Do you know anyone else on the trip?" I asked. Kyle's knees were agape between us.

"No. I prefer to make new friends on these things. It's nice to expand your circle."

I nodded supportively. "Circle expansion is certainly positive. Um, what do you think so far?" I asked, glancing at Kyle's knee as it inched, like an iceberg, toward my pins-and-needling calf.

Samantha looked at Kyle, too, and then back at me, smiling. "Well," she said, in a conspiratorial hush, "he's obviously very attractive. But of the eligible bachelors, I wouldn't say I'm wowed by the selection. Toby," she said, raising her hand to illustrate the height of a beanstalk, "is tall enough, but not exceptional as a conversationalist. I think his face is interesting, but I'm not sure interesting in an appealing way. He has an *experimental* facial structure."

"Like . . . avant-garde?" I asked.

"Exactly," Samantha confirmed.

We were getting along, now that she thought I was straight, I thought. But maybe I was being cynical. Maybe we were getting along because we weren't talking about topics in which we had absolutely no common ground. And I could be good at evaluating someone's sexual viability even if it wasn't directly applicable to me. Every not–straight person grew up doing this; every fifth grader knows what poster to hang in a locker to avoid arousing suspicion.

"And the little one is unfortunate, obviously," Samantha continued.

"He's not so little."

"Right."

"No, I just mean—" But she was smiling, and I couldn't help it. I did, too, like a cat that had just discovered an oblong square of sunlight. "Just that he's average height," I continued. "The average American man is five-eight."

"That's certainly not true."

"I read it somewhere," I protested.

"Well, I think he likes you too," Samantha said. "Or, at least, there's potential."

Say something, my heart chanted, clinching. But it was so easy to let this continue, swilling on Samantha's inappropriately founded, mirthful inclusion. I didn't want to say, *You couldn't be more wrong! I'm such a lesbian. I'm such a quintessentially brokenhearted lesbian.* I had kissed boys but I didn't remember what it was like, besides tongueier. I had been touched, but. But the bruises had faded and then I could pretend it hadn't happened, except if I saw a male figure walking toward me and I was alone and there were no stores nearby, the thing in me that thought *It's dark, and now that it's dark the rapists, and the almost-rapists, and the men that would be rapists if they knew for sure that they would never be caught, are everywhere,* as if they all staunchly emerged from their hiding spots at the stroke of sunset. At the stroke of sunset: the beginnings of Jewish holidays and the moment abusers skittered from their hiding places. But that couldn't be. Except if it was dark and I was waiting for a cab and expected a hand, a piano cord, a silk stocking, from behind, from anywhere, it could be. But.

But it wasn't happening anymore. Not. Happening. Anymore. I was sitting in an airplane with my new, straight friend Samantha, who was advocating that I try my hand at a relationship with witty, undersized Bren. I didn't want to risk the stonewalled, politically correct support and then living with the discomfort of someone who's uncomfortable with their own covert bigotry puffing steamy breaths onto Kyle's sleeping form. I didn't want to tell "my story," narrating the confusing, shameful thoughts I had about what was underneath Maude Chason's spaghetti-strap tank top until I realized they weren't going to go away. So I sat. I sipped my White Russian and listened to Samantha recap her last failed relationship, with a drunk asthmatic. He was only half-Jewish, but he had beautiful eyes, so dark and gray. I thought: the color of a shiftless sea lion's coat. I could beautify her descriptions; it was all I could do. *Keep talking,* I thought, listening adamantly, as though her every word were stricken with pulp and it was my job to sift the fruit from the juice.

A DOUGH-FACED RABBI and an eyeliner-smeared sidekick met us in the airport, holding a small green sign to demarcate their purpose. My layers bunched around my leggings. After the plane ride, I didn't give a fuck anymore. We rerouted into a bulky gray tour bus with a long, sprawling German word emblazoned on its side. It was one-thirty in the German morning. I huddled against the window seat with the least leg room, cozy and compact, prickling with defensiveness and relief as Samantha slid past me into a row farther back. The rabbi's sidekick, Jane, counted us off: one, two, eighteen. The bus meandered through downtown Düsseldorf, which twinkled with troubadours and drunkenness. I imagined all of our luggage colliding into each other in the amorphous darkness underneath the bus.

There was nowhere to be alone.

At the hostel, we discarded our belongings next to twin-sized beds and clustered into the "entertainment room!," decorated with Roy Lichtenstein–like drawings of women with exaggerated pouty lips and yellow blobs of abstract sky. The chairs were metal, hued in complementary shades of watermelon and rind. I was desperately tired in a way that promised no sleep. In the seat next to mine, the girl with the L-initial necklace was trying to subtly employ her sleeve as a tissue. The TV screen shined darkly, crystalline, reflecting our airplane-stiffened bodies inching around the rabbi. He furtively licked his lips with the burgeoning of a group address.

"We have arrived," he thundered, then cleared his throat for volume control. He told us how wonderful the trip would be; what a blessing it is for us to all be here together, studying our cultural history. In memory of our ancestors. Education, powerful, journey.

Spirit. Jewish, Jewish. *Stop criticizing the rabbi's stale vocabulary*, I reminded myself; this isn't workshop. But it wasn't just the phrasing, or
the travel-funneled exhaustion—something about his delivery seemed
insincere. Rehearsed. I was seeing the rabbi dismantled, in front a
full-length mirror, practicing where to lay emphasis on each word, a
sibilance sonata. *I don't trust you*, I thought, and wanted to cry.

At graduate school, everyone I knew was an atheist. I alone was
clandestine, anomalous, bound to ideas that the others considered
a rite of passage to deny and weave into their narratives—at best
with irony, and at worst with a brand of intellectual disdain that
was predictable and monotonous but still led my stomach to windfall
through my knees. Even my grandmother Joan, before she died, said
that she thought all "real religious people" should be institutionalized.
I did not know how to talk about God. I didn't remember how to.
Was this how to? Was believing just as much a performance as not
believing?

The rabbi paused dramatically. "Now we will introduce ourselves,"
he said, "and create a new community." His wiry fingers were a cat's
cradle. "Please, go around and tell us your name, where you're from,
what you do for a living, and what compelled you to join the Jewish
Young People's Association for Remembrance and Change. Let's begin with you," he said, gesturing to Samantha.

"I hoped to gain greater insight about the injustice that faced
my people throughout history," Samantha reeled off in a poised,
presentation-ready voice. I pushed my legs into each other until a
squashed, slow pain entered my muscles. Kyle was the first person to
say *repression*; Lauren was the first to use *atrocity*. No one was really listening, I consoled myself. My palms nipped with familiar clamminess.
Bren made eye contact with me and held it.

"My name is Willa," I started. "I am from New Jersey also. I study
creative writing at Columbia. Um... why am I here, is that what's
next? My great-grandmother Cecilia died in the Holocaust." Bren's

lips did something resembling a smile. "When I was eight..." I said, and then immediately regretted it because now I was going to tell this story. I couldn't just stop. Or maybe I could make a different story. *When I was eight, I decided I wanted to go to Germany and now I'm here. The end.*

"When I was eight," I said, "I had a Hebrew school teacher named Yael who got mad at me for wearing a red coat. It was winter, so a parka, I think. I really loved it. One day we were in Judaica class and she told me, if I were her daughter she would throw that coat out, and hadn't we seen *Schindler's List*? Didn't we know what the red coat meant? And we hadn't. She told us: that little girl died. The girl in the red coat. Yael was furious, and started talking about how irresponsible we were—our parents, that they just figured it was a history lesson but we should be talking about it, because it was going to happen again to us. Soon all of our coats would be red. She kept yelling, 'It will happen again! It will happen again!' And I ran straight home, you know, because it felt like the truth. Even to me, then; I was in third grade. But...it also felt like it had already happened to me. That I was carting around these repressed memories and it took a stranger to tell me what it was that kept me awake at night."

I had been talking for too long and no one was looking at me besides Bren, and the rabbi.

"Shit," Bren said finally. Someone shudderingly laughed.

Samantha eyed me. "You certainly have the capacity to bring down a room."

"Sorry," I mumbled.

"Thank you for sharing that powerful memory," Rabbi boomed, glaring at Bren. "It was courageous." His praise pulled like taffy, separating me even more determinedly from the group. "Courageous," he repeated, and leaned forward to touch my hand. *Do not recoil,* I thought, and held my body still. I had cemented an identity for myself. The girl who knew death was coming. He licked at his lower lip for a moment. "Willa, is it? May I ask you a question? It's of a personal nature." Rabbi surveyed the room.

I uprooted the remains of my nail polish. "Okay."

"How do you think that event shaped your relationship with Judaism?"

"I . . . I'm sorry?"

"Your relationship with Adonai our God?"

Samantha's eyebrow returned to its upward, anticipatory position.

I said, "I guess it made me feel like . . . there was something to fear. Like I couldn't just count on God to be there but . . . even when I had it, it was temporary. It could just disappear." I dug the whistle out from underneath my bottom layer and rubbed my sweaty finger over the triangular window where the noise-making air would live.

"Fear!" Rabbi exclaimed, gloriously. "As it is written: 'He who possesses learning without the fear of heaven is like a treasurer who is entrusted with the inner keys but not with the outer. How is he to enter?'" he began a meandering soliloquy about the benefits of tapping into your natural trepidation of the Almighty; that nowadays we are softened by Santa Claus iconography; a God that wants to sip tea and pet a dog's curly fur by a fireplace. We have to fear! And that fear is transformative! he crooned. That fear leads us to love and trust, somehow. The three ingredients to a meaningful God-relationship.

And look at what He can do. There is so much to fear, he added.

When Rabbi was finished, Jane added sheepishly: "Not that we condone traumatizing eight-year-olds with the threat of a repeat genocide," and the rabbi nodded. The room was silent, tension-dappled.

"And you," he said, pointing to the girl behind me, named Alison. "Your turn."

WHEN WE'D FINISHED WITH introductions, Rabbi slipped away to his private room; Jane was left with a clipboard and a Coke in a glass bottle. "Let's go around the circle and do another icebreaker," she said. "It'll help you remember each other's names better. Say an adjective that starts with the first letter of your first name. I'll go first. Joyful Jane."

I thought: *Wonderful Willa, Wonderful Willa*, as my time approached.

"West Nile Willa," I said. A pause followed, and then Bren laughed, a cackle.

"Bird flu Bren," he said next, and I beamed gratefully in his direction. Samantha and Lauren rolled with it, too, and soon we were all helping Kyle think of a disease that began with K, which was surprisingly difficult; the best we could do was "kidney disease." Next to me, Bren leaned in to whisper: "This is the best icebreaker I've ever done."

"If you hadn't played along, that would have been super awkward for me," I said as the circle split off into distinct conversations.

"Are you kidding?" Bren said. "That was so much better than *Brilliant Bren*."

"There's always *brazen*," I offered. "Or *blissful*."

"You're a human thesaurus," he said appreciatively.

"Glad to be useful."

Jane tapped her clipboard; we were officially done. "The rabbi and I have already been here for a few days preparing for the trip," she said, in a camp counselor tone. Apparently it was time for a different genre of fun. "It's the middle of the night. Now, you all have a very important job, which is to stay awake no matter what to help your body clocks adjust. It's your first evening in Germany! We're going out to Altstadt, the longest bar in the world. So let's give ourselves an hour to get ready"—Jane made a show of checking her watch, as though anybody besides hairy-knuckled men in finance wore watches anymore—"and meet back here in the lobby. It's about a fifteen-minute walk, so if you're in heels: be warned!"

Jane waited for us to depart, as if we weren't all clustering up the one shoddy staircase to our hospital-esque, co-ed bedrooms. "I know that it's cheaper, but don't you feel a bit awkward?" complained the faux-British girl. "Couldn't they be quite pervy?"

"We're not even getting to sleep tonight," Samantha murmured.

"If we're going to have an orgy," Alison declared, "it probably won't be till Berlin."

In our room, bunk beds made of gray metal nearly scratched the ceiling; slick pillowcases and thin blankets folded into neat, sterile rectangles. I had few clothes besides an alternate pair of identical leggings, a series of V-neck T-shirts, and a pink striped dress that never fit right anywhere. Peering over my shoulder, Samantha said, "I used to be a haphazard, last-minute packer, too. I'll find you something... acceptable."

"You don't have to."

"We have pre-shower time to kill, and I enjoy a project. What size are your feet?"

"Six and a half."

"Really? So small?" Samantha evaluated the size of my body thoughtfully, then proceeded to elicit donations for my going-out attire from Alison, the lone Chicagoan female, who also, as my mother would say, "carried her weight in her hips." I thought of this expression cringily, as though gravity were wrapping around our bodies like a rope.

Samantha returned with a gold sequined miniskirt that seemed suspiciously tube top–like and shiny black ankle boots. "You can really wear any of those V-necks with this, since it'll all be about your legs," she said pragmatically. Samantha pulled off her shirt, revealing a dark leopard-print bra that made her surrounding skin luminescent.

I would not stare at Samantha. But I also wouldn't look away bashfully—that would also be suspicious. We were all just body parts, near each other! How easy, how lucky, how free we were, bones and tissue in a cold Düsseldorfian room, waiting for the delivery of Jäger-meister and Red Bull.

"My legs are my worst feature," I said.

"It's extremely stretchy," Alison chimed in, from the other side of the room. "And fuckable."

In Germany, I was stretchy and fuckable. In Germany, I shed all of my layers in front of other women without hesitation, wrapped myself in a scratchy, hostel-sponsored towel. In Germany, I opened my mouth wide underneath the shower; let my wet hair sprinkle my white shirt translucent. Sequins settled over my thighs, dabbing the dim room with lesions of light.

⚘

THE BOYS RETURNED WITH Jäger and Desperados and Kinder eggs, courtesy of the Chicagoan Jewbros, Toby and Alec and Josh. Samantha and Alison received theirs first; the rest of us were ac-commodating, passing bottles and foil-dressed chocolates clockwise. Lauren toasted in German: *Prost! Prost!* I repeated, eagerly. We clot-ted into smaller circles and then rescinded this formation, pulsing around the more talkative members of the group. Toby had thin-ning hair that he continuously repositioned over his scalp as he told stories—the time he saw James Franco in an airport, the time he almost drowned in a kiddie pool after being chased out of the house by his high school girlfriend's cousin Steve. The Desperados, a tequila beer, tasted like pennies and felt like seedlings trying to bloom in my trachea. Toby handed around a bottle of Jäger and when it was my turn I gulped it greedily, until warmth passed over me like I'd unlocked a secret compartment inside of my body full of heat, an internal hairdryer.

Then Jane was saying, "Let's go, team, everybody's got to stay awake! Anything to stay awake!" she exclaimed, winkingly, before handing everyone a small slip of paper with the address of our hostel and an emergency phone number just in case; we were leaving at 8:00 a.m. tomorrow on the dot. Then we were trotting outside with our hostel keys and passports; then we were a newsprint whirlwind of clattering heels and bare legs. We headed toward the club following the faux-British girl with her Europe-compatible smartphone, of course, shouting directional commands like a sergeant, and I cloistered myself in the center to shield my body from view; we pushed forward on the gray German streets huddled as though we were running through winter. We were moving to the same rhythm as the *Amidah*, the prayer of our ancestors, to the long list of names: *elohei Sara, elohei Rivka, elohei Leah* . . . I wobbled in time, smiling like I knew a secret.

Alison's shoes were definitely not a six and a half; my feet slid like a metronome forward, back. I was exceptionally grateful that the boots were flat as the other girls steered their heels between hollows of cobblestones, the moon a pallid pendant from the sky, giant trees with their kale-like leaves dipping against bar after bar after bar, small signs for foreign beers and mysterious posts attached to streetlamps with bold red Xs: *do not!* they warned. Everyone who'd been listening to Toby's latest story laughed at the punchline and I joined in. We were in Düsseldorf!

We congealed into line for ID checks; the sound of German sharpening quieted even Toby. Yes, yes, yes, we scurried into the club with its violet lights, bass beating, snarling, my shoulders pulled like they'd slip right out of their sockets. I had never been in a group of so many people, not even the first few nights of freshman year, and it felt safe, insular, as long as I positioned myself between Samantha and Toby, where I couldn't get lost. I would not leave to go to the bathroom; I would not resist returning to the bar for a third, fourth drink even if I wanted to stop. And why would I have stopped if it was so easy to say: yes, another? My eyes were full of strobe light. Teenage girls slumped on the floor with hair curtaining their entire faces, just the sight of a sweet alabaster ear protruding.

"Look at her ear trying to escape," I said, twice before I heard how weird this was.

"What?" Bren asked, over the cascading breath of the techno.

We were within the beat, whirling like a centrifuge.

Then I was following Bren, not even realizing that I'd abandoned my resolve to stay rooted within the dancing drinking nucleus. Toby's hair rose blurrily like pixelated smoke above us. Bren was saying, "Thanks for giving me the excuse to break off."

"Break free, young one," I commented, gazing helplessly as our group fractured—Toby and Kyle and Kyle's girlfriend with one of those impossibly ordinary 1980s Jewish-girl names like Sarah or Lindsay danced closer to the DJ's speaker-clad table. Samantha's mustard-hair, spotted with ultraviolet, hips tussling into a European stranger. We were the schism-creators, I thought, and something in me was exposed, peeled; if I blinked or breathed or moved too fast I would just peel further.

"Hey," Bren said.

"Hey."

"I think we can do better than 'break free, young one.' Don't you?"

"We're breaking off like . . . South Carolina in 1860."

"We're fucking seceding," Bren boasted.

Inelegantly, my bones bounced to the percussion. Bren was barely taller than me, ropy and uncoordinated; his frame like a clothes hanger underneath his gray shirt. Why had I worn white? "I don't want to lose them," I said, then shouted, pulling at Bren's hem petulantly. Eyes wide, throat hot. Recycled air gushed from ventilated slats in the dark ceiling.

"Why not?" Bren asked sincerely. "Such a bunch of dicks. I'll tell you how this goes. Three or four girls go home with jacked-up Germans; everybody else hooks up within the group or doesn't get any. We all feel weird and gross tomorrow. Toby will make a joke that ends up the slogan of the whole trip, and we'll make it the name of the Facebook group. We'll go out for drinks or bagels when we get back to New York. Maybe a bottomless brunch, if it goes really well."

"I hate that expression," I said. "Get any. Like you could retrieve it from a box."

"Or remain sexless and alone," he corrected. "No boxes."

"Haven't you ever been forgotten somewhere?" I asked. "I don't know German. My phone doesn't work. We're going to die here," I said, my diaphragm hardening into rock, and it felt like the truth.

"What?" Bren asked. "Can't hear you."

"I just want to stay together. I'm sorry. I don't care if they're dicks." I covered my eyes, felt the crinkling strobe lights infiltrating my vision anyway. I uncovered my eyes; I led us through the crowd toward Toby's smokestack hair.

"Why are you freaking out?"

"How do you know if you're having a seizure?" I asked, turning to Bren. He followed me closely, nipping at my heels like an overeager dog on a brisk walk.

"Do you smell burnt toast?"

"No. I don't think so."

"I was an EMT," Bren said. "So if you do have a seizure, I'll know what to do. Are you foaming at the mouth? Let me see your mouth."

"No," I said firmly, before realizing the visibility of my lips. I clamped my hand tight while the breath condensed. Bren gripped my forearm until I snapped toward him, rattled. My mouth, exposed. "Don't."

"I didn't mean it like that," he said.

Peeling. The scab, a cave of barely healed pinkness. *She said, Take care of yourself, and let the door close behind her and I ran out into the hall-*

way and called her name in my hoarse tearchoked voice with my socks pulling
up cyclones of hair from the floor. Hesper, I said, and

"I don't want to be left here," I repeated. The sequined miniskirt, bandaged around my quivering self. Bren started moving again so I followed him, his steps, even though he was behind me; the occasional brush of his lithe body through his thin summer clothes.

"I didn't mean like that," he said again. "I know how it sounded, but that's not what I meant. Hey."

"Hey. Can you hear me right now?" I asked.

"Mostly."

"Two things."

"Okay."

"Please don't mention the fact that I have a body. Just think of me as a jellyfish. Like a talking, historically well-versed jellyfish that doesn't like to be touched." It was easier to say this because he was still mostly behind me, a blur of stubbled skin and dark hair. We took the circuitous route toward Alison and Samantha, who were dancing in the center of four nearly identical olive-skinned men in soccer jerseys.

"What else?"

"Please don't tell anyone I just asked you to think of me as a jellyfish."

"Let me buy you a drink," Bren said. "I was weird before. You're a jellyfish. I get that now." I turned my head, expecting him to be smiling, but he wasn't—his face was pasted with a strange, ashamed expression. "Willa," he said. "I'm sorry."

"What did you say?" I asked, leaning my head close to his, savoring the cadence of his apology as if it were the most precious gift I'd ever receive. Later, when we danced, reunited, he stood a whole arm's distance from me while the girls consolidated into a mob of curves and curls and heat, before I made up an excuse to leave. Bren paid for my Uber, and even though I wished he would come with me so I wouldn't be alone with a strange driver, I didn't ask him to. I held my breath. I paid the exorbitant fee to turn off Airplane Mode. Just in case. I watched the phone screen, the little blue dot that represented me, traveling toward my destination until we arrived.

§

IN THE MORNING, I paused in front of the continental breakfast: slices of dark, earthy bread; pots of blood-colored jams; glossy boiled eggs; folded pieces of pallid meats. Alison sidled up to me. I sampled every jam, pats of butter for my tarry bread, while Alison decided on blue-berry yogurt and hulked it over muesli. I thought of my mother, the puckered grimace of her face when she mistakenly took a sip of non-diet soda. I thought of my mother, who had written me two emails since I'd been here, sent within one minute of each other: *I hope you didn't forget the money belt.* and *Wash your hands. You don't know where the linens have been.*

Chloe's first email was punctuated with italics and all-caps quota-tions from people we knew from the writing program, absurd patrons of the bakery demanding non-fat soy lattes with fudge drizzle. *Remember the night we watched that documentary about that ballet dancer with the really glamorous coat, and then we were three minutes late to yoga so we ate black licorice instead? MISS YOU,* followed by a chain of *x*'s swim-ming across the entire length of the iPad screen. I checked, rechecked; filed the Groupons into the trash. Nothing. Her name was nowhere to be found in my inbox (the old ones stashed in a folder called DO NOT DO THIS TO YOURSELF, which I did; of course I did)— besides in my drafts folder, written in the middle of the previous night. Typo-laden, tear-heavy I pressed my slick inebriated fingertips against the touch screen: *Every time I interact with reality, the real one, the one that's in front of me, I feel like I am crawling through barbed wire because how am I supposed to have a conversation with some pretend posh bitch about whether I've ever tried MDMA when I'm with you in that aluminium diner on the cusp of Williamsburg and you're ordering a Bloody Mary and broth and how can I not be in love with you? How can I not still be in love with you? Tell me.*

Tell me.

"You totally should've stayed out last night," Alison said brightly, heaving mightily into a seat at the end of the table, next to three empty chairs. In the fourth chair, the bagel-eater was alone, coating her ham slice in mayonnaise while Kyle and his girlfriend murmured couplishly. I sat across from Alison, feigning peckishness. I wanted to swallow this bread whole.

"Lauren kissed this guy with sideburns that were just, I don't know. Grotesque. And then we all got falafel and watched the sun come up over the river. It's a river, right? The body of water we're geographically near. Anyway, it was so fun." Alison leaned until her long, dark hair nearly swept the surface of my boiled egg. "Also, what do you think of Jane?"

A mischievous smirk settled over Alison's face. I glanced at Jane, who was deciding whether to leave the second button of her chambray undone. "I don't think she's really Jewish," Alison stage whispered.

"Really," said Samantha skeptically. She deposited her plate on the table but stood for a moment with her fingers curled over the chair's back. She was still pink from the shower; skin scrubbed clean of makeup, which I hadn't realized she had been wearing a significant amount of the whole time we'd known each other, and in the moment when she pulled out her seat and twisted her flaxen hair into a knot I saw how much she looked like a Jewish version of Hesper, and that I was truly an idiot for not realizing this earlier, and I averted my eyes into the caverns between the tiny jam jars and tried to keep from blinking. If I could just fall right into the jam-jar valley, everything would be fine.

"Well, so she was showing me these pictures of her boyfriend's cockatiel Nunchuck, and flipping through them there were a bunch of shots of her with a bunch of pearl-wearing ladies drinking mysterious elixirs." Alison paused to spoon herself yogurt, crunching as she continued. "So naturally I asked her what kind of drink that was in the photo, being something of a cocktail connoisseur."

"Sure," Samantha said dryly.

"She said it was called a Greyhound? Grapefruit juice and vodka."

"Like the bus?" asked another girl from New Jersey, engrossed.

Alison leaned back, appalled. "I mean, have you ever met a Jew that would order a cocktail named after a dog?"

"I don't think it proves anything besides her affinity for acidic beverages," Samantha said. "Besides, if you're so concerned with her heritage, why didn't you just ask her? If she feels comfortable enough to saturate you with images of her boyfriend's bird, I doubt it would be an issue."

"Who said anything about being *saturated*?" Alison sniped. "And I'm not *so concerned* with her heritage, like, it's not weighing heavily on my mind. I'm just saying, it seems a little weird to have a not-real Jew leading the tour. Like, some gentile can't understand our plight." She held up her hands in an *I'm-finished-here* gesture. We chewed nervously. Samantha crossed her legs and my chair squeaked with the ripple of her body.

"I'm not against non-Jews," Alison continued. "One of my best friends is half Filipino! It's just, in this particular instance, I would rather be with one of our own." She tapped the stem of her spoon, jittering.

"I hooked up with a Filipino once," the bagel-eater contributed. "So cute."

"Other cultures have had genocides, too," I said quietly.

"Yeah, okay, but not the ones drinking Greyhounds." Alison turned toward the bagel-eater. "But did you guys *date* after you hooked up? Because I'm so non-dick discriminatory, you have no idea, but I would never seriously date a gentile."

It had never occurred to me that Hesper's gentile-ness would matter to God.

I dug my fingernails into the peel of a banana until it cracked.

"Like, hello," Alison said, "I wasn't born so I could produce a couple of halvsie heretics, using Christmas M&M's as collateral for their dreidel games. No thank you."

"Your uterus is Jewish," Samantha ruled.

"Your uterus and your soul," I said, flattening a clump of cherry with my knife.

"Your *soul*," the bagel-eater said, and the three of them laughed.

"That's right, our spiritual sister," Alison said. "That red coat story was wild. And then Rabbi just *going off*, mouthing off about the virtues of fear mongering. I'm sorry, but if there is a God, I hope He *is* just like Santa. Like a sweet, portly fellow that wants to give me a bunch of presents? Pretty good deal for the universe master."

"But having a gentile husband would make your kids heretics?" Samantha asked.

"I'm large," Alison beamed. "I contain multitudes. Someone said that, right?"

"Walt Whitman."

"Bet Willa's dated Christians," Alison said. "I see it all over you. You are like, glowing with goy-love. Goy-glowing."

"I'm not *goy-glowing*," I said. "Just enjoying the jam selection."

"At least your new buddy is one of the chosen," Alison breezed. Everyone smiled.

I made a tree out of my toast crusts. "You said if there is a God?" I asked.

"Listen to that. Just rolling on past it. Do you know any Jews that aren't atheists?" Alison asked. "Besides you."

"Are you unfamiliar with the Orthodox?" Samantha retorted. "Two words: Crown Heights."

"Not the chasids. You know what I mean. The wigless," Alison said.

"I'm not an atheist. I'm spiritual," chimed the bagel-eater. "Just not religious."

"Has this conversation not proved my hypothesis? Believer, what say you?"

"I feel like you're piety-policing me, Alison," I said, with a brittle laugh.

"Oh," she said, slicing the air in front of her plate. "That's because I'm still drunk. I'm a very confrontational drinker. But don't think I won't remember what we've been talking about. People always underestimate me. I have an intuition. I know about you," she said, holding my gaze, and flicking toward Samantha for a moment before returning to me.

Anxiety thunderclapped between my ribs.

"You don't have any thoughts about my persona?" Samantha asked, bemused. "My dating history? Religious background? Such a pity."

"Thank you again for your skirt," I said, hoping that whatever it was Alison saw, she'd stay quiet about it. *Thank you for your skirt and your participation in complicity. Your new buddy*, she called Bren, like two children who play near each other, facilitating collisions of their respective Barbies.

"It looks better on you," Alison said. "My ass is basically an overeager pancake. But yours!" she exclaimed. "Yours is so rambunctious. Your rambunctious ass was made for a gold sequined skirt."

This was the kind of thing that straight girls were allowed to say to each other.

How would I ever stand up from this table?

"Hi, ladies," Jane said, smiling broadly. "How's breakfast?"

"Alison was just describing her views on interfaith relationships," Samantha said.

"Woof! Heavy hitters. It's great that you guys are committed to seeing a variety of perspectives," Jane said, realizing midway through the sentence that Alison was starting to fall asleep at the table. "So we're going to take a walking tour through Düsseldorf in about fifteen minutes. Al, you feeling good? Okay, super. Take anything you might need before dinner."

When Samantha stood up to leave, a small corner of the jam packet that she'd been using dropped lightly onto the seat of her chair, and when the others were all safely heading in the opposite direction I rescued it, this fledgling tinfoil-y remnant of herself, cramming it between the waistband of my leggings and my downiest skin; a talisman. *Are you there?* I asked God, concentrating hard to see if I could feel the corner traveling down the ravines of my legs, my sensitive shin bones, my feeble ankles. *What about now?* I asked, slipping the whistle necklace thermometer-like underneath my tongue. It jabbed like a spear.

THE NEXT DAY WE took a bus to Cologne. We drank honey-hued beer in tall glasses, picked at French fries and caramelized onions for lunch; the locals savored slabs of pork. If no one on the trip believed in anything besides our shared bloodlines, why couldn't we eat bacon? The scent was pungent, as insistent as a red laser pointer darting into your line of vision. It smelled delicious but I didn't take any. *The believer.*

Rabbi tapped at the face of his gold watch as we waited to meet our walking tour guide, Erich. Outside, sunlight waltzed across our elbows. My skin was sticky with sunscreen, wisps of white where it hadn't fully rubbed in. I maneuvered my way around Alison and Samantha to the periphery, where Bren was snapping a square of Milka chocolate from a bright lavender package.

"Hey," I said, a little shyly.

"Hey," he replied, impassive.

"How's your blood sugar?" I asked.

"Ready for takeoff," he said, offering a square. "I always need a snack before feeling devastated by hundreds of years of oppression. I don't know about you."

The creamy chocolate dissolved in my mouth. "I'll try it your way," I said.

"You're the jellyfish," Bren said, shrugging as he smiled.

Erich was a quick walker. His English was sharp, articulate, but strangely melodic and upturned at the ends of each sentence. His blue eyes were diamond-like in the bright July day. There had once been seven major synagogues, but during the war everything was destroyed? By 1945, nearly every Jewish person had been deported or killed by the Nazis? Rabbi waddled alongside the group like a bicyclist afraid to merge into mainstream traffic. He tried to catch my eye and I tried to pretend I didn't notice. Erich continued to rattle through statistics about death. Lauren was chewing spearmint gum. Bombings; explosives. I scanned the expressions of my tour-mates; were they distancing themselves from the recollections or actually, simply, bored? The center of the city was completely destroyed in 1942? Erich said, making an arm gesture as though he were cradling an invisible baby. Every time he used *thousand* to describe the magnitude of devastation, I felt the space around my heart being ice-picked.

We clustered around the space where a synagogue would've been. Where we would've been. I dug my heels into the spongy earth. *It will happen again it will happen again it will,* said the memory, an alloy of dread and dirge. The blackened mildew I couldn't scrub off. A chorus of German voices encircled us like a shower curtain, tightly drawn; the disconsolate consonants, vowels; syncretic slush.

We followed Erich into the center of town. Uniform rows—one pale yellow, two tired musty brick—of buildings formed a horseshoe around a basin of ruins. Erich explained that in a few years, they planned to reconstruct an ancient synagogue from the thirteenth century; remake the *bimah* from hundreds of fragments that have been discovered and carefully preserved. Marbles and bones and writing on stone.

Lauren dropped her gum into the nutmeg-colored dirt; a future fossil of our visit.

In a quiet, solemn line, we entered the visitors' headquarters of the construction site. Tall, chain-link fences extended to double my height; slabs of amorphous rock with etchings housed in foggy glass cases. Someone's crusty golden earring. Children's initials scrawled in jaunty corners of rescued infrastructure; long passages of Hebrew detailing, apparently, those who had not paid their debt at a beloved bakery.

In my head, I heard a song that I'd loved during my undergrad years: Regina Spektor singing sweetly, *dead dead dead dead dead, dead dead dead dead d-dead.*

Erich finished his lecture. Rabbi initiated a circle and counted with his nimble, courteous finger to make sure we had ten men for the *minyan*, beginning to buzz with the Kaddish. We didn't. So instead of praying for the dead, we said hello to Israel, then clapped mechanically, moving past the construction site.

At my side, Bren said, "This is the point where I'd open up Buzz-Feed. Just get a series of pictures of pugs sleeping in bassinets, or a list to determine which character in *Wuthering Heights* is my soul mate."

"Cathy Two?"

"I only peruse the questions. Like a palate cleanser."

"I would accept some sorbet," I said, gravely etching a *W* in the crumbling dirt with Alison's ankle boot. From the waist down, I was dark, sheltered, my plump pink toes a thing of the past. I wanted to say the Kaddish. I did not count.

Bren smoothed his brassy hair down straight against his scalp. "This is really fucking with you," he observed.

Pointing, Lauren exclaimed, "Is that...a Korean restaurant? And nightclub?"

"Oh my God," Alison burst. "Karaoke night in Cologne!"

I glanced back toward the glass cube with the one earring. "You don't feel...affected?" I asked hesitantly. "You don't look at that earring and wonder...the rest?"

"I've gone on a lot of trips like this," Bren said.

"Honestly, who doesn't like a pedicure?" wafted toward us; a different sort of conversation.

"Like, who did that earring belong to? What were they thinking about when...And why did they deserve to die, when we get to stand here talking about pedicures?" I asked.

"You're not going to find any answers."

"I guess...I still feel like it's worth thinking about. Worth asking the questions."

"I mean," Bren continued, "it's fucking sobering. But then your emotional immune system kicks in. Every place is a different strain. And then you adapt."

"And then the security guard was like, excuse me, gentlemen!" Toby boomed.

"That's wicked," the faux-British girl commented, breathily.

"Then why do you keep going?" I asked Bren, feeling a spot in the back of my hair where the conditioner hadn't been completely rinsed away.

Jane was leading us in a direction, though I couldn't remember if it was the way from which we came; Rabbi returned from his chat with Erich to rejoin the group, wide-eyed and enthused as we returned to the town center before "afternoon free time," according to the itinerary. Sunlight hovered over us, mercilessly.

"Well, it's important. I'm not some jackass that has his blinders up like, well, it's all worked out now that we're not getting shot in the street. I just mean...you get tired. You hit a threshold where you can't empathize anymore, and then you need karaoke. Or, alternately, you don't pay attention enough to reach your threshold, and then you need karaoke differently."

"The opiate of the masses?"

"Something like that. Let's get coffee," Bren said, tilting his head toward a walking street emerging on our left; one of those cobble-stoned clusters of tall, pastel buildings with iron-cast, many-framed windows. "We're about to be told about 'afternoon free time,' anyway."

I thought of how this would look to Alison, to Samantha. *Your new buddy. One of the chosen.* Disappearing on a solo quest with one of the coveted few. Then, the guilt, like an army of fire ants on the escape from a vivarium. Why couldn't I just have a conversation without plotting how it would look from the outside?

I would've left me, too.

"Of course," I replied.

At the first cafe we came to, Bren nodded approvingly—all the best German coffee was Italian. We ordered cappuccinos and ripped open our complimentary biscuits from tiny gold packets; perched ourselves on uncomfortably shoddy chairs. I doused my cappuccino with brown sugar crystals. I felt like I was acquiring a sunburn right through my clothes. I huddled close underneath the eggshell-colored umbrella.

Bren crunched a sugar crystal between his thumb and index finger. "The real reason I keep doing this stuff is for my mom," he began. "She dropped out of high school and tried to start her own church, way out in Delaware. But then she met my dad; he was her optometrist. And they were in love; his parents didn't accept her...so she took every inch of her devotion and tried to redirect it toward Judaism. She was one of those volunteers questioning passersby during Hanukkah to see if they need a dreidel and a pamphlet."

"I always feel a little weird about that."

"Yeah. But it made sense for my mom, this avenue to prove herself as someone pious. Anyway, from what I know, my dad lorded this over her for their entire relationship—you're not trying hard enough! you're not really Jewish! et cetera—until he couldn't reasonably make that case anymore, and then he left. Growing up, most times I heard the word Jewish, it was always being hissed in the middle of an argument. But now...if I renounce religion, my mom would just see that as her own failure."

"Do you feel like you're lying?" I asked, less delicately than I meant to.

"No," Bren said, unruffled. "Because it's not like I believe strongly in Buddhism or something. I'm not betraying my true self. This is what I am. I'm just...dressing it up in black tie." He inhaled foam. "You know what's weird? I've never been on one of these trips where people actually talk about God. Or what they believe in, really. Definitely at one point the rabbi launches into a joke-filled sermon designed to prompt conversation about what Judaism means today, people volleyball some buzzwords around and then drink heavily. But you," he said. "When you told that red coat story...you're just not fucking around. I've never seen so many uncomfortable faces."

"It's a gift."

"It is a gift," Bren said, serious. "Do you know how full of shit most people are?"

"Um," I said. "Thanks." I finished the dredges of my cappuccino, savoring the sugary foam pile. "So are we at bottomless brunch level now?"

"We're ready for a brunch abyss. Hey."

"Hey."

"What does it feel like?"

"What does what feel like?"

"Believing." He tapped his ring finger against the rim of his coffee. It took a long time for me to answer. "It's like...having this restricted area of your heart, like . . . you always know that it's there, but you don't always have the key to get inside."

"So . . . do you have the key? Right now?"

"Um," I said, my eyes suddenly deluged with tears. "Yeah. I think so."

"That's cool," he said, nodding. I dabbed at my eyes with a napkin. "I mean . . . I feel obligation toward respecting your cultural origins and everything. But I don't think I've ever felt a restricted area in my heart."

"You don't think it makes me weird?"

"No. Honestly . . . I'm jealous. A jealous-fish," he said, to break the seriousness, and I looked at him in relief.

"I'm glad you're here," I said.

"I know," he said.

WE ATE DINNER AT a buffet, in a brick restaurant nestled next to a deserted racetrack. Jane introduced our guests: two rabbinical students, Erich, and his vermilion-lipsticked wife, and then I could feel the rabbi's attention coming toward me. *The Believer.* I huddled into Toby, who was giving a dissertation on the best beers in Germany and their various hoppiness and flavors, while the other guys nodded encouragingly. Kyle secured his arm around his girlfriend's waist as though she were about to spill all over the floor. It was the girls who mingled with the strangers, swift pleasantries about culture clashes, the grandiosity of Cologne's cathedral. The rabbinical students: single? Simpering, Samantha had her body angled toward the broader of the two, her wineglass tipped into the crook of his elbow.

She is not Hesper. She is not Hesper. I drank a second glass of wine.

She could be anywhere. She could be remembering anything.

Alison swaggered toward the buffet. "Lost cause," she mouthed in my direction. I followed her toward the food; the second phase of the evening, which hadn't been initiated by me. It wasn't me, I bragged to an internal interviewer; I was not the buffet-beginner. The others followed suit, and this too seemed like a shift I could take credit for. I felt victorious, scooping green beans crusted with almonds, beets glazed with honey, potatoes roofed by a layer of moon-faced cheese. When I leaned down to retrieve meatballs from a saucepan, Rabbi tapped my arm.

"Careful," he said, gesturing to my whistle necklace.

"I almost dunked it?" I asked, watching the meatball sauce contaminate my potatoes. "Dunkaroos," I said.

You've chosen the wrong person, I was trying to say. Of everyone here, I'm the one who's going to let you down.

Rabbi did not have an interest in Dunkaroos. "I was trying to make contact with you this evening, Willa," he said, beginning sternly and then catching himself, trying to sound bewitching. "I thought you might want to share the experience you described yesterday with our guests, if you don't mind."

"Why?" I asked. I nudged the meatballs from my potatoes with a wary pinky.

"It was very moving," he said, and then dropped his volume so that only I could hear.

"I don't know," I said. "I was just—I wish I hadn't said anything yesterday."

"In addition," Rabbi continued, as though I hadn't spoken, "we do have to qualify for a grant each year in order to fund this organization's mission. It would be helpful to be able to put a face to our application. One of the rabbinical students is the son of the main organizer of the Judeo-German Cultural Society for Growth and Outreach."

I tried to envision a picture of myself on the cover of a shiny brochure and couldn't. I didn't remember what I looked like, only snatches of skin. I had an oblong nose and eyebrows that stretched out, rather than in. I had a stomach that became serrated when I was nervous. But how did they fit together?

"I— It's too personal," I said finally. "I'm sorry."

"Oh. Well, of course. I didn't mean to be presumptuous." He laid a paw on my shoulder, his potato-clad plate balanced against a hip. "This is, of course, a safe space for you to discuss your personal views and memories. As a community," he continued, "we need people to feel connected to our collective history. So many young people are alienated from that trauma. I'm sure you've observed that. So I was very pleased," he emphasized, "to hear how deeply these events have resonated within your life. I'm sure that the rabbinical students and Erich and his dear wife would be interested to hear whatever you have to say. But of course," he said, "I don't mean to pressure you."

"Noted," I replied, nausea broiling into a crest. My trauma; a marketing point on a list. *Safe space.* The others milled around our conversation; Rabbi adjusted his yarmulke and cleared his throat. "These cucumbers remind me of Israel," he said, taking a few steps away from the table but continuing to look at me over his shoulder. "Cucumber, tomato, a little parsley—a perfect salad." Begrudgingly, heavy-breathed, I followed. "Have you ever been?"

"I haven't."

"It's a life-changing journey for all Jews," the rabbi said.

My cousin fucked three different Amandas and got food poisoning in Tel Aviv; posted an entire album on Facebook of himself riding side-saddle on a camel, giving thumbs ups—87 Likes.

"Maybe after graduation," I said.

"There are all different groups that explore the Holy Land. Action/ adventure groups, groups for lawyers and medical students. All inhabitants of our community, meeting together for the experience of a lifetime. It is a wonderful place to begin the next chapter of your spiritual development," Rabbi beamed. Have Jewish babies with a Jewish man, is what he meant. Goy-glowing. His hand, still on my shoulder, like a stiff block of snow.

Safe space, I thought again, but what I wanted was to be safe from ghosts. From Hesper. Maybe it never happened. Maybe my entire life had been here, choking down a tusk of potato, trying to avoid talking to a rabbi about my feelings. Foreboding accumulated like hair in a drain. I cleared my throat; took a step away from him.

"I have a question for you," I said. "Um, it's about my...sister." No one could hear me, I thought. "She's struggling with her Jewish identity ever since she came out as a lesbian."

"Ah," Rabbi said. His face was shellacked with a stoic, *I'm listening* expression.

"Do you think that means she's not a good Jew?" I asked. "I mean, acting un-Jewishly?"

He was absolutely not touching my shoulder now.

"If the question is about what the Torah says about homosexual acts," Rabbi said in a spindly, flat tone, "then it's clearly prohibited. Leviticus 20:13: 'If a man lies with a man as one lies with a woman, both of them have committed an abomination; they shall surely be put to death; their blood shall be upon them.'" He rested his plate on a nearby table, his eyes beading with concentration. It unsettled me that he had the verse memorized; he was poised, ready for this conversation at any opportunity. He was a rabbi whose voice shone when he said the word *abomination.*

Their blood shall be upon them. I twisted my napkin around my wrists.

"However," he continued, "it's generally interpreted that the *act,* not the person, is regarded as against Hashem. And, interestingly, the term in Hebrew, *t'oevah,* for abomination, is often used in reference to animals. The abominability, so to speak, comes from the fact that homosexual acts will never lead to procreation, and is therefore against God's will."

"Oh," I said quietly. I thought of how connected, how alive and pulsing and perfect it had been to wrap myself into Hesper, the scent of her skin, lovely and replete with my nerves and cells and body, alive, and how could that be where the abominability came from? Why would I have found her if I wasn't meant to be hers?

"She's still Jewish, of course. That's not affected by her...choices," he said. "Though...perhaps your sister will find her way back," Rabbi suggested.

"Right. Maybe." I could barely look in his direction.

Blood pulsed in my fingers, beneath my nails.

I made an excuse to cross the room toward Alison, even though I hated Alison. I abandoned my garland of vegetables and grabbed another glass of wine from a silver tray.

"Willa killa," she rhymed, rippling, drunk.

"I can't wait for karaoke," I said.

8.

At the hotel, we dropped off Ada's bounty of fabrics and went to say hello to Dad and Baba. Mom wanted to "rest her eyes," which meant that she was in need of a break from us. Dad answered his door and ushered us inside with a desperate, cloying enthusiasm. "Dad, look who's here!" he said, barreling from the entranceway to the bed. Baba was sitting in a chair, suspended and sedated. "We've been having a very good day," he informed us.

We prepared ourselves for the depths of that lie. But, just this once, it turned out to be accurate. Baba reached his long, quivering hands in our direction and gestured back to his heart.

"Ada," Baba said quietly. "Come."

Ada and Baba started on their paper boats, folding the complimentary Georgian newspaper into halves, quarters, making the edges sharp with their fingernails. I hung back, swinging one leg over the other. Ada turned the speaker of her iPhone on to play *Pet Sounds* and skipped the first song, so that we wouldn't all have to look at each other during the line *Wouldn't it be nice if we were older?*

I knew that I should stay where I was. Let Ada have the moment. For all their boat-constructing bonding, Baba almost never called Ada by name; just blinked wearily in her direction. She made him scarves that caused little red freckles on his neck to burst and bloom.

"Why were you crying?" I asked.

Dad said, "He seems happy. Doesn't he?" He crossed his arms, satis-fied. "That doctor said I must have a death wish. But who knows better, some fourteen-year-old at a teaching hospital or your own son?"

"You lied to Mom," I said.

"Risk, reward," Dad said. "Justified! Look how happy."

"Dad," I said cautiously. "You haven't left the hotel. Don't you think it might be overwhelming—"

"You don't need to assume that in *every single case*, your mother is right and I'm wrong. See that, Lemon?" He gestured toward Baba and Ada's industriousness. "It was the right thing. Besides, isn't this what you wanted? Not that you would tell me directly," he added.

"So it's my fault if something happens to him?"

"When did you get to be so morose?" Dad asked. "My morose Lemon."

"Moros-emon," I said with a small sigh.

"It's like when you get a cold after the end of finals," Dad said. "Because your body can push through the stress, and keep pushing, and then when you release the brake a little—there it is. That's why I was crying."

"You're mixing metaphors," I said, and he shook his head in a slow-motion swerve until, without my consent, my mouth curled into a smile.

"Why didn't you tell us earlier about the baby?" I asked, to elimi-nate the smiling. Dad blinked five times fast.

"It's bad luck."

"Since when are you superstitious?"

We listened to Ada and Baba, folding and refolding paper into ob-long shapes.

"I didn't know how to bring it up. That's the truth. I'm not at all -stitious. I just didn't want you to feel like I was . . . seeking a replace-ment family."

"Such a cliché," I said, eyeing my scuffed shoes. "Middle-aged man finds younger girlfriend. Family 2.0. Maybe you'll buy a red convertible."

"This line of conversation is what I was hoping to avoid."

"It wasn't even important for you to tell us," I said. "*Mom* told us. And we were without chairs. And that makes me think," I continued, over the beginnings of his protests, "that it didn't really strike you as critical whether we were okay with it or not. You're supposed to be able to sit for Big News. Like the news that another human being will be joining your family forever."

"I will make sure that chairs are available for you and your sister. In the future."

I didn't answer.

"Okay. You're right. I guess it just felt like . . ." He trailed off. "Like once I said it, it would be much more real than it is right now. I was afraid to have the conversation because I'm afraid of what's happening. That's as honest as I can be."

"Why are you afraid of what's happening?" I said, parroting back the complete sentence. That's always been the easiest way for me to avoid getting too close.

From the other side of the room, I felt Ada's gaze, unwavering, on the side of my head.

"Because I don't know how to change," he answered.

We watched Ada, cutting waves out of paper, creating the ocean from strips of advertisements for phone companies and Western-style supermarkets in the center of the city.

She propped up the undulating papers atop a thick burgundy Bible; Baba collected their miniature boats in a herd.

"I just realized . . . she won't know him," Dad said. "He'll be gone by the time she remembers things."

I stood closer to him, my arm around his, windshield-wiping comfort onto his back. Tears were clinging to his eyes, resisting the momentum of falling.

"They swim magic," Baba announced. Quickly Dad rushed to his side, leaving me in the little valley between room and bathroom.

I couldn't make Dad feel better, and Baba didn't need me, either. Dad was watching Ada with a steady approval, and Ada wasn't looking over at me. Brian Wilson's tinny vocals suddenly became unbearable, the organ-quality of the production, the slightly missed high notes. Toward the end of the song, a bicycle horn beeped, and I said, "I'm going to lie down," and rushed out of the room before I could see anyone's lack of response.

I KNEW I COULD call Willa, I knew she would accept whatever meager apology I happened to muster, I knew how little effort it would take for things to return to the way they had been. And hadn't they been beautiful? Sometimes exhausting, stifling, saturated with unsaid musings. I had known that she was constantly storing away tidbits for our imaginary future like a squirrel preparing for a devastating winter but it didn't seem so terrible now; what kind of person backed away saying, "Please love me less; I don't want you to remember that I prefer blackberries to pears; I don't want you to text me good night"? Wasn't that what love is? I say, "Georgia," she returns with the world's most lackluster dumpling maker in Gravesend? Maybe I would feel differently tomorrow, the next day. Part of me wanted to. Part of me wanted to take her love-terms and swiftly sign off. Tell her about the baby, about being the middle child, now; about starting over. Tell her about what it was like to watch my father realize Baba's state, how even on the best days he was almost dead, while the Beach Boys hummed in the background. Tell her about the bird, about my mother's homophobia and how it was coupled with kind of touching protectiveness, and I was fucking confused, and had never actually said the word *lesbian* out loud because I didn't have to, because I had a girlfriend and that had been like a shuttle-bus past the uncomfortable questions, and now I was transportation-less and had spotted some crusty toothpaste stain on my cardigan and was sitting in a hotel lobby with a fake fireplace, missing someone who I knew desperately wanted to talk to me and I couldn't do it because of some stupid conception of who I was. What I wanted. I scratched at the toothpaste with my fingernails, and then licked my finger and tried to rub it out that way, and then I went into a single-person bathroom and, finally, my body complied, released an electric sneeze. When I ran the tap, the water smelled like sulphur.

FOR OUR FAMILY DINNER, I tried on all of my ill-fitting Ada creations—a *Little House on the Prairie* dress that swooped awkwardly in the back, a fake mink collar to sit over a linen summer sack. But Mom forbade it, pushing a black sheath dress into the center of my chest. "Romans," she hissed, although how well I would fit in with her Italian wool, getting-down-to-business uniform seemed dubious. Ada, too, was delegated a plain, neutral-colored dress that made her skin look milky and possibly vitamin deficient.

In the mirror, we looked like three depressed executives. Ada's hair was sleeved tightly by a scarf, a babushka-style number of dark crimson flowers. Mom removed her lipstick from the mini-fridge and encouraged us to pout, slipping a slimy line of lipstick over our bottom lips.

"Are we trying to seduce them?" Ada asked.

"We want to look put together," Mom said, exasperated.

"I look like a puppet of a cancer patient."

For a second I thought Mom was going to smack Ada, an occurrence that's happened a total of four times in our lives. But instead she laughed, a throaty sound like a water bottle being crushed by a tire. She laughed and had to sit down on the bed, clutching at her knees with both palms. We stared at each other, unsure of how to proceed. This was the scariest version of Mom: hysterical over something invisible. I blotted my lipstick until it was almost gone. Ada sat down next to her, ironing out the flabs of too-loose hosiery around her ankles.

"Mom?" Ada asked.

She waved air in front of her eyes. "You can cry or you can laugh," she said. "I'm sure as hell not going to cry, Ada. But...maybe you don't know this," she said, "but I love your grandfather. I do. He used to be more than little boats and occasionally coherent phrases. The fact that you girls will remember this part—it's tragic. It's a goddamn tragedy. You do not look like a *puppet of a cancer patient*, my smart-mouthed spawn. You do not get to make jokes like that when we are all witnessing a man at the end."

"That's why I'm making jokes," Ada said quietly. "It's too sad."

"Sometimes it has to be sad," Mom said.

"Like right now, before a dinner party?" I asked. We breathed.

"Alright," Mom said. She was back, all composure and pink gloss. "You need a sweater," she instructed me. I thought of my toothpaste stain and shook my head, defeated.

"What do you mean, more than little boats?" Ada asked. "What else was he like?"

"He was very sweet. He used to build things, beautiful furniture for us. That secretary in my bedroom, the one with the etchings on the side? That was a birthday present. When your grandmother was alive, they gardened together. Little plump tomatoes. Really, abhorrently bitter arugula. He was quiet but he was funny. Deadpan. You wouldn't expect it. When your dad and I met, taking that conversational German class? Baba used to help us practice. You know," she said, "you don't have to ask the most sentimental questions right when we have to leave."

"You never tell us anything," Ada replied. "You're so pithy and re-served."

"I didn't know you were interested." Mom shrugged, clearly hurt.

"We're interested," I said, folding over the cardigan's sleeve to hide its flaws.

❧

SALOMEYA'S APARTMENT WAS OLD in a picturesque, black-and-white-photography sort of way, with thick panels of wilting wallpaper and stacks of musty hardcover books. We hoisted Baba shakily in his wheelchair up a flight of screeching stairs, and I found myself try-ing not to inhale too deep, as though lead poisoning had suddenly become airborne. The building was entrapped by grapevines, sur-rounded by strange alleys and bright green trees. Ada readjusted her head scarf with a manic ferocity. We were all nervous. Mom was do-ing the best job of hiding it, as usual. Dad was the one who knocked on the door, then petted his balding hair forward like he'd just realized that his haircut highlighted, not camouflaged, his status as middle-aged. I leaned down to Baba to make sure his mouth was free of saliva bubbles. "Where are you?" he asked.

"I'm with you," I said quickly, as though he were all the location I'd ever need.

Salomeya shooed us inside with greetings, snatched the wheelchair handle from me, and pushed Baba into her home with vigor. She was taller, rounder than I expected, with a mole on her chin that housed two spindly hairs. A long dining room table had been set up with extra leaves, jutting out into the foyer with a cluster of mismatched chairs. We parted those chairs away from Baba's wheelchair, curtain-ing the Red Sea of extraneous seating, while Salomeya's children and husband and various other, less identifiable family members flocked into the dining room with more kisses, hugs, bodily contact. My body was swarmed by well-meaning arms and lips. Their Georgian sounded different from the crisp, consonant-laden sounds I'd heard around the hotel and on the street—this was like a muddy, unfocused cousin of Russian. Everybody seemed a little hyper, uncertain about who exactly we were and trying to one-up each other with their hospitality.

Our parents had disappeared into the kitchen. Glasses were clinking, out of sight.

Salomeya held Ada by one shoulder and me by the other, leading us to chairs at the table. "Speak?" she asked, and then seemed to lose the rest. "Andro, eh—" She waved, summoning a bookish man with splotches of gray facial hair along his wizardly chin. Did we speak Russian? We spoke enough Russian to shake our heads sadly. Ada's headscarf was already sliding backward, a poof of blue hair cowlicking overhead like a lazy geyser. More guests were arriving. Somebody had brought a basket full of plums. I swiveled my braid into a bun and squeezed.

Andro spoke a languorous version of English. I knew I was in no position to ask anything from this patient, obviously benevolent stranger, but the pause in which he struggled to formulate Salomeya's rapid-fire jabbering into comprehensible phrases like "Welcome to our home," and "You are very pretty" made me feel homicidal. In the space left by Andro's translation, Salomeya kissed our cheeks again and made wide, infant-like eyes, observing us like slightly overripe apples at a market. What if he was doing a terrible job? How could so many syllables be reduced to such choppy sentences? I tried to mirror Ada's collected smile, the nonchalance of her posture in the wooden chairs. I tried not to smell the beef tongue and pastry horns full of dairy products and vibrantly pickled vegetables. Salomeya barreled toward the kitchen, as though somebody had been blowing a whistle engineered especially for her.

Andro spun his thick, 1990s-style watch so that the face pointed inward. "Is almost time for supra," he explained. "Traditional dinner feast. Many foods and wine." He rattled off some facts like a walking Wikipedia: that in more formal settings, the men and women would have to eat separately; in the countryside, this was still the case. Here in the city, we would all be able to dine as one group, he said, folding his hands inward to symbolize unity. Ada nodded, as though to say, *Yes, unity is admirable.*

When my parents returned from the kitchen, with Salomeya and her curly-haired husband and their various offspring and the little girl who was extending one of her hands as a trunk, they all descended upon the table. Slices of bread were passed counterclockwise; glasses of sweet red wine for women, dry white wine for men. Salomeya's husband had teeth the color of movie theater popcorn. He raised his glass and made a long toast in Russian, which both my parents understood and consequently bowed gratefully. There was some kind of pattern to the clattering of glasses, the moments of pause, the heaping of cold fish onto our smallest plates, but Ada and I could not master it. When my mother was a girl, she had pretended to be a Romanoff before her bedtime, twirling in a determined, two-step circle in a pink cotton nightgown and now I saw this, the practiced poise. My father was seeing this too. His face careening helplessly into shades of berry.

To God! To Georgia! To family!

We were all drunk.

I had forgotten Baba. I arched my neck to find him at the other end of the table. Salomeya was patting his wheelchair-bound knee, prattling to Baba lovingly in the time between her husband's toasts. Ada, too, was eavesdropping on this interaction, propped on her elbow. Had she known what was happening the whole time? No—I had noticed first. She was just following suit. I tried to ask Andro what they were talking about, but four pairs of disapproving Georgian eyes flashed grimly in my direction. It was no longer time for questions. Beef, lamb, crackling pans. My forehead was hot.

To friendship among the nations!

Dad slurred some vaguely Georgian-sounding words, and everyone laughed. Salomeya was leaning into Baba's ear, plentifully babbling whenever a moment of contemplative silence (uncommon) or over-whelming noise blanketed her voice. Did he understand her better than he understood us? His face was eased into a smooth smile, a stray piece of dumpling meat folded into his dimple. I tried to stay calm, and not increasingly paranoid that everyone was talking about what bizarre, rude, unenlightened guests we were. Ada was practically asleep on that goddamn elbow. Andro was taking great pains to keep the group's con-versation on track. I'd never heard so many butter knives clamoring against glass for attention.

We gulped down our wine. My headache was already brightening inside, a kaleidoscope of foreshadowing hangover. Salomeya proposed a toast, one arm outstretched onto Baba's hulking shoulder. Her hus-band's caterpillar eyebrows merged, annoyed. She waved Andro into the toast, like a reluctant swimmer being summoned to a shallow lake.

Andro took his signature pause before translating, "Salomeya... welcomes brother, offers toast to return. Many missings. Many years apart and so good to see...time has been"—he paused—"generous. Beautiful family and...the right decision, long ago."

"What right decision?" Ada asked.

Salomeya's husband expressed his displeasure at losing his talking-monopoly by knocking over a glass of wine. Three eagerly napkined women bent to clean up the mess, including my mother. Dad piled another pork medallion onto his plate. Lumps of leftover food sank into their saucy remains. Ada dropped her elbow to her side and blinked attentively in Salomeya's direction. Baba's eyes were drooping their way into sweet somnolence.

"Eli," Baba said, his voice drunk and dreaming. "Eliyana. Eliyana."

"Your grandfather is not brother by blood," Salomeya said, through Andro's translation.

"You're adopted?" Ada asked.

"*He's* adopted," Mom corrected her. "Dad's not adopted."

"I wasn't asking about Dad," Ada said, and took another long drink of wine.

"Eli," he slurred.

"Did you know that?" I asked Mom.

"I wouldn't say I *knew* that," she said. "I suspected."

"Why didn't you say anything?" I asked.

"That certainly wasn't my place. Besides, I never knew for sure."

"Why didn't *you* say something?" I pressed Dad.

Dad bowed his eyes into the heels of his hands. "Because I didn't know," he said. "Nor did I *suspect*. Just another example of your mom being ahead of the curve, I guess. I need some air." But, after an aggrieved glance at Mom, he didn't get up from his seat. He held on to the table with bulging white fingers.

"We're being impolite," Mom said. She jumped into a somersault of compliments in Russian. Salomeya's daughters nodded graciously, covering their noses in modesty.

Ada interrupted, "Adopted from whom?"

It was like even the most Georgian of our Georgian non-biological relatives could feel the insistence behind Ada's question and had to respect it. Andro repeated it in Georgian to Salomeya.

"My mother found him," Salomeya said. "There was boat... accident. Hiding"—she gestured—"full with mink skin for coat. Very small boy."

Dad's skin was turning a distinctively vomity green.

"He was alone?" Mom asked.

Salomeya fanned herself, angling away from Baba.

"There was a girl," Salomeya said. "But she expired. Previous."

Salomeya's husband barked a few sentences in her direction.

"Boat crash?" I repeated dumbly. I imagined a scaled-down, elderly Baba holding hands with a skeleton in a cherry-printed dress. Were the animal skins already made into coats? Were they fresh, still swathed in the scent of blood, of being alive? I thought of the paper boats that he'd crafted with Ada, crisply transforming slack pieces of newspaper into tiny vessels.

"I had brother who died," Salomeya explained, tearfully. "Earlier. After accident my mother find him, find them after accident. She adopt him. But...not legal, those times. Just slip child from Soviet Union? No. We keep our toes."

"Where did they come from?" Dad asked, a prickle of sweat on his upper lip.

"We think from North. From Russia," she said finally. The other Georgians guzzled their wine. "When we find him, we...didn't understand together."

I had never heard a better way to describe communicating with another person.

"Russian," I repeated. I didn't even know the blueprint of myself. I thought of Willa's efforts; all the insistent Googling to find the perfect khinkali—how futile and ill-advised it had been. Like everything, I thought, a nihilistic spasm in my shoulder. We were from the land of Putin and Pussy Rioting. We could've gone to the Russian Tea Room, slurped caviar. There was nothing novel about my background. There was, maybe, nothing novel about me.

Salomeya's husband was making another grand toast and even though my internal organs were seizing into a complicated knot, I drank again.

"You are still welcome," Salomeya's husband stumbled.

"I'm sorry," I said.

"How did he end up in the U.S.?" Ada asked. Somebody has replaced our scraps of meat with clean, white plates. Large, presliced fruits on a glittering platter: berries and grapes and browning chunks of banana. Salomeya's youngest daughter brought out dessert wine. Salomeya explained a long sequence of events to Andro, who summarized: no one knew that part. Goddammit, I thought. There was no way that she'd only said, *We don't know anything else.*

"Perhaps through Turkey?" Andro said eventually. Georgia wasn't so far from Turkey's border.

"Many things happen," Salomeya said. "It was difficult time."

"Did he have papers?" Ada pressed. "A fake passport?"

"He never mentioned any of this to you?" I asked Dad.

"He never talked about it. Salomeya, but . . . not this."

"God watched over," Salomeya's husband said.

"God watched over," Salomeya echoed. "And brought back."

"It was a different time," Mom said. "In terms of identity fraud. It was easier."

"What did he do when he got to America?" Ada asked. "How did he meet Nana?"

Dad breathed in through his nose, out through his mouth. "Please," he said. "Stop asking so many questions."

"But I want to know."

"Ada. Later. Give us a minute to process."

Salomeya's lip trembled ominously. "I am happy to meet," she announced. "He had quality life."

"He's still alive," I said, but my voice clung to the wall. No one seemed to hear me.

Dad reached across the table to take her hands in his. "Thank you," he said.

I scratched at my skin through the woolen dress.

"I need some air," I announced, and pretended not to notice the scowl on Salomeya's husband's face, or the appalled expression of Salomeya's daughters as I stood up. I wormed my way through the tiny, clustered kitchen onto the balcony. The night was darkening. Stray huskies circled the streets. Even from outside, I could smell the wine, the wafting of leftover fish carcasses in the garbage. When I heard the footsteps, I knew it wasn't Ada—so much heavier, clumsier than her gait—but I still expected her to be there, maybe with a rescued cluster of grapes in a cup, here to say how confusing and horrible this had been. Not just tonight. All of it.

But it was Salomeya, who was flushed and teetering. She lowered herself into a plastic chair and leaned her head back in its mole-spotted glory. For a minute, we listened to the city that existed underneath us—the chirps of insects, the purposeful footsteps of people returning to their apartments, dragging their feet across a welcome mat before scuttling into slippers.

"Do you know everything?" I said.

She laughed, although from poor comprehension or wisdom, I'll never know.

"Who was the girl?" I asked. Her face was the same, twinkling, impassive.

"Was her name Eliyana?" I asked.

"Eliyana," Salomeya repeated, pursing her lips.

"Tell me," I said.

"Tell me," I repeated, and reached for her.

"Hesper," Ada called. "What are you doing out there?"

Salomeya gestured with a long, heavy arm toward my sister. Her kerchief was pulled back just enough to show her natural, tawny color and the blue that lurked just below. She looked ridiculous. Glassy-eyed and, I could tell, much drunker than she'd realized before she tried to step out onto the balcony.

An alloy of voices followed her through the open door. Salomeya's expression changed from that of a confidant to that of a robustly sleeping person. She slept with her head cocked to the right, her lips puffed fishily outward, just like Baba did. Orange haze quilted the hills of the city, above the buildings and dark landscapes.

"Why did you leave me alone in there?" Ada asked. "It's too weird for a solo mission."

"Salomeya knows who Eliyana is. I could tell."

"Lemon. Give me a break. Break me off a piece of your Kit Kat bar," Ada said, giggling.

"Why did you drink so much?"

Ada swatted at me. "Because it's culturally appropriate."

"I was really getting somewhere," I said, suddenly feeling close to tears. "I was about to find out something important."

"Maybe Salomeya thinks *you* know who Eliyana is," Ada said. "Did you think of that?"

I hadn't.

"I don't understand you at all," Ada said. "We get this influx of crazy information about Baba tonight. Right? Just...a mountain of weird, tiny conundrums. Conundra? Anyway. The hills are *alive* with questions of Baba. How did he get to Georgia, who did he pretend to be to get to the U.S., was he actually from Russia? I'm spit-balling. That's not even touching how Salomeya's brother died, or what lies Dad was told growing up to cover all these tracks. But you," Ada said, wriggling her fingers in an octopus-wave, "you want to know about Eliyana, who might not even be a person. You just fly past Baba's whole life because you think you found the juicier story line. You're such a writer, Hes."

"Thank you?"

"No. I meant that pejoratively, little one. You are just traipsing around in search of a plot twist. Like, why are you sitting out here with Magicless Sal—"

"You shouldn't call her that."

"It's your nickname!"

"I'm revoking it."

"Fine. Why are you sitting here with *Salomeya* when our actual, flesh-and-blood father is sitting inside, trying to figure out where the fuck he came from?"

Guilt paraded through my chest. "Dad has Mom," I muttered. "For comfort."

"Dad has Mom like Willa has you," Ada said.

I felt like Ada had turned my spine into an accordion. She knelt forward to retie the kerchief, closer to her head, and resumed her upright position with a smug, I-know-I've-won-this expression that I remembered from playing board games with her all through elementary school.

"Fine," I said. "But should we just . . . leave her out here? Sleeping?"

"Why not? It's her house."

"Just seems weird. Doesn't it?"

I waited for Ada to give me a cue. As a little sister, my whole life had been girdled by her instructions. But she had nothing to say, just propped her chin into her palms and smiled. I could tell by the way she paused that she was about to hurt me; that whatever inhibition she usually exercised had been unlatched by the wine, the endless, unfamiliar night. Languorously Ada rested her head back against the balcony. She said, "You can leave her. That's what you do."

DAD KNOCKED ON THE door in the morning as if he expected a swarm of hornets to greet him. I answered, the only person already awake; of course I was, perpetually awake, thirsting through a montage of memories: Willa's expression, tarnished with disbelief, as I left her in the hallway. How she'd stood with her arm still propped in the door since she didn't have her key. How she'd called my name, splashy and sibilant: *Hesper. Hesper.*

"Good morning, ladies," Dad boomed. "I brought coffee—"

Lifting her head from the pillow, Ada said, "Please leave and don't come back for many hours. Please. Triple please."

Mom emitted a grunt that sounded vaguely affirmative.

"Lemon, what do you say I wheel Baba in here and the two of

us can go for a walk?" he suggested. "Since you're up and dressed already. Meet you in the lobby in five minutes?"

I couldn't deny that I was up and dressed already. I'd tried on every article of clothing I'd packed, and some of Ada's clothes, too. A restlessness stirred throughout me, the kind that made it impossible to concentrate on reading or a non-formulaic TV show. I wanted to whittle a piece of wood into the shape of a duck, peel a zucchini into long ribbons. For hours I'd been imagining myself as Mrs. Dalloway—tossing a black shawl over my shoulder and fucking booking it, buying the flowers myself. Tasks, a million tiny, shimmering tasks, to fill the day. The ability to chatter about nothing. But now, with the opportunity presented to me, I wasn't sure I wanted to leave. At least I knew what to expect from a claustrophobic suite with Ada and Mom. Dad was impulsive, and hard to talk down from a plan once he got started. Veganism, mountain biking, camping. But eventually he lost interest. That part, at least, was dependable.

"Okay," I agreed. I could tell that he was surprised, and part of me was, too.

⚜

"This coffee is disgusting."

"The cafe culture here is . . . new," Dad said. "At least that's what the guidebook says. It used to be that they would give you a little packet of instant coffee with an American flag on it and a cup of hot water. This is an improvement."

"It's . . . was it supposed to be iced or warm?"

"It's a singular Georgian temperature called *tepid*. I ordered it especially for you."

"So generous."

We petered through the back streets of Old Town, into the small circles of tourists like us. We moved like a school of fish, examining

all the brownish storefronts and restaurants with jovial, overly wel-
coming names—*Friends Cafe! Georgia Food!*—through the winding
streets. White filigree balconies on every building; carpets of curly
green ivy, climbing up the sides. The streets directly in front of us
looked a little like the Europe I pictured in my head, those clusters
of sidewalk cafes spilling into the center of the thoroughfare, people
nursing a single, green-bottled beer with sunglasses on. But when I
looked up, to the hills in the distance, everything looked like castles
made of mud or terra-cotta. The occasional tin roof, shaped like a
compressed umbrella top. Thick valleys of moss-green water. It was
like we had been dropped into a Disney park that hadn't been well
maintained.

"I thought we could get up on the funicular," Dad said, after about
a half hour of walking with only the street noise between us. "The
concierge recommended it. Get the true panoramic view of the city.
There's an amusement park up there, too. If it's good, we can take
Mom and Ada later and pretend like we didn't do this already."

"Trial run."

"Exactly."

"Did you tell Mom where we were going?"

"No, I . . ." he said.

We were, the two of us, hoarding secrets.

"I just wanted to get away for a little bit. She'll be asleep when we
get back, probably." Dad flashed a waning smile in my direction. He
looked, in the breeze, wispier than I realized; age haunting those circles under his eyes. "Doesn't it feel good to unplug? Go for a walk
without little plastic buds in your ears, reminding you of all the re-
sponsibilities you left behind?"

I struggled with the urge to contradict him out of habit. "Yeah. It's
nice here."

"So it seems like you're a more competent drinker than your big
sister," Dad said.

"I wasn't trying to keep up with her pace. That's the trick. Did you get the vomit off your shoes?"

"I hope so. They're my only pair."

Around us, construction crews propelled their workers up on cranes. The newer buildings were painted in more cheerful colors, mostly a cotton-candy pink that made me think of Lip Smackers. One tall, gold-domed castle peeked at us from the top of the highest hill. Dad consulted his guidebook to make sure we were going the right way ("taking the scenic route," he confirmed). It felt like we had been gone a long time. I wondered whether I should say something about it—getting back to Baba, to my hungover tart of a sister. But it did feel good to detach; to not have to think past getting to the funicular.

"How are you doing?" I asked. Dad didn't turn his head, and at first I thought he hadn't heard me. "With all the weird, new information about our family history, I mean. Dad?"

"That's the entrance!" he said. "Right over there. See it?"

"I see it."

It was typical of him to evade emotional questions, but I was still put off. I thought—if ever there were a time, wouldn't it be now? He'd invited me on this strange avoidance quest, led the wandering path across the tourist destinations. We got onto a sleek, black train labeled TBILISI that crunched over an enormous number of steps uphill with unexpected gusto, and then we settled into what looked like a space capsule: a small, dark orb that barely fit the two of us. Frigid air created goose bumps all along my arms, my exposed collarbones.

The city below us appeared as if it'd been spackled with gold. A smattering of pointy church roofs beneath a crisply blue sky. Mosques and convention centers; burgundy, light gray, cinnamon. Our seat dangled from the wire and I felt the rush of our height swarm my throat.

"I didn't feel much of anything," Dad said. "I thought it would upset me. Even as it was happening, I knew: I should feel betrayed. Or at least invested. But the thing is, my father never spoke about his life before he came to the U.S. Everything I knew felt like a fiction, anyway. So to find out these strangers aren't the strangers that share my actual twine of DNA...it's not so monumental. It's like we walked into the wrong house by mistake. I'm grateful to them, of course. Without Salomeya and the rest, we wouldn't be here. But am I devastated to find out Dad was adopted? I'm nonplussed, Hesper. I'm not at all plussed."

"Maybe you're in shock."

"I'm depressed," he said. "Everything I experience is...it's like watching it from afar, happening to a leading man who happens to resemble me." He stared out at the city through the glass rectangle on the side of our space capsule before rubbing his knees, as if he could scrub the confessional quality out of the conversation. "Lovely up here, right?"

"Right." I squinted to see what he was looking at. "Are you... Have you talked to..."

"What about you?" he asked. "Do you want to talk about it?"

I kept my gaze fixed firmly through the window space. All those oddly tall, Georgian taxis, skittering along the road like toys. "It's weird to think how close we came to not existing. And horrible, the idea of Baba...hiding under a pile of furs with a dead person. It just seems like the beginning of a really wretched fairy tale."

He nodded. "It's hard to picture."

"I just hope that's not where he thinks he is," I said, my voice catching. "Now. I want him to think we're all with him, you know, soaking up the sun in Italy or something. Fishing on a completely placid lake. I don't want him to be stuck for the rest of his consciousness, waiting to be found under some animal hide." I pulled my bottom lip under my top teeth, like a rabbit, and bit down until I was sure I wouldn't cry.

Awkwardly, Dad attempted to sling his arm around mine. It felt like we were on a very uncomfortable first date. "He hated fishing," Dad said, finally. "And the sun."

I laughed, and Dad looked relieved that the moment had passed. We were almost done with the funicular path, and I realized that neither of us had brought a camera.

"I wonder if he liked San Francisco because of all the hills," Dad mused. "It looks a little like here. That big river, the Bay . . . doesn't it?"

"It's pretty to think so," I said.

Beside us, the river twinkled greenly, and we started to descend.

ON THE WAY BACK to the hotel, Dad wanted to stop into a jewelry store we'd passed earlier that morning. Glass cases with long, dangling gold chains covered the back wall. A garrulous, stately shopkeeper asked all about our itinerary so far, bobbing as Dad spoke, and showed us to her "special collection."

"We should get back, Dad," I said. "It's been hours." I imagined how many paper boats Ada and Baba could have assembled by this point; an entire fleet. Mom would be mad enough to say *fuck* out loud.

"We're practically there. Only a few blocks away. I just want to pick out a gift." He smiled self-consciously at the shopkeeper and followed her into a smaller, well-lit room in the back. It took me a second: this is where the rings were kept. Only pendants and crucifixes were close to the door.

"Hesper. Lend me your fingers," Dad said. "I like that one. What do you think?"

The ring in question was gold; almost all of them were, and strikingly geometric. It was a small pearl encased in a gold-barred box, with enough space you would wiggle a pinky into the infrastructure of the ring—an inch or maybe two, mounted on a gold band. Or one pearl in a see-through box and another, dangling freely, with a weird gap between the left and right side of the band. An infinity sign, made of tiny pearls, atop a gold band. So much gold. All of them looked like they'd been created by either an extremely high-fashion designer or a ten-year-old.

"This is your . . ." the shopkeeper began, with a timid smile.

"Daughter. My youngest daughter," Dad said, plucking the ring from her and slipping it onto my finger.

The gold made my skin look jaundiced, and the metal felt slimy and cold. I hated it. I felt exposed through the weird open space between the pearl and the gold box, as though anybody could reach into the ring itself and scoop out the beautiful part, leaving only the outline of what it was supposed to be. But more than that, I hated even trying on this symbol, this marker that said: *I belong to someone. I belong.*

I could already picture Christina's Instagram: her, with this ugly ring, drinking a glass of seltzer. The gold glinting. Christina with her ringed finger and a perfectly executed manicure—probably red, or maybe pink, knowing her taste. Christina with a faux-surprised face and her ringed finger up against it, or maybe against her not-yet-showing pregnancy belly. A dual announcement.

The pearl kept looking at me with its gleaming, uniform shine.

Pistachio-lemon cake. For me.

"Does it fit?" Dad prompted.

I nodded, wormed myself free of it. My knuckles squashed and rumpled beneath the ring.

"I want to go home," I said, and Dad nodded eagerly as he handed over his credit card.

ADA WAS SMOKING OUTSIDE of the hotel. "I thought you quit," I said.

She let the cigarette sag from her lipsticked mouth. "Mom's going to kill you," she said.

Dad handed me the guidebook and rushed into the hotel. "Good luck," Ada called after him.

We stood, our heads tipped toward the sky. From the entranceway of the hotel, an abundance of lights sparkled from the high altitude in the distance. Trees looked almost like pine-colored fur. The buildings around looked sculptural, towering with the edges of clouds crowning the roofs.

"Did you have fun?" Ada asked. Her voice sounded sludgy with hangover.

"You were sleeping," I said. "I wouldn't have left without you, otherwise. You know that."

"I didn't say anything."

"I know you. I see your face."

She hovered around the cigarette, anticipating the next drag. "You're supposed to be my emotional team, and you left with *him*. For like, six hours. You know Baba doesn't like me. Nobody can calm him down besides the two of you. And where did you go, anyway?"

"We went on a funicular."

"A funicular," Ada repeated. She tapped a string of ash loose with her pinky.

"I'm still your emotional teammate."

"Yeah," she said, staring down at the sidewalk. "You're my only sister. You have to be."

"Ada. Come on."

"I take care of you all the time," she said. "Or have you forgotten all of those nights, sneaking into my apartment with your pupils dilated like a lunatic's? So that you don't have to sleep by yourself, or keep chugging along on your hamster wheel of denial? Whichever combination it is. I'm not saying you owe me anything, Hes. I love you. Obviously. But just . . . don't desert me so much. Don't walk away from the table and hang out with a non-English-speaking stranger on the balcony instead of riding out the night with me. Don't go on a super weird tourist journey with Dad without leaving a note, at least. Just *consider me*. Occasionally."

"I'm sorry."

She handed me the cigarette nub, which I accepted. Nicotine trickled through my body, rampant and ebbing. "It's okay."

I was gearing up to tell her about the ring as she said, "Christina had a miscarriage."

"What?"

"She called the hotel, eventually. I guess Dad wasn't answering his phone."

"He left it," I said, an eerie sense of disbelief creating a canopy over us. Even though it had only been rattling around my consciousness for a day, it still felt like an abrupt shift to adjust back to our old truth. Was I supposed to be sad? Angry? Instead I had this distinct, emotional whiplash, as if time had rebounded. Reset. So everything would be the way it had always been, but horrible. But luminous with the loss of what wouldn't be.

"Typical," Ada said.

"Jesus," I said. "I . . . feel like I don't know what to do with that."

"I know."

"When?"

"Last night. It's not that uncommon, Mom said. She was still in her first trimester. The baby was the size of a bean. But it had ears."

"Stop." I waved her off. "How can you be so . . . clinical?"

"Because Mom and I spent all morning talking her through a fucking meltdown on speakerphone, and it was the worst conversation I've ever had, but you got to go on a touristy tramcar up a beautiful mountain. I was empathetic for the first hour. But it's

not ... maintainable, Hesper. You get desensitized. Listening to somebody cry is boring."

"God," I said, but I had already stopped thinking about Christina.
I knew how easily that could apply to me, too. Or Willa. Who was
listening to Willa' cry on the other end of a phone line?

"I know that makes me sound like a bad person," Ada said. "But
it's true."

Just because it's true doesn't mean you need to say it, I thought.

"What's going to happen now?" I asked. I thought of the ring, the
single floating pearl.

"I mean, I assume we'll all fly back on the next plane out, right?"
Ada said. "There's no reason to stay here."

"What about Baba?"

"We'll have another chance to push the Ambien on him, I guess."

"But we ... there's so much more we don't know about him. Or
his life."

Ada clamped a hand on my shoulder. I could feel her thumb
tweedling my bones.

"Not all mysteries get solved, Lemon," she said.

I DON'T KNOW WHAT we expected, but there was Dad, kneeling on the
floor in front of Baba's wheelchair with a wet washcloth, exhuming his
face of all crumb-debris. He had tasks and he was doing them. It seemed
almost as if his knees were rooted to the carpet. He peered into Baba's
cement-gray eyes with unwavering focus. "Girls!" he said. "Care for a
pomegranate seed? I picked up some fruit from a stand next door."

Ada fastened a look in my direction that said: *Of course this is how
he'll be.*

"No takers?" he said. "That's okay. We're on our way to dinner,
aren't we, Dad?"

"Ess," Baba said. "Essp."

I rested my knuckles on his bald spot, the way I knew he liked best, and he crackled.

"Eliyana," he said.

"Eliyana," I said back.

"There's supposed to be a beautiful restaurant in an old mill, not too far from here," Dad said. "And there's a huge waterfall, too, the concierge said. 'You can dine with the river sounds,' is how she put it. Isn't that lovely?"

"No river," Baba yelled, abruptly. I jumped. "Not in river. You can't take me."

"No river," we cooed at him. "No rivers allowed."

"Where's Mom?" I asked, and Dad straightened suddenly, hyper-vivid and wildly tall.

"She went to make a reservation for us. It's a very exclusive restaurant. Cash only!"

"That's like, every coffee shop in Williamsburg. Not a sign of exclusivity."

"Maybe it is here in Georgia," Dad countered. "Let's go, okay? You ready?"

"Um," I said slowly. "Dad, are you—"

"Hungry?" he suggested. "Yes, I am. Worked up a real appetite. Put on your best clothes. I'll meet you downstairs in five minutes."

THE INTERIOR OF THE restaurant was dark, with tall, ivory columns smattered throughout the large space and a square stage set up in the center of the room for performances. The chairs were abnormally high, and required a finagling of muscles. They made me feel like I was in first grade again, unsure how to gauge the space between my body and its destination. I wheeled Baba so that he wouldn't be facing the window while Mom, harried and cloaked in a scarf, ordered a plate of appetizers that would be suffused with herbs and walnut paste and two bottles of wine. Ada and I exchanged an uneasy glance.

"So, Lemon," Mom said, over Dad prattling about how good dinner had been the previous night. How had that only been yesterday? "How has your day been?"

I kept my eyes fixed on the plastic menu. "Eventful," I answered, in relative honesty.

"We haven't gotten a chance to talk, since."

"Sorry for disappearing this morning," I said, quickly avoiding the subject before Dad could hear. "I didn't mean for you to be worried."

"Worried?" Mom asked, slipping on a sarcastic smile. "When my youngest, relatively reckless daughter disappears in a foreign country for six hours? Why would you presume that? Yes," she confirmed to the waitress, "that wine is very good, thank you. A little bit more. More. Perfect."

"I was with Dad. I didn't disappear."

"Seline, it wasn't her fault," Dad cut in. "I was the adult."

"You're both adults," she said, nearly knocking over three identical saltshakers. With a rickety exhale that seemed to emerge from the recesses of her empathy reserves, she continued. "But it has been a stressful trip, and I can understand needing some time to process."

"Thank you," he said. She itsy-bitsy-spidered a hand nearer to his, and took it.

After we finished three plates of khinkali and scraped the filling of stuffed Bulgarian peppers in vinegar sauce and watched the Georgian dancers stretch around the main floor, and drank the first bottle of wine, and the second bottle of wine, Dad clattered his fork against his wineglass. His front two teeth were smeared violet.

"I would like to make a toast," he said. "To my beautiful family. Ada, you are the smartest, best clothes-designer I have ever been in proximity to. Everything you create looks like an angel could wear it.

And it brings me so much pride to know that you're so giving, and compassionate, while also being unafraid to stand up for yourself. I wish I were as curious and uncontainable as you are."

Ada blinked, bewildered. "Thanks, Dad," she said, and gulped down half her glass.

"And to you, Lemon," he said. "You have such a sharp eye. I think the way that you see the world is a very special, particular thing. I see so much of myself in you—how invested you get in things, and then pulled away into other interests. You know, it's a gift to feel deeply. You don't have to flee from that."

"You're also brilliant," Mom chimed in, after a pause. "And uncontainable."

"God help the man—sorry, person!—who tries to contain you," Dad added.

We drank. I sliced into an egg, which shivered on a triangle of freshly baked bread, and the yolk oozed.

"And to the woman who made these two possible," Dad continued, flourishing his wineglass higher up in the air. "I don't know what my life would have been like if we hadn't met, all those years ago in that repugnant foreign language building that looked like a prison. I think back," Dad said, his voice thinning, "to all of the tumult that we have come up against, and I'm grateful to have such a strong, supportive, *unending* person as you in my life."

Mom clasped the stem of her wineglass. "Thank you, Martin. That's very sweet."

Has he forgotten? I wondered. Forgotten Christina, forgotten their divorce?

"And I feel," he continued, "that I've never gotten over you for a reason. That our relationship has suffered the trajectory of a yo-yo for far, far too long, Seline, and with the way that...other factors in my life...have turned out, it's impossible for me not to interpret this as a sign."

"Martin," Mom said. "I don't think—"

He held up a hand. "A sign from some higher power—I'm not sure if I believe in . . . well, that's neither here nor there—that my life is meant to be with you. You and our daughters, and you know I . . . you know I've tried so hard to change, this past decade or so, to be more open about my emotions and to say what I need when I need it, and I'm listening, Seline, I've listened and I'm changing and I'm ready for this, I'm ready for what it is that you need and what our family can be if we're reunited. I mean, just this morning," he said, swooping his free hand into his pants pocket, "Hesper helped me pick out this ring for you. Seline, we actually went for a walk and we discussed real . . . we had a real conversation, didn't we, Lemon?"

"Wait," I said, trying to swallow a croak. My heart thudded manically. I sounded like a machine. "Wait, I didn't . . . I didn't have any idea that was—"

"What the fuck," Ada said, her mouth forming a perfect donut-hole. She stared at me, aghast. "Are you serious?"

"Martin," Mom said. Her face, forever unruffled. "Maybe in private, we can—"

"When we were young, my priorities were so askew. I know I didn't appreciate you enough or give you the space you needed to pursue the opportunities you'd worked for, professionally and . . . in every way. I know that now. I came out of our divorce just . . . spelunking for kindness, for attention from anyone. I don't want to spelunk anymore, Seline. I don't just need a kind heart to come home to. No one has ever challenged me, or pushed me to be a better man. I need that push," Dad said. "I want it back. I never stopped carrying a candle for you."

"We know," Ada said.

"We will discuss this later," Mom said. "In a non-public arena. Without our children."

"We belong together," Dad said, so fast it was almost impossible to understand him. "To our new beginning," he toasted, and tossed the ring box on the table with a clank. The black velvet box narrowly avoided our plates of filmed yogurt sauce and cubes of carrot.

"To new beginnings," Mom amended, and Ada and I queasily raised our glasses. Mom leaned her weight forward, trying to catch the attention of any waitstaff, and drew an exuberant check mark in the air. *We are finished! We are! Finished here!* her body language broadcasted.

"She didn't say no," he whispered, behind a cupped hand. "Lemon? She didn't."

"I thought that ring was for Christina," I said. "I can't believe you, Dad. Seriously."

He looked at me for a minute, as blank and unknowing as if I'd spoken in Georgian. "Did you look at the ring?" he bellowed toward Mom. "Open it."

The waiter slid the check toward Dad. It startled him.

Mom examined the gold ring with rapt attention. She dipped her pinky into the ring-space to graze the little lambent pearl, just as I had thought an onlooker might. Until she glanced upward, it hadn't occurred to me that she might say yes. That stupid ring. My father's absurdly unwavering love, or codependency, or whatever had been stringing him toward this drunken outburst all these years. Or, at the very least, the attention. Knowing he would be waiting for her. He stuffed a pile of lari into the credit card holder and sauntered, a little wobbly, toward the door with Baba's wheelchair and a reluctant Mom.

Ada took my elbow. "Hesper," she said. "I don't even know where to start."

"I know the feeling," I said. We scooted our chairs inward.

"Is this like, what grief does?" she asked. "Should we be pitying him? Or..."

"I don't know. Grief can turn you into anything, right? Like a magician. Grief-ician."

"I think he's an asshole," Ada said. I could see her eyes brimming with tears. "An asshole that we can't fucking trust with anything. He doesn't think, you know? He doesn't think what it'll do to us. Say they do get back together—"

"You think Mom would—"

"—and then what? What if it doesn't work a second time? Where does that put us?"

"Back at the aquarium, I guess," I said. Sympathy tears were springing up in me. Or maybe they were real, too. An acrid taste flowered in my mouth; the flavor of the wine clung to my teeth. It was feeling more and more like our lives had been held up by a really shoddy, stapled-together bracket and in Tbilisi, something had quivered out of place. At least these were different problems, I thought, grasping around my neck for a chain that wasn't there.

THAT NIGHT, MOM SHOVED her traveling pajamas and her preferred toothpaste (Colgate; never Crest) into a pillowcase and told us she would be staying with Dad and Baba until the morning, to "work through the evening's declarations." She moisturized her arms aggressively, digging her fingernails into wide, concentric circles of lotion-application. "I just want you both to know," she said. "I have no intention of remarrying. Not your dad, not anyone."

"But the ring was so beautiful," Ada said. She scrunched a laugh down.

"Ada," Mom said. "Obviously the ring is not the issue." But after a minute, her trademark smile emerged and she let the lotion settle into her skin. "But it is hideous, isn't it? Like a gag gift."

"I tried to tell him. Well, not with words," I said.

"Your face is so expressive, though," Ada said. "You're like a cartoon. Those big eyes."

"He wasn't really looking. He was very focused on . . . whatever he was planning."

Mom's expression buckled. "It's sad," she said finally. "The extent to which he's willing to go in order to fuel this decades-old fantasy." She folded her scarf into fourths, sixteenths. "You heard him, slamming me onto that same pedestal as though I've never made a mistake. Don't ever do that. It's the quickest way to poison your relationship."

But you came here with him, I thought.

"You still love him, though," Ada ventured. "I mean, don't you?"

She folded the top of her pillowcase down into an envelope, the corner of the toothpaste jutting out in a sharp point. "I do. You're old enough for me to tell you that I do. But you know what else? I would never marry someone who would propose to their ex-wife the day after their girlfriend has a miscarriage. I couldn't do that to another woman. Even a woman I don't like who has a pet lizard. Grief, depression, what have you—that's all well and good. At the end of the day, you're responsible for your own goddamn happiness. And the truth is, depression makes you selfish. All your father sees is himself, and some bodies around him."

"Why do you look at me when you say that?" I asked, itching with interpretative possibilities. The air in our hotel room smelled of coolant and butter. Mom shook out her bun into a crown of crimped waves.

"My eyes had to settle somewhere, Lemon," she said.

⚜

WHEN SHE LEFT, ADA keenly extended her torso all the way across the bed. Her legs were flaccid and draped oddly toward the floor; she looked like a mismatched set of body parts. "Do you think I'm just like him?" she asked.

I curled on her opposite side, lapping up the softness of her blue hair as if it were a cherished pet's coat of fur. "Like Dad? How do you mean?"

I'm the one who hurts everyone I try to love, I thought. I'm the emotional destroyer.

"Because I can't get over Charlie."

"You've barely mentioned him."

"That's because I've learned to stop mentioning him. But I think about him constantly. It's almost like a tic. When I wake up in the morning, I'm like, how long can I go without thinking about Charlie? But, you know, as soon as I think that, I've already lost my own challenge." Ada nestled her face into the quilt. "When I go online and I see a profile of somebody like him, I get this rush, like maybe it could actually work with this OC, this time. Maybe he'll smell the same, and just love me better, but I could already have the same...foundation of intimacy, I guess. I could already know which bagel/cream cheese combo was his. None of that like, preference exchanging, dillydallying. Just a straight shot into real stuff."

"The dillydallying is the best part," I said. "I could've stayed with Willa forever if all she wanted from me was a ranked list of my favorite beverages." I started to braid a plait into Ada's hair without even realizing I was doing it; slipping one strand under, over, a comfort mechanism that I'd used since we were little, sharing a bed like the one we did now, knowing that our parents were lambasting each other in a nearby room.

"I think," I said, "getting over somebody happens excruciatingly slowly, so you don't even realize it until it's almost over. Like when a headache disappears and somebody has to offer you an Advil before you know you don't need it."

"Yeah?" Ada asked, a note of desperation sneaking into her voice.

"Yeah."

I braided in silence for a second before she asked, "How are you... doing? With that?"

"I don't know," I said. "There hasn't been that much time to think about it here. That's one benefit to this trip being a total shitshow." Ada sighed. "I could stay here forever," I continued. "Imagine how weird things could get. We'd find out Baba has an evil twin who's also an alien."

"All Our Tbilisian Children," Ada said. "Hey. We're free of parents, maybe we should go out?"

"Go out, go out?" I asked dubiously, patting her nest of braids. My head still felt heavy from the interminable taxi ride home after Dad's disastrous toast. "You mean put on shoes again? I can't."

"I'll put on your shoes. Just do this for me. I want to have a story about being in this fucking city that doesn't involve someone in our family having a meltdown." Ada squished my right foot stubbornly into a leather ankle boot. "I want to kiss somebody who in no way resembles Charlie." She searched my face for resistance. "Please."

9.

We upholstered ourselves in slinky synthetics and finished the Red Bull and Jägermeister from yesterday. Yesterday? Time, elastic, deceitful. I returned to the gold sequined skirt; I was pretending it was a signature look instead of my only option. I was ebbing, flowing, trotting out of a cab and into the bright Korean restaurant, I was trudging down a winding narrow staircase into a room with a single diaphanous disco ball in the right hand corner. Organ-like light fixtures, configured as though they were dripping from the ceiling tiles with tiny bulbs. Toby ordered shots for everyone while we perused the karaoke selection: solid with early 2000s hits, our wheelhouse. I knew I was the drunkest one there having abandoned my dinner in pursuit of space from the rabbi. Then I was cornered by Alison, whispering in my ear: *"How's our Jewish star?"*

So: after dinner, heads tilted back as we did shot after shot, and high fives for everyone, and Alison was saying, *Samantha, where's your rabbi friend?* while Samantha blushed and Bren pointed to a mysterious dark square balanced atop a speaker built into the wall, asking: *What do we think that is? Surveillance? We're famous!* We waved to our hypothetical audience. Was it a heater? It could easily have been temperature-related. Possibilities of the dark square ground against us, Kyle and his girlfriend and Alison and Toby started off with that French song that's mostly requesting a threesome and we were convulsively clapping, sweat ribbons underneath my gray T-shirt, I was reaching my fingers into my sternum expecting the texture of a pincushion but all I discovered was bone.

So: Bren cautiously not touching me when he asked am I okay and of course not but couldn't I just pretend, couldn't he just pretend I was doing a good job pretending? I was ignoring him, pushing my hair across the back of my damp neck, I was ignoring him when I went to the bathroom and smeared more kohl across my eyelids. I was ignoring him until he was gone, where was he? and Alison was side-hugging me like a binder clip fastened to a term paper. Muscles, tissues, tendons, we were crawling up the walls, the dark square exhaling a puff of steam. *It's a fog machine!* Toby yelled. It smelled of rubber and chemicals and we hid our mouths in the built-in handkerchiefs of our elbows until it cleared. *No,* I whispered. *Anything but the fog machine!* Toby bellowed, on its second burst, and I knew this was the slogan that would eventually become our Facebook quote, there was no Bren in sight to share a satisfied glance, and why was I surprised, that I'd managed to alienate my one real friend here, and I thought of Chloe, that prickling enmity when I thought *You're going to leave me, too,* and the scent of a car wreck leaked from the fog machine until it felt like it was inside my lungs, like it was emanating from my chest and the fog machine, syncopating.

I was getting onstage with Alison and Lauren, Kyle's girlfriend, I was vaguely shoulder-shuffling, the clunky piano opening and then synth, snapping, suction as Alison burst into Christina Aguilera's voice and we rambled after her, the long-memorized lyrics: *come, come, come on in, let me out.* I held my mic down so no one could hear me while we declared ourselves genies, while we begged for intruders, for release. *Come come come on in let me out,* then it was over and Bren was shyly chatting up Samantha next to the bar, then it was over and I was coughing with the fumes of the fog machine, hoping everyone saw Bren flirting, maybe even successfully wooing, Samantha, Samantha who was almost-Hesper, and the terrible sliver of my heart that thought *I wanted you for myself even though I didn't want you for myself.*

I was mincing, meandering up the stairs, I was pressing hard on my diaphragm to remind it please, please work, oxygen, carbon dioxide, nothing fanciful or unique, *come on in, let me out,* the sky was the color of sapphire and three hairgelled men in their tight shirts were smoking cigarettes on the corner, watching me, eyes trickling. I told myself not to worry because there were people here, it was practically Times Square, the tall bouncer with his steampressed stern expression, Italian teenage girls limberly reeked of tequila, tender-mouthed, *don't worry* but I was pulling down my gold sequined fucking skirt trying to inhale, exhale, when the boldest one came over and asked in three different languages: what's my name?

"Cecilia," I answered, my tongue thick and wooden. I turned to go back inside. This would not happen to me. I would not let this happen to me.

"Cecilia," he called. I was walking fast, faster. "You're breaking my heart!"

But I shouldn't have been walking away. I should have been walking back, toward the people that I knew, toward the fog and the cocktail napkins and bottles of people I knew, and I jolted quickly trying to weave myself in the space between the bouncer and the side of the building but he was nimble, his skin was sallow, the jawline of a soldier, he swiped at my arm but I dodged past him with a fumble, those fucking shoes as slippery as if they were made of melting ice, and he said again, tramping toward me: "Cecilia. What's your number?"

"Don't touch me," I said. But I sounded placating, sanguine, as if I were delicately reminding a kindergartener to tidy his cubby at the end of a school day.

"If you change your mind," he said, scooping my arm toward his.

The touch of him turned me frigid. I couldn't reach the whistle, it was tucked beneath the underwire of my bra and the touch of this stranger was the mirror that turned Medusa to stone, I was a pillar, I was disappearing from myself, and he scrawled digits on my inner wrist in ballpoint pen and I was too close to sinking onto my knees and feeling the stubble of the cobblestones on my face to do anything but watch him. The pen pressed into my skin. He had trouble with the last digit, a six, and swept the ink in a curve, a bunny slope, over and over until it was legible, and then he let me go.

But I felt him everywhere, still, I felt him and his fingernails carving tiny moons into my wrist and I toppled through the club and to the bathroom and smeared the pen into a concrete-hued rectangle, until it was nothing but a watercolor of gray against my inner wrist and it didn't have to mean what it meant but what if he were the same man, what if he were an incarnation of the boy who followed me home with his red hoodie and brooding eyes, his breath hot as he fumbled underneath my self and if I couldn't get away from him here, could I get away from him anywhere? Was he going to follow me here, into the bathroom? Was he underneath the tiles? Behind the graffiti-stickers? But. Even posing as Cecilia, I was still me. The song went: *Come and set me free, baby, and I'll be with you.* What if he heard me singing it, what if he heard the karaoke and he knew the message? What if it was my fault?

Of course it was: my fault.

In the bathroom, Samantha and Alison rushed in, Alison playfully hipchecking me at the sink, both of them carting small plastic cups of vodka soda, suddenly in sync, reapplying lip gloss with identical leans over the faucet to get closer to the mirror and I swabbed my arm with as many paper towels as I could grab and tried to look normal, at ease, a person neither plagued by trauma nor having difficulty breathing. Alison was describing the kissing technique of Lars, a Swedish man she'd been dancing with who had surprisingly soft lips, and she offered me her tube of lip gloss as if I had been involved in the conversation, which of course I hadn't been, but I accepted and applied it anyway, bruising my lips a burgundy that I never would have chosen for myself because it looked painful, overly pink on my already pink skin, but here I was, following suit, I was reemerging, awake, wide fucking awake, and then Samantha asked me a question I couldn't quite hear over the painful incessant vibration of the bass, staring at my mirror-self I was thinking, *I regret not being you.*

"What?" I asked.

"Do you mind if I hook up with your little friend?" Samantha repeated. Her lips glinted.

"Bren?" I said stupidly. They both laughed, and Samantha drew herself toward me. I tried to hold my breath so that I could imagine she smelled just like Hesper. "I thought you said he was unfortunate."

"Burn," Alison exclaimed, and then clasped a hand over her mouth. "That's almost his name!"

"Unfortunate may have been too harsh. I can be hasty with my first impressions." Samantha revealed a tube of mascara from her bag and swept her eyelashes into an upturned forest. With the mascara applied, she looked so much less Hesperine; it was easier to consider what she was actually saying, to unhelix the thing in my heart that said *you you you you.* "I don't know. It was nice talking to him, and his eyes are that pretty grayish blue."

"They're just gray," I said. "No blue to be seen."

"I asked if you were okay with it as a courtesy," Samantha said. "You can at least answer me directly, Willa."

Alison configured herself to face me, the actual-me, while Samantha and I continued to watch each other in the mirror. She stroked the texture of my skirt, suddenly enraptured by the fabric, and I wondered if maybe they had taken other, more exotic drugs, or whether my drunkenness was just another experience I had that was different from everyone else's.

"You're right," I said. "Sorry. I'm used to avoiding questions about myself."

"You're still doing that, Willa Killa," Alison said.

"No," I said. "I'm not okay with it. Please choose someone else."

"Then just fuck him already," Alison said. "I'm exhausted."

We were both surprised, I could tell. Me, more than Samantha, who nodded swiftly and pursed her lips in the mirror, returned to the task of trying to create volume in the underbelly of her hair. I couldn't believe I had just said that; how easily the words had dropped out of my mouth. I had never voiced, so simply, what I'd wanted from someone and had them listen. I knew it was unfair to sequester Bren from romantic, or not-romantic, possibility from Samantha, but I didn't care, not yet, not while we were still here and I knew that when I found him he would be unencumbered, ready to banter, ready to leave if that was what I wanted to do or pace the parking lot or flail, flail as if it were dancing, and that I was his jellyfish and for the moment everything could stay as it had been between us.

"I should go back to Lars," Alison said. "My mouth misses his mouth."

Samantha gave her a fretful look, then finished the icy sludge that remained of her drink.

"What was so special about his mouth?" I asked.

"Oh," Alison said. "Maybe it was more a question of his manner of kissing. Like this," she said, and before I realized what was about to happen her body was pressed against me, I could smell her Garnier shampoo, I could feel her tongue slipping underneath mine, flickering, probing from top to bottom. It was a kiss of hubris. It was a kiss that erased Hesper's kisses and it meant my lips had already forgotten hers, that my lips might never know hers again, the texture of her skin, the way that she couldn't quite open her mouth wide enough, and I wanted to cry when Alison pulled away, smiling like a miscreant.

"See?" she said. "I have to get back to that."

I wanted desperately to wipe my mouth. But it would mean that I needed to get the kiss off of me, I thought, and that was suspicious. And I couldn't say anything about how she hadn't asked permission, either, for the same reason. I had to pretend it meant nothing, that it woke no sliver of me up, that I wasn't tilting with chthonic wanting. But she knew; you knew when someone returned your kiss. I knew she knew and I felt limp. My eyes roasted fatty tears. "That was demonstrative," I finally said.

Alison laughed. "You're so funny, Willa," she said, weaving past me toward the exit.

Samantha tossed her empty cup in the garbage and held the door for me. "Coming?"

MY FEET WERE HEAVY but I followed, unmoored, fused to Samantha and Alison because I was afraid but also I wanted to turtle into my own shell, I wanted another drink, I wanted to cross myself out. Were the men outside still waiting for me? The numbers smeared on my forearm. They were waiting for me. I followed Samantha and Alison into the second, larger room of the club, sprawling, where the fog had made a tapestry, the fog collapsed into the walls and our lungs and rendered us detritus, the fog baked us into stripes and cells and I felt myself choking, we were going to die, here, they were going to lock the doors and slowly we would lie down and never wake again, we were stripped and shaved and bodies, we were gold stars in a shower of steam, and how did no one else see it, how did no one else know? My body stood still but Samantha and Alison pushed forward, deeper into the crowd where they would die, and I thought: *I have to find Bren, I have to save him, I have to save us both.*

Dead dead dead dead dead dead, dead dead dead d-dead dead.

Every second it took for me to find him was another second we would not get back. I shuffled through the bulk, dancers and drinkers and people mincing their tongues together and dipping their asses into each other's laps, searching for him until there he was, taller than I remembered and, yes, maybe Samantha had been right and there was a blue undercurrent to his eyes, steely, searching for why was I talking so fast, why was I pulling at his collar and interrupting his conversation with Lauren, why was my wrist sullied with pen marks, the percussion in the song that was playing bleared like car horns, and in the disarray he surrendered and let me lead him outside and when we got there I checked to make sure there was no one else around, that the men were gone, and I couldn't get enough breath into my body, sucking the oxygen up as deeply as I could.

"Hey," Bren said. He held me by my shoulders but I was still writhing.

I was trying to get a better view of the fog, pouring from the building into the sky. I didn't want to smell us, burning, burnt. But the club only shone with strobe lights, and the thumping house music, and from here it seemed normal, it looked just like any techno-tattered dance establishment but I couldn't stop gulping the air, the non-fog filtered air, and I crouched down to get closer to the swarthy scratchy earth and Bren followed suit, and he had been saying *what's wrong? what's wrong?* but I only just then heard, and was surprised, and found that my voice still worked and I said, "I rescued us."

"Rescued us from what?"

"It's a gas chamber," I whispered. "It's not a fog machine. Inside."

"Willa," he said. "That's not funny, like, at all."

"I'm not trying to be funny. I'm trying to help you."

He blinked, and took a long breath. "Thank you," he said.

"You're welcome," I said, and twisted to reexamine the sky. "We're safe here."

"We are safe here," he said.

"Can I ask you something?" I asked. *This is not a good idea,* I thought, but knew what I was about to say, and that I would say it anyway.

"Sure. Can we stand up?"

We stood. He lifted his hands from my shoulders in a formal, almost ceremonial gesture.

"Do you want to kiss me?" I asked.

His expression was saturnine, withdrawn. "Do I *want* to kiss you?" he repeated. "Are you requesting that I kiss you, or asking my general opinion?"

"Both, I guess."

He shook his head. "You send out so many mixed signals, I just— I don't know where you stand. You freaked when you even thought I was looking at you, that first night. But you want to spend all this time together, which is cool. I like being your friend, okay, but now— what? You think there's a Holocaust reenactment going on inside and you want to make out? Because you're scared? Is that it?"

"Aren't you?" I asked. "Scared?"

"You must know I like you," he said, memorizing the texture of the ground.

"It's not..." I started. "Alison kissed me, when we were in the bathroom. It made me feel really weird. I want to nullify it."

"That's really homophobic," Bren said. "It doesn't make you gay just because somebody kisses you, Willa."

"No, no. I'm gay. That's why it made me feel weird, like, vulnerable. Because no one else knew, but now Alison does, and you."

"If you're gay," he said, "why do you want me to kiss you?"

"I just don't want the last person I've kissed to be Alison."

He paused. "So you're asking me if I mind being used?"

"I'm sorry," I said. "I didn't mean it like that."

"I'm not a support group," he said, his voice tremulous. "I have feelings, you know. You're not doing me any favors."

"Bren."

He shook his head. "Let's forget this, okay? I'm going to go back inside. I'll see you."

"I've been really heartbroken," I said. "It's making me horrible. That's . . . one of the reasons why I came here. So I could see something else, besides me."

Bren finally looked at me. "Well, I hope that you will," he said, and left. I caught the first cab that I could find. In the cab I swept my knees up to my chin, not caring that the skirt was tiny, not caring what anyone could see anymore. I sunk my teeth into my thighs.

10.

Yelp and Facebook and TripAdvisor all told us to go to the same club, crammed into a building that looked like a tenement. Even in the dark, the rusted pipes were conspicuous, along with a heady tower of air-conditioner units mounted to the back. It was, of course, Go-Go Dancer Night, which I extracted from the jabbering, extremely drunk crowd behind us. Surrounded by tight, cotton dresses that were basically stockings, I was especially out of place in Ada's latest dress creation—one with beaded feathers for sleeves and a skirt, with a latticed overlay that moved without my consent. I looked like a lacy owl.

"It's very cold," Ada shouted at a host, once we were inside.

"You will drink to warm," he said, and brought us toward the bar.

It had four floors, and we were on the most danceable; it was dark everywhere besides a string of blue lights around the ceiling and spot-lights on the dancers, who were both on a stage and encased in glass, somehow. Tall, long-legged women danced in either black or white lingerie, dipping forward into each other's hips, necks, breasts. Long, hairsprayed locks, swaying to the mounting bass lines. The way the spotlights were set up, you could only see silhouettes of their faces. Around us, intersections of men were rapt, adagios of cheering as the women nearly kissed, nearly grazed, nearly, nearly, and I thought: they're here for entertainment, they're here for consumption, they're here only for one reason and that reason is for men, not for each other.

I hated looking but I also kept looking.

No one here knows you're gay, I thought; no one knows, no one knows. But.

Torn to shreds, Mom had said. *Don't Google it.*

I thought of the times that a stranger's gaze had lingered on us; of the stilted moments after Willa had taken my hand and put it atop the table instead of under it, of the moments when she'd kissed me by the subway and a man had called "Let me take your picture" and we had to pretend not to hear him because he could be angry, because he could be dangerous; when she'd brought me a cone of snapdragons by Union Square and a guy had followed us down the block toward the park calling us cunt-lickers and Willa still had a headphone in so I had to decide whether to tell her; and the look on her face when I did, a whirlpool of disappointment and fear.

"Ada," I called. "Can we dance on a different floor?"

"This is the best floor, Hesper," she said. "That almost rhymes! Did you hear it?"

"Please," I said. "I feel... weird here. I'll buy you another drink."

She brightened. "A mixed drink?"

"So mixed that you won't know what hit you."

⚘

EVERYTHING WAS TOO LOUD, too expensive, sound and smell and bass-crunching from every direction. Sensations crawled over my nerve endings. We were parched and arid and dancing, receding from the crowd and then swallowed by it, buoyed among white-teethed and determined men, will you dance with me? Now? What about now? Hands like seat belts. But I let them because this is what my sister wanted, to be a set of fingers and a warm wet zero, and it's not

so bad if you thought: this was someone else's body, this was someone else growing numb from the same weight-shifting beat. One
two, one two, muzzy house music from a decade ago but it was still
dance-worthy, wasn't it? And with the dancers out of sight it felt like
undergrad again when I thought maybe a taller, red-haired, blond-
haired, guitar player, oboe player, poet, was maybe my type and I just
hadn't found it yet, blue collar, white collar, champion skier, pun-
constructor, but that wasn't it, was it? Remains of the past filled my
mouth like an accidental gulp of seawater. Had we been here for
an hour or four hours, and then Ada finally got her wish, and even
though we were old enough, for this not to feel strange, it still did,
this block of man with his bulky arms crawling over my sister's waist,
his hair sharply shaved in the back, and kissed her neck and her collarbones and her mouth, wrapping himself around her like a tetherball,
and she reached a hand like a branch toward me and said: "I'll text
you when I'm ready to leave, okay?"

I thought of volleying myself between them. But I didn't. I said
okay. I was free of witticisms and I wanted to take a bath. A lavender-
scented, luxurious bath, with a moat of gleaming bubbles.

Instead I found myself climbing many stories of stairs, sidestepping
the karaoke floor and the troves of women wearing bows as big as
Minnie Mouse ears, until I reached the terrace. Seats draped in black-
and-white striped cushions surrounded large glass tables; a small bar
was situated in the corner, rendered nearly invisible by all the people.
Men in pastel-plaid shirts leaned into the bartender's space, impatient. Disquieted, I huddled into the smallest free chair and capped
my knees to my chest. The dress rubbed its leagues of fabric over my
knees. I was the only person there alone and I didn't even have actual
Internet data, since we hadn't bothered to buy a proper phone plan
for Europe. Fuck you, I thought, and switched off the Wi-Fi-only
button in a scintillating blitz.

There, in my inbox: Willa.

Nausea ping-ponged from my head to my throat to my stomach and back, and I tried to rest my neck deeper into the space between my knees, tried to find the support in my own body and it was not there, it was not anywhere. Just the sight of her name beckoned me right back into her bedroom, where we'd broken up; the din of her neighbor's alarm going off, off, off, the leagues of heat leaking from her radiator even though it was unseasonably warm, the maze of emotions on her face as she struggled to understand: but how? but how could I? when we were? And even though I closed my eyes, even though I quickly shut out of my email before I could read past the preview (*Dear Hesper, I know it's a faux pas to begin an email this way but last night I dreamed—*), I still felt shaken, shadowed by all of it, all of it again. I wanted to say leave me, Willa, leave me alone, but of course I already was alone. I was in Georgia. The air was saturated with cigarette smoke and the city looked golden, peppered with glints of light across rows and rows of trees, and I drank the drink I'd bought for Ada and surrendered my seat (though no one else came alone, probably it would be there when I returned, I thought hesitantly) to go to the bar again.

The bartender eyed me and called for someone else to help me. It was that obvious.

"How may I order you?" the replacement server called, darting over from the other side of the bar. At first, I couldn't figure out why she looked so familiar, until I noticed the dimpled sheen of burned skin underneath her uniform's collar. It was Lali, the girl from the flea market who'd sold me her sister's bird figurine.

"Rum and Coke?" I asked. Willa's drink. But it was too late now. I set my hands to work, trying to untangle the lanyard of my hair created by the insistent wind on the roof. Lali squirted some Coke from a hose into a not-terribly-clean cup and then tucked a napkin beneath it.

"You look familiar," she said, in Russian, after I nodded encouragingly.

"You sold me...at Dry Bridge Market?" I said, alternating between Russian and English. "It was a very pretty bird."

"Yes! That's right," Lali said. We both nodded exuberantly. We had established a connection! I felt satisfied and also, suddenly, very lightheaded. I gripped the bar with the hand that had less chipped nail polish and continued to smile. Don't stare at the burn, I reminded myself, but maintaining eye contact felt equally incriminating. She had thick eyelashes on and liner that made her look like illustrations I'd seen of Cleopatra.

"We charge Americans extra," Lali said apologetically.

"That's okay."

"Will you go home with me?" bellowed the man next to me in Russian. "Single, I see."

"No, thank you," I mumbled. Lali accepted my change. I watched her tuck it into the pocket of her uniform slacks. The fabric, snug against her body.

I knew I was lingering, right on the precipice of creepiness. But I had nowhere to go.

"Do you want food?" Lali asked. She pushed a laminated menu toward me with the same glossy, stock photos I'd seen in cafes that Dad and I passed the day before: graceful glass bottles of Coca-Cola, triangles of pizza with yellowing cheese, a salad crested by thinly sliced purple onion. I didn't want any of those things. Lali's eyes were sultry and dark.

"My sister is downstairs," I lamented. "I don't know when she wants to leave."

"My sister is the same," Lali said. "But in Turkey."

I sipped my new drink. It was clunky with ice.

"I have U.S. candy," Lali said suddenly. "Do you want?"

"U.S. candy?"

"Peanut M&M. I have in back room. Yes?" she prompted.

"Yes," I said.

She doesn't know, I thought. That wouldn't even be on her radar, on her grand spread of options. This is a gesture of kindness in a country proud of hospitality. It's like putting out new sheets for a guest. Lali yelled something at her burly coworker and emerged from behind the bar. There was a small sliver of skin between the bottom of her shirt and the beginning of her pants that I was not staring at. No, I was not. Her hair billowed behind her in the rooftop breeze, like a rope I was meant to grab on to. Down the narrow stairs, I could hear my knees cracking in the pauses between songs.

The back room was a patchwork of supplies—paper towels, boxes of liquor that hadn't yet been opened, cleaning supplies with Georgian lettering in bright red. I touched my favorite letter-shape, the one that looked like a tiny carrot with a crown on top. Drunk, I knew, but it made me want to float away. Leave Ada, leave Georgia, become completely unmoored from everything I'd ever been and would be, if things continued how they were. I rested my head against a stockpile of toilet paper and smiled. Everything in here, too, carried the scent of stale cigarettes, but now it seemed familiar. We were blotted with the light emanating from a single, ambient bulb. Lali emerged from her excavation of the peanut M&M's and held them up in victory.

I thought of my father, raising his wineglass. We would be mummified in that fucking toast for the rest of our lives.

"Tear it," I said, gesturing. Smiling, lupine, she pulled the wrapper open until it ripped, a snowstorm of peanut M&M's unleashed into her open palms. I waited. She popped one into her mouth and crushed it.

I'm too drunk, I thought, and pressed my hot lips into her hand. I sucked the peanut M&M into my mouth like a vacuum cleaner and she laughed and I did it again, chewing, my muscles moving, her skin warm and salt-laden, and she smelled different than Willa, which for some reason I did not expect, and the reason was that I thought it would feel exactly the same to be in love and to follow a stranger into a closet for exported candy, and I kept doing it and she moved the M&M's into a trail, along her forearm and into the bend of her elbow, her laughing, the tintinnabulation of her laugh, and I didn't know what would happen when I stopped, so I didn't, until one of the M&M's skittered from her arm-space onto the floor and I could see that I could kiss her and I tried to breathe but all I could see was Willa, the way her hair spread beneath her on the pillow like cobwebs, the face she made when she crumpled a piece of paper and tried to toss it into the garbage and missed, and I knew if I kissed Lali it would be erased and I blotted my lips against the side of her cheek and she blotted her lips against the side of my cheek and it was a game, and she was still laughing, and then it was about to happen, so I ran, peanuts and chocolate heavy on my breath, I ran down every steep stair of the nightclub and found my sister, my horrible, lovely, blue-haired sister and said: we are leaving right now, and she listened, and we were gone.

⚜

A SORENESS DEEPENED, SETTLED below my sternum; my body, exhausted. It felt like I had been crying all night, only through my rib cage instead of my eyes. Track marks of mascara lined the bottom of my pillowcase. Ada's repeated demands that we take aspirin and drink an entire water bottle before finally, finally going to bed around 3:00 a.m. had mollified my hangover, but a pressure crawled over my temples.

"Big night last night?" Mom asked, plunging another sugar into her instant coffee.

"I could ask you the same question," I said, flicking the crystals in their paper container.

She took a deep sip. "I wish it could stay like this."

"Evasive?"

"Early," she said. "And...still."

I nodded, and we caffeinated silently. I wanted to hold on to it, too. As I watched Dad and Baba and, finally, Ada, join us, the peace dissipated. Plates were scraped for eggs and slices of warm, hearth-baked bread; Baba was trying to roam the dining room and we had to hold his limbs in place until he finally surrendered. Dad was embarrassed, and avoided eye contact with all of us besides Baba. He kept saying things like, "You can't walk, Dad," and "You're not going anywhere," and the more insistent he became, the more that sense of captivity expanded to include all of us. I felt the sparks of those sentences, clamoring for our attention. I kept my eyes downcast. Even though I had brushed my teeth last night and twice this morning, I still felt the lingering saline taste of Lali's skin, of the peanut M&M's. From beneath her cloud of hair, Ada looked at me guiltily.

"Hold still," Dad said, and put his hand over Baba's forehead, as if he were feverish.

"Martin," Mom said, once Baba sat, obsequious and attempting to eat a piece of cheese. "Wasn't there something that you wanted to say to the girls?"

He scraped the prongs of his fork across the tablecloth. "Did we say that—"

"We did, yes. Whatever you're about to protest, please reconsider."

Dad's expression looked frayed, and strangely inanimate, as if he'd been made into a sculpture. "Yes. So we did. Ada, Hesper...Dad," he said, arching to include Baba, "I believe I owe you an apology. I was not in the best shape last night, and I know I said some things that were...that had extreme consequences for our relationship as a family, and...that it was unfair to drag up my relationship with your mom in so much detail. That I should really work on my boundaries," he said, whatever ardor-driven enthusiasm he'd begun with starting to deteriorate. "Obviously, it was not the right time for me to propose to Mom. And I should"—he examined her disposition somberly—

"I should be more careful about what kind of example I set for you both."

My teeth clanged into my coffee cup. Ada said, "So are you going to propose to Mom at a better time? Is that what we're supposed to take away from this little speech?"

He paused, then watched Mom to gauge whether he should answer.

"That's not the foremost concern right now," Mom said, shredding her sugar packet. "Your father's in a committed relationship, and he should take care of his partner. It would be wrong to even discuss it, at this point. She's barely in any shape to go to a store and buy Triscuits. It's unethical to consider ending it. Just...unethical," she repeated. But I noticed that she was wearing her wedding ring, the original one, with its diamond facing out, and I wondered if she were trying to reassure herself as much as us. If there were two things that bound this family together, it was the ability to lie excellently, fluidly, both internally and externally, and the sprinkling of freckles over our eyelids.

And she had stopped saying Christina's name. It was like she was already starting to become a shadow on the wall, rather than a person that was waiting in an empty, apparently cracker-deprived apartment on the other side of the world for Dad to return home. I ripped a corner of bread and let the carbohydrates soak up last night, Lali, the Willa-guilt, and swallowed it. Soon she would be just my ex-girlfriend, I thought, and then my ex, and then an anecdote. Once I knew a person who took me to a Georgian restaurant. I could get there; I could wait. As long as we were here, it would heal, wouldn't it? There had to be a way for guilt to dwindle.

Dad said, "After this we'll go to visit Salomeya and their family. They want to see Baba again before we leave."

"They're your family, too," Mom said.

"We're going home?" I asked, at the same time Ada's smile burst across her face like a stampede. She leaned back in her chair in lavish relief.

"Tomorrow," he said. "If we can fly out, that is. There's supposed to be a big storm."

"We're from the West Coast," Ada beamed. "We can handle a little rain."

"It might not be just a little rain, Ada," Mom said, wincing at the bitter dredges of her coffee.

"But we haven't seen so many of the things that people talk about," I said, my voice wobbly. "In the guidebooks. Remember? There are a lot of churches here, and a castle. An ethnography museum."

"You want to stay to check out the ethnography museum?" Ada asked.

"Well. This is a surprise," Mom said.

It was only Dad, with one of his hands fluttering up, ready to jerk Baba back down into his wheelchair if he floundered, that seemed to understand. Of course it was Dad, the person I wanted least to relate to, who gazed at me with sympathy, a sympathy that said: *This is how I am, too.* I felt foggy, away from myself, as if I'd already watched us eat breakfast and it had been excruciatingly boring. My sister was haggling to upgrade to business class, and I would have to decide whether I could go home by myself, or if I would return to sleeping on Ada's futon, knowing her roommates hated me but were too polite to eject an emotionally turbulent little sister back up to Morningside. I remembered the papaya sitting in her fridge and wondered what color the mold was blooming into, without us.

11.

At 5:00 a.m. I woke up, at once thirsty and desperate to pee, a flat sheet twisted around my waist so that getting up became an acrobatic event. My heart felt riddled with adrenaline. I worked to coil each breath into Mississippis. M-I, M-I, I counted, palm soothing my heartbeat into submission. *Am I? Am I?* In the dingy, cupboard-sized bathroom I rested my fingertips in the soft center spot where I'd have a pen jabbed in the event of an emergency tracheotomy.

Dear Hesper i feel like i am writing you this letter every minute of every day, every time I finally sink doughily into sleep or see a trinket you would like, a tree made of ivory or limestone. Dear Hesper I feel like you are becoming not a thing that you are because the real you walks around and has bad days and feels annoyed by things i don't know, or understand; the real you is so much more like, dimensional and complicated than i could ever imagine up. but a you that i carry around because it's the best you that i can do. I realize you are artificial and sad. but it feels better than a real other-person who has no you in it. I don't believe you don't love me, I don't believe you're not coming back because how can I? You never came to New Jersey to try the Korean fried chicken place that opens at 9 AM and has radish cubes that smell like erasers. I don't know where you are but you need a radish cube. You'll see. xxx

I had written it, edited it, emailed it. 2:42 a.m.

I scrubbed my scalp with olive oil–coriander shampoo, a tiny gift snuck into my luggage by Chloe, until it felt like my skin was peeling. Shaved my legs with a rusted pink razor decorated with dancing daisies, reveling in the razorburn. Scraped the dead skin and dirt from underneath my nails until I was clean.

I had a life before this. I triumphantly tossed breadcrusts at ducks puttering around a circuitous, algae-laden pond and rejoiced when my mother bought me aquamarine platform Skechers. I staged a coup in fifth grade against a music teacher who asked half the room to harmonize as we sang a prayer and I refused, urged others to maintain solidarity because it sounded better in a minor key. It did! I was right. I tried, I was trying, what else can I do? I was more than the carrier of Hesperpieces. I could be.

BREN WAS IN THE hallway next to the boys' room, gloomily leaning against a wall with a toothbrush in hand. His little case to cover the bristles was shaped like a cute animal I couldn't identify. If I knew for sure he didn't hate me, I would've asked what it was. Probably a bear. I waited to see if he would say something but he didn't.

"Hey," I ventured.

"Hey."

"I owe you an apology," I said timidly. "I wasn't thinking. I was so, so drunk."

"I was too," he said. We were both exaggerating out of kindness, and it felt good.

Bren blushed, then covered his toothbrush-holder with his fist. "Listen."

My eyes were wettening. I had to open a little extra to keep the tears steady.

"Are you sure that you're okay?" he asked. "Because some of the shit you were saying yesterday was really intense. Trying to warn me that the fog machine was actually like, a modern day gas chamber," he said quietly. "That's not exactly a normal sad drunk revelation."

"I'm a snowflake," I mumbled.

"I'm not saying I don't want to watch out for you. But we haven't done the hard stuff yet. We've looked at a lonely earring and some dirt. Are you sure that you're ready to go to Sachsenhausen? Because we're supposed to leave in an hour."

"I just needed to sleep," I murmured. "I was tired. The jet lag."

Bren didn't say anything.

"I'm not used to traveling."

"If I stay quiet, will you find more excuses?"

"I can construct a mountain of excuses," I said, relieved to feel the mood amenable again.

"It's not like I've never been the depressed asshole who's crying into his Dippin' Dots, but then you don't even remember. And I try to talk to you about something and you just shift the subject," he said. "I don't even know if we have a real fucking friendship. It's like you just need a partner for banter badminton. You just want a way to hide."

"I was trying to help," I said.

"There wasn't anything happening," he said. "I think you need—"

"We have a real fucking friendship. Okay? I'm sorry. I'm really sorry."

"Okay," he said. We didn't look at each other, until we did.

"I can't drop everything to help you every time you need someone," he said. "It's not fair."

"I understand."

"Willa," he said. "Trying to help you is like taking a bite of an asteroid."

"I'll try to be less work," I said. "But I'm not leaving. I want to see everything. I'm not weak."

"I know."

"Can I stand next to you while you brush your teeth? I'll close my eyes."

I followed him. I listened to the sound of Bren's brushing; imagined him hawking the plaque particles into a soft, foamy pool of white.

⁂

THROUGH THE FENCE, BETWEEN the curling space where flowers would be, I was turning electric. I was the last duckling, scuffling behind the rest of the group. The sounds of Rabbi and our tour guide, Dennis, surrounded us, speaking about the panoplies of persecution—the disabled, the red triangles, the pink triangles—and here I felt my throat start to harden, calcifying, as I thought of all the members of the queer community who had been taken, who were still being taken, scattered within history and right now. Wanting to be seen; wanting to be equal. *You, at least, could make this easy for me, Willa.* Because to want to live in plain sight was to make things hard.

We skirted a giant obelisk, grasshoppers in weeds, on the route through the camp. Dennis introduced three characters for us to follow, to make the visit more personal. Rabbi's gaze pirouetted around the group, landing on mine. I found my sunglasses. Judith was only fifteen...Dennis began, sluggish with foreshadowing and Bren was moving, Lauren and Kyle and Toby, Jane and all the girls I couldn't name, stirring forward.

I pushed my thumbs together. *Cecilia, you're breaking my heart.*

The camp was diffuse, marked by long archways of pebbles and bronze statues of soldiers. Spiny maple trees arched their necks into the sky. Aside from Dennis, we were silent. Other tour groups milled in the background. My whistle necklace smacked the soft skin of my torso. Everyone else was fine. Everyone else with their sloped noses and small waists and puckered mouths were fine and we crowded into low-ceilinged barracks with white shuttered windows and the green feathery trees behind us, beyond us, we crowded inside and ogled rows of beds, uniforms on a mannequin with numbers emblazoned over the breast pockets. How could everyone else breathe as if we were doing something mundane—playing charades, pouring wine into goblets? *Move your right foot, then your left,* I thought. I thought it three times before anything happened.

Effortfully I placed one foot and then the other foot into movement but felt like a different-self, the puppetmaster of my organs and appendages but not–Willa Greenberg, I was a leg and foot slipping into a puddle, I was hearing Dennis's voice, the gentle trudge of his baritone from far away, I was pulling the sounds apart from English to not-language, as though extracting a clump of cotton candy from a whirled funnel of fluff. I was standing in an enormous gray-walled structure with the rubbling remains of ovens, I was a leg, a foot, my mother's oval face and my father's moled skin slipping, my heartbeat clacked like typewriter keys, wind whipped across the roof of the crematorium until we left, my insides were tightly turning to glass, Dennis explained that at the upcoming track the prisoners but especially the pink-triangled prisoners had to "test shoes," slide their feet into too-small shoes. *Especially the pink-triangled prisoners,* I thought, looking at my toes shining pinkly in the flip-flops like they were swelling, swollen, just another reason why I would be here—if not one, then the other. I closed my eyes and felt the weight of carrying sandbags with matchstick arms over cement, centers, broken stones, the ground ahead of us, tubercular gray, cracked with moss, my mother's oval face, my father's freckled skin, a leg, a foot.

Cecilia.

Then I felt it:

death-kissed.

Against the azure sky the tall trees clustered around the outskirts of the camp, reaching like fireworks into the night, ready to burst and I stayed and I stayed until I could not anymore. *What am I doing?* I thought, but I knew.

I was leaving them, I was farther and farther and farther away,

thicker, I disappeared into the enormity of the woods. I was going where God wanted me to go.

I lugged myself around like a mattress, the sign reminded visitors that anyone crossing the line will be shot, diamond-shaped specks of light whispered in through the perimeter-walls. I was bowing underneath the weight of the sunsplit leaves, I was shaking with reverberation of sounds I couldn't hear, I was into the trees, I was not:

dead not dead, not dead, not *dead dead dead d-dead*, I sang, soft. I looked up and all I could see was trees,

thick in the thimble so far from anyone I knew; I could see nothing, and I was transported:

my fingers slid into Hesper's and our knees shook, we were encrusted with light, we were possibility tangled into knots and now, the hush of those memories slid away and I was left, and I could leave, I could take one step then another and be with Graham in Berlin sleeping on a foldout sofa. I squinted deep into the forest looking for someone coming, a man through the bars of bark. He was coming for me and he would . . . he would—

I held the whistle in my mouth under my tongue, the grime of gold sweet, and I blew—

and I blew, and I heard the sound of myself and I had never felt so unstuck in time; I was windmilling across the sky, I was aviating into clouds made of no one, I thought: I have never died,

I have never died,

I have never been Cecilia. I could find you, in Chloe's inbox, in Tbilisi, with your blue-haired sister and magicless Salomeya; I could find you but I didn't need to find you because I could be, without you; I am not an afterthought, I could be and keep being—

And I breathed into the whistle until I was nothing but the impetus for the sound, the whistle that said: *help me*

12.

In the daytime, Salomeya's apartment seemed even more cluttered and overly patterned: the ornately floral carpeting in the main room clashing with the flower-spattered wallpaper; a bookcase in which everything was double-stacked and then piled higher to the ceiling. Even more people were here than last time. Ada and I were tightrope walkers, dipping around piles of newspaper; Mom was busy trying to rebutton her cardigan in the midst of a swarm of kisses. Around us, the splendor of a language we didn't understand pooled in the air. Baba was awake and extended his hand into the relative-sea and they clasped it. A woman with a puggy nose tried to teach me how to say "My name is Hesper." My name is . . . what? Hesp-er. *Chemi saxlia Hesper*, I tried, and she laughed with a cranking snort, a snort that sounded like it was going to lead somewhere. No, no. *Chemi saxelia Hesper.*

"What did I say?"

"You say your home is Hesper," she explained, and handed me her tea.

I felt a shyness around Salomeya, though I could feel her looking over at me and I knew she could feel me looking for her, too. I remembered that conversation on the balcony with a similar, guilty hum that percolated through me when I thought of Lali; that I'd stumbled into a moment that was hyper-charged with feeling and possibility and had to abandon it right as the gears were starting to shift. But then there was the melee of two dozen people, oscillating through a two-bedroom apartment with their wine and their tea and their swinging limbs, wanting to hear me say *My home is Hesper* in a feeble attempt at Georgian, and someone started singing and Baba knew all the words, every pause and clap, and when he began to cry I couldn't tell if he was overwhelmed with love or sadness. Ada went to find more wine, with a promise that she'd return in a minute. And it was then that she found me. Andro was at her side, chittering and stroking his wizard-beard. "Salomeya has a journey for you," he said, over her insistent, prolix sentences that included several finger-jabs into Andro's elbow.

"You," Salomeya said, herself. "Come."

I followed her. Andro walked jumpily, his back to the wall, as if a predator would emerge from within the apartment itself. A long hall-way snaked through a bedroom into a closet, filmed with dust along rows of envelopes and white shoeboxes. The windows were open, and the soupy breeze practically bubbled inside the little room. Rain was sludging against the side of the house, pattering the pipes in a rhyth-mic background glaze. She knelt in the closet, leafing through the altar of boxes with uncompromised focus. Water damage had created pockets in the ceiling, cracks that looked like pinwheels in midspin.

Salomeya emerged with a box in her hands. We were closer than we had ever been. She had a crisp, earthy smell, like juniper berries and musk, and she touched my cheek with her papery hand before she began to speak to Andro. He lowered himself onto the floor, cross-legging it, and I followed his lead. Underneath her bedframe, another collection of boxes spread as far as I could see. It was like an underwater museum in here, I thought, and remembered suddenly that I had done this, too, when I was really small: stored away my receipts and seed beads and stray doll parts and preserved them all, everything, imagining that someday an observer would reconstruct my entire life from these, the artifacts of my existence. Plastic and paper, the occasional packet of DO NOT EAT jingling unknown particles that came in boxes from the Internet. And even though I knew that Salomeya wasn't my great-aunt through DNA, it warmed me to see that we had the same hoarder-like habits, developed independently, thousands of miles and decades apart.

She spoke for a long time before Andro said anything.

"Salomeya is complaining I am not good translator," he explained. "She says she can tell."

We all laughed. Then a curtain seemed to draw around Salomeya, and she started to speak in longer, flourished sentences, using her hand to circle the distance among us. Andro didn't interrupt her, or try to translate simultaneously along with her telling; there was no halting, just the sound of Salomeya imparting some kind of information or wisdom that held him, rapt, unwavering. When she was finished, she placed her hand on my shoulder and I felt the weight of her body, the effort that it took her to stand in place in this dusty, small room and tell me. I had said, "Tell me," and here we were, listening to the voices on the other side of the apartment growing louder and then quiet, stretching into wisps.

Andro took the box from Salomeya and placed it between us on the floor.

"When your Baba left Georgia," he said, "he made Salomeya promise never to tell this history to anyone. No souls. She feels...her chest is knots, breaking this promise. Do you understand? But he is gone," Andro said, touching his heart and then his forehead. "And we do not want the past to be gone for always, too."

"I understand," I said. My chest was knots, too.

"Baba's family, they had money. They were enemies of the state, under Soviet rule. So they bribed someone to take the children on a train when they knew they'd be relocated. The train was supposed to be north," Andro said, shaking his head. "But Baba and Eliyana, they got on a wrong train. Coming here. Less safe. Train ended up

going through Russia and...they knew it was wrong. They gave all
the money they had to try to get back. Someone took pity, put them
on the boat with other women and children. It had been sent from
a village where the men were killed by troops. But the families with
money, they paid off the army to smuggle out their wives, babies,
put them on voyage to Europe, under cover of many furs. Company
that sold animal skins, you see? But boat got lost, turned around in a
great storm over Black Sea, and those who lived...found their way
from landing in Batumi. Your Baba and Eliyana—she was very sick,
by then."

"And Eliyana," I echoed, straightening. "She was alive when they
landed?"

I looked at Salomeya, who nodded. "Eliyana," she said.

"They snuck on a train here, last stop was Tbilisi. In those days,
you must think: orphans everywhere. It was different time. In Soviet,
seven million orphans...it was normal to see. Begging after trains, at
churches, orphanage." Andro shook his head, then glanced around, as
if anyone were listening to us. "Very different. Dark time, in the past."

"They were alive?" I prompted. I thought of him, small and
sinewy, enveloped in a fur coat ten sizes too big. "They were alive and
came to Tbilisi on the train."

"Salomeya's father worked at the train station. Conducting. He
found them, in back, and heard Baba crying. She did not...she could
not live so long, hidden, very sick. Not so much air, in the car. So
Salomeya's father, he sees Baba and Eliyana, this small, dead girl, and
he had lost his son, not so long before. He feel...he felt a connection,"
Andro said, windshield-wipering between my heart and his. "He felt
he knew Baba, from earlier life. Another loss person, needing."

Salomeya's lower lip quivered. "We bury her," she said. "We cry
for her, too."

She reached for the box and handed it to me. "They come from
professors," Andro said. "Ah, how you...studying words."

"Linguistics," I said, thinking of the Mad Libs we'd played, so innocently, on the airplane. Inside the box, a photograph, pocked with water damage and curling on all ends, was wrapped in a napkin. Baba and his sister, Eliyana, sitting on a porch. She had on dark shoes with straps across the front; he had a checkered shirt and a diaper that poofed around his meaty baby legs. In the background, a tree tousled with bands of leaves appeared tall and idyllic, like a stereotypical picture of New England; snow was still on the ground beneath them. Weren't they cold? I wondered, and then felt immediately ridiculous. They went through hell. The cold in this picture was the last thing to dwell on. Maybe this was the happiest they ever were.

"You look very much like her," Andro said; his own observation. His translations were labored, filled with pauses, but his own English came at a different pace. I did. Once he said it, I saw the resemblance seamlessly: the wide, heavy eyes; the fluffy, unruly hair that photographed a weird shade of gray in pictures since it was almost every color, a reddish-auburn-blond that gleamed bright in the summer. Even the expression on her face looked like mine, protective and, at the same time, disengaged, as if the present couldn't unroll fast enough.

"Take this," Salomeya said, tucking the napkin around the photograph and pressing it into my hand. "And this," she continued, laying a lone, skinny braid atop it. "We rescued."

"Rescued?" I asked Andro.

"They saved a piece of Eliyana's braid, before they buried her."

Eliyana's braid stared up at me, and I thought of braiding Ada's hair the night before, weaving the strands of blue through, over, under, how methodical and comforting I had always found that gesture and then I realized I was crying, too; fat, sentinel tears. I edged the photo and the hairpiece away from my dripping face and a slight, tubercular whimper came from my mouth.

"Why didn't he take this with him?" I asked. "How could he have left it here?"

Andro hesitated. "Perhaps you are not this way, Essp, but—some people find it more easy to leave clean. Start over with no past. Otherwise, you carry so much with you, there is no time to begin again. You lose someone, they become part of you, but it can be—to talk about it can be the undoing. Every time, step back, forward. You understand?"

"Yes."

"When he left, they lost touch many years. In war, even if you live, you die."

"From Russia, they think?" I asked.

"Boat came from Russia, but...don't know if that was only where it came from. They were so light. It was probably Belarus, farther, even. It was a long, long journey."

I swallowed. "When did he find you again? How did you reconnect?"

Salomeya tapped at the box again and presented me with an envelope, thick with paper. It was in Georgian, swirls and cloud-tops neatly printed on pastel blue lines. *1999*, I read on the postmark. The year that our nana had died. Chirpy, loquacious Nana, always wearing a wide-brimmed hat if we were going to a restaurant, even McDonald's. She finished every meal with two white Tic Tacs.

"Found us on Google," Andro said. "I hope you will read letter, somehow. Find a translator in New York."

"Better translator than Andro," Salomeya said with a barking laugh.

"Do you remember what he said?" I asked Salomeya, who answered in a rush.

"She knows every word of letter," Andro summarized. "It is... very dear. He said...he looked for them everywhere, even though he knew it was no hope. But that he had beautiful family. A life to fight for."

"Were there other brothers and sisters? Besides the two of you?"

"Three other brothers. Older. But they are gone now," Andro replied.

I stared at the photograph for a moment longer. I wondered whether it should feel creepy, running my fingers over the hair of a long-dead girl. It was as smooth as the inside of a seashell. "I don't think I loved him enough," I said. "When he was well enough to know it."

I couldn't even remember if he had been at my high school graduation. He must've been. But I didn't have any memory of it. We had spent so little time together and I had asked him nothing. When I thought of him, swollen with hunger and nestled behind an animal hide, it made me physically ill. My own life had been so pampered with down comforters, frustrations about wavering Internet connections, and sold-out concert tickets. And I would be that way again; if not tomorrow, then the next day. Braid or no braid, I would never be able to grip tight enough to this type of realization to let it truly adhere, and I was disappointed in myself before I even got the chance to attempt it.

Salomeya brushed a strand of hair behind my ear, talking to Andro but staring at me.

"She says this has been true every day of her life," Andro said. "It is not enough. You keep try."

"I'll try," I said. Slowly, I felt Salomeya dragging her heavy legs against the floor; the painful lumber of someone with arthritis. She walked to me until she was close enough to stroke my hair over each shoulder; then slowly, tenderly, she braided it into two plaits.

"You will keep these things," Andro said. "They are better for you to have."

When she was finished, she patted the top of my head, just as I did with Baba, and ushered me out of the room. I kept the box tucked underneath my arm, the sharp corners digging into my rib cage, and Andro led us back into the party. Ada was sitting on the floor, helping one of Salomeya's granddaughters mend a torn hem; her mouth was puckered to keep a piece of thread safe and easily found. Outside, the rain was beginning to thrash dramatically against the side of the apartment building; the sky glowed a dirty, celestial green.

I knew I should let him see me; I knew I should let him think I was Eliyana. Bring him comfort, bring him peace. I wanted to be the kind of person that would allow him this kindness. But I couldn't help but think that, if I did, I was sealing some permutation of a curse; that I would die too, and horribly, and mar the lives of the people around me with the ache of missing something that's never, never fucking coming back, and wasn't that already what I had done? And what would he do, glimpsing Eliyana-me? Maybe he would cry, that nebula of wrinkles in his chin protruding as he escalated into a torrent of sobs. Or maybe he would scream. It could fail, I rationalized. It would be better not to try.

I piled my braids underneath the elaborate cape that I had promised I wouldn't wear in front of company and tightened the bow as hard as I could. I couldn't undo them, could I? We looked so alike with our hair identically braided. Wouldn't that be saying that I didn't care about our history? When it wasn't that I didn't care. It was that it felt like an indictment. This was just another opportunity to be generous that I couldn't bring myself to take.

I hid in the bathroom, trying to shrug myself out of visibility, until Mom found me and said we needed to leave before the water rose any higher; she didn't want us to get stuck here, since there was nowhere to sleep. I imagined our bodies piled, stacked against the floor of the train to Tbilisi; wondered what it smelled like, how slowly the train must have moved back then. The braid shivered in my pocket every time I moved, and when it was time to leave, I stood outside so I wouldn't have to see Salomeya's face as she said goodbye to Baba, again and again. I shook my hair into its usual, almost-curly state, and felt the raindrops starting to come down faster.

ONCE IT STARTED, IT got worse fast. Dad had called for a cab already, one with ample space for Baba's wheelchair, and the driver had the bravado of a prizefighter. "Speak Russian?" he asked, and Mom nodded, allowing him to release a tirade that I understood was admonishing us for traveling when the flooding had already begun, and then to negotiate for an additional fee because of the inclement weather conditions. Relentless raindrops slashed across the windshield, the back windows, blurring the world around us into light and not-light. The sound of the storm was making Baba agitated and he started to bash his soft fist against the side of the door. The cabdriver child-locked us inside, and we slid down street after narrow street.

Water gushed around the car, the current creating a rocking motion that felt both terrifying and vaguely soothing, like a porch swing if a porch swing might also lead to your uncertain death. Dad was silent, leaning his entire body forward so that it rested on his knees, while Mom continued to fight with the cabdriver in Russian. It seemed like she'd really hit a stride, in this time of absolute crisis, back into fluency. Their conversation seemed like a tennis match of hostility. As we attempted a third left-hand turn, the license plate unhinged from the cab and was swept furiously away.

"Are we turning into a river?" I whispered to Ada as the car glugged toward the left, onto a street I recognized as nearby the hotel.

I could see she wanted to make a sarcastic comment but couldn't. Fear had pinched her face into a sweaty, anxiety-flecked arrangement that I'd only seen a few times in our lives. The pebbly pounding of rain grew louder, and I held her hand in mine. Our bodies were cold with the rain that had maneuvered its way onto us even beneath umbrellas, and our bare knees knocked together as we slid to a stop in front of the hotel. Mom handed the cabdriver an extra four bills and he scowled with every inch of his beady face. It was hard to see the ground, densely layered with mud over the uneven, dilapidated sidewalk, and Ada and I both nearly lost our balance coming out of the car. Our shoes were ruined, and Dad had to hail an extra set of hands from inside the lobby to help him jerk Baba's wheelchair inside. Already, branches had fallen in the center of the road, like a fence separating us from the rest of Tbilisi.

Inside, we swaddled Baba in towels, tried to hush him to sleep. Nothing worked: no song or head patting or number of warm, Downy-scented shirts from Dad's suitcase. The hotel seemed smaller, more fragile, in the midst of the storm, and even though I knew it wouldn't happen, I kept feeling like the infrastructure might just blow away into the rolling, unflappable waters. The rain purred outside, a kitten desperate for our attention, and Baba was crying, hitting the table in front of him, until Dad shooed us out of the room. "Go upstairs," he said, holding Baba by the shoulders. "I'm going to give him an Ambien in some applesauce. It'll be okay."

"He's okay?" Ada asked, twice, over the sound of his moaning.

"He'll be okay. It's been a hard day for all of us, right?" Dad asked.

"I'll stay with you," Mom volunteered. "You might need help with him."

Ada looked between the two of them and her mouth set into a firm, clenched line. I knew what she was thinking: that of course they would cling to this, their last opportunity to be together, without Christina, without anyone, while they still could. While they had Tbilisi around them as an excuse. That Mom was only pretending to be an upstanding moral citizen for our sake, or so that she could feel satisfied with herself as a role model while still having everything that she wanted. The ring sparkled at us like a dare. But before Ada could say anything, I threaded my arm with hers and led her away. I didn't want to hear her accuse Mom of being a hypocrite, a homewrecker. I didn't want her to be right.

DEAR WILLA, I IMAGINED writing. But it had been too long; and I didn't have the beginnings. Even if I wanted to tell her, it would be too hard to begin now, without context. And the longer we were apart, the more this would be true, until if she asked me how I was, I would say fine, and she would say good, and it would have to be.

IN OUR ROOM, WE shivered out of our wet tights and skirts and shoes and lined them up by the radiator. I had never been more glad to see my checkered pajama pants, the polka-dot socks that I'd almost not packed because they seemed too warm for this time of year. When Ada wasn't looking, I slid Eliyana's braid and the photograph in between pages of the journal in my carry-on. The rest of Salomeya's things were hidden underneath a coat she'd given me as a gift. We fashioned ourselves capes made from bath towels and watched the flooding from our window. The water was moving so fast, from high up, that it was striped with foam. Objects dunked in and out of the stream, picking up speed as they flowed downhill. Fragments of trees and branches were visible, but mostly it just looked like vats of mud, sponging down the slope. We could hear yelps, yelling. The angry splash of water as it swept through unlucky parts of the city.

"See how it's moving?" Ada said, nudging her body close to mine on the carpet. "That means it's not going to damage the hotel. It's moving away from us."

I needled my foot underneath hers and said nothing. Wind kazooed from a crack in the window. If I closed my eyes, all I could think of was Baba—the velocity of his crying, the sound of his skin smacking against the glass as he tried to get out. Eliyana. But if I kept my eyes open, it was surges of brown, thrumming water, branches and the occasional discernible objects—a bicycle, a broom—rushing past us as if in a dream. The air was frigid and I couldn't get warm. I couldn't stop looking.

"Maybe we should watch TV?" Ada suggested, swishing the curtains closed with smooth, older sister authority. I splayed each blanket on the comforter and squirmed deep underneath the layers, tightly contained in fabric. Rain plunked loud, louder, a crash of a cymbal. The percussion of our first real natural disaster, I thought. Probably the power wouldn't stay on for much longer. On the blinking, thick television, the first channel was blasting shrill, warning-sound notes of news coverage. On the other side of the city, cars caked in mud, buildings with holes in the center. A large-haired news anchor swept her arm over a satellite picture of Georgia with a solemn, wooden expression, and then it cut to a different reporter in a poncho, gesturing into the sweeping waters.

"Is that..." Ada said, peering at the screen. "Are those..."

"Animals," I said, watching footage of a dead bear, its corpse snagging on an air-conditioning unit. "The zoo must have flooded."

"Holy shit. Holy fucking shit," Ada said.

Squads of policemen in dark uniforms, equipped with what looked like tranquilizer guns slung over their shoulders, were shown getting out by foot, following a lost hippopotamus down a major highway. A broad, regal white tiger with its stomach missing, blood trickling down its hind legs, in front of a store selling designer jeans. Mostly they were corpses, it looked like: a menagerie of dead bears and wildcats. Ada cupped her hand over her mouth in horror.

"We can't leave here," she said finally. "They must be all over the city."

"They're dead," I said, my voice a tiny whisper. "They're just dead animals."

Ada shook her head. "They're showing the ones that are dead. Who knows what's left, wandering around the streets?"

"Ada. We're safe," I said.

"They'll be hungry," she said. "They've never been out on their own."

"I bet they were well fed at the zoo."

"What if they attack us? On the way to the airport?"

How the fuck are we going to get to the airport? I didn't ask.

On the news, a man and woman were hoisting their black Labrador onto a stretcher made from branches, pulling him above the water, while one of their neighbors struggled to move his legs through the viscosity of the mud. They were forming human chains, working to combat the pull of the water, and I thought of standing in rows like that in elementary school to play Red Rover, against the biggest tree in the schoolyard. And then I was back, here, my sister crying into my neck, the chorus of ambulance sirens and car horns from people who didn't have time to get out of their cars but had no other escape options.

"What do you think they're saying?" she asked, clutching my arm until it ached.

I hit the off button, firmly, and it sizzled into darkness. "If you can focus, and give all your attention to the rain. If you listen to the sound," I said, "it's like a noise machine. To help you sleep."

"A noise machine?"

"Just try it. Just think of it as an aural blanket."

"An aural blanket," Ada repeated. She scurried to the wall to turn the lights off, and returned to my side with a fervor I hadn't seen from her since we were children. Her knees were knobby and sharp. Outside, the wind whipped across the side of the building, like a dress unzipping. Like a thousand dresses, unzipping simultaneously.

"We're never going to get to leave here," Ada said, and although I knew she was in pain, although I knew there was destruction everywhere and a tiger missing his organs and soldiers waltzing through mud-lakes and screams, screams of people who needed help and couldn't have any, that I was so stupidly lucky and couldn't appreciate it, couldn't stop my brain from skipping over to the next obstacle to analyze and untangle, retangle; and that my parents were making mistakes knowing they were mistakes and not caring, not caring at all, and that Baba was afraid and the world was pooling, vicious, indomitable, I couldn't help but feel a tiny orb of pleasure, too; a tiny bit of me that thought: we'll stay here and I won't have to change, to face an empty bed or call my dealer or handle the bruised, decaying papaya or wonder if every brown-haired person is her—because we'll· be here, cradled in an igloo of linens; knowing things will happen but not yet, not while we're right here, in Tbilisi.

13.

"Willa," Bren said, rushing up to meet me in the forest. "Willa, just...hold still—"

But I couldn't, slipping like an eel out of Bren's grasp, my hair in my mouth, *dead dead dead dead d-dead*, Bren's hands were warm on my wrist, the ink still smeared from the night before over my pallid forearm skin. *Shhh*, he said, swiping the whistle from my lips and meaty breaths shook all of my torso with their effort, the splash of air in my lungs, we were marching into death, we were marching back to the bus, we were marching on and on and on. Before we reunited with the group Bren held me by the shoulders with his firm grasp and I could feel the muscles in his hands and I said, *Don't touch me*. I said it again: *Don't touch me. Don't touch me.*

The boy knew I wouldn't say anything and here I was, finally able to say: *No. No.*

It was the wrong person to say it to. But it still counted.

"Okay," he said. "I'm sorry. Can you—"

"I disappeared," I said. "I'm disappeared." I cupped the beak of my nose in my hand and felt the warm congealing of snot rushing from my nostrils from the crying. "I do need a tissue," I whispered, and Bren wrangled a crumpled white rectangle from his pocket and I tried to mop up my face.

We scampered into the main area of the camp with its little cabins along the outskirts; I could see the model of the train that brought them here and I wanted to be sick but there was no time. Into view came the silhouettes of normal people who I didn't recognize and then I did, Jane's body holding a clipboard in front of the bus. Gasoline and rubber, the chatter of Alison and someone talking about basketball. Silently I followed Bren up the little stairs of the bus and he took a step to the left, so that I could sit in the window seat, and in the bus I folded in half and the past fogged over me. I thought of piles of hair and shoes and stripes and bones, I thought of Cecilia, and I said the Kaddish under my breath because it didn't matter to me anymore that I didn't count.

"You have to go home," Bren said in my ear.

"Where?" I asked.

"Yeah," he said. "I know what you mean."

WHEN WE ARRIVED IN Berlin, I was the first one off the bus, avoiding. By now it was evening, and the bus driver hauled our suitcases from the innards of the bus onto the sidewalk with gusto. Starry skies traipsed over us like a joke, as if to say: *What a beautiful night after your afternoon of historical torture porn.* Bren was flanked by questioners—they were gossiping about me; I could feel the heat of their eyes fixed directly above my head. I didn't want to know what I looked like. My sleeves were damp with that distinct mix of perspiration and the aftermath of using your shirt as a tissue. Jane approached me cautiously and dropped a soft hand on my shoulder as she said, "I understand the experience of visiting a concentration camp can be very emotional for some people."

Fuck off, Jane, I thought.

"The rabbi would like to speak with you tonight," Jane continued. "If you're willing to discuss your emotional reaction. He feels a great connection to you, Willa, and would like to be a spiritual resource for your journey." .

"I want to leave," I said. "I think my trip is finished."

Jane's expression looked as fragile as a rose petal. "I'm not sure that's wise, Willa. Here, you're surrounded by your peers of faith. And, of course, we'll have an opportunity to share our responses to the visit this afternoon, and I'm positive that your experience will be valued here. We need someone to represent the rawness that this—"

"I don't want to represent anything. I don't want to be the reason that your funding is renewed," I said, my voice snapping open like a stubborn jar that's been twisted too vigorously. I thought of my contents spilling onto a wide open floor. And although there was so much I wanted to say, so much I had felt and continued to feel in stupendous gusts, a tornado of feelings that I didn't know I had suppressed inside myself, I could only say: "I feel this great... pressure. I'm dying here."

"Willa," Jane said slowly. Her disposition tense. "I know you're not trying to be insensitive, but... people *actually* died here. Millions of them."

"You think *I'm* insensitive?" I said. "You're the one trying to milk my inherited trauma for a board member. You think I don't see you grooming me for some kind of marketing campaign about the value of discovering your historical umbilical cord?"

"This is my job," Jane said, in a low voice. "I don't relish approaching you like this."

"You can't keep me," I said, close to a growl. In my peripheral vision I saw Bren, excusing himself from the tangle of Alison, Samantha, and Lauren to rescue me. Again. A murmur of guilt bloated in my chest. "I have a friend in Berlin and I'd like to leave the program. I'll see you at the airport next week when we all fly back together."

"Willa," Jane said, attempting to placate me. "I really feel that—"

"You can't make her stay," Bren jumped in. "You must see the

irony in forcing someone to tour concentration camps and historical
sites commemorating the destruction of our people, right?" His face
flushed with intensity. I wished, so much, that even a little fraction of
me wanted to have sex with him. I'd never had such a loyal friend.
Not even Chloe. Not even Hesper, at her apex of loving me, would
have argued so vehemently for my agency. With Hesper it had always
been a fight for her, not for me.

"Of course," Jane agreed, twisting to try and catch the attention of
Rabbi, who was deep in conversation with one of the quieter, taller
boys from the group, "we can't *force you* to continue on the tour with
us. It was never my intention—nor my implication, Bren—to make you
feel like you're in some kind of prison situation here. We're going to an
Indian buffet tonight. There will be samosas," she added pleadingly.

I watched Bren attempt to turn his face to granite. He was a samosa
aficionado.

I saw how he wanted me to stay. But God wanted me to leave.

"Let me at least get the rabbi," Jane said. "He'll want to speak with
you before."

"Okay," I said. Then, with her back turned, I looked at Bren. "I
love you," I said. "I'll write to you." And then I ran from them both;
I captured my suitcase from the pile on the sidewalk. I knew if I
stopped, even for a moment, I would lose my resolve. The rest of
the group went silent as I crossed their path, except for Alison, who
asked: "Willa Killa? What's up, buttercup?"

My gaze downcast, veined with adrenaline. I didn't want to ever
see them again. I didn't want to see Samantha, especially; her Hesper-
ness. But even that seemed far away now. I needed to disappear. My
skin was as thin and useless as cellophane. But I could still breathe;
I was still breathing. The suitcase trotted behind me as I ran to the
first major street I crossed, got into a cab, and handed him my phone,
pulling up to the note where I'd recorded Graham's address. I said the
only thing I remembered how to say in German. I said thank you.

PLEASE BE HOME, I thought, slinking my finger over a worn gray buzzer. An intercom clinked noisily; then a low hum allowing me into the building commenced. Graham's apartment was on the fifth floor. Inside, the apartment was a display of attractive decay—paint chips and exposed beams. Steep stairs ricocheted in my hip creases. Then I switched to the staccato rhythm of prayers, a few slabs of Hebrew for every stair I climbed. I rummaged deep into my lungs to find the air to continue. Before I knocked on the crisp red door, I licked my palms and scrubbed whatever makeup remained on my face with my damp saliva hands. I wanted to be clean of it. I wanted to be as light and delicate as gossamer spun by spiders.

The person who answered the door wasn't Graham. A tall woman with a slicked-back, tiny blond ponytail stood in front of me, wearing a black sleeveless turtleneck and a floor-length skirt. She seemed impeccably chic, and also slightly ugly. Her mouth and eyes were so close together, the rest of her face a moat of empty space around these features. "May I help you?" she asked. Her English had the clipped practice of being immaculately studied in school for many years.

"Hi, I'm...a friend of Graham's?" I suggested. "I'm meant to be staying here for a bit."

"Are you?" she asked, but not snarkily. "Graham is in the shower. I am his roommate Anneli. Please come in," she said, extending the door open for me. My suitcase trailed in after me, clunky and obtrusive where I'd meant to be easily ignored. I remembered Chloe describing how small the apartment was—*sardine syndrome*, she'd said in her trademark chipperness—and felt betrayed. Was I misremembering? No. With sleeping bags, two or three visitors would be able to comfortably slumber in the large, gleaming living room. A little balcony with two small metal chairs opened into the city, surveying all of the mismatched buildings in the neighborhood. A hallway swept into the bedrooms, a kitchen, a bathroom with its water gurgling from Graham's shower. Besides the bookcases, everything was white—the furniture, the walls, the light fixtures. It was like a minimalist design blog had come alive. I thought of the ugly, burnt shade of orange of my suitcase and was glad it had flipped onto its side.

"Thank you," I said to Anneli as she brought me a coffee cup full of water. "I hope I'm not bothering you."

"It is not inconvenient for me to have an additional visitor." Anneli jerked my suitcase upright and smiled in my direction, a wiry crescent on her slim face. "I will be happy to share my bread and cheese, for this first night. It seems you have had a long trip."

I glanced to my left to say to Bren, *Not inconvenient!*

But.

"Thank you for your hospitality," I said. "I really appreciate it." Anneli was already departing from the living room, her Scandinavian body waifing back down the hallway toward her bedroom. In the bright, white light, I could see the dirt from underneath my fingernails glow in a grim dark line. I wondered how much earth from the camp had found its way into my body, how much debris I would carry with me. I drank my German water from its German cup. I checked my account balance using precious international data. My student loan money bobbed in my account, the funding for my most grand boondoggle. Creative writing classes seemed an eternity away.

I listened to the shower's trickle truncate. I listened to Graham's footsteps.

Please, I thought. I slid my hand underneath my shirt and felt my heart, beating.

When Graham emerged, his blondish hair dark with wetness, he smelled oddly feminine—like the cucumber melon scent from my adolescent years spent sampling Bath & Body Works products at the mall. I'd become so used to seeing him pixelated, his face in a small rectangle hovering in the lower right hand corner of Chloe's screen as she boiled water for linguini, that it was a surprise to see the resolution of his actual skin. I could barely meet his eyes.

"Greenberg," he said. "I—wow. I didn't expect to find you in my living room."

"I thought Chloe would tell you I was coming," I said, inspecting the blur of periphery behind him for an eavesdropping Anneli. "Didn't Chloe tell you?"

I was not a good liar, but we didn't know each other so well, after all. Graham lived in a studio in New Haven, and Chloe mostly trotted to his apartment on weekends with her laptop and a few pairs of underwear jammed into an NPR tote bag. When we did talk, we feigned greater intimacy than we'd established for Chloe's sake, and besides we knew so much about each other through Chloe, it was almost as if we were real friends that had just forgotten to spend time together.

"She didn't give me exact details, but...well." Then he did look at me, evaluating what his response should be. Tears lingered just behind my blink. "Cool, man. It's good to see you." Graham busied himself with refilling my water and shuffling a handful of crackers onto a salad plate. "How long are you staying?"

"I'm not sure yet," I creaked. "Is that...okay?"

"I'll ask Anneli, but I think it will be. It's a big space for visitors," he said, glancing at the sofa and its pillow pile. "Not very private, but..."

"It looks great," I said, filleting every bit of enthusiasm I had into my voice. "Thanks."

"How was your magical mystery tour?"

I did my best to be nonchalant. "Full of mysteries."

He gestured back to the small white table next to the balcony and we sat, in stiff chairs meant for a showroom and not for human bodies. I nibbled politely on a cracker cloaked in seeds while Graham exalted the virtues of the neighborhood we were staying in. Wedding, he said, had historically been in this area of Berlin that tourists were told to avoid, but now was filled with artists, microbreweries, an old school bus renovated into a restaurant that sold tacos and cakes. Everything was chipped, marketed for its dilapidation; but it was still cheap enough to live here for the immigrant families who always had, Graham emphasized, not like what had happened in Bed-Stuy and Fort Greene. Gentrification was one of those topics that was easy to fly into and mumble and nod along while my heart thought: *Now I'm living in a place called Wedding, and I haven't thought of Hesper for hours.*

"There are a lot of things I'd miss about America," Graham landed eventually, "but I would think about staying here, if I could." His hand buzzarded above the crackers and scooped several into his mouth. "There's all this nature around—parks and lakes just outside the city. It's so much cheaper to live here, and there's everything you didn't know you wanted to be enchanted by—there's a whole abandoned airport."

"Why would you want to go to an abandoned airport?"

"Why *wouldn't* you?" Graham asked.

"I thought you were really invested in the zoo."

Graham pinkened. "I guess I'm getting sentimental because I'll have to leave soon," he said. "My course is almost over. And before you say anything, of course, I'm looking forward to seeing Chloe— she's the best thing." He wiped the napkin crumbs with the hem of his T-shirt. "But I don't feel *enchanted* by New York when I visit her. Not the way people do in movies."

I nodded. "I haven't been feeling that way lately, either."

"The garbage smell," he said. "In the summer. It just—"

"It mushrooms," I finished. "And the rats. I can't even look at the subway tracks."

"That weird tunnel at Union Square where Chloe's tulips got stolen?" Graham said, smiling hugely. "Doesn't it feel like you're not going to end up at the L, but like, in purgatory instead?"

"Those poor tulips," I said. "Her favorite."

"I got her new tulips," Graham said. "She was okay."

"I'd miss her," I said. "If I didn't go home." I gathered the crumbs remaining on the plate and made a little grave in the corner. Graham watched, quietly. "Chloe, and . . . the blueberry pancakes at Community. And Central Park, I guess—that little bridge near Ninetieth."

"That's a short list, Greenberg."

"Everything reminds me of her," I said, hoping I wouldn't be pressed to identify the antecedent. He didn't ask for more information but he did retrieve two beers from their refrigerator. "It's kind of nauseating. You know?"

"Yeah. Sure. Everybody's had that," he said, as if we were discussing chicken pox.

"Getting an MFA is pointless," I said. The foamy beer dripped down my narrow throat. "I only wanted to go to grad school because I didn't know what else came next. Now I feel like I'm going to be paying a hundred grand to delay working a job I hate. My life doesn't mean anything, you know?"

"Jesus," Graham said. "You're a real ray of sunshine today." He swiped the beer bottle from my hands. "I'm cutting you off prematurely."

"That's fine," I sighed. "I just . . . I wish I could stay here in Berlin. Everything's better here."

"Are you . . ." he began. "Serious? About not going back?"

"Why not?" I asked, possibilities trilling around me.

"Well. You would be here illegally, just . . . for the first thing. So you wouldn't have health insurance or any way to find work besides under the table." Graham put his beer bottle down on a white coaster and tapped the rim with his finger as he thought. "But you wouldn't be the only one in that boat, of course. I guess you could be a nanny, or work in a shady restaurant washing dishes."

"I'd be a good nanny," I said. "I can do CPR."

"Or I bet you could get a master's in English . . . literature or some-thing," he said after a minute. "I know they have graduate programs for science taught in English."

"Bingo," I said. "I love literature and some things."

"Say you get in. Then you'd need somewhere to live. Say you stayed here, and took over my sublet," he said. "Which I guess you could afford to do. The problem would be your half of the lease with Chloe."

I shrugged. My heartbeat whipped, wild. "Everyone at school loves Chloe. It wouldn't be hard to find a new roommate. The apart-ment is only seven blocks from campus. And that weird basement is a selling point."

"Don't you think Chloe would be . . . upset?" Graham asked.

"I don't know. Do you?"

"She'd forgive you," he said after a minute of thought. "She's re-silient. But . . . okay, you can't decide to live here without seeing Berlin properly," Graham said, an authoritative note drifting into his voice. "Just because I have a high opinion of it, that shouldn't influence your decision. What if you're allergic to German mold? What if all the parks have some kind of special Berlin organism decaying in the leaves, and you've decided to live here?"

"I guess I'd stay inside. Or buy allergy medication."

"Metaphorical mold."

"Metaphorical allergy medication."

Graham dug a pair of keys from his jeans pocket. "Go explore. Then you can decide. I would go with you," he added, after a beat, "but I have to study for our final exam. Are you . . . Will you be okay, Greenberg?"

"I just need to," I said, and when the silence had eclipsed the be-ginning of the sentence, it was as if I hadn't spoken at all.

BERLIN. I WAS ENCUMBERED by nothing; I was surrounded by leaves. It was a trial period, I felt myself flowering down winding streets, the rush of bicycles, of pedestrians choppily chattering in German, the swish-swish of their German growing louder made me sweat, but then a harmony of Arabic, of Turkish, of English would find its way into it, the rhythm of the city, and I could breathe again. As long as no one yelled in German I could breathe. Everything was farther away than it looked on the map and everyone was dirty-haired, buns propped up with colored elastics and beards coiled with red hairs in a sea of brown. My joints and muscles twitched, unused to walking so much after the hours of bus-sitting from the tour— but I wasn't going to think of that. I was a passive explorer, I was scoping out my future home, I was eating a samosa and the group wasn't here, by now they wouldn't ever be here again.

Apotek: pharmacy. Tiergarten, S-Bahn, if you let your gaze fall to the rubbly ground for too long you could miss a cathedral, a palace; Charlottenburg, Potsdamer Platz. At Checkpoint Charlie a mustached man sold fruit smoothies from a tinny stand. Did I like it here? Did I just find comfort in a place where the history felt like part of the horizon? Wind. Wind gathered the scarf around my neck and nearly scraped it off into the street. So what? So I might lose my scarf. So I had a sofa to crawl back toward, and nothing else. I was elastic. Grad-uate school applications opened in October. October: it would have been my one-year anniversary with Hesper. What would Hesper say when she found out I was gone? But not now. Now! I was at an art gallery that was once a crematorium and it was beautiful, pointed red roofs of grand buildings surrounded by untrimmed grass, trees from so high up it seemed they'd dripped from the sky itself. At the crema-torium I had a slice of blackberry cake.

I would have to tell Chloe. I would have to tell my parents.

Tomorrow. I would be able to tell them tomorrow.

On the way back from the Reichstag—columned, glass-domed,

plunked from a history textbook—I found it. The memorial. I knew
of it but I hadn't known what it would feel like, to enter, to be surrounded by the slabs of concrete in all different sizes, how as you
advanced through the memorial it was like being swallowed. Into the
graves with the negative space, I fled into their open concrete mouths.
Thousands of slabs, some tall and some small, as I followed the alley-
ways. I felt God buzzing in my chest, knowing: I'd been rescued in
the forest but now, alone, I had to find it myself. The way out. In the
corner of my eye I spied: two little girls, one in red, one in purple,
playing freeze tag along the tops of the shortest slabs, the girl in red
chosen, frozen, with her hand outstretched. *You're it.*

14.

Margaret, whom I'd slept with a total of thirteen times, was throwing a party. It wasn't *our* party, but hers, and I'd been recruited to help: scoops of vanilla ice cream embedded in pools of root beer, cupcakes with thick foamy icing in pastel blue. Maraschino cherries bobbed in cocktails housed in triangular glasses. It was not, Margaret emphasized, a *Mad Men* party. That would be *hackneyed*. This was an ironic, 1950s *bash*, she said, coating her lips red with swift, deft strokes. When the first round of drinks were made, each cherry stabbed with a decorative, swordlike toothpick, deviled eggs sprinkled with paprika, Margaret unfastened the Mary Janes she'd just put on and sighed. She leaned her whole body on one elbow.

"What's wrong?" I asked, although of course I already knew.

"I don't think anybody's coming. No one replied on Facebook or email."

"It's barely eight."

"It's not the *time*, Hesper. It's the *atmosphere*." Margaret spoke in italics. I could feel her wide, actress eyes moving from me, to the window, to the lack of potential guests on the sidewalk in front of her Upper West Side building. She had the runtiest one-bedroom in the building, she explained cheerfully to anyone who would listen; the apartment on the eleventh floor right next to the elevator, so all day she could hear the sound of people entering and departing. It was only runty to Margaret and her trust fund film friends, though; I saw it as palatial space for one person in Manhattan, with enough room for a dining room table that sat six. She had a closet with a built-in organizer. She made me hang up my coat on a hanger fattened with a cushion to prevent the protrusion of hanger-spots.

"I should've bought striped straws," Margaret lamented. "The cute kind. Candy striped."

"The straws wouldn't affect your guest list."

"I know that," she said, wounded. "It's the stupid election. No one wants to have fun."

The day after the election, everything had been quiet. The tension felt like a mist, tiny droplets cast over everyone. Usually the trains were saturated with micro-motions: light bopping to enveloping music; fingers traveling over screens in the maze of *Candy Crush*; students highlighting pertinent facts in their textbooks. That day everyone seemed to be staring straight ahead into the future, feeling the mist settle across their cheeks.

Margaret, without looking, swatted my hand away from the cocktails. "I get that it's a catastrophe for liberty and everything, but we can't be expected to stop having fun in the meantime, can we? I don't want this to ruin my party."

She was just as shallow, as selfish, as I was, and I kissed her. In relief. In appreciation.

"My lipstick," she whispered. But she acquiesced, one hand reaching for a napkin behind my back, so she could be prepared when the kissing stopped and her makeup needed to be reapplied. In a minute, the first guest would arrive, fickle and clanging with a six-pack of beer that Margaret hated.

All of Margaret's friends were performers—comedians, actresses, the occasional aspiring singer-songwriter. Uniformly adorned with little gold earrings and long chains piled atop their bony chests. It was my first time hanging out with them in tandem; so far I'd met them by chance, pre- or post-plans, with Margaret's attention ping-ponging between me and the friend to make sure I was approved. I didn't mind. These conversations were numbing; exchanging riffs about hypothetical scenarios ("what if all the chairs spontaneously burst into flames? Are your clothes flame resistant, Hesper?" etc.) and quoting articles, movies, media. Quoting was a way to have an entire conversation without saying anything at all besides that you paid enough attention to parrot accurately.

I didn't ask: how are you? because there may have been a true answer, and no one wanted it.

She asked: did you grab a Manhattan? Those cherries are real. They're imported from Croatia.

By the end of the night, eighteen people came, not counting a Canadian that Kate had met on Tinder who asked, "Are there meatballs?" excitedly when he saw the plates of food, but there were no meatballs, and this poor guy was branded *No Meatballs* and the jokes, the jokes. They were meek, a little unfocused, but they were there, and they were ceaseless.

"This is my latest, Hesper," she introduced me to No Meatballs, and it felt more like a prize than an insult, somehow. How ebullient I was, knowing that she wouldn't use the term *girlfriend*. How safe, and secure, I was in this arrangement.

We drank. Kept drinking. Bourbon bit my throat.

Margaret had covered her boatneck with a blazer, and the bulbous brass buttons on Margaret's blazer rubbed against my spine.

She draped her toned arm around me and gently pushed my body deeper into a circle of bodies I didn't recognize. She licked my earlobe with her pink tongue and the crowd clapped in booze-fueled approval. Margaret was very recently out and I was here, the evidence of her queerness, crowded in the crook of her arm. Each time we kissed, or she slid her thumb across my shoulder blades, I felt gazes hot on us. It was the opposite of losing yourself in wanting. It was a performance, like everything else.

I glanced over at the arrangement of deviled eggs and wormed my way around Margaret, and No Meatballs, and whoever his guppy-mouthed date was. I thought of Baba, that first breakfast in Tbilisi. Ada's mannequins were now dressed in clothes fashioned from the street market, and I remembered Lali—the moment with the M&M's, and how fast I had run from her. I was still there, watching the blood pool from the zoo animals that had drowned, or had been killed in the street. When we left, they were still shooting the animals. Mom haggled a cab to take us any way to the airport for a thousand U.S. dollars. "I don't mind if we come *close* to danger," she emphasized.

I thought again of the streets as we slowly plodded toward the airport. The entire van sloshing into mudbanks, the cabdriver assuring us that soon we would be past the worst of it. On the outside, volunteers in orange vests, mopping up what used to be part of the city. Scowling at us, the escapers, shielded by gray-tinted glass. We didn't *just* get to drive away, I thought, fighting it out with every strained face we passed. We'd been stuck in the hotel for days. Power-less. Baba spitting up pomegranate seeds into his lap; he didn't want to swallow anything. But we did get to drive away eventually, and we did it without seeing whether Salomeya's house was damaged. If she even had a house anymore. Nobody mentioned helping her. We had pretended to call from the airport after arriving in the U.S., squatting in the bathroom so she couldn't hear the rain, and that lie brought forward newer, scragglier lies, and those scragglier lies became the truth.

When the power went out, we'd played cards by candlelight, and Baba finally stopped crying. But that only lasted so long. "He thinks we're on the boat again," Ada said, and we plugged his ears with music so he wouldn't be back there, nauseated, hiding underneath piles of fur. *Eliyana*. But he plucked them back out. We couldn't fix anything with our fucking earbuds.

I gulped down two paprika-laden egg halves so that my mouth would be busy again. Margaret crinkled her kitteny face in my direction; she thought of food as decorative, the part of the party you curated for guests. I hadn't been invited to stay over. Margaret had kundalini yoga in the morning, a meeting with her experimental theater troupe at noon in a coworking space with a knitted hammock. I slipped behind her and whispered in her ear: "I think I might go home."

"It's early!" Margaret said. "If you leave, there won't be enough of us to have three conversations going simultaneously," she whispered in my ear.

"I'm tired," I said. When that didn't stick, I continued. "I have a headache."

"Okay," she gave in, eyeing the rest of the party. "Text me when you get home." She tucked a stray hair behind my ear. "You look hot in that outfit," she whispered, flitting her fingers underneath the triangle of my silk collar, and I looked down to see what I was wearing because I couldn't remember.

I WAS DRUNKER THAN I'd realized, no longer fluent in the language of fitting keys correctly into locks. The strap of my handbag slipped from my shoulder and hung, pendulum-like, against my elbow. I rested my warm face against the cool, chip-painted door of Ada's apartment. Well, now it was mine, too, I guessed; I'd moved in when Ada's now-former roommates Nicole and Jessica left to cohabitate with their boyfriends at the beginning of fall. But I still felt like a visitor who couldn't remember which key was for the top lock. The sensation of Margaret's blazer lingered over the small of my back. Ghost buttons.

"Just let me do it," Ada said from the other side. Her voice had the nasally lilt of our childhood. Ada's face was stark with impatience. I sank into her arms, though she hadn't initiated a hug, exactly. She was chewing something that smelled familiarly salty.

"Are you eating Goldfish?" I asked, my chin still bent into her shoulder. She tilted the bag toward me. "And butterscotch? That's just exactly what I wanted. How did you know?"

"It's the salt," Ada said. "The perfect combination."

"How'd you come up with it?"

"You did," she said.

"I don't remember," I said, lolling against the wall opposite the front door. Without speaking I trailed Ada to the living room. Without speaking we knelt, identically, onto the embroidered burgundy rug, even though the sofa had a copious amount of room for two small people. Ada piled Goldfish and butterscotch chips into her open palm, then into mine.

"You got a letter," Ada said flatly. "I went to put it in your room..." Her voice was scrubbed of all inflection. She'd been practicing this conversation, I realized, probably for a long time before I came home. I felt like a piece of cud that had been passed back and forth between cows and spit up in a grassy crater.

"I went to put it in your room," Ada repeated. "And I saw you had a ton of letters there. All from Salomeya."

"You don't know that," I said floppily. "They could be from Andro. Remember him? He looked like Dumbledore. You're a wizard," I said to Ada. "You're a wizard, Ada!"

"I can't believe you didn't tell me she's been writing you," she said. "And... you're just collecting them? You're not going to find out what she wants to tell you?"

"People don't really write letters to other people. They write to themselves," I said. *Dear Hesper, I feel like I am writing you this letter every minute of every day.* I was her diary. I was the diary she'd had, and now she would always have a different diary-me, a person that responded predictably to every statement or revelation because she could only imagine me so much, so well, and I would never change, except in the ways she wanted me to.

"Don't be fucking wistful," Ada said. "It doesn't suit you. When your older, formerly unknown relatives from across the world write you page after page, it means something. It means something to me. The least you could do is not hide it from me. I don't understand," Ada said, one lonely tear dribbling insolently from her eyes. "I don't understand why she would choose you and not me. I would have already hired a fucking translator. I would go back, if she asked me to."

"It's because you didn't care about Eliyana," I said. "You didn't believe she was real."

"How was I supposed to know that it was real?" Ada asked.

"I don't know," I said. "But I did. Maybe I'm just more... connected. Spiritually, or something. Can I have more Goldfish?" I asked, reaching for the tinselly bag. I wanted to hear the crunch.

"I don't want to share my fucking Goldfish with you."

"I'm too drunk to have this conversation," I said pitifully. "Can you be mad at me tomorrow?"

Ada inspected my expression. Her nostrils looked like they could encapsulate little pearls, I thought tenderly. The bag of Goldfish tipped precariously, then all at once onto the rug. Those small, salty crackers shaped like animals. I thought again of the zoo; the shots; the blood. Only in dreams I returned to those moments: inhaling the smell of the debris, listening to the ambulance sirens stuck in the feet of mud and scraps of infrastructure, listening to the faint but persistent screams from our balcony. We were Rapunzels, we were ordering room service that came with half-moons of honeydew to make it seem like we weren't trapped, we were indulging! We were indulging and it was fine that we stayed with Baba while Mom and Dad were together for so long. He just liked us better. That was all. Ada was the one who had the nice speakers to plug into her computer, so music had its proper dimensionality. That was all. We just wanted him to be able to listen to *Pet Sounds* as Brian Wilson intended. Under no circumstances were we going to admit any other possibility. Not then, not now.

The thought of them: kissing, shedding their respectable parental clothes, merging into each other again while we babysat Baba during the middle of a calamity that was sweeping dogs into the street and drowning them, it made me sick. It sickened me.

But what happens in Tbilisi during a natural disaster when your girlfriend has a miscarriage and your father's dying stays in Tbilisi during the natural disaster when your girlfriend had her miscarriage and your father is still dying.

You can pay anyone to take you anywhere. Right up to danger but not one hair past it.

Sometimes, when I couldn't sleep, I Googled the flood and saw its hideous, brutal aftermath and thought about how stupid and lucky I was, how I couldn't appreciate anything, and knowing that I couldn't appreciate anything just made it harder. The carpet crunched. I herded the Goldfish into my palm and blew off any debris.

"Let me research them," Ada said. "If you're not going to. Please."

"They're my letters," I said. "It's my choice to read them or not. That's how it works."

"You're unbelievable," Ada hissed. "You are so selfish. I feel like you're getting worse, Hesper. You're immaturing." Spittle danced from her lips to mine. "All you care about now is exercise classes and costume parties. I don't know how anybody can be so self-facing, right now. Honestly. It's like the country is crumbling, and all you want to know is where you can get some imported fucking fruit."

"Cherries," I mumbled. "They're Croatian."

Ada swept the last Goldfish from my palm. She blew on it with gusto. I had given up inspecting them for traces of dirt minutes ago, and I knew she wanted me to see her prudence and agree that I was reckless. "What do you even care about?" Ada asked. "There must be something."

I wanted to answer her. I didn't know how to say it. Sometimes, when I wasn't jettisoning with Margaret to her barre classes, or having my aura read by a healer named Raisin, I felt like I could disappear. I tried to write stories for class, but all my characters were stolid, austere. Lamenting their lives while sipping espresso in corporate cafes. I couldn't remember what happened next to people. I stole plotlines from TV shows meant for teenagers. *Little did he know that his half brother would soon arrive in Illinois as well,* I'd type, and then painstakingly delete one letter at a time. Then I'd hit undo all the way back. I crocheted a scarf that turned into a very narrow blanket. It was marred with holes.

"I don't know."

"I liked you better before," she said, and I knew she meant the me I'd been when I was with Willa.

"Yeah," I said. Truth scratched my throat like an allergic reaction. "I liked me better before, too."

THE NEXT WEEK IT was my turn to be workshopped. Besides Chloe, my class this term was the misfit group—a cluster of the most argumentative first-years and the shyest of mine. Nine grim faces watched me as I read the first three paragraphs of my submission. I'd used the distinctive and unnecessary adjective *admonishing* twice. "As he drove toward home, the cornfields seemed to take on a sinister quality," I read, "and Michael wanted to disappear."

My professor, a slinky-bodied woman with a gray lob, thanked me. "Who has compliments for Hesper?"

"I loved the description of the orange on page three," Chloe said. A few nods scattered around the room. "Sheathed in light—so pretty."

"Can I say something?" Megan said. She put both palms flat on the table. Each of her fingers wore a bejeweled silver ring. "Is this story...I mean, are we supposed to take it at face value? It has to be a satire, right?"

"What makes you say that?" the professor asked.

"It's just such an...aggressively superficial story," Megan said. Her rings clattered against the table. Our paper package of Swedish cookies hopped in place. "John learns who he's become after his unknown half brother arrives in town? Come on. It's completely devoid of any issue that's facing contemporary society today. No race, no class, no socioeconomic or religious diversity, no struggle. It's an examination of white, male, Christian identity; a surface-level exploration of un-challenged masculinity. So my thought is, Hesper must be presenting this story to critique the socially irrelevant, literary-magazine-curated ennui faced by upper-middle-class drone people. Otherwise, how could you take on this attitude at a time when our society is reaching a fever pitch?"

A silence churned in the classroom. I watched the empty chair across from me and realized I expected Willa to appear there. That first year, she never let a critical word about me go unchecked with her polite, question-filled deflection methods. That clarinet, she'd argued, her face splotching with pink, was a *metaphor*. And Megan had backed off for the rest of the semester, disinterested in picking a fight with Willa. Now there was no detractor. There was just me.

"Where do you see that like, in the text?" Jennifer asked. "I like that idea but I'm not sure there's evidence to back up your interpretation."

"It would be socially irresponsible to write this without some kind of angle," Megan said.

"Okay," the professor interjected. "Let's—"

"We're not here to critique what she didn't write."

"Of course we are," Megan said. "That's what workshop is. Funneling avenues for improvement to the writer. The satire's working, it just needs to be more distilled—"

"It's not satire," Jennifer said. "It's just a small worldview."

"Let's hear some other views about—"

"You could not, at this moment in time, write a story like this in earnest," Megan repeated. "It would show a blithe disregard for the political climate. What kind of artist could—"

"What kind of disregard?" I asked.

Megan hesitated. "Blithe," she said.

"You mean BLY-the?" I pushed.

"Hesper, please respect the cone of silence," the professor said, drumming the hydrangea tattoo that swam directly underneath her collarbones.

"It's not satire," I said. "Call me whatever you want, Megan."

"Let's move on," the professor suggested.

WE TOOK A TEN-MINUTE break between workshopping stories. My heart still felt like it was being voraciously plunged. *Aggressively superficial.* I wanted to hide in the bathroom stall, even though the third-floor women's bathroom was always spackled with stray hairs stuck to the divider between the two toilets, something Willa hated.

In front of the two sinks, Megan, Chloe, and Jennifer lingered. I maneuvered awkwardly around their bespectacled bodies to pee in the less-gross stall, and as I was finished, I heard Jennifer say Willa's name. Just her name. The same way you might say "grocery list" or "caffeine-free." *Willa, you remember her? Willa Greenberg?*

"How long has she been there?" Jennifer asked.

I debated whether I should flush now. I waited. I wanted to know where Willa was.

Chloe was suspiciously quiet. She knew I was in here. I felt Megan examine my shoes, the only part of me that was visible. Black. Scuffed.

"Been where?" I asked, despite myself.

"Berlin," Megan answered. I dunked the flusher down with my thumb. *Berlin?*

"I'm so jealous," Jennifer exhaled, twirling a new paper towel from the wall-mounted dispenser. "I went there during study abroad and *loved it.*"

The door bobbed halfway between open and shut. I shuffled between them, held my palm open. A stream of pink soap drooled leisurely from its pump. Megan watched me in the mirror, violining a piece of icy blue floss between her two front teeth.

"Everyone loves it," Megan affirmed. "Think of the street art. And the beer."

"But why is she ... there?" The disbelief in my voice pulled like an unraveling thread.

"Why not?" Megan said, tweaking a glob of plaque into the sink. "It's like a cheaper, better, greener New York."

"She went on this ... Jewish group thing," Chloe said quietly. She was only looking at me now. "They went on a tour of Germany and afterward she stayed with Graham. When he was taking that course in Berlin. When he came back for the fall semester, she moved into the place he was subletting. I guess she's applying to do a master's program there now. Instead."

I felt as if I were watching myself through a keyhole, trying to configure my expression appropriately. Megan twisted her used floss into a tight circle around her ring finger, her smile tilting a fraction toward being a smirk.

"Well, I'd love to be in Europe for the next few years," Megan said. "It's going to be an absolute shitshow here soon. Not that Hesper's too concerned about that."

They went on a tour of Germany. And afterward, she decided to stay.

"We should get back," Jennifer prompted. She paused to see if anyone but Megan would follow her, and when it was clear Chloe and I were staying behind, she shuffled away in a hurry.

"I didn't think you wanted to know," Chloe said. "I thought your policy was ignore away. I didn't mean to do the wrong thing, Hesper. I...it's hard. Being in the middle." But she was more Willa's friend than mine, and we both knew it.

"No, I get it. I haven't mentioned her. There's no reason why you would."

"Yeah."

"Is she...I mean, how is she? Does she...like it?" I asked.

"She's good. She likes it." I watched as Chloe decided whether she should smile. Instead she rolled another rectangle of paper towel from the wall dispenser, even though her hands weren't wet, and rubbed the dry paper against her palms. "Um...there's a cafe near her apartment that's inside an old school bus. They have caramel walnut cake."

"That sounds cute," I said. My voice on the brink of crumpling.

"Yeah. I think it's really cute."

Chloe gazed at me in the mirror with a pitying kindness that I felt all the way down to my toes.

"Yeah. Good. I mean, I'm glad. I just...yeah. I'm glad she has caramel walnut cake."

Chloe left and when I was alone, I crept back into the stall and stared at all the reproachfully arranged stray hairs against the back of the stall's door. Most of them were long, coiled curls. I thought of how Willa's hair looked, pooled on her lavender pillowcase in the morning, like a mermaid's. Maybe she had new sheets now, too. Maybe you needed new sheets in Germany.

There were so many decisions she'd made without me already. I had envisioned her back in New Jersey, in her childhood bedroom with her painkillered dad sleeping in front of a TV somewhere on the other side of the house. I'd never been there, I realized—I was supposed to see the town where she'd grown up. The empanada place with the green sauce. The nail salon with the decorative stoplight in the window.

"This is bullshit," I whispered. I was the one who'd recovered completely, not her. I was the one with a new not-girlfriend to fuck and exercise next to. I thought Willa would be faint, fumbling. Instead she was a fucking expat, a student in a totally new university. She must have papers, a visa, a new lease and mailing address. I didn't even know where to send her a birthday card. Why had it been so easy for her to move on? I thought she'd wanted to have my goddamn baby. I thought she thought we'd be together forever, and it surprised me how betrayed I felt. It was one thing to be fucking someone else. But it was another to start a new life in a new country. It was another to eat caramel walnut cake in a refurbished school bus–turned–cafe without me.

I sat up. I washed my hands until they pruned. *You don't get everything,* I thought.

MOM CALLED, AT FIRST once a week and then twice, three times. I ignored her, even when I could hear Ada chatting with her from the other side of the apartment and I wanted to go to the bathroom but if I went to the bathroom I would need to say hello so I didn't, I didn't. I would give myself a UTI before I let her reach me.

It wasn't exactly that I didn't want to talk to her. It was just easier not to. We were too alike. I remembered that conversation at the flea market, while Ada admired the Georgian fabric. That hazy, tangerine film cast over the nearby buildings. Mom had said, *I wanted to do things alone. I wanted to do things on my own terms without someone waiting to ask me fifteen questions about my day.* I thought about it all the time; the truth from her webbing into the truth about me. I didn't want to turn into Mom, invited to pose on an extended misery tour with my ex-partner. Casting out emotional devastation like a bath bomb, sizzling fuzzy pink salts in every direction. I didn't want to be put in the position of fucking someone who still loved me, who would always love me, that pathetic, galactic love that Dad and Willa had in common. I knew if I were put in the position I would do exactly as Mom had. I wouldn't be able to say no.

"I want to have Thanksgiving in New York this year," I told Ada, who was still mad at me but had, at least for the time being, dropped the issue with Salomeya's letters. I checked the mail compulsively, first thing when I woke up, before I left for class, after I came home. I was going to keep the problem out of view, where it belonged. That was the thing about fighting with Ada: she tired easily. She wasn't naturally punchy and hostile. She wanted to feel Tibby lick her hand, but she always retracted her touch before Tibby's nibble turned to a bite.

"You do?" Ada asked. "You don't want to go home?"

I could see her counting the traditions we wouldn't be able to do: the walk through Chinatown for our circuit of the greatest dim sum in the city; all of us pretending to be Edvard Munch's screaming figure at the whistly noise that the BART made in the tunnel. Riding to the ninth floor of the de Young Museum and looking down at the city through the glass walls. Mom's pistachio thumbprint cookies. Deep frying the turkey in sesame oil. It wouldn't be the same.

"I feel like I can't get on another plane," I said.

Ada's surprise twisted her lips together. She reconfigured her expression. "Oh. That makes sense. But—what if Mom can't change her flight?" Ada scrubbed her butter knife in the weird way she usually did, making a sponge-sandwich around its metal blade, and I watched the suds trickle around the clogged drain.

"I don't care. Maybe I'll stay by myself, then. You can go. I'm not feeling very . . . celebratory."

"No, I—we can't be separated for Thanksgiving, Lemon. Can't you just . . . try? For me?"

"No," I said honestly. "I don't think I can."

"You need to call her," she said. "She's really worried about you."

I dropped my crumb-laden plate in the sink for Ada to wash. "I'm meeting Margaret at spin class," I said, although I was still in my pajamas. "But tell her I said hi, okay?"

"Hesper, come on," Ada said, but I'd already left the room.

THEN, FOR REASONS I couldn't explain, I called Dad on my way to spin class. The Brooklyn air was cold on my cheeks. *What am I doing?* I thought as it rang for the second time. *I should just—*

"This is a surprise," Dad said.

"Is it a bad time?"

"No, no. I...well. I've been meaning to..."

A pause hung between us. I didn't know what to ask. Neither of us were the ones who reached out; we were the ones who waited. My lips felt gummy in the silence.

"Your mom thinks you're struggling," Dad said finally.

I appreciated, at least, that he wasn't throwing around the word *depression.*

"Pot, kettle," I said.

"She says you won't talk to her."

"Then how can you trust her depiction of my struggle?" I asked, in victory.

"Ada told her you've been bouncing around the city, taking on any hobby you can find. You've been hoarding letters from Salomeya. You know, you really can't...outrun your—"

"You have no right to tell me how to cope, okay?" I interrupted. "I know what you're like. I remember a certain person who took my mother away during a certain natural disaster to act like a honeymooner."

Come at me, I thought, that adrenaline of a good fight starting to whistle in my chest.

"What are you talking about? What kind of *honeymoon* would that be?" he laughed. It was a deep, prolonged laugh, the kind that folded a person's body in half with its strength. "Oh, Hesper. Jesus Christ. What kind of honeymooners were we acting like? We were stuck in a nightmare."

"You were gone a lot," I said. "Alone? When Baba was having his trauma flashbacks, and it was just me and Ada to try and distract him?"

"And you think that alone time was . . . seductive?" Dad asked.

"It's not funny. I can hear that you're trying not to laugh. I hear you."

"I'm just trying to imagine what you think was going on. The reason we left you, it was because I had a panic attack. I didn't want you to have to see me . . . like that. And then your mom got obsessed, I mean obsessed, with us setting up some kind of trust . . . trying to figure out who would take care of Baba if something happened to me. Mom kept saying, when I get stressed, I get practical. She was saying, 'What am I going to tell your daughters? That their extremely responsible father had not updated his will since 1995?' So. That's what we were doing. I thought one of us might die. We were in a natural disaster. If we had stayed at a different hotel, in a different, less elevated part of town, who fucking knows if we'd be here to have this fight. We were barely gone four hours, Hesper. We were there with you almost the entire time. Days. Jesus, it was the furthest thing from a honeymoon that I have ever experienced. It was certainly not some kind of . . . tryst."

"Oh. I guess I didn't see it that way."

I filled my mouth with air. I hadn't spoken to my mom, not properly, for months, because of this thing that hadn't happened. Sometimes I still felt stupidly, embarrassingly young when it came to reading between the lines. Just often enough that I couldn't quite forget what it was like to be a kid, eavesdropping at the top of the staircase, trying to determine what was a fight that ended with a slammed door and what was a fight that ended with somebody laughing and treating us to ice cream. "You hadn't updated your will since 1995?" I asked finally.

"Death just seemed far away. And then I guess I was waiting," Dad said. "To see...what would end up happening with my life."

"Yeah," I said. That was the attitude I'd adopted most recently.

"You know what the worst feeling in the world is?" Dad asked. "It's hearing your daughter speak to you with just unparalleled disappointment. You can't imagine what a lonely feeling it is to have a child with such a low opinion of you."

"Dad," I said. "I just...I feel like...I ruin people. I'm a ruiner. I'm Mom. You know? And I don't want to be close to people anymore. I don't want to have to look at them after they're broken. But then I find out...that they're in Germany? That they don't even care the way that I thought they did. They're at a new master's program, eating walnut cake...and maybe I...maybe I shouldn't have let them go. Maybe it was better to be loved too much than to be guilt-less."

"Hesper, I'm not ruined. I'm not a building after an earthquake. Your mom and I, we have a complicated relationship, I won't deny that. But it's not...it's not so easily divided into roles that way. Your mom isn't a ruiner and neither are you. And that girl in Germany eating walnut cake isn't ruined, either. You don't get one shot at a relationship. You know...maybe one day, you will find someone whose love doesn't scare you."

"But you didn't," I said.

The line was quiet for a long time.

"I love Christina," he said. "It's just, sometimes, I forget that a whirlwind eventually...gets less windy. Then I look at your mom, and I think of the person I felt I could be with her. I never felt that I could be that person with anyone else. That's the honest truth, Hesper. That's the reason it never works out with your mom."

"That's really dark."

"They both know it," Dad said. "That's the dark thing. I can't hide it, even if I want to."

"What am I supposed to do now?" I asked, after a long pause.

"You know what you need?" Dad asked.

Therapy, I thought.

"You need to get those letters translated," he said. "Or work on doing them yourself. I don't doubt you can do it. Put yourself into a project that matters. Baba, he's . . . when he's there, you're the one he remembers, Lemon. A lot of other things are fading into the background, but I think . . . it means something that you haven't. Not to him and not to Salomeya. And don't write to her," Dad said. "To the girl in Germany with the cake. Just let it go. A clean break is the best break."

"Just let her eat cake?" I said. Even though we were on the phone, I could hear him smile.

"That wasn't the important part."

"Okay. I'll do both of those things. I promise I will."

Dad paused. "Don't forget to have some protein," he said, and I knew he meant that he loved me, and that he was sorry.

We talked for a few more minutes as I descended down the hill toward the spin studio. Dad filled me in on Christina—how she'd started going to a support group, and they'd moved to a new apartment, one with a garden so she'd have somewhere to grow ficus trees. She was repainting the walls a color called *Coming Up Roses*. Her iguana had befriended a millipede that they'd named Ralph. I said Ralph was a good name for a millipede and he said he'd tell Christina I approved. I didn't say the word *miscarriage* and Dad didn't mention the fact that he'd sent the engagement ring home from Georgia with me instead of her. I didn't hear Ada coming up behind me until she tapped my shoulder with one cold, manicured finger. "Boo," she said. "I knew I recognized those ratty sneakers."

"I've got to go," I said to Dad.

"Okay, Lemon, love y—"

Ada knitted her lips together. "Who were you talking to?" she asked suspiciously.

"Where are you going?" I asked at the same time. I tried to dodge her inquisitive hands, already halfway into my sweatshirt's kangaroo pocket.

"To a meeting about female solidarity," she said, slipping my phone out of my fingers before I could stop her. Her new political-ness had taken the place of her Charlie obsession. Every comment could circle back to the news. If she hadn't been so preoccupied with snooping, I knew, there was a lecture coming about my lazy complicity being just what *they* wanted.

My passcode—my birthday—unlocked the most recent calls. "Are you serious?" she said. "You're talking to Dad?"

I looked hopelessly across the street. The light had just changed to red; a vibrant hand flashed, then paused, to warn against oncoming traffic. Ada stood with her arms akimbo, already halfway through a tirade about Dad's *character*, what a terrible partner and lackluster father he'd been, how he'd dragged us through hell because of his stubbornness. It was all true, basically, and that was why it had felt good to talk to him. I didn't want to adventure near the moral high ground. I didn't have to worry about his judgment. I knew how the world looked from the muddy, baseless middle.

"He's sorry," I murmured. "He probably thinks all the time about how sorry he is. How, if he could do it over . . . he would be a different kind of person."

I saw Ada staring at a discarded bookcase on the sidewalk next to us that was littered with candy corn. I thought about how, if she didn't hate me right now, I could have made a *cornucopia* pun. Each of the little kernels looked discarded and sad, abandoned even by the hungry rodents of Park Slope. I felt her twisting, trying to decide what not to say.

Ada opened her mouth, but closed it quickly. "We're supposed to be on the same side," she said finally. "But lately, it's like...I don't have any idea what you're thinking."

The light changed. I expected Ada to continue on my path, but she stayed right where she was. By now the blue part of her hair had grown out a few more inches, and it made her look like she was a creature molting her original skin. She shivered underneath her gray coat, hands jammed into her pockets, and somewhere deep in me, a younger version of myself imagined kicking her right in the shins.

"Let's be on different sides, then," I said.

"Someday, you're going to push people away so hard, they'll never come back," she said.

"I know," I said. I crossed the street.

⁂

WE DIDN'T TALK AFTER that for a few days, but eventually she gave up. It took more effort to ignore me than it did to move on. Mom emailed me her flight change; it turned out that I'd won the battle of Thanksgiving. Mom booked a red eye flight and landed in New York at 6:00 a.m. the day before Thanksgiving and planned to pick us up from Brooklyn to go to the Hudson Valley for the long weekend. Waiting for her to arrive, I chewed spearmint gum until my mouth ached. Ada sat down next to me by the window and we watched the tall, bountiful trees of northwest Brooklyn with their leaves sleepily swaying in the November wind, until Mom arrived in her rental car.

"Hi, my beautiful ones," Mom said, squeezing Ada's hand from the driver's seat. Ada's backpack jingled with pins for all of her new causes: reproductive rights, health care, racial equality. My backpack was silent; my hand was untouched. Mom looked so small, sunk down in the rental SUV. "Don't laugh at my car choice. There are not so many options for renting a car during a major holiday at such short notice."

"You're destroying the earth with the gas this car uses," Ada said. "Think of the earth!"

"The earth is already destroyed," I said, but they both ignored me.

"Yes, I'll keep that in mind, Ad." Mom toggled the rearview mirror to see better and I caught her gaze. She broke it off right away, which meant she was too hurt to pretend. I thought of how many times I'd ushered her calls straight to voice mail.

"So, Hesper," Mom said. "It seems that your vocal cords work."

"Only in large cars," I said. "Once we're out of here, it's touch and go."

Ada buckled her seat belt. "I told you," she said.

"Well, I guess we'd better make the most of this drive, then," Mom said. We pulled away from our building, a crust of clouds beginning to form over the skyline. It was midmorning, awash with shades of luminescent gray. Mom's rental car pressed onto the highway and edged closer to the BQE.

"I booked an Airbnb this time," Mom said. "I thought it might be a nice change of pace."

"But I love hotels," Ada sighed. "The bathrobes! The room service. The little soaps. That was supposed to be the only good thing about staying here this year."

"It's a cottage in Beacon, Ada, not a tent we're pitching outside a train station. Plus, think of the waste of all those little soaps, and the energy they use to clean your sheets and towels every day." Mom looked at me then, or she looked back to change lanes and decided to keep her eyes near me. I felt the heat of her, watching, scoping out something in me that I didn't know how to say. "I thought maybe a hotel, after last time . . . that it might be difficult for you."

"Tbilisi is ruined for me," Ada said. "Not *luxury*."

"Maybe," I said at the same time. "It might be . . . hard. To go back right now to little soaps."

"I brought you a bathrobe," Mom said to Ada's drawn face. "We'll have a bathrobe-d Thanksgiving, Ada."

"It doesn't even feel like Thanksgiving this year," Ada said, curling her fingers around the door handle. "Everyone's depressed about what might happen after the inauguration and there's so little we can do about anything. And we're in the wrong city because Hesper refuses to get on an airplane, even though everybody knows planes are safer than just about any other form of transportation, including this car. But never mind. Let's throw out all of our holiday traditions for the person who disappears whenever things get even remotely challenging."

"Get on a fucking plane, then," I said. "Enjoy the hills and ten-dollar toast. Be my guest, Ada."

"It's not about that. It's about how you don't care about anything anymore. All of those letters from Salomeya, just sitting in a pile. People choose you, every time, and you don't do shit about it. You sit around wearing Christina's engagement ring, watching life go by—"

There was a long beat. I hadn't known that she'd known about the ring. When I found it, tucked surreptitiously in my luggage, I wondered if it had been a mistake. Dad had sent it off with a note: *better off with you, Lemon.* I couldn't explain why I liked wearing it. Maybe it was a little like pulling off a scab, even though you knew it would bleed. *Nothing's going to work out for you!* the ring seemed to exclaim on my finger. *Don't forget! Nothing works out for anyone!*

Finally I said, "I'm going to work on the letters. I've just been..."

"Inundated with your busy schedule?" Ada suggested sarcastically.

"Alright," Mom said. "Ada, stop harassing your sister."

"I'm not harassing her. I'm *pissed* that we have to change all of our plans. I'm pissed that I'm always having to watch over you like you're a delicate little flower and not a grown woman. Do you know how often I have to be the intermediary? It is *exhausting.* And Dad's the one who should be doing all the work to keep this family together, not me. Dad is the one who—"

"Ada."

"I hate him," she said.

"Why are you even talking about Dad?" I asked. "I thought you were mad at me."

"I'm not angry with him anymore, and I wish that you wouldn't be either," Mom said to Ada. "I'm...disappointed, and I want better for Christina, and I sure as hell want better than this for both of you if you end up in long-term partnerships, but there it is. People disappoint you. People do inadvisable things under stress. He's still your father."

"Well, one of his daughters has completely forgiven him," Ada said. "One of his daughters is keen on avoiding *you*, instead, for some mystifying reason."

"I don't want to avoid you, Mom," I said quietly. "I mean, not *you*, in particular. Just—everything. All of it. I don't know when I got to be so...weak."

"Lemon, that's..." Mom began. "That's not true at all. You've been having a hard—"

"You're supposed to be a fuckup," Ada said bluntly. "You're the baby."

"Stop telling Hesper she's a fuckup," Mom snapped. "Don't you realize what power that kind of narrative has in someone's life? Look at your sister's zombied expression and have a little compassion, Ada. She's *radioactive* with depression. Don't you see that? You *live* together. I knew it and I hadn't heard from her in months. Ada...you can't let your political awakening blind you to the people that need you that are sitting right in front of you."

The phrase *radioactive with depression* made me look down at my palms, as if they would glow.

Mom cleared her throat. The GPS interjected our silence with crisp, British-voiced directions to weave onto the George Washington Bridge. The city was smudged with fog, peaks of skyscrapers a faint, steely gray. I tried to notice everything so I wouldn't have to think:

radioactive with depression. It was the kind of phrase I wished I'd written myself. And it was true. I was the aftermath of at least one disaster, and I couldn't conjure the energy to disprove the assertion.

"Is it true?" Ada asked, craning her neck to see me over the back of the passenger seat. "Should I wear a hazmat suit?"

I rested my head against the cold, shaky window glass. "Gloves would suffice."

Ada unbuckled her seat belt and climbed over the seat divider. "Ada, Jesus. Some warning," Mom said, guarding her coffee cup with her non-driving hand. Ada plunked herself next to my backpack and clamped her arms around me in a side-hug. She smelled like she always did. I hadn't realized, not even a little, that she'd been crying until I saw the wetness reflecting on her face in the dim, battery-powered light. My big sister. When we were kids, she'd locked me in the pantry with all the canned goods because the cat liked me better. But here we were, and she was in the backseat even though I knew it made her nauseous, rubbing the top of my head to give me static-scalp.

"Tell me what's not okay," Mom said.

"I don't know. It started with Willa, but...then it didn't stop with her. I don't know. Baba went through so much to get away from...whatever was so bad, wherever he was coming from. I mean, it had to be bad enough for them to risk everything in hopes of getting anywhere else. And I think about him...and the level of pain he must have gone through, and how he hid it from us for his whole life until he's...not really alive anymore, and how I'm such a selfish ass-hole," I said. "How it took two generations for me to be completely spoiled. I don't appreciate anything. I'm not a good daughter or a good sister or a good friend and part of me likes it that way. Part of me just wants to be...really alone. It seems better for everyone."

"I'll kill you if you kill yourself," Ada said, pinching my arm. "I mean...you know what I mean."

"I'm not going to kill myself," I said. "I just wish that living felt different."

Once we were safely on the Palisades Parkway, Mom pulled onto the shoulder and turned the engine off. "Hesper." She scooped her thumb into her keyring until it flushed white with pressure. "I love you. I don't think you're more selfish, or more of an asshole, than most twenty-three-year-olds wandering this country right now. You're not the terrible consequence of a rotting humanity, Lemon. Baba never thought of you that way. Not ever. You're growing up and you're not your full self yet. And people who think that isolating themselves is a benefit to society are just narcissistic. You should know that. It doesn't affect the world very much if you're really alone or really not."

"You don't have a real personality until you're twenty-six," Ada gloated.

"That's not it. It's that your personality is changing more rapidly and then it gets . . . set."

"You don't think I'm doomed?"

"I definitely do not. Do you think she's doomed, Ada?" Mom asked.

"I mean, probably," Ada said, but she bopped the tip of my nose with her finger. "Let me in," she said, and even though I wasn't sure that this is what she meant, I opened my mouth so she could scrape the inside of my cheek with her nail.

⟡

WE MADE ANTI-THANKSGIVING plans. We each got to pick something to bring us comfort. "I want to pretend like there's no outside world," Ada said, and we bundled our cell phones in a plastic bag and double-zipped. I picked Meg Ryan movies, the ones where she looks the most like an early '90s lesbian. I loved the flounce of her hair, the piddling, hostile expression on her face whenever she talked to men. Mom's choice was no Thanksgiving foods, since she always spent hours pacing the kitchen while cooking the turkey just right, and the texture of stuffing was always too wet. We prepared microwave popcorn in a red striped bag, *You've Got Mail*, slipper socks, and a blanket that felt like a cloud. We merged into one many-legged creature and stayed that way, close enough to each other on the sofa to feel the aftershocks of someone laughing so hard their body quaked. I still felt it, the sadness that pulsated underneath my thoughts, but I also was the person laughing, I also was the person scuttling my feet over Ada's legs so they'd be more comfortable and I remembered all of the other times in my life that I'd done that exact thing, and thought how glad I was to have a sister, a fellow memory-keeper, another rolodex of micromotions and insignificant memories that formed the backdrop of who I'd been and who else I would be, hopefully.

We finished *You've Got Mail* and went straight for *When Harry Met Sally*. As we waited for the movie to download enough to start watching without the dreaded streaming catch-up, Mom said, "Maybe you should come spend the whole winter break with me in San Francisco. You know, if you feel like you want some more time away."

"You think so?"

Mom shrugged. "Winter in New York is bad for the soul," she said. "That's what I always say."

"You've literally never said that, Mom," Ada pointed out.

"Well, I definitely meant to."

"Yeah," I said. "Maybe."

As we hit play, the three ads we had to sit through popped up. The first one was for a home-based genetic testing service, with a beautiful, ethnically ambiguous woman draped in freckles smiling as she uncovered her surprise Irish genes. "I can't believe I'm Irish!" she said. "I had no idea!" We watched, silently, snickering at first with how campy the marketing was, and then individually lost in thought.

I felt the mood shift from light to cloudy with possibilities. I could still feel the part of my cheek where Ada had stripped me with her fingernail.

"So you just send them your spit?" Ada asked. "And they analyze it and do a full comparison of your genes with every other person that's done it, in some kind of...registry?"

"I think so," Mom said.

"That's so crazy."

"Science," I said distantly. But I already knew. By the time we got home to New York, Ada would have express delivered the kit to our apartment, and I'd spend all night trying to gather enough saliva to reach the fill line of the little tube. We'd flip a coin to see whose DNA would be analyzed—since it would be the same results, it didn't make sense to pay twice—but we both knew it would be mine. That was just how things went. We'd joke about it—*goodbye, saliva!*—while we sent it away. They wouldn't send me an email, or a letter, that my results were ready. They'd just be there one day in my online account: the full expanse of my genetics, laid out across the screen, as unceremoniously as the menu at a coffee shop. Northern Irish, Welsh; French, which surprised me; British, which didn't. And: Estonian/ Baltic Finnish. Baba had been from Estonia. Hadn't we just been talking about Estonia? I asked Ada. Not me, she said; that must have been someone else.

I didn't remember. Then I did: *The president of Estonia went to my high school, Willa said.*

Estonian. We researched hesitantly, wading into forums, trying to understand what this information meant. A quick survey of stereotypes: they liked sour cream. They were stony, cold, slow. Quietly kind. It seemed that the bulk of conversation about Estonian identity had to do with whiteness. Were they white enough, asked the white supremacist websites. They categorized shapes of noses, the fair quality of Estonian skin. Pages of genetic comparisons to Finns, Poles. It made me itch. White compared to what? White enough for whom? Not white enough for the Germans, and depending on who you were, you were deported under the Soviets in the 1940s: nationalists, kulaks, *enemies of the people.*

Baba hiding under a tarp of fur, waiting. How the fuck did they end up in Georgia? Wherever the train was meant to go, the journey from Estonia to Tbilisi must have taken months. They would have stumbled across Russia, past Moscow and any other city names I could recognize. Maybe they hadn't realized they were going in the wrong direction until they got off and whoever was supposed to meet them wasn't there at all. Maybe they'd been misled on purpose. This part, we would probably never understand. Genetics only told you who you were, not how. Not why you and not someone else.

I would spend hours clicking on all the names of unknown places, pictures snatched from strangers' lives, cars and churches and bright-ballooned parties. Most people from Estonia who got out ended up in Finland, I read, and imagined another, cleaner life, an IKEA catalog of Baba and my look-alike great-aunt, drinking soup from white porcelain bowls before going to a sauna in the snow. But that hadn't happened.

I'd checked the box that said: *I wish to be connected to any close genetic relatives that have also used this genetic testing service.* I would wait for the emails that said: *I think we come from the same place that doesn't exist anymore. I think our families' ghosts used to breathe the same air.*

My family had run from the Nazis, too; and then they had to keep running from the Russians. They had run, just like hers. That was what I would have told her, if I could. Maybe they'd been able to tell Baba looked Estonian the way that people could tell that Willa was Jewish. But I didn't know; there were some things I wouldn't know. I wouldn't click through to see what kinds of cancer I was more likely to get, or whether I had a longevity gene or the cilantro allergy that made it taste like soap. I would send the results to Dad and Mom and

Ada; I would sign up for a class on Estonian history in the post-Soviet studies department, and another in basic Georgian language, when I got back to New York. I would write back to Salomeya's letters. I would sign them: *Yours, Hesper.*

It was still true, what I'd written to her all those months earlier. In the beginning, I couldn't stop thinking of her. It was just different, now.

But that Thanksgiving, we watched as many Meg Ryan movies as we could find until Ada fell asleep, and I asked Mom for my phone out of the Ziploc. I took a picture of the Wi-Fi password; I told her I wanted to call Margaret and wish her a happy Thanksgiving, and I snuck outside with my backpack. I stood in the cold garden, surrounded by dead, crispy plants, and grass so neatly mowed that I could still see the creases against the blades. I folded myself in half on the floor of the gazebo and tried to connect. *Come on,* I thought, placing both hands on my diaphragm. From my backpack pocket, I wiggled the gold ring from its velvet jaws and felt the weight against my finger. A child playing dress-up, admiring it: the strange height of the ring that had failed to mean anything, except that now it was mine. That the only thing I was bound to was the past.

Then I nestled my cell phone to my ear and called.

"Hello?"

"Baba," I said. "It's me."

"It's you," he marveled, and I opened up my laptop so I could translate it; so I could tell him I loved him in a language that wasn't mine.

15.

Then it was August, and I realized it wasn't so easy, after all—
trying to find a way to exist, legally, in Berlin. I followed all the
directions I'd scrounged from Google: registered my address at Bür-
geramt, paid for health insurance through KKH. In my pre–graduate
school life, I'd worked as a proofreader, tweezing unnecessary commas
from letters and legal briefs. Room after gray-carpeted room, I stood
in line. I was stamped in; an almost-student with freelance potential.
I'd never felt more guilty, more privileged, more blindly fucking
lucky.

I could apply for a master's in English Studies, Literature, and
Culture, but my qualifications weren't right as an American. Before
my transcript could be evaluated, I needed to pass an assessment
exam, which included learning German and attending special classes
four days a week. In some ways, it was a relief to have so much
of my time automatically accounted for. Conjugating verbs was as
soothing as combing out the knots in my whistle necklace. I was; I
am; I am not.

"Talk as much as possible," our tutor Stefan instructed. "Quiet
people learn slowly."

Nearly everyone I interacted with spoke English and waited, bemused, as I tried to practice my German. I could buy a coffee. I could
apologize.

It was only a problem to hear the German out loud, that swift, gut-
tural sound that swept me right into the dustpan of history. My throat
tightened, especially with men. Speaking. Looking at me. I inched
backward. They evaluated: *Where did you come from?* But, in class, it
was a different German than I spent my days around; carefully pronounced, languorous and practiced. German with a foreign accent
wasn't so painful; it had a hesitant swish to it that reminded me of
Hebrew. Most of my classmates were from Turkey, some swathed in
dark hijabs, their iPhone earbuds a bright surprise snaking out from
modest outfits. Our class drank tall, cedar-y beers from glasses at a
biergarten and chattered. We had nothing in common but developed
a strong camaraderie. We were all tracing the directions of grammar
with such care. Nominative, accusative, genitive, dative.

I had three months left before I'd need a visa. I knew no one and
I was free of the looping anxieties that had tethered me to home.
I found that I didn't want sex. The possibility of it, simply excised
from my life. What I wanted was to never be emotionally vulnerable
again. A cool, precious numbness enveloped that other, older Willa,
the one who had lived in New York. Here I had a mouth that would
never taste another mouth; would never experience that dangerous
sparkle that came from an unexpected kiss. Sometimes my previous
life felt like an elaborate, immeasurably long film that I'd been forced
to watch dutifully every day up until now, and I loved the feeling that
the film was over; that I could leave the theater and never come back.

§

Two minutes before our scheduled Skype date, the laptop gurgled
its familiar underwater tune. My mother was impeccably early to
everything. More than her anger at my recent departure, I hated being
able to see her face throughout the duration of our talks. I hated the
feeling that she was culling all of her energy from within to evaluate

the backdrop of my bedroom. She didn't like the window overlooking the street: couldn't anyone just see in? And why were there so many *trees* in this neighborhood? she'd asked, incredulous. Anything was evidence that our corner of America was superior. Her eyes were hooded with sleeplessness.

"And how are you?" she asked.

"Gut," I said instinctively. It was our most common practice question. "I mean, good."

She vigorously stirred her yogurt. *Tap tap,* said the spoon. "I don't understand why—"

"For the certificate," I said. "So I can be considered for the degree—"

"But you got into Columbia, Willa. Well, as a master's student," she added, a sprinkle of spite. "You'd think they would jump at the chance to have you in whatever German—"

"It's not that simple as an international student."

"I thought you didn't even need to speak German."

"I don't. My classes are in English. But first I need the certificate."

My mother pinched her lips together into a lip-sandwich. "The thought of you . . . my only child . . . speaking that hateful language," she said. She paused, and I waited it out. I would not rise to the wriggling worm. "If you had to run away, you couldn't have gone to Israel?"

"No," I said. "I couldn't have."

"When your father was here, he wouldn't even let me see a German movie in theaters. Remember when I wanted to watch— what was it? The artistic one about the kindly Stasi officer. He said, 'Roberta, we do not give our money to those who'd rather we were dead.' "

"Dad is still here," I said hoarsely. "He just has trouble—" but I wouldn't have known how to end the sentence, and I was grateful when she interrupted.

"You know very well what I mean."

"It's illegal to deny the Holocaust here. There are memorials all over the city. There are as many memorials as there are Starbucks in Manhattan." I watched my mother scrub an imaginary smudge from her laptop screen with a nub of tissue. "The people who are in charge now, they weren't even alive when it happened. They were just born into this...climate of tragedy."

"It's easy to be forgiving when you've lost nothing, I suppose," she said icily.

"Mom," I said. She was trying to sow an entire garden of doubt in me and it was working. "They were my family, too." I had never told her what happened in the forest. I didn't know if there were words I could use to describe it. It would be like trying to describe the specificities of a long-ago nightmare. *Dead d-dead d-dead dead.*

"I just couldn't stay there," I said. "I couldn't stay anymore."

She leaned closer to the screen. "Is this about your friend? With the peculiar name?"

"I don't know what you mean," I said, bunning my hair against my neck. My *friend.* "I haven't had any issues with my friendships lately."

From across the ocean, we stared at each other. Three promising pimples, in a straight line leading from my hairline to my eyebrow. Soon they would bloom tiny white buds. I felt the brittle ground of her antagonism and I said nothing. Berlin Willa didn't engage with timid homophobia. Berlin Willa let her skin breathe.

"Frankly, I'm worried about you," she said finally. "What if something were to happen to you, Willa? There's so much tension in Europe. All of those immigrants, crowding in to try to start a new life, while the people already there grow increasingly resentful. Do you think that in the midst of all that, Berlin is hankering for another lost-soul, artistic Jewess?"

"That's the exact same situation that's happening in the U.S., Mom. The anti-immigrant rhetoric is just as toxic at home. It's not just immigrants; it's anybody that's not white. Have you been watching the deba—"

"It's just hot air here, Willa," she said impatiently. "Nothing's going to come of it. *We* don't have a history of genocide. *We* are about to elect the first female president."

"Actually, we do have a history of genocide," I suggested. "The Native Americans—"

"It doesn't make any sense, what you're doing—"

"They gave them smallpox blankets, Mom."

"No sense whatsoever," she said over me.

"Hello, Turnip?" Dad broke in. He leaned over my mother's shoulder like a bumblebee in slow motion. His hair was fuzzed in a gray coif. "Is that you?"

"It's me, Dad."

"Look at that," he said, tapping the screen with his thumb. My mother winced.

"Willa was just telling me about how nice the weather's been on her trip," she said.

"Wonderful," he said.

"All that sunshine," she said. "Are you putting on enough sunscreen, Willa?"

"I'm taking good care of myself."

"You don't want to get burnt," she said. I swallowed the cinder block in my throat.

"It's sunny here, too," Dad said, smiling hugely at my appalled expression in the square that hung on the lower right hand corner of the screen. "A lovely summer. Are you still—away?"

"I'm still away, but we can talk, Dad."

"Wonderful," he said. "Just wonderful. Have you met my cat?"

"She's not a real cat," my mother said. "God knows I couldn't take care of anything else. Besides the day nurse, I have no help, you know that, Willa?"

"I know that," I said softly.

"She's a robot. But we have warmed to her."

He held up what looked like a stuffed animal—glassy plastic eyes, soft gray fur. Long whiskers, like the strands of a violin bow. "She purrs when you touch her face," he demonstrated, and we all listened to the robotic whirring of my father's new pet. I thought of Hesper then; of Tibby, lunging with her paw at the unseen enemy beneath the refrigerator. And then, with only a dollop of the old pain, the thought rolled away, and a new thought appeared in its place.

"She's beautiful," I said.

IN OCTOBER, ANNELI, THE woman who'd been Graham's roommate and was now my roommate, informed me that she would be hosting a visitor for "the next three weeks or so. I will hope that it is not a problem, considering the circumstances in which we became acquainted," she said. I goggled at her command of English. Of course, there was nothing I could say to dissuade her from introducing a new element—Sofie—to our living room. Sofie was Anneli's cousin. She wanted to be a journalist; she was nineteen and wore harem pants and pink sneakers. She was always home. She loved American news and lounged in the common space with her iPad and her laptop tuned to different sites, comparing coverage.

"Willa," she said, each morning as I herded my slice of bread into the toaster. She pronounced my name *Villa*, and at first I found this charming, the image of a grand Italian getaway. "Willa, will you please explain how this is—? Who will be voting for this—?"

I tried to answer things the best I could. I resented the deluge of questions first thing in the morning, before I lowered the French press down, Sofie was blogging about her American friend and the interesting perspective she was gaining on U.S. democracy and continued to needle me whenever we crossed paths: *why? why? why?*

"I believe she will lose," Sofie said. "I do not believe Americans respect women."

In the warm recesses of my memory, I felt his breath on my neck. I bit down on my tongue.

The daily fear of a woman. You got on a bus and you went to events at night alone but all through the event you strategized about whether it was safe to get home, whether it was safer to be in a cab, in a cab you were alone with a strange man in a closed box, on a subway there were witnesses if something should happen and you could go to a different car, a different stop, a different block. In both scenarios you might have to run. In both scenarios you thought: it's not over until it's over, until the door is locked behind you and no one is standing there with his hand ready to clamp across your mouth.

If he wanted you, he could just grab you. Just grab you and do what he wished. That was the American dream that I'd grown up with: you were close enough to grab and too polite to spoil dinner.

"They don't," I said. "You're right."

§

I DIDN'T LIKE SOFIE, but when she offered to help me with German, I accepted. Soon I was able to construct actual sentences in something akin to real time. She was a relentless quizzer of vocab and I didn't want to disappoint her, or worse, have to be corrected in perpetuity. When it came time for my test, I knew I would pass, and I did. It came as both a relief and a prelude; now I would have another application, another task to keep me in limbo. But first, Sofie and Anneli took me out for Korean food in Prenzlauer Berg to celebrate. Sofie and Anneli wanted to talk about nothing besides the American election.

Our bibimbap was served in black stone bowls; eggs like jewels shimmered atop grains of jasmine rice. It made me homesick for New Jersey, for the heavily Korean town that I'd been raised in. I breathed in the scent of fermented pickles. We toasted in German: *Prost!*

I tried to change the subject, but Sofie always twisted it back. "How can you think of anything else?" she asked as the waiter served dessert. "The fate of your country is terribly undecided."

I chewed on my miso-toffee crisps. "No one knows what will happen," I said.

"You must be glad to be here," Anneli said.

"I am."

"And now you will pursue a master's in English literature?"

"If all goes well," I said, crunching desperately on my dessert.

"Oh, nothing goes well," Anneli said. "What would life be then?" she asked, and plucked a piece of toffee from my plate to try herself.

WHEN THE ELECTION RESULTS came in, I locked my door. I didn't want to talk to Sofie.

I didn't want to talk to anyone.

He could just grab you. Just grab you and take you, I thought. There was no pretending that it mattered anymore.

I put on Simon & Garfunkel's greatest hits instead, loud enough through my iPhone buds that it made my eardrums hurt. *Oh, Cecilia, I'm begging you please to come home. Come on home.*

I DREAMT OF THAT night. Of the tree, and his hands.

Or maybe it wasn't a dream. Maybe it was the glimpse of another life: a life in which he'd had less shame, more time. A life in which he wasn't afraid of being caught. I couldn't see his face and I was filled with him, a sharp pain that bent me in two, and not just in two but into a million, unretrievable pieces, a mosaic of me let loose into the street. Willa confetti. In the dream I looked down at myself and saw the roundness of a pregnant body and I thought: *Who is that? Whose body is that?* and I held my hands over myself and waited to see if I could feel anything, but I couldn't. In the dream I saw my future and it wasn't mine at all. In the dream I dove into a garbage bag to retrieve a moldy orange and scraped the mold away under the tap because I couldn't afford a new, non-moldy orange for my baby, and I woke up saying: *There, that's not so bad, is it.*

IN THE DAYS AFTERWARD I wanted to stop reading the news. I wanted to but I couldn't stop myself.

My vision intertwined with Facebook, that solemn right-hand bar alerting me of trending stories and all the stories were: we're going to die. This can't be happening. Voter fraud. The world laughs at America. Health care, women's rights, climate change, build a wall, build a wall, a wall. Scrolling up and down and back. I counted my breaths the way my mental health apps instructed, puffing out my diaphragm and slowly lowering back in. I thought of my father, the small white pills he took to sleep, to dull his chronic pain. The pain that stopped him from bending down to get his own glass of orange juice, never mind anything more arduous; the pain that defined him now. And when they came for him—and there it was, the first time I thought it and then I couldn't stop thinking it. When they came for him, how much would they need as a bribe? Would it be an internment camp, the way it had been for the Japanese, or would it be worse? Would they have medicine there? Would my parents be brought to the gas chambers? Wasn't it better to be gassed, quickly? Should that be what I wished for?

And I squeezed my eyes shut tighter, realizing that all over the country, all over the world, people were engulfed in the same, spiraling panic. *When they come for us.* How many hands were pressed over hearts at this very, intolerable moment, trying to think of a prayer more elegant than *Please, help me, help us. Help all of us.* Nothing united every community like fear, a fear that buoyed through you and rose like a hot air balloon. Fear because of what your skin looked like, your religion, the texture of your hair, the gender of the person that slept next to you at night. The gender of the person that stared back at you in the mirror. The passport you didn't have. Maybe political safety was like good health; it was there until it wasn't, and you never knew if it would return once the absence was upon you.

It felt like it was just beginning for me, but it had been happening this whole time, hadn't it? Just because it occurred more slowly, just because there wasn't necessarily a camp to visit and take a selfie in front of a notorious iron gate, that didn't make it a different thing. There were already so many names of innocent people, innocent people that were now hashtags pleading for social justice. Innocent people whose names I'd never know.

I stayed in my room as much as possible. I knew Sofie would be perched at the kitchen table, ready for an intellectual debate. Ready to unstitch the current geopolitical climate and try to identify what would happen next. Eventually I couldn't wait any more for dinner, or to use the bathroom. I couldn't talk about it. I couldn't stop thinking of my Hebrew school teacher, how insistent she'd been to a room full of eight- and nine-year-olds: *It will happen again. It will happen again!*

And how I'd thought she was crazy and now I thought she was right.

In Philadelphia, the city where my mother had grown up, storefronts were cloaked in swastikas on the anniversary of Kristallnacht. I couldn't stop reading about it. SIEG HEIL 2016, loopy black letters against a muted brown wooden store display. It wasn't just this. It was etched into doors in the West Village, in Brooklyn, all over the country. Every sweet-eyed racist that had covertly posted online now armed with spray paint, with a little pocketknife, ready for their time.

It had only been a week. What about next week, next month, next year?

The world wavered and quivered and threatened to burst into flames. That's what Virginia Woolf had written in *Mrs. Dalloway*. I was still a few months away from applying to my graduate program and now, I thought: what if I didn't get in? But...even if I did. Then what? Berlin would be the place that saved me, as the U.S. had saved my mother's family in the 1930s, while my family, my community, were swept out of view?

I had been raised to think that history was a series of events that had passed, instead of a ravenous snake that slinked out of eyeshot, ready to snap us up at any capricious moment. I'd thought that I was here because I was impulsive; mercurial and afraid of returning to heartbreak. How stupid I'd been, to think that hearts were the only thing that could be broken. I controlled nothing. I was only safe because I'd been too afraid to see Hesper again, coming at me from the other side of the quad, in a coat I didn't recognize.

"I LOVE THAT WHEN I talk to you, it's already tomorrow," Bren said over Skype. It was the middle of the night in New York, but I could still hear the sirening of an ambulance in the background from his bedroom. He had a new pair of tortoise-shell glasses that kept slipping down the slope of his nose.

"It makes me sound like a fortune-teller," I said. *"Willa, show me the future!"*

"God," he sighed. "I wish you could show me the fucking future, Willa."

I chewed at the inside of my mouth, wishing I could make a joke. "I don't know how I'm supposed to go to work," he said. "I don't know how I'm supposed to focus on *sales reports* like anything that mattered last month matters now. Everything feels like it's covered in a . . . sheen, you know? Like you can't even see what it used to look like."

Bren adjusted his glasses, examined my expression from behind glass and screens.

"Can I ask you something?" he said.

"Yeah."

"Did you know?" he said. "That day in the forest, when you decided to stay, did you . . . did you think that something like this was going to happen?"

"Are you asking me if I *am* a fortune-teller?" I said weakly. He tried to smile.

"Kind of. I meant more, does God talk to you," he said, dropping his gaze from mine.

"I don't know," I said, after a pause. "It's like . . . sometimes I get this really strong feeling and I can't ignore it or explain it. It just tells me where to go. Or whether to go." I pulled the whistle down as far as it could dangle against my chest. "But I don't always know . . . if it's spiritual, or if it's instinct. I don't know until after."

"So what was it that day?" Bren asked. "In the forest?"

"I don't think that was me. I think it had to happen exactly like that. Maybe all of it was designed to bring me here. Maybe that's the only reason I ever met Hesper," I said. "Because I had to be in Berlin now." I was surprised to hear myself say it. Was that really what I thought? How long had I thought that?

"I wish I had gone with you," Bren said. "I feel like . . . a bad friend. For leaving you."

"You didn't leave me. I left you." I paused. "Can I give you some advice? You need to go to sleep. You look horrible, and nothing gets solved when you don't sleep. If you take care of yourself, you can go

to protests, and volunteer and help people that need help more than
you do, and—run for local government things I know nothing about,
but definitely exist. But you can't make any positive changes in the
world if you're a zombie person. You can't make any positive changes
if your own pain renders you useless."

"Okay," Bren said. "I'll write that down." I saw him scribble
SLEEP AND THEN BE A HELPFUL HUMAN in curly script on
a Post-it.

"And also—you need to stop feeling guilty about me. You're the
only person I have ever been close to that ... felt so much. About
leaving me. And I appreciate it, but I don't want it to become this
thing between us that like, shifts the ... dynamic. When you think that
you're shit, and you're indebted to someone, and that someone needs
you, it sours. And I don't want it to be sour."

"What about ... tart?" he asked.

"No. We've got to strive for neutral—pH 7."

"Have you noticed that, even when we start talking about big
things, it still winds up being about you, or about me, or us?
Like ... we just drift back into being stupid and small."

"It's because we are stupid and small." Bren didn't respond, his expression turning more crestfallen by the second. "It's because we've
been lucky. Maybe it's a blessing. Even if everything devolves now, and
there are swastikas all over our synagogues and subways, I mean ... we
still had that. Right? We still had something. That's more than a lot of
other people have gotten. Like, a *lot* of other groups never got to live
in the safety cocoon."

"The safety cocoon," Bren repeated. "Wait, but—if it's a cocoon,
don't we have to escape it?"

"Yeah," I said. "I think that's part of it. Now we have to do more.
Now we have to do everything that we still can. Post-cocoon."

"Willa Killa," Bren said. "You said something a little optimistic. I
mean, almost."

"Sorry to break character."

He smiled, but I watched that smile fade. Worries reappeared on his pale face.

"Wait, I wanted to tell you something," I said. "I feel like I'm going to forget."

"What is it?"

I leaned as close as I could to the screen, close enough that I was a blur of dark hair and pallid skin. There was a freedom in watching yourself pixelate; a certain brand of digitalized depersonalization. I could have told him, *You can always stay with me if it gets too bad.* I could have told him that everything was going to be alright. That I knew, the same way I had known to stay in Berlin, or to be his friend on the tour, or that God had come back to me, that day among the copse of tall, thin trees. But I didn't. "I like your glasses," I whispered. "They look just right on you."

"Thank you."

"You're welcome."

"I don't want to get off Skype yet," he said.

"We don't have to."

"Maybe we should look up different foods that have a pH near 7. Just for research."

"I feel like . . . avocado?"

"I'll check," he said.

⁂

Dear Hesper,

Last night I dreamed of you for the first time since I moved away. It wasn't a memorable dream—no concrete details. A flash of your tawny hair, puffing out from beneath your winter jacket's collar in a little bubble. I don't know if I was me, or if I was a camera. Do you dream like that? I don't usually. I woke up confused, and a little disappointed, and I stole some of my roommate's licorice tea from the kitchen and drank it all even though it was too hot to drink. It was like the dream bent something in my chest into a shape that didn't quite fit with the rest of my shapes. So I'm writing to you. I'm not sure what to say, even though I haven't shaken that feeling that I carry around with me all the time that I have so much to tell you. But you're not you, anymore, you're an imaginary audience with preferences I've memorized, but sometimes I can pretend you're still you, and that I'm learning new things about the you that you are. Laundry detergent that makes your skin prickle with red bumps. Your favorite planet, your favorite childhood outfit. Mine was powder blue: a matching turtleneck and corduroys. I looked like a walking crayon.

I wonder what you know. It's a big program, our MFA group, but everyone scavenges information about each other, and I bet Chloe let it slip that I'm here, in Berlin. I bet you know her new roommate, too, the one who's wearing a CamelBak backpack in every picture even though sitting in a classroom is far from the type of expedition that would need a portable water supply. I didn't know I would be here; I thought the next time I came to Europe, I would be in Tbilisi, with you. I get travel alerts from our trip, a brightly colored triangle announcing that the flight prices are up or down for June 2017. I know I should unsubscribe. I get emails from Groupon, too, from that time I bought you a massage. Don't forget Hesper's birthday! *the email says. It makes me think, you know—how no one ever really disappears on the Internet. Not the way you can disappear in real life.*

Sometimes I'm still mad at you. It's a blustery, fleeting sort of anger, like the air right before it rains in the fall. Mostly I'm grateful for you; grateful that we got to love each other entirely, even if it was for a short time. Mostly I want you to be happy, even if that means being subsumed in someone else, but I want that happiness to be invisible to me. Which is easier now, since I won't run into you across the quad, those steps in front of Low Library where you'd sit with your notebook on your lap and your water bottle next to you like an obedient pet.

The other day, I heard myself tell a friend that I was grateful to you because it brought me here, to Berlin. Running away from you did, I mean. And if I were in New York, I would be so scared to be myself. I saw an ad, online, for an officiant for gay weddings under the heading, "Get Married While You Still Can!" and it made me queasy, the idea that our rights could be plunged away so easily. I don't know whether it's scarier now to be gay or Jewish—every day it feels like a pendulum, swooshing between possibilities to be marginalized differently.

My mom called me crying. I haven't heard her cry since I was a teenager, not even when my dad first hurt his back and we realized he'd be on the painkillers forever, that there was no way to treat the cause, only the symptoms. She was crying now. She was telling me that she wanted to be cremated because she didn't want some neo-Nazi in a beanie kicking over her gravestone. I didn't know what to say. I thought of whether you would have known what to say, and felt good when I realized you wouldn't.

Maybe what I want to say is that I have just realized that I've taken every basic element of my life for granted. But I realize now I was lucky; that I've had almost three decades of luck and never stopped to say thank you. The only thing I ever actively, moment by moment, appreciated as if it were about to vanish spontaneously—that was you. Us. The us that we were.

I want to say: thank you. Thank you for bringing me across the world. I feel safe here. The longer I stayed in New York, the more I felt like . . . I was turning to liquid, like I couldn't contain myself in the body I'd been given. Do you know what I mean? Suddenly I had so many feelings, and I'd spend the entire day trying to come up with some totally banal reason to stay alive, like, I couldn't jump into the street into oncoming traffic because I really needed to buy asparagus. Time to go to five grocery stores and compare the quality of asparagus and the size of their little spears and that was what I had, play by play asparagus shopping, that was all I had without you. I'm not telling you to make you feel guilty. I'm telling you so you know that now, I'm better. If you were worried, you don't need to be anymore. I thought loving you would make me a better person, but it was losing you that did it.

There's the possibility, even though I'm trying not to think of it, that I'll have to come back to the U.S. if I don't get into a graduate program here this year. I want you to know—maybe it doesn't matter, maybe you aren't looking for me around every corner in the Upper West Side the way that I had been searching for you—that I won't come back to New York. Maybe I'd move to Chicago, somewhere that you've never been either, so it could just be mine. I like the idea of a city that's bitterly cold in the winter but is filled with lakes. I like that it's called the windy city, since wind can always scatter whatever's left away.

I think of what I would say if I saw you. Maybe I would say: Hesper, do you remember when you left my apartment for the last time? I was wearing your socks. They were ivory with red toes. I was wearing your red-toed socks and calling your name, only my voice didn't sound like my voice, and I was standing in the hallway with my hands empty, trying to say your name loud enough that you wouldn't be able to leave.

I'm sorry that I never gave you your socks back.

Or maybe we'll be lucky, and we'll find each other after all of my grief and anger and sadness have caramelized into acceptance, and I'll see your hair peeking out from the back of your jacket collar on a real street, in a real moment, and I'll recognize you, irrefutably. And in that moment I'll know just what to say, even if it's just as simple as a smile, and raising my hand to say: it's you, it's you, and I am still me; hello.

ACKNOWLEDGMENTS

Thank you, first, to my brilliant, supportive, and in-all-ways-exceptional agent, Stephanie Delman at Sanford J. Greenburger Associates, for your wisdom, lightning-fast email replies, and supply of donuts. I am honored to be your client and am so grateful for your help in making my lifelong dream a reality. Thank you to Maddie Caldwell, my fantastic editor, for your editorial expertise and your incredible vision for what this book could be. From that very first phone call, I knew you were the one. I could not be happier with what we've come up with together.

Thank you to Anjuli Johnson, Jordan Rubinstein, Morgan Swift, Anne Twomey, Lisa Forde, and the rest of the Grand Central team: I so appreciate all of your efforts in bringing this book into the world. Thank you to Hsiao-Ron Cheng, who created the cover of my dreams. Your work is an inspiration.

For those who read through many early drafts of this novel, I am endlessly grateful to; Victory Matsui, Jessica Lanay Moore (the original coiner of "shamomille"), Essie Chambers, Angelica Baker, Cary Gitter, Breanne LaCamera, and Emil Ostrovski, with a special thank you to Kerry Cullen, who gave this project so much love and attention. Thank you to Cosmonauts Avenue for first publishing an excerpt of this novel, "Turnip," in 2015.

For the support throughout earning my MFA at Columbia, thank you to my teachers, Porochista Khakpour, Karolina Waclawiak, Sheila Heti, Rebecca Godfrey, Sonya Chung, Stacey D'Erasmo, Christine

Schutt, John Freeman, Josh Weil, Alan Ziegler, and most importantly Heidi Julavits, who guided me through my thesis and whose energy and dedication to craft continue to inspire me years later. Thank you to all of my classmates, too many to name here, from whom I've learned tremendously. You make me want to be a better writer every day; I couldn't have done this without you. Thank you to my eighth grade language arts teacher, Mrs. Elbert, for taking the time to read my lengthy melodramatic stories, and making me feel like I could do this. I owe you so much.

Thank you to my family for your support, especially my parents, who are two of the most indefatigable, driven people on this earth and showed me how to keep going, always. For your love and encouragement, I am grateful to the Greenbergs, Rosenthals, Feltmans, Barcellonas, and all the others in the mix. I am endlessly lucky to have you on my team. Thank you to Dani Barcellona for your unbeatable Goldfish and butterscotch combo.

To Caroline Moran, my best friend, who keeps me from being forlorn and was the original brain behind the flood; and to Addie Guiliano—watching you grow up is one of my greatest joys. Thank you to Paige and Elisabeth Plumlee-Watson, for more than I can say. Our friendships are truly the best outcome of a nine-hour road trip to the country. Thank you to Allison Castelot, Kelli Trapnell, Ariel Hubbard, Mina Shaghaghi, Larissa Belcic, Jose Nieto, Kacie Medeiros, and the rest of my Leonia family, for being stellar friends and sharing in all of these ups and downs. Thank you to Brian Farkas, for your love and relentless Vassar pride; to Dana Byerwalter, for being a source of positivity and fortification throughout the editorial process and a perfect pen pal; and to Sara Lyons, my oldest friend and the Ashley to my Mary-Kate. I'm so proud of everything you do. Thank you to my wonderful colleagues at *Poets & Writers*, for their enthusiasm about this project and pep talks in the kitchen; I'm so glad to spend my days with you all.

Thank you to the musicians and writers that have inspired me throughout working on this project: Björk, Tori Amos, Lia Ices, Wilsen, Daughter, Peggy Sue, TV on the Radio; Virginia Woolf, William Faulkner, Ali Smith, Leslie Jamison, and Miranda July. I could never have found the heartbeat of this novel without your work.

Finally, thank you to Christine Barcellona, for everything. You are the happy ending I never thought I'd reach.